About the Author

Robert Nuttall was born in Manchester; he now lives in Surrey with his wife, Kim, and dog, Billy. A director of a media company based in London, he retired in 2016 and shortly afterwards began writing novels.

Previous work by this author, *Wandsworth Common*

Robert Nuttall

Robert Nuttall

The People at Number 53

Vanguard Press

VANGUARD PAPERBACK

© Copyright 2024
Robert Nuttall

The right of Robert Nuttall to be identified as author of
this work has been asserted by him in accordance with the
Copyright, Designs and Patents Act 1988.

All Rights Reserved

A CIP catalogue record for this title is available from the British Library.

ISBN 978-1-83794-278-7

Vanguard Press is an imprint of
Pegasus Elliot Mackenzie Publishers Ltd.
www.pegasuspublishers.com

First Published in 2024

Vanguard Press
Sheraton House Castle Park
Cambridge England

Printed & Bound in Great Britain

Dedication

Dedicated to my first grandchild, Sienna Nuttall xxx

Acknowledgements

To my family: wife, Kim, Guy, Lucy, and Sienna. Myles and Amelia, and pet dogs, Billy and Pablo.

Prologue

Present day is prior to the Russian invasion of Ukraine.

Joseph Furber Makin, an only child, raised in the family home in Wide Open, Newcastle upon Tyne. Wide Open is off the A1, just north of the Newcastle Racecourse, aptly named because it was wide open to the bitter, freezing winds coming in off the North Sea. It was a bloody cold place to live. Joe's dad, Alan, a Geordie born and bred, would say about the weather: *"There are only two seasons up here, winter and July."* His middle name Furber; was his mother's maiden name. She said there were too many Joe Makin's in Britain, and he needed a point of difference. So, Furber was the point of difference – fine, until it became known at school. Then had the piss taken out of his middle name mercilessly. He couldn't blame them; it was a strange name. So, he took the name-calling and the bullying, that was only until he grew big and strong. Then he took his revenge on the bullies; after that, they wouldn't dare take him on, and he became popular in stopping all bullying in the school.

Joe's dad, Alan, was a coal miner who eventually retired through ill-health caused from the coaldust in his lungs from years of working down the pits. This was aided by the huge amount of alcohol he would consume after a day's work. When Joe's mother, Norma, died, his dad never got over losing her. He decided to join her by stepping up his alcohol intake and eventually drinking himself to death. Surprisingly, this took him some time, but he finally achieved it nearly three years after Joe's mum's demise.

During this dark period before Joe's dad's death, Joe's two aunts on his mother's side, Marie and Hilda, took over young Joe's upbringing. They would buy his clothes, collect him from school, take him back to their terraced house, feed him and help him with his homework. Later in the evening, they would take young Joe "home" put him to bed, and collect his clothes that needed washing. They then waited until his dad came home; Alan would join the other miners in the pub when his shift finished. He would stay until closing time and then stagger home. Marie and Hilda had long given up trying to tell him he had a responsibility to young Joe, and more than ever, his son needed his father's love and guidance. It broke their hearts. All he would say on the matter was there was nothing to come home for since Norma died.

When Alan eventually died, Joe moved in with his two aunts and never spoke about his dad from that day on. Joe loved his aunts; they reminded him of his mum. He always said he was lucky he had two mums. In return, they showered love on him and were so proud of him. They doted on him and watched as he grew into a polite, respectful teenager who hadn't been scarred by his very young childhood days, or so it seemed…

Joe was a good scholar at school, although his teachers always remarked that he would be much better if he applied himself hundred per cent. Like most Geordies, he loved his sport, and he was a regular of both the school rugby and football teams, playing for the "firsts" three years early. Everyone at school knew of Joe's circumstances; the teachers and parents were considerate and kind to Joe's situation and what he had gone through. Unfortunately, children could be cruel, and Joe sometimes got into fights reacting to snide comments about his mum and dad.

Apart from Joe's aunts, another influence in his young days was his headmaster, Mr Potts. He would take a sympathetic approach to Joe's behaviour, knowing full well it was caused by verbal bullying. Trying to depress Joe's quick temper, Mr Potts would tell Joe to rise above the comments and not resort to fighting when he heard them; he was better than that.

Young Joe respected and liked Mr Potts, apart from his aunts, he wasn't used to having people on his side. It worked, and the fighting dropped off, and so did the nasty comments. Joe was growing up mentally and physically, and because of his sporting skills, he was becoming a hit with the other pupils.

The younger days had toughened up Joe, but he knew he had his devils in his head to deal with, a legacy from his parents. One thing always stuck with Joe when he was in

Mr Pott's office after a playground altercation. They talked Joe's unfair upbringing and how other children had bad childhoods also. It was up to them to turn that negative into a positive going forward in life. Mr Potts said Joe could drag it around with him for the rest of his days and let it weigh him down. Otherwise, he could shrug his shoulders and say to himself, "Shit happens," and be determined to turn the bad start in his life into a positive. Joe was shocked; it had never occurred to him that teachers were human and used bad language. He once said to Joe, "It's not where you start off in life; its where you finish up. You've had the worse start, but use that experience to drive you on to have a great life. Joe, you can do it; you've got the ability!"

It worked, and Mr Pott's advice that afternoon always stuck with Joe. From that day, whenever Mr Potts saw Joe around school, in the corridor or playground, he would give him a sly wink; it always made Joe smile and feel special, like it was their secret. In Joe's latter school years, no one was more pleased at Joe's sporting and academic achievements than Mr Potts. The sporting trophies Joe helped the football and rugby teams win for the school were his way of paying back Mr Potts for his friendship and guidance over the years.

His teachers, and especially his headmaster, Mr Potts had high hopes that Joe would make it professionally, but it didn't happen for two reasons. One his lack of total application, and two the main reason for his lack of hundred per cent, girls! He was a good-looking lad, one-eighty-three metres tall at fifteen years old, mousey hair, pale blue eyes, a strong jaw, broad shoulders, and a good athletic body, thanks to his sport and gym workouts. The ladies loved him, and he loved many of them back with ease. His popularity with the ladies made him equally popular with his school friends and local mates.

Leaving school, he tried a couple of jobs, not really sure what he wanted to do with his life. He eventually joined the police force; he liked helping people and also enjoyed the respect he got from the public. His life was going well; he was settled in his job and had money invested from the sale of the family home after his dad had died. His two aunts never took a penny off him for housekeeping. He met the love of his life, Stella, a pretty young lady from the other side of Newcastle. A dark-haired girl with a look of Catherine Zeta Jones; a real looker, and she knew it. Her looks were complimented by a bubbly personality; if she had a fault, it was that she was flirty around men. This wasn't lost on Joe's aunts, both of them thought he could do better, and they told Joe of their reservations when they realised Joe was starting to get serious about her.

But Joe was in love and happy, so they never brought it up again and accepted Stella. After going out with her for twelve months, Joe proposed, and was delighted when she said yes. He paid for a big engagement party on St. Valentine's day and invited family and their friends. They bought a semi-detached house near his aunts in Wide-open and married in August.

Later that year, things started to go wrong; his Aunt Marie died of a brain tumour, followed by his Aunt Hilda four months later. They had left everything to Joe – their neat little terraced house, all their possessions and savings. He took their deaths badly; they were everything to him, and he loved them both dearly. He had always told them he would be there to look after them when he grew up, just like they had always been there for him. This was when Joe's drinking started to become a problem' unfortunately, he had inherited the family's alcoholic gene. His mum's death was from liver failure, followed by his dad Alan drinking himself to death.

Joe worked hard at keeping the drinking under control, but sometimes he just had to have a blow-out, especially when things went wrong and got him stressed out. Joe left the police force after being suspended for being drunk on duty. He decided to jump before he was pushed.

His departure from the force came about when three months after the deaths of his beloved aunts. His life went from bad to worse when Stella ran away with one of his good friends. Joe later discovered they had moved to Spain after emptying their joint bank account. Adding insult to injury, Joe also found out Stella had pawned his mums engagement and wedding rings to help pay for the flight tickets and her new life abroad. He called on the pawn shop and bought back the rings, the owner had heard the story of the break up, and felt sorry for Joe. It appeared that most of the locals had heard about Stella running off abroad, gossip travelled fast in Wide-open. Joe struggled to cope with the talking and sniggering behind his back from locals, and also his circle of so-called friends. It appeared some locals were jealous that he had come into more money from the passing of his aunts.

He finally stopped drinking, hiding himself away, and feeling sorry for himself. He realised he was following in his parents' footsteps of drinking himself to death; he needed a fresh start away from Newcastle. He put his aunt's house up for sale, sold all the possessions, and he left for the bright lights of London. He enjoyed the buzz of the capital and quickly settled into London life. He loved that there was always something going on, especially the nightlife with the many bars and clubs. He soon realised that he was a big hit with the ladies down there too, not only because of his looks but also his Geordie accent; they loved it. He settled well into his new-found life and was certain he had made the right decision to move south.

After his aunts dying and Stella running off *(his aunts were right after all; they had told him she wasn't good enough for him),* there wasn't anything to keep Joe up in his birth place. Newcastle would always be home to him, despite bad memories from his young, shitty life. He always managed to blot out the bad times, except they would always come flooding back when he was drunk. He would remember how alone and lost he felt after his mum died, he had nightmares about having to go into an orphanage. His father never showed him any love and emotion after she died, when just an occasional hug would have made all the difference and lifted Joe out of his sadness. Creeping downstairs at night time after the nightmares had broken his sleep only to find his dad still dressed, passed out in his armchair. His face ghoulishly lit up in the moonlight streaming in through the window, the room filled with the stench of alcohol and sweat. After failing to wake his dad, Joe would go back to bed, alone and afraid, cover his head with the blankets, praying he wouldn't have the orphanage nightmare again.

All the happy memories were thanks to his two lovely aunts doting on him giving him all their time, something his mum and dad could never do. If it wasn't for his aunts, he would have ended up in that orphanage for sure; he had a lot to be grateful to them for. They would go to watch Joe playing rugby and football at school; they looked so out of place, two old ladies cheering Joe on amongst all the younger parents. They brought light and love back into his life; he would be grateful to them lovely old ladies, forever.

Chapter One
Rob Fee

Rob Fee was from Solihull in the Midlands; he was an only child to James and Sarah Fee. Young Rob thought it was normal to see dads hit mums; he lived his younger years in fear of his abusive dad, James. His mum, Sarah, was a lovely lady, a pretty petite blonde with a heart of gold. She was ashamed of what her husband did to her and would hide the bruises from her friends and neighbours. Sarah was born and raised in Maidstone, Kent. She moved up to the Midlands with work when she was twenty-four. Her legal company had relocated to Birmingham. She loved the job and had worked for the company since leaving school. After meeting James at a nightclub, they started dating, he's was tall, and good looking, funny, kind. She got pregnant, and they married. After little Robert arrived, Sarah gave up her job and became a stay-at-home mum.

James had a good job; he was head of sales at his brother's car dealership, but he liked to drink, and that's when the demons took over. At first, he would smash things in the house when he came home drunk to upset Sarah because he knew she loved her home and was house proud. When she stopped reacting to his drunken rants, he started to knock her about. One night, when he came home late and started hitting her, she ran out of the house in her nightdress to get away from him. It broke her heart to see young Rob running after her, barefoot and in his pyjamas, in the rain, crying out her name. James was always so sorry the next day, and tried to make things better that would only last until the next drinking session. Rob's mum made him swear not to speak to anybody about what his dad did to her; it was their little secret.

In his early teens, his dad would also hit him when he tried to protect his mum that was when his mum started defending herself to save Rob from a beating. This only made things worse, and the house ended up like a battleground. He never hit either of them in the face; the bruises and marks on their bodies and arms could always be hidden from view. Rob decided to join the boxing club at school, and over time, he became a good amateur boxer and often represented the school. He was fifteen when he in his own words, *he finally stopped the bastard hitting his mum for good.* As usual, his dad came home drunk, and shortly afterwards, an argument started with Rob's mum in the kitchen. When he grabbed her by the throat, Rob ran in and grabbed his dad's shoulder, spun him around, and punched him in the face. His dad's legs buckled, and he fell to the floor. He shook his head and looked up at Rob in utter amazement. He jumped to his feet and darted towards Rob; the second punch came from the shoulder. The force of it sent his dad reeling backwards over the kitchen table, flattening one of the chairs under his weight. He staggered to his feet, his nose bleeding heavily.

Unsteady he shook his head once more, he glared at Rob, grabbed a kitchen knife from the worktop, and shouted through gritted teeth, "You, little bastard, I'll fucking kill you."

Rob's mum, who had stood crying near the sink, screamed, "No!" but it was too late.

When Nigel lunged at his son, Rob moved quickly to his left. The first punch caught his dad under his chin, the second was hard to the side of the head. His dad went down for the third and last time, and he lay unconscious on the floor. Panting, Rob lowered his fists, looked from his dad lay on the kitchen floor to his mum and said, "He will never hit you again mum, I promise you that, it's over." Rob was good to his word; his dad never touched his mum again.

Three weeks later, his dad left the family home, apparently to live with a woman he had met, when she bought a car off him at the showroom. At least he did the decent thing, probably out of guilt, and carried on paying the household bills, and Rob and his mums living expenses. After the divorce, Sarah got a job at a legal firm not far from home, and married one of the partners two years later. She deserved happiness and to enjoy the rest of her life without violence and in peace.

Rob left school and studied accountancy at Manchester University, after passing his exams he worked for a small family company in Birmingham for three years. Like Joe, he felt there was more to life, his mum and stepdad were happy and settled. They had paid for Rob to go through university, so he didn't start his working life in debt, for which he was eternally grateful. He had itchy feet, and wanted more to life than being born in the Midlands, worked there, got married and lived there, and eventually died in the Midlands. He made a decision to try his hand in the capital, he moved south to London. He was drawn to London with the hope of furthering his career, having a better life, but most of all change. What did he have to lose, he was young, didn't have any ties, his stepdad was kind, loved and looked after his mum, so she was fine, it was now or never! The salaries were far better down in London, and he wanted some excitement, before his life got serious with responsibilities. His first job was working in the accounts dept of a London conveyors office. It bored him silly, but it at least it paid the rent on his flat in Lambeth, and more importantly funded his social life. So, that made it okay to be bored at work, it worked while he looked around for a better job. He wanted something that was a challenge, where he would be the head accountant, the boss. So, for the meantime he was happy being bored during the day and having the time of his life at nightclubs at the weekend. The Atlantic Bar off Piccadilly Circus was one of his favourites with its fantastic restaurant, and a nightclub downstairs, this was the place where he first met Joe Makin.

Chapter Two
The Boy Did Well

After several jobs in the Smoke, Joe used all his savings to start his own business, one man and a van at first doing service deliveries in the city. After five years, he had a fleet of twenty-five, delivering all over London, from Business mail to deliveries to banks and businesses. Then later newspapers and magazines to hotels, which was very profitable. His hard work was very rewarding, life was good, and he bought a terraced house in Clapham. He also treated himself to his lifelong dream of a black Porsche, second hand with only twelve thousand miles on the clock. Mr Potts was right as usual; you could turn your life around for the better.

It was about this time that Joe and Rob Fee's paths crossed, in Battersea. They had separately chatted up two women who were friends in a nightclub on the South Bank and went back to the women's apartment nearby. A few nights later, they met again in the nightclub and got chatting. Rob was five-eleven, black hair, olive skin, with a slightly crooked nose from his boxing days, which didn't spoil his looks, also a very natty dresser, he lived not far away in Lambeth. Joe and Rob became good friends, two good looking guys with funny accents, the ladies loved them.

They discovered they were kindred spirits, as far as their childhoods were concerned. They both had a shitty upbringing, because of the effect of the booze on their parents. Possibly, because of this they had the same attitude to life, sod what happened in the past, live for today and let tomorrow take care of itself. Joe met a woman called Dawn one night in The Atlantic bar, five-six a pretty blond blue-eyed young lady from Rotherhithe in the East End. She had a gorgeous smile, and a figure that would stop a prison riot, like most East End girls she was really good fun to be with. They couldn't keep their hands off each other, and three weeks after they met, much to the Rob's disappointment, she moved into Joe's place in Clapham, and three months after that they were married. Joe proposed with his mum's engagement ring that he gave to Stella. When he asked Rob if he should use the ring again, Rob said, "Sure why not, it's not like it's jinxed or anything like that is it? After all, it is a beautiful ring." But deep down he thought it might be jinxed, you never know! He felt guilty thinking like that.

Apart from losing his clubbing partner and wingman, Rob had again grown tired of his current job; he was complaining to Joe about how boring it was. Joe's business was going from strength to strength, it was growing and expanding out over London town. So, it made sense, he asked Rob to join the firm as the company accountant, he felt a little guilty about getting married. When he first told

Rob, he was going to propose to Dawn, he said, "Are you bloody mad, you've have only just met her, you don't really know her, also what about me?" Joe looked at Rob with raised highbrows and a smile, Rob realising what he had just said, they both burst out laughing.

Joe's mocking reply, "Don't worry, I will still love you too," only made them laugh more. They were still close and always in each other's company outside office hours, with Rob's current girlfriend, they would go out in a foursome for dinner or to a nightclub. They went on holidays together; Rob would have different girlfriends, but Dawn got on well with whichever one Rob was with at the time. Which Rob appreciated, but it made him feel guilty about what he thought of Dawn. The way she was always getting Joe to buy her things, Rob felt she was a gold digger. Joe was so in love and doing well in business, he bought her whatever she wanted, and she always appeared to want a lot. Rob would see the expense because Joe put it through the company, but Rob never raised the matter. Joe was easy going and so smitten with Dawn and after all it was his company and his money to do with whatever he wanted.

For the next eighteen months life was good, but Joe didn't know that fate was lying in wait to give him a kick in the teeth again. This time, it came in the form of his best friend and trusted accountant. Rob had started to dabble in drugs, and his "habit" over time had progressed from occasionally smoking weed to snorting coke. He had managed to keep his "problem" a secret without anybody at work suspecting anything, least of all Joe. Unfortunately, Rob's troubles started to become Joe's troubles; he began creating fictitious management accounts. He fooled Joe to believe all was fine, all the client's accounts were in order, showing a healthy company. With hundreds of small accounts Rob was showing them with income coming in but in reality, he hadn't invoiced them for months. To keep the company running, he had continued to invoice the big accounts so the company was bringing in enough cash to cover all the costs and salaries. But these accounts amounted to only forty-nine per cent of the total due income. Has Rob's drug problem got worse, the invoicing followed suit, the problems had gone on too long. The cracks inevitably started to show when Rob stopped invoicing some of the big accounts. When Rob realised, he couldn't correct the mess he had caused, things started to wobble. He went AWOL before his best pal Joe found out the mess Rob had put the company in.

After not hearing from Rob for a few days, Joe was worried and tried to get in touch with him. He left massages on his company phone, after another day of no contact. Joe went to Rob's flat and found out from a neighbour that he cleared it out and left. Joe couldn't understand why Rob had disappeared; they were good friends, Rob was Joe's best man when he got married, they had never had a cross word from the day they first met, Joe couldn't understand why he would disappear and not say anything, he hadn't mentioned any problems he was having. Rob had always appeared happy working for the company, he was paid very well. There was never any pressure from Joe, business was good and things were going from strength to strength. In Rob's abrupt absence, Joe decided he would do the accounts until Rob turned up or until he could hire another accountant. It soon became apparent the company had big problems and that was why Rob had disappeared. Joe needed professional help; he brought in an independent accountant to assess the damage. She quickly uncovered a financial car crash that a company the size of Joe's would find it hard to survive, without a huge injection of capital.

Despite all of his efforts, Joe lost his business, even after some companies paid up the invoices that they hadn't been billed. Joe had thrown everything he could at it, he felt responsible for all his staff. Trying to do the decent thing he carried on paying them full wages *(much to the anger of wife Dawn)* right up to the company officially going bust. After losing the company, next went the house, his building society and bank pulled the plug on him, he had sold his Porsche so he could pay the weekly wage bills. Then, when he was at rock bottom and thought it couldn't get any worse, he also lost Dawn.

The final straw came when he told her he would have to sell her Range Rover, a birthday present he had bought her. They couldn't afford to run it any more and the money would help pay rent on a flat until things got better. She said, NO! Adding that she wasn't going back to work to come back in the evening to a shit hole of a flat, she was leaving him.

Joe pleaded with her to stay, promising he would soon be back on his feet. He would start up another business when he was allowed to and the good times would soon return. Her reply was she couldn't stand to look at him because he was such a loser! The next day, she left with three suitcases of clothes, all the jewellery he had bought her and the Range Rover. She didn't even say goodbye or leave Joe a "*Dear, John*" letter. It was at this low point in Joe's life that he came to the conclusion after finally sobering up following a three-day binge. He was shit at choosing women and vowed never to fall in love again or have a drink again, although the later was sworn with less conviction. A psychiatrist would probably blame his mother's early death for the reason for Joe falling in love so quickly and proposing. He knew that he would turn his is life around and the good times would return, but he still had the demons from the past that he couldn't shake off.

In the meantime, Rob "the man" had disappeared off the face of the earth. Months later a mutual friend told Joe about Rob's drug habit that had spiralled out of control. Also, that he had moved out of London after having a breakdown trying to get "clean." Joe didn't blame Rob, if anything he felt guilty, he should have seen that his pal was having problems and been there to help him. He missed his Brummie pal they had so much in common, and more so now Dawn had fucked off. He had no one to talk to about life or what he should do about his troubles. Which was

28

ironic really, when it was Rob who had caused the troubles.

Anyway, as far has Joe had been concerned, it wasn't as if Rob was embezzling money from the company. His life just got fucked up because of the drugs, everything had just got out of control, and he couldn't cope. The poor bugger had enough problems now trying to sort out his life, just like Joe did, it was what it was! There was no point in bearing grudges, Mr Potts had told him all those years ago, and he always remembered he had said, "It was just a waste of good energy."

Joe had stopped feeling sorry for himself and was starting to get on with his life the best he could, working all the hours just to survive. London was a fantastic exciting city, but when you didn't have much money, it was a harsh place to live. Despite his problems Joe still loved London and was determined to sort his life out and get back on track. The one exception being his wife, she was a selfish bastard. Unfortunately, Joe didn't see it until he needed her support, all she did was bail out with everything he had paid for when things were going well. He realised now he was well rid of her that was one thing Rob had done for him. If the problems hadn't come along, she would have just continued living the high life at Joe's expense. Whenever Joe brought up the conversation of starting a family, she would just say she wasn't ready. Saying life was for enjoying not ruining your body by having kids, Joe was in love and in his defence working his balls off every day, and he just didn't see it. When Joe told her about the mess *they* were in, she corrected him and said, "You mean the mess you are in." He thought it was just because she was upset, and she would help out trying to save the company that was until she had left with all her belongings that Joe had paid for.

Chapter Three
One Door Closes and Another One Opens

Joe had moved into a flat in Hackney, in the East London a friend rented it to him for a ridiculously low rent. Joe was grateful and promised he would make it up to his pal when he got back on his feet. The flat was sparse furniture wise, a couple of paintings that Joe hadn't bothered to hang were leaning against the wall. He hadn't planned to be living there for long, always the eternal optimist, he had been there now for seven months

Joe had a job behind the bar pulling pints at The White Hart pub on Chancery Lane next to the Holborn tube station. Lunch time was a busiest time of the day with business people having lunch meetings in the restaurant or just to socialising with a couple of drinks and a bar meal. Jimmy Daly was one of Joe's regulars, he would have one drink with lunch in the bar Monday to Friday. He was a funny character, talked very slowly and kept himself to himself. Jimmy was has regular as clockwork; he would come in at one p.m. on the dot, sit on the same stool at the bar. He would have one Gin and tonic and a meal off the specials board and leave at 1.55 exactly. Joe would have his G & T ready for him when he walked through the door, and he also put a reserved ticket on Jimmy's place at the end of the bar. For this personal service Jimmy would give Joe a £2 tip when paying his bill, he always paid in cash.

Joe was surprised when found out that Jimmy had his own business, Daly Private Investigation services; his office was just around the corner above a betting shop on Brook Street. The last thing Joe had his "funny" shy regular customer down as, was a private eye. Joe assumed he had a boring job like an accountant or office equipment manager, not a private "dick". Over time through chatting over the bar, Joe and Jimmy became friends and hearing Joe's story about losing his business and his wife walking out, Jimmy felt sorry for him. He explained that he was a private investigator and that it centred mostly on marital problems, cheating, divorces, tracing, the odd missing person cases and insurance frauds. Once, he even had a case on a missing Labradoodle, which the owner paid handsomely for the recovery of his four-legged friend.

Jimmy started to give Joe a few jobs on his days off from working in the pub, Joe was grateful for, the extra money, it certainly helped. To start with the jobs were nothing difficult, just things like following husbands, wives, girlfriends etc., that Jimmy's clients suspected were having affairs. Joe enjoyed the work and would type up in-depth reports back in jimmy's office after each surveillance job. He made sure the reports were thorough quickly learning that Jimmy was a stickler for the detail. He would tell Joe *the devils always in the detail*, don't leave anything out, even if it seems irrelevant. Reminding

Joe, that it was usually the little irrelevant points that cracked the case.

Jimmy Daly was a fifty-seven-year-old Londoner, born and raised in Kings Cross, he moved to Maida Vale after he married the love of his life, Anne Marie. She was from Highgate, and they met at a dance at the Roundhouse in Camden, everyone said they made a lovely couple. Jimmy knew she was the one for him, quickly realising she was a "keeper." He plucked up the courage and proposed, luckily, she felt the same about him. Jimmy's business gave them a good income, after the honeymoon Anne Marie quit her job as a secretary to become a housewife. They didn't have any children, it just never happened for them, they were happy and doted on each other.

They would go on a three-week cruise once a year for their holiday, they always dined at The Ritz on Christmas Eve. Not having children did have its benefits, but they would have given up their good life for a child. In later years Anne Marie developed thrombosis in her knees, it got worse and restricted her walking, and she ended up housebound. It didn't spoil their life, so they couldn't go cruising or dancing at weekends. They still had each other that was the most important thing, they just adapted. That's what people of their generation did, they never complained, they just got on with life whatever shit hand they were dealt, never the victim. Jimmy's good looks had long gone with age, he was now thin on top, with bushy grey eyebrows, and he had small round eyes and thin lips. He was overweight, this being the reason his suit jackets never fastened, he had a pot belly. He was now widowed; He was a kind man, but he always seemed sad. Joe just put it down to him being a bit misery, some people just were.

But Jimmy's secretary Harriot told Joe Anne Marie was his life, and he was never the same after he had gone home one evening and found her dead in her chair from a heart attack. She said a light went out in Jimmy's eyes after that, and he changed forever. Despite appearing miserable, when you got to know him, you realised, he was a wonderful kind human being. His only fault being when he spoke it was ever so slowly as if he was deliberating over every word, he was about to say. He was so good at taking in every small detail and also looking like nobody on the street, made him ideal for his role of private investigator.

Jimmy's secretary/receptionist/food shopper/dogs' body, Harriot McKenzie-Parkes, enjoyed Joe's visits to the office to write up his reports and briefings with Jimmy. Harry, has she liked to be called was originally from Brighton, she inherited a tidy sum when her widowed Mum passed away. She had looked after her elderly mother until the end. Three months after the funeral she sold up, moved to London and bought a flat for cash in Kennington. She didn't need to work and certainly not for what Jimmy paid her, but she loved the idea of working for a private eye! She found it all so exciting after her dull existence in Brighton, the job, the buzz of working and living in London was such a different way of life to what she had been used to, it gave her such a thrill. She was probably late twenties, early thirties, and super model thin, but with full breasts. She was attractive, but not what you would call a real beauty, she had perfect skin and striking dark brown eyes. Also, she never wore make up, well, not until Joe started coming into the office. Then she started to wear a little blusher and red lip stick, which she thought was really daring, and made her feel a little slutty! The more she got to know Joe she would fantasise about having a wild passionate affair with him. She absolutely loved it when he called her H instead of Harry. Apart from a couple of school romances, she never had a real lover. She was always busy looking after her mum, she didn't have any regrets, that's what children of her generation did.

She was always smartly dressed if very conservatively; she would wear her auburn hair up in a bun topped off with glasses, surprisingly with stylish Ray ban wayfarer frames. She tried to make the best of what God had given her. What the Almighty had given her in abundance, was a wonderful, warm, kind personality. She was one of those people who was instantly liked and won over everybody she met within a couple of minutes; she was a genuinely lovely human being. Once Joe got to know her, he put her at mid to late thirties, she as actually late twenties.

Jimmy told Joe he was a natural PI, and he was very pleased with the way Joe had handled the jobs he had been given, also how he had conducted himself with clients. Joe was a great help to Jimmy who was starting to find the job hard work now in his later years, he put it down to he was getting "on", and he was certainly not as fit as he used to be.

He taught Joe what he had learned over the years in the business. Not before too long Joe was doing more investigating than bar work. He didn't mind, he enjoyed the PI work more and Jimmy was paying him more than what he earned in the pub.

One day, not too unexpectedly Jimmy finally offered Joe a full-time job in the business, which Joe gratefully accepted, Harriot was thrilled and couldn't stop smiling all day. Jimmy discussed with Joe and Harry that he would step back and do more of the office-based work seeing Joe was now ready to do the field work. It was unanimously agreed to be a good idea and the best working combination. Jimmy applied for a Licence for Joe now he was to become a full time Private Investigator. PI licenses in the UK are issued by the SIA, Security Industry Authority. Joe attained the necessary IQ level three award and that was it, Joe Makin PI! The Agency did good steady business, Joe took to the job like he had been doing it all his life. Sometimes, he would bend the letter of the law to get a "result" but did his best to keep it from Jimmy, who would have been horrified. Profits were up and Jimmy offered Joe a full partnership in the business, to which Joe graciously accepted.

The first thing Joe did as a partner was give Harry a twenty five percent wage increase. She reacted by bursting into tears and was comforted by a startled Joe with a gentle hug, which she secretly appreciated more than the raise. The second thing Joe did was to finally get Jimmy to let Harry update the office, and he would do the same with the business; everything needed a complete modern make-over. She did a great job, replacing everything except in Jimmy's office. He *liked it just the way it was,* and said the clients wouldn't be going into his office anyway, that was Joe's role now. The finished job was classy, a modern black wood grain desk for Harry with light grey filing cabinets behind. Harry was the first thing clients saw on entering the office. A new soft Leather sofa in cream was to the right of the reception just past the photo-copier under the double window. In front of the sofa was a modern glass and chrome coffee table with current magazines on. This was the waiting area in the reception for the clients to relax until Joe was ready to meet with them. Joe's revamped office on the left used to be the old storeroom, it was now his bright classy looking office. A big modern black desk, a high-backed leather chair greeted you as you walked in, another leather chair was situated on the opposite side of the desk for the client.

To the right was a cream leather sofa and coffee table, which matched the ones in reception, the walls were painted pale grey. Joe would speak with the company's females' clients on the sofa. Harry said, it would make them feel more relaxed talking about their case, male clients sat facing Joe at his desk. The office looked very modern, but still business like and most importantly like a modern professional successful company. The grubby front door had been replaced with a smart grey wooden door with a glass panel in the top half. Sat proudly in the centre of the door below the glass was a brass plaque engraved Daly & Makin Private Investigators. Joe thought the glass panel looked like the PI's office door in the old Raymond Chandler films. He wanted to have the glass sign painted, but sadly H over ruled him on that one, saying it would look tacky and dated. The third and last job, Joe had a website designed for the agency to bring it into the 21st century, within six months it had trebled the business. The Modern front website page carried the ABI Logo: *Association of British Investigators, upholding professional values,* for impact and reassurance. Jimmy was delighted and from then on gave Joe carte blanche to do whatever he saw fit with the business.

Monthly board meetings were held on the last Thursday of each month. The three of them would discuss all the months' business and upcoming jobs. The meetings were usually held at a top restaurant; this month's meeting was at the OXO Tower. It was a good excuse for a nice evening together, something Harry looked forward to and always made an effort to look as glamorous as possible. Joe stated for the record if business kept improving at the current rate, they would have to take on another person, this was duly noted.

He then went on to briefly go over the recent cases and outcome. Harriot would run through the finances, company "accountant" being one of her many roles, Jimmy would run through AOB. Business concluded it was Cognac all around after dessert, then taxi's home, Jimmy headed back to Maida Vale. Joe and Harry would always share one, dropping H in Kennington and then on to Joe's place. Harry asked him on the way home why he was still living in Hackney, he told her he should have moved somewhere more central, but just hadn't got around to doing it.

Joe thought about what H had said, he was earning good money now, but he had been so busy he hadn't had time to look for somewhere else to live. The next morning, he asked Harry if she would sort a place out for him, she was excellent at getting things done. She loved the idea of finding Joe a new apartment and day dreamed of him asking her to move in with him.

He told her his budget and also that he fancied living in Chelsea or Fulham, he liked both areas, and they were quite central, Harry got on the case immediately.

A couple of months later he was moving in to his flat in Fulham, Vanston Place was a quiet street just off Fulham Broadway. It was a modern block of eight apartments, Joe was on the second floor, a light airy two bed, two bath and good size lounge with balcony. Harry had done a fantastic job finding the place for him. It was an Ideal location and a great apartment; Harry even helped him shop for all the new furniture.

He made a mental note that he must take her out for dinner one night, the big bouquet of flowers he sent her was definitely not enough. The problem was he was certain she had a massive crush on him, and he didn't want to give her false hope by going out for dinner. She was such a lovely lady, but not someone who Joe would date; for a start she was too good for him.

He thought, *I date women who run off with good friends or leave when the money runs out.* He knew Harry wouldn't do anything like that to him, but he didn't want to spoil the great working relationship they had. Anyway, Harriot McKenzie-Parkes deserved someone far better than an occasional pisshead like Joe Makin. Once Jimmy and Harry got to know Joe better, they realised he had a drinking problem. It was sporadic though when he was stressed or under pressure it was a kind of release for him. Jimmy had a heart-to-heart chat with him about it, he told Joe it concerned and saddened him. Joe promised it was something he managed to keep under control most of the time. But sometimes when things just get too much, he would crack and go on a bender. He also promised Jimmy that it wouldn't affect his work or the agency, he wouldn't ever let that happen. Jimmy smiled at Joe and eventually said, "You can get help for your problem, you know; I don't want you to come to any harm, Joe. I think too much of you."

Joe smiled back and replied, if his "problem" ever got too much, he would seek help.

Chapter Four
A Usual Job

Monday morning, Joe was at his desk checking his workload for the week, Harry arrived and shouted through *good morning* and shortly afterwards brought him his first cup of coffee of the day. Despite sending Joe a text and a message to his mobile, she thanked him again for the beautiful flowers he had sent her.

Joe smiled and said, "You are more than welcome; it's the least I could do after you found my new place for me; it's perfect, and H's great taste strikes again."

Blushing, Harriot replied, "Are you settled in? I would have gladly come around over the weekend, and helped you."

Joe shook his head. "H, you have done more than enough; I'm in now, and it's a smashing flat. Thanks to you, it looks good, and it's a great place to live. Thank you again."

There was an awkward silence as Harry lingered, just smiling at Joe, so he smiled back. She jumped when the silence was broken by Jimmy shouting, "Good morning, all, and to all, a good morning!" to which they replied in unison, "Morning." Harry turned and hurried off to make

Jimmy his cup of coffee, and Joe started up the laptop on his desk.

After answering a couple of client e-mails and sending one to Harry and Jimmy. Looking in his diary he had an appointment at eleven-half with a Mrs Elizabeth Harrington. After lunch some paper work regarding closing two competed cases, then clear until a late afternoon meeting with Jimmy. Joe picked up the Manilla file that had been sat in his in tray, the cover carried the usual white sticker with Mrs E. Harrington typed on it together with the date. He opened her file that Harry had prepared when the Lady had contacted the agency for an appointment. Mrs Harrington lived in Mayfair, number 53 Adams Yard, married to husband Nigel for twenty years, two grown children. Husband Nigel was the reason for the appointment she had told H.

Harriot's checks had shown Nigel Harrington was a Director of the German Investment bank LPZ based in the city. The Bank operates throughout Germany, with offices in London, New York, Hong Kong and Singapore. LPZ provides banking services to large corporations and Mittelstand companies, financial institutions, and Asset management customers. *Almost ninety per cent of companies belong to the German Mittelstand and over fifty per cent of them bank with LPZ. Therefore, it was safe to say LPZ are a heavy hitter in the banking world,* Joe thought. The check on Mrs Harrington confirmed she was a housewife, with no employment records.

The family home in Adams Yard had no mortgage on the property. Joe was impressed, it was a much sort after area, up behind The Dorchester Hotel, a very pricey place to live. He knew his way around Mayfair from his work and also his social life. The properties in Adams yard an exclusive cul-de-sac cost million, probably starting at £15 million plus for one of the "smaller" houses there.

Joe decided there and then that if he took the case, he would double the highest fee that he had ever charged a client. Mrs Harrington could obviously afford it and business was business, Jimmy wouldn't have agreed, he was too much of a gentleman. He felt a slightly uneasy about the job, only as far as old Nigel sounded like an important influential man. Someone who could cause trouble for anybody who caused him trouble! Joe decided he would see how the meeting went, before deciding whether to take the job. A big fee was very nice, but not if it was going to bring a shitstorm in its wake. Jimmy had always drilled into him if a job doesn't seem right, walk away from it and don't look back. Joe decided he would discuss it with Jimmy at their afternoon meeting after he had met Mrs Harrington.

"I wonder what old Nigel's been up to?" Joe said in a low voice, closing the file. He had a drink of coffee sat back and looked up at ceiling. This looks like a usual case of suspicious partner who wants to know if hubby is cheating. Well, we will find out at eleven-half when his lady wife comes in.

Chapter Five
Mrs Harrington

Joe's phone rang on his desk at 11.34 precisely. It was Harry letting him know Mrs Harrington had arrived, Joe appreciated punctuality, Jimmy always said it was sign of good breeding. He thanked Harry, asked her to give him a couple of minutes and show her in. Joe walked over to the small wardrobe over by the sofa. He checked his hair and tie in the mirror on the inside of the door and then put on his suit Jacket. His office door opened, in walked Harry followed by Mrs Harrington, perfect timing.

Mrs Harrington was an attractive lady, impeccably dressed, late-forties maybe a little older, blonde hair up in a bun, five-eight, medium build. A very good-looking lady and most likely a real stunner when she was younger. She was exactly how Joe had imagined her, classy and oozing money and style, Joe thought she also smelt delicious. He shook her hand catching the huge diamond ring on her finger, apologising for his clumsiness, he offered her a seat on the sofa. He turned and thanked Harry asking not to be disturbed, and she left closing the door behind her. Joe sat in the chair on the opposite side of the coffee table. Picking up his pad and pen, he asked, "Now, Mrs Harrington, what can I do for you today?"

She cut straight to the chase and replied, "I think my husband is having an affair, and I want to know if my fears are correct, or if I'm being over sensitive."

Joe noted a slight European accent, but couldn't place it, possibly Polish, Hungarian. He wrote down notes, this was for the benefit of his client, a tip from Jimmy *having an affair dash, but unsure* on his pad looking he up asked, "And what are the reasons for your suspicions, Mrs Harrington?"

She let out a little sigh, looked up at the wall behind Joe's head and then back at him, she eventually replied, "This is quite embarrassing speaking to a stranger like this, 'erm, our sex life has always been very good. However, these past few months he hasn't come near me and that is very unusual."

Joe wrote on his pad; the case is pretty flimsy I would be surprised if old Nigel is bonking his PA or *anybody else for that matter. I would think the answer is he's stressed or over worked, easy money, maybe.* Joe didn't really have to write anything more on his pad, but he did, it looked professional and thorough.

He explained his fees and expenses for taking the job, She never blinked at the fees, and probably a couple of lunch bills with her friends, he thought. He explained depending on what he found it could take a few days or a few weeks, again she didn't appear concerned. Joe added that he would provide photographic evidence. She asked about the confidentiality of the firm and insisted that all records of the case be handed over to her and none kept on

45

file. Joe reassured her the company's reputation was built on confidentiality and mutual trust, with many satisfied returning clients. He also agreed not to keep any record of the case on file, which was a lie. Jimmy always insisted they wrote up a brief conclusion of each case which were then put in the client's folder and filed.

After making a few more notes, he closed his pad, he looked up at Mrs Harrington, smiled and said, "I'm sure we will be able to take the case and will be back to you tomorrow morning with the decision." Adding that *he hoped to be able to show her that her husband still loved her very much and wasn't involved with anyone else*.

Joe had decided there and then to take the case, but out of courtesy he would speak with Jimmy later that afternoon for his thoughts. It sounded like excellent money for an easy case, he hoped for a positive decision and was sure they wouldn't regret it. He would have it put on the agenda for the afternoon meeting.

Rising from the sofa, Mrs Harrington smiled and replied, "That's very kind. Thank you, Mr Makin, also it's very sweet of you trying to reassure me. I love my husband very much; he is the world to me; it would destroy me if he left me for somebody else. I'll wait for your call tomorrow morning; I'll be abroad for a week to ten days at the end of the week, visiting a relative. My husband will probably use the company flat in Docklands with me not being home. If my husband is betraying me, he has the perfect opportunity, don't you think? Hopefully, when I return, you will have finished your investigations, and we can conclude our business. If that is the case, Mr Makin, I will pay you a £500 bonus, I want to know one way or the other as soon as possible."

Joe thanked her and smiled, thinking with your looks and money, you would have guys queuing up to date you. He finally replied, "Good, our receptionist be in touch first thing, then we can go over the details that I will need, the address of your husband's workplace in Canary Wharf, his movements, office hours, etc. I'll need an up-to-date photograph of him, the make and registration of his car, and anything else you might think relevant. Also, you mentioned he will probably be staying at company flat not far from his office in Canary Wharf; I'll also need that address, please."

Joe walked his new client to the door; he shook hands and reassured her he would most likely be able start on her case after the weekend. Whereby he would text her mobile once his preparation work was complete and was ready to start the case. Closing the office door, he turned to Harry who was sat behind her desk typing and said, "What did you think of her, H?"

Harry looked up and replied, "She's a very classy lady and obviously extremely wealthy, did you see the size of the diamond ring she was wearing, oh wow?"

Joe smiled and said, "See it, I nearly broke a couple of fingers on it when I shook her hand."

Harry laughed and asked, "Are you going to take her case?"

Joe was walking back towards his office and replied over his shoulder, "Yea, I think so; it's very good money and shouldn't take the least ten days she's out of the country. All for a run-of-the mill case of is the partner cheating or not?" Little did Joe know that those words would come back to haunt him big time.

At their afternoon meeting, they eventually came to the last item on the agenda of Mrs Harrington. Joe explained the case, the fees he had agreed to charge and asked Jimmy for his thoughts. He knew full well he could have gone to the toilet and then make a coffee by the time it took Jimmy to dwell on the question before answering

Jimmy scratched his chest over his shirt then looked at the ceiling and then the wall and eventually replied, "It appears to be a case and for a heavy fee, was she okay with that?"

Joe replied, "Yes, nothing to her, very wealthy lady, you should have seen her jewellery!"

Jimmy had satisfied the itch on his chest and after inspecting the ceiling and wall again, carried on. "Her husband sounds like a big hitter; could he be vindictive and cause us problems? What do you think?"

Joe smiled. "Great minds think alike Jimmy, the thought did cross my mind to, but if we catch him out on his wife's instructions, we're just doing our job. I can't see any comeback, certainly not legally, can you?"

Jimmy shook his head stood up looked at Joe for a good sixty seconds and replied, "No, I don't mean legally, but just be certain everything you do is above board. If they live in Adam's Yard, they are obviously very wealthy, we don't want any comeback if he is fooling around. That way we shouldn't have any problems, okay, let us take it, why not, it doesn't sound like a difficult job, let's do what she asks and take the money, we would be silly not to."

Joe promised he would do everything by the book and declared that was it, nothing else to report. The meeting was over thanking God, Joe loved Jimmy like a son would his father, but he took so long to speak. Surely, nobody could be thinking about something that long, he would take so long to reply to a question, that their brief meetings would sometimes run to over an hour, when twenty minutes would have done. The job.

Chapter Six
Easy Money

Joe stood on the corner of South Audley St at the entrance to Adam's Yard, after having a good look around at the area, he turned into Adams Yard. Walking along the left-hand side looking for number 53 on the opposite side of the Cul-de-sac. His first thought was it was always a problem "Staking out" a Cul-de-sac, very conspicuous, you stood out like the preverbal Bulldogs balls. He saw the house on the opposite side, a double fronted four-story white painted Town house, beautiful and obviously worth a fortune. Steps going up to large Shiny black painted double front doors, finished off with two perfectly trimmed bushes in large square black pots either side. Elegant heavy draped curtains in all the Georgian windows. It looked like a photograph in an Estate agents window everything pristine and perfect, nothing out of place. Next port of call was Nigel's offices, he took the tube to Bank, then changed onto the Docklands light Railway (DLR). Coming out of the station Joe walked the short distance to the offices of LPZ Bank. Just set back in the right-hand corner of Canada Way, it was very impressive a glass fronted building fifteen stories high. A large reception area with a glass atrium, on the left-hand side sat six receptionists. On the way back to Holborn, Joe text Mrs Harrington to thank her for all the information she had provided, and he was ready to start the job on Monday morning, he wished her a good weekend.

Monday morning, Joe stood across from LPZ's offices in Canada square and saw Nigel speaking on his mobile and enter the main glass doors. His wife had told Joe that her husband took lunch a one p.m. each day and finished for the night usually at seven p.m. After returning at 12.45 p.m., he saw Nigel leave the office at 1.10, Joe followed, but Nigel called at a Pret, bought a sandwich and returned to the bank. Nigel left the office at seven p.m. and boarded the DLR followed by Joe, again from a safe distance. Once on board Joe took the chance Nigel didn't suspect anything and sat a little further down on a bench seat across the aisle.

Joe had a prefect view of Nigel, despite the tube being busy. He had Nigel at 5–10, medium build, dark hair with a little greying at the sides, strong jaw. A reasonably good-looking bloke most ladies would think, and probably in his late forties, early fifties. An expensive navy-blue overcoat covered his equally expensive dark grey business suit, he had an air of authority about him, like most senior bankers do, must be the pay and bonuses they are on. Perfectly polished black Loake shoes, his briefcase on the floor behind his legs looked like crocodile skin. Joe thought altogether Nigel and Eve Carrington were a rich good looking power couple!

They got off at Bank and Nigel crossed the busy road and entered 1 Lombard Street restaurant, which took its name from its location. Joe saw the Nigel wave to a large man sat at one of the tables, walking over he sat and joined him. The man despite his bulk was also in a sharp expensive suit, he also looked like a banker. Two hours later Joe followed Nigel back to the company apartment in Canary Wharf. Hungry and tired he decided he would it a night, and headed back home to Fulham.

He was back on look out at the bank at 6.45 p.m., this was the job, boring, most of the time. When he told people his job, they always said how exciting it must be, but in reality, as boring as hell. Nigel left the office at seven-half p.m. having spent his lunchtime probably at his desk in his office. He leisurely walked down Canada square, swinging his briefcase he crossing the road to the apartment block to the company flat.

Joe hung back and had Nigel in his sights 6 metres in front as they walked towards the impressive Glass building, which was Westferry Apartments. Nigel walked through the front doors acknowledging the uniformed concierge sat behind the reception desk. Joe waited ten minutes before walking up to the glass entrance, Danny the concierge, waved and buzzed him in. Joe shook Danny's outstretched hand and asked, "Anybody arrive before him, Danny, or anyone expected tonight?"

Danny came from around his desk, smiling replied, "Nope nobody at all, Joe, if anybody was due, he usually tells me on his way in, so I can expect them and let them go up." Adding, "Like I explained on Friday Joe, he doesn't have many visitors when he stays except the attractive dark-haired lady, I told you about; she's called a couple of times in the last month and left after him the next morning, though no pattern to her visits."

Joe thanked Danny, and slipped him two twenty-pound notes that he already had in his hand. "Okay, Danny, you've got my number, if you have anything to report send me a text as we agreed, okay?"

Danny slipped the notes in to his trouser pocket, smiled broadly, and replied, "Sure, no problem at all, Joe. Thanks very much, appreciate it."

Danny Sumner had been one of the concierges at Belgrove court, Westferry Circus apartments for five years now and enjoyed the job, it was easy work. He lived with his wife Alice and their three-year-old son Arthur in a three-bedroom council house not far away on the other side of West Ferry. They were childhood sweethearts from Jamaica Road who had never managed go get out of East London. They made an odd-looking couple; Danny was a 6' 1" beanpole with a shaven head after his blonde hair had started to go. Alice stood at 5' 4" not too bad a height for a woman until she stood next to her tall husband. She had jet black hair, a pretty face, still carried a little weight from the birth of young Arthur. But they were in love and happy with what little they had in their life. Danny was not one of the brightest men, but one of life's genuine nice guys who unfortunately never got a break an even if he did, he would probably cock it up. No matter how hard he tried, when things were looking good, it would always go tits up. They were just starting to get on top of things when Alice got pregnant again, to make matters worse she announced she was expecting twins. Danny couldn't believe it, he said, "We can hardly afford to live as it is without two more children, Alice." Then he felt guilty when Alice started crying and told her he was sorry. His heart melted he hated it when she got upset, he told her not to worry, and they would get by somehow. He wished he could give her a better life, he loved her so much, and she deserved a lot better, she never ever complained about their life and how hard it was.

He worked all the extra shifts he could at the apartments, then he *got* an evening job behind the bar at the local pub, until the landlord sacked him and gave his job to his nephew. So, when Joe turned up out of the blue and told Danny he was a private detective on a case and gave him £100 with a promise of more for information Danny couldn't believe his luck and jumped at the offer. When Danny explained that he knew the tenant and that he sometimes had a lady visitor, he was given another £40. The extra money was a life saver with Alice due in a few more months, Danny couldn't wait to finish his shift and get home to give Alice the £140, he told her to buy some baby stuff for the twins and treat herself. Alice was worried when he explained where the money had come from, frightened that Danny might lose his job if his bosses found out. He promised her he would be careful, and they wouldn't find out, it was easy money that they really needed.

Joe didn't receive a call from Danny that evening, and was outside the banks head office the next morning to see Nigel walk into the reception greeting one of the receptionists who looked up and smiled at him. She was a pretty dark-haired woman, and Joe wondered if she was the mystery visitor Danny had seen a couple of times at Nigel's apartment block? He made a mental note to ask Danny later if she came visiting again to try and get a photo of her on his phone.

Tuesday and Wednesday were much of the same, Nigel went to the office didn't come out for lunch and went back to Docklands in the evening. Where he remained all evening, and according to Danny no sign of the mystery dark haired visitor. Joe began to doubt if old Nigel did have a girlfriend, if he did, he wasn't in any rush to meet up with her, considering his wife was out of the country. On Thursday evening though, Joe had a result, after work Nigel left the office and walked to the DLR. Getting off at Bank he walked through to Monument and then took the Central line to Sloane Square. Walking up the Kings Road, Joe followed at his usual discreet distance. Crossing the road at the Old Chelsea Town Hall, Nigel turned right onto Sydney Street, half way up he stopped and rang the bell at number 44. A smart terraced house in the middle of a row of similar houses, but in this part of town it probably cost upwards of £3 million. The front door was opened by an attractive blonde woman in her late-thirties, she greeted

Nigel with kiss on the lips, and they both went inside. Joe thought to himself, *Bingo! So old Nige has been very busy, this blonde and then there's the mystery dark-haired visitor who would stay overnight at the apartment.*

Joe was in luck two doors up on the opposite side of the road was a posh Bistro. An ideal place to sit, watch and hopefully learn *what Old Nige was up to.* Joe sat at one of the five outside smart tables covered with blue gingham table cloths and a small glass vase with daffodils in, it was a perfect spot, Joe got comfortable, took out his phone and relaxed enjoying the warm summer evening.

Emiliano's Bistro offered a good selection of traditional Italian meals, also light snacks and sandwiches, they obviously served excellent coffee. Joe ordered a toasted cheese and ham ciabatta and an Americano. He couldn't believe his luck at finding such an ideal stake-out, it certainly beat standing on a corner, even on a nice evening like this. Half way through his ciabatta the door opened across the road at number 44 and out came old Nige and the blonde girlfriend. Nigel had changed into Chino's and a check shirt; the blonde wore the same pink floral summer dress that she had answered the door. Joe made out he was checking his phone, but was actually videoing them walking down the street with their arms around each other, like a couple of young loves.

Paying the bill, Joe took a quick slurp of his coffee and grudgingly a last large bite of the delicious toastie. Wishing he would have had time to finish it, he contemplated taking it with him, but it wasn't that kind on neighbourhood. Following on the opposite side of the road, he slowed as they stopped at The Beaufort Arms pub on the corner of Sydney Street and Cale Street. It was a typical London pub, large semi leaded windows, highly polished mahogany bar with a large brass hand rail with a matching brass foot rest running the length of the bar. Black wrought iron tables and stools scattered across the bare floorboards. A restaurant section had been added and was separated from the "pub" area by brass poles with red ropes, the dining tables covered with red table clothes. The blonde sat at one of the empty tables outside while Nigel followed by Joe went inside for the drinks. Their table was at the junction of the two roads the fourth table back on the Sydney St side was vacant, which was ideal. Joe came out of the pub and took a seat before Nigel returned with the drinks; he would have struggled otherwise to keep an eye on them from across the junction. A waitress served a meal at the next table to Joe, he caught her eye, and she nodded back. Joe had a clear view of Nigel's' table, he had returned with two glasses and a bottle of white wine, sitting down he gently kissed his companion on the lips,

Joe smiled; he had caught the kiss on his phone. He ordered another bottle of lager and a gin and tonic from the pretty blonde waitress noting the nametag on her uniform, Sally. When she was walking away to get his order he shouted after her, "Oh, Sally, could I also have two menus, please." She turned to Joe smiled and nodded; Joe smiled and thought what a pretty lady Sally was. She had thick blonde hair neatly tied back in a ponytail, a lovely fresh face, very little make up, deep blue eyes and a sexy cheeky smile, not too tall about 5–6 and a great figure.

The G & T and the extra menu made it look like Joe was waiting for someone to join him, it looked much better than a guy sat drinking on his own, simple but effective. The evening wore on, Nigel and "Blondie" were having a good night, deep in talk, very tactile and very kissy. Joe had some good photo evidence for Mrs Harrington when she returned home. He was pleased with how it was going and the £500 bonus, like he had told Jimmy it was an easy case and money for old rope. The smile dropped from his face; he was so pleased with himself that he hadn't thought about the effect the news would have on Mrs Harrington. He remembered when she was leaving the office, she had told him that she loved her husband deeply. He sat back, said under his breath, "Shit the poor bugger will be devastated."

Sally the waitress appearing at his side from nowhere made him jump, they both laughed and she asked, "Are you ready for another drink." He had been sat there for over three hours drinking and watching old Nige and Blondie kissing and cuddling without a care in the world. He had progressed from pints to whisky about an hour earlier and was beginning to feel the worse for it.

He smiled up at waitress Sally and replied, "Why not, but only a single this time, please, Pet."

Clearing the table, she took the empty glasses and both menus. Joe was sure she was flirting with him, but he did feel quite drunk so he could be wrong. He remembered a few drinks back she did ask him if he had been stood up, so maybe. Anyway, he would give her a good tip for looking after him so well all evening. Before she came back with his drink, Nigel and his lady got up and started walking back down to the house, they walked past Joe's table without a second look. Joe turned sideways in his chair just in time to see them going into number 44. He was happy with how the evening had gone and the photo evidence would close the case. Old Nige hadn't been very discreet. The pretty waitress returned with Joe's drink. She smiled asked, "Are you a Geordie? I just love your accent," Joe told her he certainly was and asked what time she finished work, he thought, *Well, it would be rude not to!*

Joe opened his eyes and squinted, the sun shining in through the curtainless windows dazzled him. Trying to get his brain in gear, he wondered where the hell he was. He looked to his left away from the glare of the bright morning sun and saw Sally's beaming face looking back at him. Now he remembered! He smiled back and said, "Good morning, what time is it?"

She kissed him on the lips, replying, "Just after seven. I've got to get ready for work now." Within that she climbed out of bed and walked over to the bathroom closing the door behind her. Joe admired her naked body and smiled remembering the night before, he had all the evidence he needed to nail old Nige the two-timer. He celebrated by getting drunk at the pub and to top it off came back to Sally's for a great night of sex. "It doesn't get much better than that my son," he said to himself. He shouted through to Sally, "Where do you work then?"

She shouted back, "At the White Company on Oxford Street." He heard the pump on the shower start up, so he lay there looking up at the ceiling.

They shared the tube ride down to the West End, Joe promised he would ring her, and they would go out when she had a night off from her evening job at the pub. He had been drunk when they went back to her flat, but sober, he decided he did like her, she seemed a genuine warm open person. She had told him on the tube journey that she was twenty-seven, was originally from Leicester and had moved to London after University.

Her mother had married again after her father had died and didn't have much time for her, so she rarely went back "home" to Leicester. Her dad had left her some money which helped her survive London prices. She had made some good friends in the five years she had lived in Kings Cross. Also, some of her Uni friends lived in London, and they kept in touch and met up regularly. Joe asked her if she remembered the couple sat at the corner table last night. She told him she had seen them there before having a drink and also in the restaurant a few times, adding they probably lived locally. He thought to himself he would ring her, unlike other occasions when he had said that, but really had no intention of calling. She gave him her number, he put it directly into his phone, promised he would call, they kissed and said goodbye.

Chapter Seven
Case Closed; A Job Well Done

When Joe opened the door and walked into the office, Harry's beaming smile turned into a frown. "You've been out all night again, haven't you? And drinking by the look of you," speaking to him like a mother would to a naughty child.

"Actually, I was working last night on the Harrington case for your information, but yes, I have been out all night!"

Joe replied, giving her one of his smiles that she could never resist. "Don't worry, I've had a shower already, and I'm going to shave and change my clothes, Could you drop this suit off at the dry cleaners at lunchtime for me, H, please?"

"But, of course, sir," she replied feigning anger. She couldn't stay annoyed at him for long, but her heart ached wondering who he had spent the night with. Joe always kept a toilet bag and a full change of clothes in the wardrobe in his office, for occasions like this, which cropped up quite often.

Changed, cleanly shaven and a crisp white shirt he stood in front of the reception desk smiling at Harry. She looked up from her PC and said unimpressed and straight faced, "Your eyes are still bloodshot, I'll get you some drops from the chemist, after I've dropped off your suit"

His smile grew, he replied, "You're an absolute star, H, tell me when is Mrs Harrington back in the country?"

"Monday," Harry replied, not even having to look in the diary.

"Excellent, can you arrange a meeting with her on Monday ideally? Is Jimmy in yet?" Joe asked, looking in the direction of Jimmy's closed office door.

Harry followed Joe's glance at Jimmy's door and replied, "No, but he shouldn't be too long now, I'll let you know when he arrives." With another beaming smile Joe turned, and went into his office and closed the door.

He had downloaded the photos onto a USB of randy old Nige and blondie kissing and cuddling from the night before. His mind drifted to Sally and their romp back at her place, a big smile on his face as he leaned back in his chair and looked at the ceiling. He realised he spent a lot of time looking up at ceilings, she was very sexy in an innocent sort of way and wow what a body. His carnal thoughts and mental images of the night before were shattered by the phone ringing on his desk. Jolting forward he picked up and then dropped the receiver on to his desk, finally answering the call, it was H's irritated voice to say Jimmy had arrived. Joe replied, "Thanks, sorry, I dropped the phone."

Harry frostily told him, "I know, my ear heard the commotion," and hung up. *Blimey, she's in a bad mood today,* Joe thought, collecting up his laptop and the USB, he headed for Jimmy's office.

Harry brought Jimmy his good morning tea and a coffee for Joe and then left closing Jimmy's door behind her. Joe was running through the night before in Chelsea with randy Nige and the blonde from number 44. Joe finished and took a drink of his coffee, waiting for Jimmy to comment on what Joe had just told him. As usual Jimmy sat silently drinking his tea looking at Joe, placing his China cup back on the saucer he cleared his throat and finally spoke. "When will you be giving Mrs Harrington the news about her cheating husband?"

Joe replied, "She's back from a trip abroad on Monday; H will get in touch her to arrange a meeting, hopefully on Monday." I'm certain she will want to hear the bad news sooner rather than later.

Jimmy looked at Joe for what seemed a good two minutes and nodding his head, finally said, "Good work, any further on who the dark-haired woman was who visited him a few times in Canary Wharf?"

Joe was surprised to be asked about the other woman, he shook his head and replied, "No, she hadn't shown up before old Nigel went to meet his blonde."

Jimmy smiled at Joe and said, "Okay, like you said, Joe, it was easy money. Well done."

Chapter Eight
To Be Expected

Joe arranged to meet Sally on Saturday night, he was going to ask H if she would book a table for two at Hush in Mayfair, but thought better of it and booked it himself. Hush was an excellent restaurant perfect for a first date, not too flash, excellent food and reasonable prices for Mayfair. He picked Sally up at her place in King Cross, he told the black cab to wait and rang the bell to her flat. She came out kissed him on the lips, she looked lovely, Joe had told her it was a casual dress, nothing too fancy kind of evening. She wore a white and pink floral summer dress with a white handbag and matching shoes, her thick blonde hair in a ponytail again, simple but very attractive, Joe thought, *You look perfect!* The cab headed off to Mayfair.

They had a great evening, got on as if they had known each other for months and ended up back at Joe's flat in Fulham. Sunday morning Joe cooked breakfast, early afternoon they strolled through to Chelsea and had a couple of drinks on the Kings Road. They chatted about their families, backgrounds, aspirations, Sally was quite shocked that Joe was a private investigator. She asked him to dish the dirt on the cases he had worked on, he teased her for being nosey, and said he was sworn to client secrecy. Joe never admitted it to anyone, but he always got a buzz out of telling people he was a PI. It wasn't your run of the mill occupation, it sounded exciting, mysterious and most woman found it quite sexy, shame most of the time it was boring and mundane. She asked him was being a PI the reason he had asked her about that couple at the pub on the night they met? She playfully hit him when he pompously replied, "I couldn't possibly comment on that, young lady!"

Joe looked at his watch and said, "Wow, is that the time I've got a bit of work to do for tomorrow?" He paid the bill, they said their goodbyes, and he put her in a taxi then headed back to Fulham. Thinking about the weekend, Joe smiled and thought, he would ask Sally out again, next weekend if she was free, and he really liked her. After a light dinner of pasta and a couple of glasses of red wine, he went over his notes for the meeting with Mrs Harrington he was due at Adams yard at eleven a.m. the next morning.

Jimmy sat down on the sofa in Joe's office and asked him, "So, how did it go, did she take it badly?"

Joe shook his head and replied thoughtfully, "No, not at all; she was very calm, I expected there might have been a few tears, but nothing. Strangely, it was if she expected it, or as if she knew."

Jimmy looked beyond Joe and out of the window behind Joe's desk and finally said, "Obviously, a classy lady, you know, I've never guessed it right even after all these years; you never know how the client is going to react to news you give them about their case. The ones you think will break down don't, and the hard-faced ones are sometimes devastated and cry a river. I once told one woman her husband had been cheating on her, and she jumped up and attacked me. For God's sake, you just never can tell."

Joe, sitting back in his chair, put his hands behind his head and said, "A very cold lady; she paid in cash and £50 notes, also insisted that I handed over all the details and wanted assurances that none would be retained on file."

Harry walked in with Jimmy's cup of coffee, and said excitedly, "Go on then what was the house like?"

Joe laughed out loud and replied, "It was stunning, a big marble black and white hall, a beautiful staircase that looked like it was out of a Hollywood Movie. I expected a man in a Tux and a woman in a ball gown to come dancing down the stairs any minute. The maid showed me into the drawing room, where Mrs Harrington was waiting. Again, beautifully decorated and furnished, stunning, very high ceilings a huge white marble fireplace and a big gold patterned sofa. All in all, H, it really opened your eyes as to how some people with lots of cash live."

Harry sighed loudly, looking dreamily at the wall behind Joe's desk. Gathering her thoughts, she looked back at Joe and Jimmy. She said in a sad voice, "All that wealth, possessions and lifestyle doesn't mean you're happy, does it though? I bet you broke her heart this morning, Joe, when you gave her the news about her husband."

For a moment, the room was silent while they all thought how true Harry's words were. It was Joe who broke the silence; he said, "Yes, that's true, H, but I wouldn't mind betting she'll bounce back. She strikes me has a tough cookie our Mrs Harrington; she never flinched or got upset when I gave her the news. She never let any feelings show whatsoever. Sitting there so elegantly, she thanked me, took the USB and gave me an envelope with the cash in which included the £500 bonus. I bet she will make old Randy Nige pay through the nose for cheating on her."

Harry jumped in quickly with, "Serves him right, for cheating on her; what is it with, men? They have a gorgeous wife, and it's still not enough?" Jimmy and Joe looked at each other and burst out laughing. Harriot blushed deep red.

Joe said, "All right, girl, mind you, don't fall off your soapbox." They all laughed.

Joe and Jimmy had finished their drinks. Harriot collected the cups, and Joe placed the envelope on the tray and said, "Make sure you bank the money, won't you, H? We don't want it staying in the office, a sad ending to the case, but at least it was a very profitable job." They all nodded in agreement. Harry and Jimmy left and went back to work, leaving Joe to go over the brief of his next case. It was an insurance company job, they wanted surveillance on a man who was suing them, claiming he couldn't walk after a car crash. Joe had done quite a few of these for the company, and it never ceased to amaze him at how stupid some of claimants were. Pretending they were bed ridden and then get caught playing Sunday football for their local pub team. Joe always enjoyed these jobs, they were boring, and he never felt   guilty when exposing the cheats, after all, honest people were paying sky high insurance policies because of these dishonest bastards.

Chapter Nine
A Bolt Out of the Blue

The claimant in question, a Paul Severs lived in Putney at the back of the High St in a terraced house on Lifford St. *Nice area,* Joe thought, driving across the bridge and onto the High Street. He turned left on to Chelverton Road, and half a mile up he found Severs Street on the right. Severs lived at number 40, a nice, neat terraced house similar to all the others on the street. Outside number 40 was a Volkswagen Golf which the brief told him belonged to his man, Joe parked up on the right with a clear view of the front door of Severs place. He looked at his watch nine-half, time for breakfast, he poured himself a coffee, from his flask, opened his plastic container and decided on an egg mayonnaise sandwich, he would save the Tuna and sweetcorn for lunch.

At 11.35 a.m., the front of number 40 opened and out stepped a skinny dark-haired woman, Mrs Severs no less. Joe thought, *Here we go,* and got his camera ready. She closed the door behind her, Joe watched her walk down the street in the direction of the High Street. He pondered her choice of dress, *Why would you wear a black jumper and black leggings in this weather?* As she disappeared around the corner of the street. Joe shrugged his shoulders and took another drink of his coffee and started to think about lunch. 1.10 p.m. his phone rang, he saw Sally's on the screen, he pressed the green button and said, "Hi, how are you this lovely day?"

Hr heard Sally's lovely giggle, she replied, "I'm fine, I've just popped out to get some lunch and thought I would give you a quick call, what are you doing?"

He smiled and said, "I'm working, I'm on a stake-out."

He smiled, when she excitedly asked, "Really, can you tell me about it?"

Holding his phone closer to his mouth, he lowered his voice and lied, "It's a famous politician who the government think is passing secrets to the Brazilians."

Sally squealed excitedly, "No! Who is he? Tell me his name; go on, please." Joe had to clamp his hand over his mouth to stop himself from laughing out loud.

Controlling himself, he replied, "No, I can't; I've told you too much already; I might have to kill you now that I've told you what I have done already."

He looked in his rear-view mirror and saw Mrs Severs appear at the bottom of the street, struggling with two loaded shopping bags. Sally replied, "Oh, get lost; I don't believe you anyway; you're nothing but a big liar, and I bet you're really a bus driver!"

Joe laughed and said, "Now, you're just being rude and mean, and I was just about to tell how I was going to kill you…slowly in bed on Saturday night."

Sally's laugh down the phone made him smile, she said, "You dirty little devil, I'm going now, and I've seen a nice dress I want to, but for our date at the weekend, bye." With that, she hung up.

Day two of the stake-out nine a.m., Joe was back in Lifford Street; he had decided he hated stake-outs they were always so bloody boring. He decided he would give it another half hour before he would have his breakfast and a coffee. He had made himself a bacon and fried egg bap, which now didn't seem all that appetising, cold, but he was hungry so he would eat it anyway. He called it a day at eight-thirty p.m., the only thing to report was skinny Mrs Severs going out again dressed all in black, she returned two hours later. He wondered if Paul Severs was actually in the house, he hadn't seen anything of him, his car was parked outside though and hadn't moved.

Days three to six followed the same dull pattern, Joe sat in his car on Lifford Street half expecting, half wishing to see Severs come out in shorts and a vest and jog off down the street, but no such luck. At least he had his newly purchased crossword book to while away the hours. Monday morning, day eight, Joe tucked into another bacon and egg bap for breakfast, he had grown to enjoy them, despite their greasy look. Closing his sandwich box, he poured himself a coffee from his flask and glanced up the street at number 40 and sighed in boredom.

No sign of life at all and the downstairs curtains were still drawn, the tall blonde girl next door at number 42 came out and hurried off up the street, probably heading to work. Joe's mind drifted back to the weekend he had spent with Sally. He was becoming quite keen on her, she was a lovely lady and good fun to be with, and he thought he might give her a call at lunchtime. He looked at the clock on the dashboard 9.38, he thought it was later than that.

He looked in his rear-view mirror and saw a man walking down the street towards his car. He cleared his sandwich box and flask off the passenger seat into the footwell, he didn't want draw any interest from a possible neighbour. He needn't have bothered the man walked straight passed without a glance towards the line of cars. Joe's heart skipped a beat, he quickly pulled out the photograph of Severs from his inside pocket, he said to himself, "Bloody hell, it's him, the cocky bastard, he just walked right passed me." Joe caught him on camera walking down his street with his rucksack on his back. He stopped at his car and put the rucksack in the boot. Putting his key in the front door, he opened it and disappeared inside number 40. Joe smiled; he had half a dozen photos of Severs, and he said out loud, "That's why there wasn't any sign of you last week, you weren't bloody well there, you? You cheating bastard!"

Joe opened the office door, striding in he said, "Hello, H, how are you, my little beauty? Good, I hope?"

Seeing H's smiling face was infectious, Joe broke out in a broad smile, Harry looked truly glad to see him and replied, "I'm all the better for seeing you. Have you cracked your case? Is that why you are gracing us with your presence?"

Joe threw his backpack on the sofa and declared, "It certainly is H, and another potential fraudster bites the dust; the jobs a good One. Is Jimmy in his office?" Not waiting for a reply Joe knocked and walked into Jimmy's office.

Jimmy looked up, smiled, took off his glasses and asked, "All done, then, young Joe?"

Joe plonked himself down in the armchair against the wall facing Jimmy's desk and replied, "Yep, banged to rights, the cheating bastard. The insurance company was well pleased; they said they've got another job for us next week."

Jimmy sat back and looked at Joe for a good thirty seconds before replying, "Good news, those insurance jobs are good money for old rope. So, what's your plans, out celebrating tonight?"

Joe stood up, dusted off the seat of his jeans. Smiling he replied, "Yep, I am that Jimmy, I'm going out for a nice meal with my lady friend."

Jimmy replaced his glasses and without looking in Joe's direction, replied, "Have a good time; you deserve it. Now go and bugger off and let me finish up what I'm doing, so I can go home at a decent time."

Joe's face broke into a smile as he spotted Sally enter the main door of the restaurant, she spotted him waving and headed on over to the bar. He kissed her and whispered in her ear, "You look lovely tonight."

Sitting on the bar stool, she straightened her skirt and looking up at Joe as he sat back down, replied, "Well, thank you, kind sir, you look very nice too."

Joe laughed. "What would you like to drink?" Without waiting for a reply, he summoned the barman and ordered a large gin and tonic with a squeeze of passion fruit in it.

Sally had a good look around. Taking her drink off, Joe she asked, "Are there any celebs in tonight? This place is always in the papers with photos of different stars eating here."

Joe smiled and teasingly replied, "Well, tomorrow's paper, might have a photo of the two walking out of here."

The Ivy in Covent Garden was the place to be seen if you were lucky enough to manage to get a table. Joe knew the Maître de Gabriel Arquette, a suave handsome black-haired Parisian, which guaranteed him a table whenever. He had hired Joe about a year ago to check up on his English wife. When Joe reported back, that she wasn't having an affair but was secretly attending night school to learn French to surprise him.

Gabriel was so relieved that he couldn't thank Joe enough. They became good friends and stayed in contact with each other, socialising every few months or so. Whenever Joe went to The Ivy, Gabriel made sure Joe always got one of the best tables and was always made a fuss of by the staff. Especially if he was with a lady, Joe loved the attention, and it always impressed the hell out of his date.

After finishing their drinks at the bar, they moved to their table and enjoyed an excellent meal. They were having coffee and brandies after Sally had finished her dessert when Joe's phone rang. He glanced at the caller ID, excused himself and took the call at the table. Smiling at Sally sat facing him, he said in a low voice, *"Hi, Jimmy, what's up?"*

The smile disappeared from Sally's face soon after Joe's did, she was worried from the look on Joe's face it was bad news. She leaned towards him and touched his hand resting on the table, she silently mouthed to him, "Is everything okay?"

Joe gave Sally a wry smile and said into his phone, *"Okay, Jimmy, I'll be in first thing tomorrow,"* and ended the call.

Sally stroked his hand and said, "What is it? You look like you've seen a ghost?"

Joe rubbed his mouth with his napkin and placed it on the table. He looked up at Sally and replied, "I worked on a case a couple of weeks ago; a woman suspected her husband was having an affair," Sally interrupted, "and was he?"

Joe took a drink of his wine, wiping his mouth this time with his thumb and forefinger, he carried on, "Well, as a matter of fact, yes, he was. That was Jimmy on the phone, it's just been on the news. The man who was found dead in Hyde Park last night, the police have released some details and named him, it turns out to be the man I was investigating, my client's husband, Nigel Harrington."

Sally looked at Joe, and he still looked pale and troubled; he was deep in thought, and she held his hand again and said, "Oh my God, that's awful. Do you think his wife killed him?" She realised she was speaking too loudly when she got a surprised look from the couple on the next table.

She lowered her voice and leaning in closer to Joe, asked him again, "Do you think she killed him out of jealousy for having an affair?"

Joe looked up at her and smiled, he replied, "I don't know Sally; she didn't appear too surprised or upset when I gave her the news about him seeing someone else. If she was jealous, she made a good job of hiding it."

Joe paused, realising what he was saying, and quietly said to Sally, "I really shouldn't be telling you all this; it's confidential. Promise me you won't repeat any of this to anyone!"

Sally looked surprised and answered, "You don't have to worry; I wouldn't say a word to anyone, I promise, I find it all quite so exciting. Am I terrible for saying something like that about a murder? I'm so sorry!"

Joe squeezed her hand, smiled and said, "No, not at all, I suppose it does seem exciting. I'll have to get in touch with the police tomorrow and tell them everything I know."

Sally stroked his hand and asked innocently, "Will you get in any trouble over this?"

At least she made Joe smile, he gave out a little laugh and said, "No, you silly thing, I'm a private detective, I can't get in trouble for taking on a case for a client. Unless you do something illegal in your investigations." Sally blushed at her silly questions, but she was happy that she appeared to have lifted Joe's mood.

Chapter Ten
No News Yet!

Joe opened the office door and saw H's worried face trying to force a smile for him. He gave her a big reassuring smile and said, "Good morning, H, are you okay?"

She could only manage a half smile and replied, "Yes, not too bad; isn't it awful about Nigel Harrington? It's so shocking, Jimmy is in his office; he was already here when I got in. He said you were to go straight in when you arrived. I'll bring in the drinks."

Jimmy looked up from the desk as Joe walked in and sitting down, he said, "Morning, Jimmy, how are you this bright morning?"

After a good thirty seconds, it took Jimmy to take off his reading glasses and clear his throat twice. He finally replied, "I don't know, Joe. Ask me in a week or so if I'm okay. This business with Nigel Harrington is a real worry. I've been on to Andy for any news on the murder, but he's not working the case, and nothing's been released yet apart from who he was." Andy Sherry was a DI for the Met; he was an old friend of Jimmy's, and he and Joe got on well. They would feed each other information, which helped on the cases they were working on. If Andy needed info on a suspect, who better to ask than a private investigator. If

Jimmy or Joe couldn't help, they would use their network and ask colleagues who worked for other detective agencies in town. They were all friends, and it was a tight-knit community, and they all looked out for each other and shared information and "news" that was out on the street. They all had their own friends in the police force, and information crossed between them on a regular basis; one hand washed the other.

Some of the "friends" on the force might have got backhanders from the agencies for information, but Jimmy ran an honest business, and all Andy ever got for sharing info, was a case of his favourite red wine (Portuguese Crausto) for his birthday and a hamper from Fortnum & Mason at Christmas for Mrs Sherry, Andy's wife. He was good, honest cop who had been on the force for more than twenty years. He was a portly chap, 5–10 tall, with a big, jolly face on top of three or four chins and thick, unruly dark hair. He liked his job, especially working for the Met, all he had ever wanted to do was be a policeman. He lived behind Kings Cross Station in a flat with his wife Betty, she had worked in the ticket office in the railway station down the road. Jimmy lived close by, they drank in the same pub on York Way, that's how they became good friends many, many years ago.

The Sherry's had a son Paul, he was killed in a hit and run in Clapham when he was fifteen years old. Betty never got over it and gave up her job at Kings Cross station to be a housewife. Andy dealt with it in entirely the opposite way, by throwing himself in to his work. It seemed to work for them, they had a good marriage and were happy in their own way. Andy's would keep his pain buried deep inside; he had lost not only his son, but also his best friend Paul. They did everything together, season tickets at Fulham FC going to the match at weekends, fishing trips down in Dorset. Betty would go along with them when they went down to Poole. When they went out fishing for the day, she would relax on the beach or go shopping over in Bournemouth town centre. In the evenings they would have a nice family dinner in one of the many local restaurants, they were a happy close family. Andy missed all that so much, he missed Paul terrible, but worse he had also lost his wife. The will to live left Betty when Paul died and sadly it never came back.

Jimmy was very supportive of Andy in those bad old days and was always there for him. Jimmy's wife, Anne Marie, would call around to see Betty and sit with her and chat. Apart from food shopping Betty never wanted to leave the house. Despite Anne Marie's pleading, she was happy to just sat at home with her memories of how life used to be. The visits stopped when Anne Marie's thrombosis worsened and restricted her walking and despite their friendship, Betty never once went to visit Anne Marie at her home in Maida Vale.

Andy liked and trusted his old friend Jimmy and was happy with their "arrangement" it was good to have ears on the ground on what was happening on the streets and info in the police stations and courts that didn't make its way into the newspapers, the relationship worked well for both of them.

Jimmy didn't wait for Joe to reply, he asked Joe again, "How was Mrs Harrington when you gave her the news about her husband cheating on her?"

Joe was sat back with his hands behind his head let out a huge sigh and slightly shaking his head, replied, "Like I told you, Jimmy, she appeared very calm, not shocked and certainly not upset at the news. Why you don't think it was her do you?"

Jimmy rubbed his chin, deep in thought, he looked up at Joe and finally said, "It's not up to us to guess at things like that Joe, it's our job to tell the police all we know and explain about the case we took on for his wife. I'll give it day or so before I give Brian the reporter a call" and see what he can tell us.

Brian May was a reporter at a national newspaper another of the Jimmy's contacts who was a big help at supplying helpful information on what was happening. What with Andy and Brian they had a good little network going which at most times was a great help to all concerned, it was always a two-way street. Joe and Jimmy always cleared it first with Andy if it was okay to share with Brian any information Andy had passed to them.

Brian May had worked on the nationals for twenty-two years now, he did his "apprenticeship" at the Surrey Times in Reigate before moving on to the national newspaper scene. His early ambitions had long gone, now, in his early fifties he lived alone in a flat in Sutton, south

London, close to the mainline station. He had never married and now referred to himself has a confirmed bachelor. At 6 ft tall and painfully thin with a stoop. He always had a look on his face that he was carrying the troubles of the world on his shoulders. When you got to know him, he very likeable and a bit of a wit, not too much, but better than the miserable persona he gave off. He resembled a villain out of one of those old black and white Sherlock Holmes movies. The villain who disappeared into the fog of old London town after the loud piercing scream from some poor female victim.

He didn't enjoy his work any more, but it paid the bills, what he did enjoy was the social side of the job, a liquid lunch every day together with a sandwich at the bar with his colleagues. After the papers news pages were locked ready for printing it was back to the pubs with some of his fellow reporters. The truth being he wasn't in love with his job, but with the drinking culture that went with being a national Newspaper reporter working in the capital. A culture that apart from his looks was also the reason he was single; he had never found a woman that he cared enough about to marry. He was relatively happy with his life as it was, both his parents were long dead, he was an only child, he was pretty much used to being alone. He was to set in his ways now to share his life with anybody else. Despite his large dependency on alcohol and being pissed for most of his waking hours he was a good reporter and well-liked by the editor Hugh Whitehall because of his one big break.

His claim to fame was he had covered lots of big stories in his early enthusiastic days. Brian broke some big stories, and he enjoyed the celebrity status that went with being top reporter. There would be TV interviews on a couple of the big news stories. Colleagues admired him, wanted to be like him, and bought him endless drinks in the Fleet Street pubs. Those were the days, he loved every minute of the fame and milked it for all it was worth, television interviews, appearing on current affair programmes. He won Newspaper awards, he was invited to the top London society parties and introduced has Fleet Streets ace reporter. He wished he had a pound for every time he was asked who his sources were, and where he his stories from, he would smile and just say, "I couldn't possibly reveal the names my sources."

Sadly, those heady days came to an end, he loved every minute of his celebrity press life and wished it would have continued for ever. However, all things come to an end and now he is just a hack, telling his stories to anyone at the bar who would care to listen. People who didn't know him, thought he was a fantasist, just a sad drunk who made up stories about I life he wished he had.

Joe agreed with Jimmy there wasn't any point chasing Brian yet, he would need a day or two before he got any information from his contacts in the police that were on the newspaper's payroll. He sat up straight and asked Jimmy, "When are you going to speak to the 'old bill' about our case on Nigel?"

For once Jimmy replied quite quickly, well quickly for him, after a twenty second pause he said, "I'll ring them shortly, I wanted us to speak to you first, they'll think it's a hell of a coincidence. His wife hires us to follow him and see if he's having an affair and then soon after, he ends up murdered."

"There isn't anything you want to tell me about the case that you missed in debrief is there, Joe?"

Jimmy's question shocked Joe, he stood up and looking down on Jimmy sat at his desk, replied, "No, absolutely not, Jimmy, I wouldn't hold anything back from you, I never have done, never would. Also, I played the investigation by the book just like you told me to."

Jimmy smiled and standing up said, "Okay, Joe, of course, you did, but I had to ask, you know as well as me, the police are going to be all over us like a rash because of us taking on the case for his wife, just before her old man got himself murdered."

Joe was sat in his office, thinking, *What a great start to the early part of the week, involved in a murder enquiry.* Then he thought about poor old Nigel, he seemed so happy outside the pub with blondie. Little did he know the clock was running down on his life rapidly, so much to live for, but someone decided that he had lived long enough! Life was really shitty sometimes, his mind drifted to happier times and the evening meal with Sally the night before. He had enjoyed her company, a beautiful woman, great food and top wine, what more could you ask for and then the phone call from jimmy that ruined the evening.

The door opening broke Joe's thoughts, it was Jimmy, he sat down on the sofa, gave Joe a tired smile looked around the office and eventually said, "I've just phoned the police and explained we might have some information that could help them in their enquiries in to the murder of Nigel Harrington."

Joe interrupted with a big smile and said, "Bloody hell, Jimmy, you sound like a newscaster on the six o'clock news, what did they have to say?"

Jimmy's chest jumped as he let out a chuckle and said, "They want you to go to the yard tomorrow at ten-half for an interview

Joe shook his head. "Shit, can't they do the interview here?

"You know what that means, don't you? I'll be sat in a bloody, drafty corridor on an uncomfortable wooden chair for an hour or two, waiting for them to get around to me."

Jimmy stood up, smiled, headed for the door and replied, "No, you won't; it's the Met. You know New Scotland Yard, remember? Let's just get it done, Joe; we don't want any problems with them, it's our duty to surrender any information that might help."

Joe shouted after Jimmy smiled, "I know... I know, and you could have closed the bloody door behind you!"

Walking out into the reception to make a coffee at the machine, he looked over at H. He was worried about her and asked her again, "Is everything okay, H? You really do seem very quiet."

Harry stopped typing and looked up from the laptop, replying with a fake smile, "No! I'm fine, thanks, Joe. I was just a bit shocked at last night's news about Nigel Harrington. Will it reflect badly on us?"

Joe sat down on the sofa, had a sip of the hot coffee he had just poured himself and said, "I can't see how to be honest with you; we took on the wife's case and did everything above board. Have we any chocolate biscuits left?"

Harry smiled at how relaxed he was about the awful news and said, "No, but I'll get some at lunchtime when I go out for a sandwich. By the way you owe the tea money, £10; you didn't pay last week, and before you deny it, you know full well you didn't."

Joe stood up, and with fake indignation; he gave Harry a ten-pound note. Walking back into his office, he shouted to her over his shoulder, "Anyway, I don't drink tea; I drink coffee."

Harry laughed and flicked an elastic band after him, shouting, "Well, you should pay more; your coffee is more expensive than teabags."

Joe laughed and shouted back at H, "I'm out of the office most of the time earning the money, while you two sit in here all day drinking tea and eating all the biscuits. Also, H, can you get me a copy of the file for the Harrington case, I'll need to take it with me tomorrow."

Harry smiled again and shouted with false sarcasm, "Yes, sir, I'll bring it in straight away, Your Lordship."

Chapter Eleven
Helping with Enquiries

Joe hated the smell of police stations it made him feel nauseous, even when he was an officer, it was a strange smell, he couldn't describe it, and it was just awful. It was the probably the same musty smell in all old buildings, they all had a stale smell. However, he had never been to the Yard before, and he was well impressed. Scotland Yard was different it didn't have that horrible old smell, it was just like any other modern office block, all fresh and air conditioned, like a posh solicitor's firm in the city. He smiled to himself, the smelly stations are for the rank-and-file coppers, not the top dogs of the Met, only the best for them. Except, he had still been sat waiting for over forty minutes, he was in two minds to get up and leave. He didn't because it would only piss off Jimmy, and he hated doing that, he always felt bad the way Jimmy would look at him when he did, like a disappointed father.

Joe's concentration returned when he heard his name called out. He looked in the direction of the call and saw a man leaning out into the corridor from a room, gesturing to him. Joe walked down to the man who shook his hand and introduced himself as DI Ian Mooney, and he stepped aside and ushered Joe into his smart office. The detective inspector asked, "Would you like a tea or coffee? And I'm sorry for keeping you waiting. It's been very hectic, as I'm sure you can imagine."

Joe replied, "That's okay, I'm sure you are busy with the murder. Any leads yet? Oh, I'd like a coffee, white, no sugar, please, if you don't mind." The DI pressed a button on the key board of the phone and ordered a coffee for Joe and a cup of tea for himself. Joe looked at the DI, smiled and asked him again if they had any leads on the murder yet. DI Mooney looked at Joe with a deadpan look and ignored the question at the second time of asking.

DI Ian Mooney was fifty-four years old; average height, darkish hair greying at the sides, blue eyes and still a handsome man for his age. Always immaculately dressed, today was no exception, he wore a dark blue business suit with a stripe shirt and a plain red tie. Joe thought he had more of a look of a successful Barrister or Trader boss than a police inspector. Ian had worked his way up the Met to detective inspector over the past thirty-four years he had been with the force. The Met was his life, his wife and children came a close second, he was well respected by his superiors, colleagues and also quite a few of the villains he had put away over the years. The family home was in Surbiton, Surrey; where he had lived since marrying his childhood sweetheart Cybil. It had been the family home to their two children, Alfie, and Ruby, who were now grown up and had flown the nest to live in Richmond and Tottenham.

When Ian first met wife Cybil, he was taken with her looks as much as her bubbly personality, he fell head over heels in love with her. She was quite tall for a woman at 5, 10, thick long honey blonde hair, fabulous green eyes. She was a real stunner and women envied her looks, but loved her because of her personality. Ian was in awe of her, and although he was a good-looking man, he knew he was punching above his weight when he finally married Cybil. At forty-nine years old now, she was still a looker despite gaining some extra weight over the years, she could still turn men's heads wherever she went. Ian was so proud of her and loved it when colleagues said what a smashing woman she was and great fun too. He had been contemplating early retirement and living the good life, tending the garden, growing his own vegetables that he had been promising to do for years. Enjoying holidays abroad every four months or so, they could afford it on his pension and savings. However, Cybil wasn't too sure, she said he would miss his work, Ian thought the real reason was she didn't want him "under her feet" every day.

The door opened, and in walked a pretty policewoman with the coffee and tea. Joe made eye contact with her and thanked her. Taking his cup from her, he was sure he was met with some encouragement when she smiled back and replied, "You're welcome."

DI Mooney coughed out loud which worked in regaining Joe's attention. "Let's get started, shall we? Your boss, Jimmy Daly, phoned yesterday and reported you had some information on the Hyde Park murder.

Would you mind telling me everything you have that could help us with our enquiries?"

Joe started at the beginning with the appointment and went through the case right to the very end, making sure not to miss anything out. When he finished with all the details of the case, he gave the DI a copy of the Harrington file together with the photograph evidence proving "Old Nigel's" affair. DI Mooney scribbled away, making notes, pausing occasionally to clarify a point in Joe's story. The officer looked long and hard at the file that Joe had handed him again making, a few more notes. He closed the manilla folder and looked up at Joe, gently rattling his pen on his teeth. He finally spoke, "And you say Mrs Harrington didn't appear upset when you told her of her husband's liaison with the blonde lady in Chelsea or the visits to the company flat by the dark-haired woman?"

Joe slowly shook his head and recollecting, replied, "No, not at all; like I said, it was as if she already knew something was going on and was just getting her suspicions confirmed."

DI Mooney wrote down something else and looked up back at Joe. He asked, "And you say the address she gave you was 53 Adams Yard, Mayfair?"

Joe nodded this time, replying, "Yep, that was the place, and one hell of a place it was too!"

DI Mooney asked, "Did you go to the house for any of your meetings with Mrs Harrington?"

Joe nodded again, and a little irritated, replied, "Yes, like I have just told you, the first meeting was in our offices in Holborn at Mrs Harrington's request. Then, when I went to present her with what I had found, it was at her home in Adams Yard, why do you ask?"

Closing his notebook and placing his pen back into his inside jacket pocket he continued to look at Joe sat opposite him. Joe didn't much care for the way he was being looked at, the detective had a sort of a smirk on his face. Joe knew a lot of the police didn't like private detectives for some reason, and it looked like DI Mooney was one of those policemen. Joe asked the detective, "You have a look like you know something I don't; would you care to share it with me or maybe not?" The "smirk" turned to a smile; he appeared to be enjoying Joe's discomfort, and he was tapping his fingers on the desk. He held up a photo from Joe's file of Nigel and the mystery blonde walking to the pub.

The inspector finally said, "Well, yes, happy to share with you. I know a couple of things you don't; one, Nigel Harrington didn't live in Mayfair, and he lived in Chelsea at 44 Sydney Street, to be precise. And second, the blonde girlfriend you photographed him with that evening is, in actual fact, his wife, Amelia. She is the real Mrs Harrington, and not the woman who came to your office claiming to be his wife."

Joe slumped back in his chair; his mouth dropped open with shock. He stared at his photo. Detective Inspector Mooney was holding up; he wasn't expecting that bombshell. He finally closed his mouth and replied, "WHAT! No, that's not possible, are you sure? Why would someone ask us to take a case on regarding their cheating husband when they weren't even married to them?" Hearing the words that had just come out of his mouth, Joe realised just how stupid they sounded. Joe's thoughts were all over the place. Of course, somebody could arrange that if they wanted to, but why, for what purpose, to have Nigel Harrington murdered?

DI Mooney's voice interrupted all the questions swirling around inside Joe's head. "Well, if what you say is the truth, at this moment I don't have any reason to doubt you; I think we need to find out, don't you?"

Joe was taken aback with the officers' comments and blurted out, "What? Why would I make something like that up? Don't forget, I came in to try and help you."

DI Mooney leaned forward and interrupted Joe, "Relax, you are helping us; you're not being accused of anything yet!" he said menacingly.

Joe didn't like the "yet" one little bit. The inspector continued, "I suggest we arrange to go to Mayfair and speak with your 'Mrs Harrington'. Let's pay her a visit and hear what she has to say about the murder of her "husband, shall we?"

"Fine by me," replied Joe, starting to regain his composure and feeling well pissed off with Mooney's attitude.

DI Mooney's car pulled across Park Lane and continued across the front the Dorchester Hotel; it turned left onto South Audley Street, heading up towards Adams Yard. Conversation on the journey so far had been sparse which gave Joe time to digest what had happened in his interview. He kept asking himself the same questions. *Why would someone hire a private detective to follow a person that they were going to murder? It didn't make sense; why not just murder him? She obviously knew a lot about poor old Nige already because of the details she gave Joe in the meeting. Also, if she wasn't Mrs Harrington, just who the hell is she? And who is she working with or for? Did they hire me to be the fall guy or muddy the waters after they murdered poor old Nige?*

Joe started to get a little worried about what he was involved in; this was getting serious. It didn't help that the murder was all over the newspapers and television news, Joe hoped it would start to die down in a day or so. The silver BMW pulled up on Adams Yard a little further up from number 53. DI Mooney placed a card reading "Police on Official Business" on the dashboard to stop the notorious Mayfair traffic warden's having the car clamped and towed away. As he got out Joe wondered if the car was a squad car or Mooney's own personal car. They climbed the steps to the big, shiny black front door. DI Mooney rang the bell, and turned to Joe and said, "Let me do all the talking, okay?"

Joe nodded and replied dismissively, "Sure, no problem, fine by me."

Noise and shouting could be heard from inside the house and eventually the door was opened a tanned dark-haired boy in his early teens wearing shorts and a tee-shirt. He had under his arm a bulky black leather pouch, he looked uninterestingly from DI Mooney to Joe and then back at the policeman. The inspector said, "Good morning, is your mother home?" The boy turned and walked back down the hall leaving the pair stood on the doorstep.

Throwing the leather pouch back down on to the hall table, he shouted in a strong European accent, "Mum, it's not the estate agent, it's someone for you!"

A pretty middle-aged lady appeared, gave them a big smile and asked, "Hello, can I help you?" She also had the same accent as the teenage who came to the door.

DI Mooney flashed his warrant card, introduced himself and asked, "Is there a Mrs Harrington at home?"

The smile had disappeared from the woman's face when she saw the warrant card. She replied, "No, I'm sorry, just us, me, my husband and our three children, we're her in London on holiday. Joe's heart sank at her reply. He had a haunting feeling that this situation he found himself in, had just taken a turn for the worse.

DI Mooney asked politely, "Would you mind if we came in and ask you and your husband a few questions."

Back in the car, DI Mooney looked at Joe, who was rubbing his neck, and was deep in thought. The detective broke the silence. "That went well, don't you think?"

Joe looked at the detective and replied, "What can I say? Everything I've told you is true; you've seen our agency's case file. I even described the lounge furniture, the curtains, the mirror, and table in the hall, didn't I?" Joe had glanced at the bulky leather pouch the son had thrown on the hall table; it had Mayfair Letting printed on it in red letters.

DI Mooney started up the car and pulling away from the curb, replied, "True, but all that proves is that you've been in the house; we'll check with the letting agent and see who had rented the house before this family, that covers the time when you say you visited your Mrs Harrington there." Joe just shook his head and returned to his thoughts as the car pulled into the traffic on Park Lane. Dropping Joe at Victoria, the detective said through the open passenger window, "We'll be in touch soon, and also we'll need to speak to your partner at your office."

When Joe walked into the office, Jimmy was standing at Harry's desk in reception discussing something. They both looked Joe stood in the open door. Harry spoke first, "Jeepers Joe what's happened, you've got a face like thunder?" Joe closed the door behind him, he looked at Harry and then to Jimmy and replied, "We've got a problem; our Mrs Harrington isn't Mrs Harrington, and she wasn't married to old Nigel. Oh also, just to make it even more confusing, he didn't live at Adams Yard in Mayfair. Old Nigel and his real wife Amelia, who it turns out, that she was the 'mystery blonde' he was drinking with that evening, lived in Chelsea, where I followed him to. Our Mrs Harrington appears to have disappeared and I've got a detective inspector from the Met who thinks I'm or we possibly we are involved in this somewhere along the line. All in all, it's been a bit of a shitty old day so far!"

Finally taking a breath, he asked, "Any chance of a cup of coffee, H? It's been a mare from start to finish today."

They were all sat in Joe's office Joe and H on the sofa, and Jimmy facing them in the armchair. Joe explained everything about how the morning had panned out from the interview to going to Adams Yard and meeting the family who had rented number 53 for a month's holiday let. He relayed Mooney's message that he wanted to interview both Jimmy and probably H tomorrow. He finished with the conundrum why would someone hire a PI to investigate someone they were going to kill? Jimmy finally broke the silence in the room saying, "If our Mrs Harrington was involved, maybe she or whoever didn't actually plan to kill Nigel. Also, we haven't got anything to hide from the police when we meet them. Okay, it looks like we've been duped, but that doesn't make us guilty of anything."

Joe smiled at how methodical Jimmy's thinking was and that he was always relaxed, nothing ever phased him. He supposed at Jimmy's time of life he had seen it all and that's why he took everything in his stride. Joe asked, "Jimmy, are we okay to investigate what's going on, with it being a murder investigation?"

Jimmy stared at the wall behind Joe and H and finally replied, "We would have to be very careful not to interfere with the police investigation. Otherwise, yes, we would be in trouble, why what are you thinking?"

Joe said, "Well, for starters, I would like to speak to the letting agency Mayfair Properties, before the met do and find out who they had down on their books as renting the house before this family who moved in at the weekend. Also, I would like to speak to some of the neighbours in Adam's Yard and see if they remember seeing our Mrs Harrington or anybody else at number 53."

Jimmy scratched his forehead, looked at his finger nails on his left hand and replied, "We need to be discreet, Joe because if the Met get wind of us snooping around their investigation and warn us off, that's it, we will have to step back, do you understand?"

Joe let out a big frustrated sigh and replied, "Yes, Jimmy, I understand completely. H, did you check the ownership of the house?"

Harry replied, "No, just if there was a mortgage on the property, I can do it if you want."

Standing up, Joe walked over to sit at his desk. He said, "Yes, please, if you would; it would be interesting to see who it belongs to; we wrongly assumed it was the Harringtons. Jimmy, would you mind speaking to the letting agents about the previous rental? You're far more subtle than me. Also, it might be a good time to speak to our contacts in the press and also Andy Sherry to see if they have any news on the case."

Jimmy smiled at how Joe had taken the lead on the investigation and replied, "Yes, Joe, I will do it first thing tomorrow, promise."

Before he left for the evening, Joe rang Sally, and arranged to meet her at his place, when she finished work. Thankfully she was free and seemed happy to hear from him. He just needed to clear his head of everything that had happened during the day. He needed a diversion, and she was a perfect one, just what the doctor ordered. He called in at Wholesale Foods on Fulham Broadway on his way home, to buy some lamb and vegetables. He always had drinks in his flat so the wine and spirits for the evening were sorted. He had promised Sally, he would cook her a romantic meal if she stayed over for the night. She let out that sexy laugh of hers down the phone and agreed only if they gave each other a naked massage after dinner. He smiled, his head was beginning to clear and his mind had stopped racing with the events of the day. He decided he would try and take everything in his stride like Jimmy appeared to, don't think about things so much. Jimmy had always told him, "Don't worry about things that you can't change, just try and deal with them rationally." He was looking forward to seeing Sally, he would try to put all the Adams Yard bollocks out of his mind and have a nice relaxing evening with her.

Chapter Twelve
Chasing Shadows

Joe phoned the office and asked H to put him through to Jimmy, but not before asking her if she had checked out the ownership of number 53. Her answer wasn't what he was hoping to hear, it possibly made the case harder to work out.

The house in Adam's yard belonged to a company registered in Panama. Joe was pissed off that this wasn't picked up by H when she did her prep work for the case, but he didn't say anything, she would only get upset. Why just check if there was a mortgage and not who owned the property, this would have been a big factor to taking on the case? She was usually always very thorough; it wasn't like her to miss something as important as the ownership. So basically, it meant that any chance of finding a possible connection between "Mrs Harrington" and the actual owners of 53 Adams Yard, if it wasn't her had just run into a brick wall. A purchase like this on most occasion's means there is no available records on the real owners. The lack of owner information means it was impossible to ascertain any links between these anonymous companies' individual persons.

London's property market is a safe haven for corrupt individuals and companies through anonymous ownership. Latest statistics showed s a large amount of London land titles were owned by overseas companies, over seventy-five per cent of these companies are based in Panama or the British Virgin Islands. This recently caused concerns over Tax avoidance

To follow-up on the owners of number 53 would have been a massive factor in finding the disappearing "Mrs Harrington" and indeed in the case of the murder of Nigel Harrington. These important leads were now off the table and could jeopardise clearing Joe and the agency's name in a bloody murder enquiry. That was one line of enquiry that Joe and Jimmy could now cross off the short list, thanks to Harriot not doing her job properly. Jimmy's voice broke Joe's train of thought, "Morning, Joe, any joy with the neighbours, did any of them remember seeing our 'Mrs Harrington' at the house?"

Joe sighed and replied, "Morning, Jimmy, I never got the chance to speak to any of them, the ones that were at home wouldn't entertain speaking to me. I managed to speak to some of the staff working in a couple of the adjacent houses. I had a bit of luck with one, a butler in service at number 46, he remembers passing the house one day when our Mrs Harrington was supposedly in 'residence'. He told me he saw some men in smart business suits come out and get into a 'large' Mercedes car. He remembered because two of them were speaking to each other but not in English, he said it sounded Eastern

European. He didn't recognise the language, but the butler is Italian and also speaks Spanish, German and Portuguese, so we can rule that out all of those! Not too much to go on, but it I suppose it might be something, 'Our somethings are pretty thin on the ground at the moment'."

Jimmy hadn't had any more luck than Joe had, the letting agent (for a hefty tip) had told him the house was booked by a Russian family for four weeks before the current family. Although, they were delayed arriving and only stayed in number 53 for the last two weeks of the Let. One thing the agent remembered was that they didn't want any staff in the house during their stay. Which was unusual because the Let came with a butler, maid and chef included in the price.

The agent said the let had and been done over the phone and e-mail, they had paid the rent by BACs through a company in Moscow. Jimmy had tried to check out the company, but has he expected, it didn't exist. He said, he would get in touch with the letting agency again now Harriot had told him the house was registered in Panama. Although, he didn't hold out much hope the agency would share any details regarding where the rental payments were paid. They were probably paid into a company bank account in Panama or the Cayman Islands. Jimmy ended the call with Joe saying he would be in the office tomorrow, and maybe the men the butler saw was speaking Russian, so that could be a lead, and they could have been one of the Russians who had booked the house. He was going to contact the butler again and try to get him to ask around his friends who are in service to see if they had any sightings of the mysterious Russian family. He wasn't sure if she was Russian; her English accent was good, but she did have a slight accent.

That afternoon as arranged DS Mooney and his trusty sidekick D.S. Alan Brown called into the office to take statements from both Jimmy and Harriot. They were pretty much routine questions, what did Mrs Harrington look like? When did she visit the offices? Did either of them think anything was suspicious about the case? Did they think it was unusual she didn't want any records kept on file about her case? If it was a common request, then why did they always keep records after assuring clients that they wouldn't? Jimmy thought the main purpose of their visit was to see the office and ascertain what kind of operation they ran. Otherwise, they would have taken the statements down at the Yard and not made a "house call" to Holborn.

Joe was back in Adams Yard, but this time calling at number 46, he wanted to speak to the butler again. The maid who answered the door invited Joe into the lounge and went to fetch the butler. Joe looked around the room, it was a similar house to number 53, but obviously with different furniture. It was more traditional than the furniture at 53, Joe guessed the owners were probably in the late fifties or even sixties. There were some photographs in silver frames on the Steinway piano in the far side of the room, Joe was about to get up and look when the door opened. The butler appeared without his jacket and wiping his hands on a towel he was flustered, he said, "You shouldn't be here, the maid shouldn't have let you in. You must go now immediately; her Ladyship will be home very soon. With that he ushered Joe out of lounge and down the hall to the front door."

At the front door Joe turned and said, "I need to ask you a few more questions about number 53, can we meet up for a drink or something when you finish work?" The two folded fifty-pound notes that Joe pushed into the butler's waistcoat pocket did the trick.

The butler replied, "Give me your phone number, and I will call you, and we can arrange something." Joe thanked him and gave him his business card and was then literally pushed out of the front door, which was slammed shut behind him. Joe walked down the steps smiling to himself at how panicky the butler had been, the smile quickly disappeared when he realised, he had just laid out £100 on the promise of a phone call that might not come! He reassured himself that the little bugger would call me and if not, he knows where to get hold of him at his place of work, ladyship or no bloody Ladyship.

Chapter Thirteen
Looking for a Way In

Joe walked into the office at eight-thirty on the dot and, "Good morning, H, you okay."

Harry smiled and replied, "I'm good, thanks, and you?"

Joe sat on the edge of desk which always annoyed her and asked, "And how did the questioning go yesterday with sarky Detective Sergent Mooney?"

Pushing Joe off her desk and wiping away non-existent marks, she replied, "He wasn't sarky at all, in fact, he was charming and quite handsome with it, thank you very much for asking."

Joe let out a loud false laugh and said, "Oh my God, you fancy him, don't you, H? He is married you know; didn't you see the wedding ring?" Holding up is left hand and wiggling his third finger. His actions had the desired effect, Harry's face went bright red, and blushing she jumped up and started hitting Joe which just made him laugh even louder. The loud "Ahem" behind them stopped the horseplay immediately, they both turned and sheepishly looked towards the office door.

Jimmy was standing there feigning an annoyed face, he asked, "What's going on, shouldn't you both be working? It wouldn't have looked very good if I had been a prospective client now, would it? Harriot, I'm very surprised at you, I expect it from that dope, but not you."

Joe laughed and tucking his shirt back into his trousers, he replied, "I'm glad you saw that, Jimmy; she's always knocking me about she made me promise not to tell you about it."

Harriot was still blushing from Jimmy's remark, clipped Joe around the back of his head as she pushed past him to get back to her desk, she sat down straightened her hair and glasses, then smiling up at Jimmy, she cleared her throat and said in her poshest receptionist voice, "Good morning, Jimmy, would you like your usual, a cup of tea and a chocolate digestive biscuit?"

Jimmy smiled and walking into his office replied, "Yes, please, Harriot."

Joe followed Jimmy into his office sitting down he waited patiently for Jimmy to settle himself down and open the shop (as he always put it) to do the business of the day. He watched in amusement as Jimmy sat down, arranged his pen and notebook in their usual place on the left-hand side his desk (he was right-handed) and turned on his computer. After clearing his throat loudly, he ran the palm of his hand across his hair (left to right) twice and finally straightened his tie, he was ready, finally. He looked across at Joe and said, "Do you want to go first?" Joe explained that he had been to see the butler again at number 27, but received short shift because he had to leave before her Ladyship returned home. He was hoping he would get a call from the butler after giving him his card and some cash. He then continued saying would then arrange updates on any activity at number 53 and hopefully try and attempt to get descriptions of the men he saw getting in the Mercedes. Joe wrapped up his debrief saying he was also going to try and get the butler to speak to the other servants in Adams Yard to see if any of them had seen "Mrs Harrington" at the house.

With that he looked at Jimmy smiled and said, "What about you?"

Jimmy looked at Joe for a while, cleared his throat again then reached for his notebook, before he opened it, he finally spoke and asked Joe, "Who is her Ladyship who lives at number 46?"

Joe replied, "I haven't a clue, I'll make a point of finding out though."

Jimmy shrugged his shoulders and said it might be an important fact, let's check out who she is. Clearing his throat yet again Jimmy started his debrief with, "I spoke with the letting agent again, and he wouldn't give me any details of where the money for the rentals of the house is paid. The only thing he would say was it was a company account abroad, which we had previously assumed it would be. I spoke with Brian at his newspaper; he told me he had heard there was talk that something dodgy was going on at old Nigel's bank, but didn't know anything more yet!"

Joe sat up in his chair and interrupted Jimmy, he said excitedly, "Well, that's something positive to explore then, Nigel might have been involved and that was why he was killed. Sorry, Jimmy, go on, that's the first good bit of news we've had yet regarding this case."

Jimmy smiled and continued, "I also met Andy Sherry for a drink after work last night, he said, he had heard from colleagues that the German bank where Nigel worked are not being overly co-operative considering one of their directors had just been murdered in a London Park. At this moment in time, they didn't have any leads, no murder weapon, and no witnesses. He was killed with a single shot to the chest from close range which could mean he knew the murderer and was talking to him when he was shot. The wife doesn't appear to know anything or isn't saying much, she doesn't have any idea who would want to kill her husband and the police think she is telling the truth." Jimmy closed his notebook and the silence was deafening as they both digested Andy Sherry's information.

Joe was the first to speak, he said, "Do you think Nigel was embezzling money from his bank, Jimmy?"

Jimmy opened his notebook once more and wrote something in it before replying, "I don't know to be honest, Joe and if he was, the bank would deal with it quietly internally. It's not good for business to make a big song and dance about a director robbing off his own company especially when the company is a bank."

Joe sighed a replied, "We seem to be getting nowhere fast, it's like swimming in treacle, what are we going to do?"

Jimmy looked at Joe and smiled at his frustration and announced, "We do what I've always done, when I can't make progress in a case. I put my head above the parapet to see clearer or to see if anyone takes a pot shot at it."

Joe was intrigued, he leant forward in his chair, he asked, "Really, what's our move then?"

Jimmy began to explain, "From what we've dug up so far on old Nigel's murder, which granted isn't very much. I think, our best bet is trying to speak to his bank, and hear what they have to say and also to try and ascertain if they've got anything to hide. You can't just walk in and ask to see someone; they will just call security and march you straight out of the door. We need to intrigue them, phone up and ask to speak to Nigel's boss or a fellow director that he worked with. Then explain to them that someone hired us to investigate Nigel, but don't say who or what we were hired for. If they've got anything to hide, they will want to know what we had found out, if they haven't, they will just tell you to go the police.

Joe sat back and let out a long whistle he hadn't thought of that he said, "Oh, I like that, Jimmy, I like that a lot, and I will give them a call this morning. What do we do if they don't have anything to hide and refuse to see us, what then?"

Jimmy stood up and said, "If that's the case, don't worry, there will be other parapets that come along where we can have a peep over, now you'll have to excuse me, I'm going for a pee!"

Joe went back in to his office, on the way past he asked H for a mug of coffee and a couple of chocolate digestives. When she came in with his drink, he asked her to get him the number for Nigel's' bank LPZ. He was about to ring the bank after going through the conversation in his head about what he would say. He knew he only had one shot at getting them to meet with him, when his mobile rang. He looked at the screen, but didn't recognise the number, his face broke out into a smile, and it was Lorenzo the butler. The tip must have worked, Lorenzo had kept his promise to call Joe, and they arranged to meet up on Thursday evening at a pub in Covent Garden. The butler did mention that the police had been making house calls in Adam Yard to see if anybody saw the people at number 53 a few weeks ago. He also added that he didn't mention Joe's visits asking the same question, Joe ended the call and thought good old Lorenzo is pretty switched on, he might be a good asset.

Chapter Fourteen
The Meeting at the Bank

Joe looked the business in his smart dark blue Canelli business suit, he kept it for occasions like this, very important meetings or when he wanted to impress clients. He also had his fake Mont Blanc briefcase just to finish off his professional look. He was on his way to Nigel's bank in Canary Wharf, he had phoned them yesterday. They asked him what was the nature of his call, when he said Nigel Harrington, they put him straight through to the HR department. When he wouldn't give them any details of what his business was about in relation to Nigel. He stressed he wanted to speak to a director about Nigel Harrington, they took his name and number and said someone would him call back. They did, less than five minutes later, the female caller told Harriot, she was Claude Zimmerman's PA, and he was a director at the bank. Joe took the call and the PA transferred him through to a chap with a strong German accent. Joe explained briefly that he was a private investigator and that his firm had been hired to investigate Nigel Harrington shortly before his death. Just like Jimmy had said, that magically worked and opened the doors for him at the bank. He was invited to meet Zimmerman at their offices at eleven-thirty a.m. the next day (Wednesday). When Joe went and told Jimmy the news, he agreed that this could be the breakthrough they had been hoping for, or at least they could cross off the Bank from their list of possible "suspects." Jimmy then ran through what Joe should discuss and tell them at the meeting making sure he didn't give away too much information.

On his arrival, Joe was taken up to the ninth floor by one of the receptionists after signing in and receiving his visitors pass which he had to hang around his neck. The offices were very plush all the furniture was modern and very expensive. He didn't look out of place amongst the sharp suited bankers in the lift with him. Coming out of the lift on the ninth they turned left and walked down to two large grey wood grained doors, they also looked very expensive. The receptionist tapped gently and from deep inside the room a voice called out *enter*, Joe recognised the strong German accent from his phone call the previous day. Joe followed the receptionist inside and smiling looked around the room, it was a large conference room probably a boardroom with a huge grey grained table the same as the doors, with at least twenty grey high-backed chairs around it. The walls were decorated with expensive looking oil paintings of country scenes. *Possibly German country sides,* Joe thought. On the right-hand, wall was a huge screen, probably for business presentations Joe assumed. Still smiling Joe stopped behind one of the chairs in front of him, on the opposite side of the huge table three of the chairs were occupied. The man in the middle smiled back at Joe then stood up and walked around the huge table and shook Joe warmly by the hand introducing himself has Claude Zimmerman. He then introduced his two colleagues on the left of his now empty chair was Heinrich Wagner and on the right Manfred Schmidt, Joe waved to them and said, "Please don't walk all the way around here, it will take too long." They both said hello, and falsely laughed at Joe's remark.

Claude patted Joe on the back and said, "Please take a seat." He then walked back around the table and took his seat in the middle of his colleagues.

Claude announced that Manfred was the HR director (he smiled and nodded to Joe) and Heinrich was the banks head of security (he didn't smile or nod, but just gave Joe a cold stare). He went on to explain that due to the reason for the meeting he felt it was important they both attended. Claude looked the part and explained he was the MD at the bank. He was tall six-foot, medium build, blonde hair and dark hazel eyes, dressed immaculately in a chalk blue pinstripe suit, Joe guessed he was mid to late forties. Manfred on the other hand was overweight, mousey thinning hair, average height, a jolly round face, he also wore an expensive suit, grey mohair, which looked untidy and ill-fitting due to his size. Joe thought that Manfred was one of those men who no matter how hard they tried, they always looked like a bag of shite.

Joe noted that he was sweating heavily, even though the room wasn't that warm. Sweaty Manfred could have passed for a middle-aged English man, but for his strong

German accent. Then there was Heinrich, tall, very short fair hair, dark eyes, and heavily built.

He looked like a bag of shite in his suit, but unlike Manfred it wasn't because he was overweight, it was because of his bulk, he was obviously a powerful muscly guy. Joe came to the conclusion Henrich was ex-military, and he probably wasn't has expensively dressed as the other two Germans, his suit was more functional than stylish. Joe decided the way Heinrich was looking at him that he didn't very much care for Joe, but Joe didn't mind because the feeling was mutual.

Joe started by saying he was very sorry about Nigel Harrington's death and asked if the police had any leads as to who killed him, and then went on to ask if they knew why anybody would want to harm Nigel? This was exactly like Jimmy had predicted, and it had the desired effect, it unsettled the three men sat opposite him. They didn't expect to be asked such blunt questions like that and certainly not from someone they had met only a minute earlier. They expected to be the ones asking the questions and for Joe to tell them everything he knew about Nigel Harrington. After a couple of sideways glances between Manfred and Claude, Claude leant forward let out a large exasperating sigh and spoke Joe, "Mr Makin, we agreed to meet with you because we thought you might have some important information that would help us bring the killer of Nigel to justice. We didn't expect to be grilled about our colleague's death and in such a direct manner as if we were suspects."

113

Joe smiled as if a little shocked and said, "Forgive me, gentlemen, I didn't mean to be so forthright, it must come from earlier days of being in the police force, before I became a private detective." This information again raised sideways glances amongst the three men, Jimmy was spot on again. Joe continued, "I can assure you that our agency wholly joins you in wanting the murderer of Mr Harrington brought to justice."

It was Claude again who spoke, "That's good to know; your agency is in Holborn, and you are a partner of the company with a Mr James Daly no?"

Joe smiled to himself; crafty old Claude had come right back at him, showing that they had done their homework on the agency. Joe nodded and replied, "That is correct, Mr Zimmerman; we are a long-established private investigating agency, but I'm sure you already know that too."

Joe was caught a little off-balanced by Manfred asking the next question, and he also got straight to the point. "What can you tell us about the investigation you carried out on Mr Harrington and also who was it who hired you?"

Joe got the distinct impression he was quickly wearing out his welcome at the bank. He replied, "Well, I'm sure you gentlemen are aware more than most that we have client confidentiality in our business, just like yourselves." Staring straight into the cold eyes of Heinrich.

Joe continued, "But, what I can tell you is the nature of the investigation wasn't regarding his business here at the bank, but more of a private matter."

Claude asked the question this time, "And is that all you are prepared to tell us?"

Joe smiled sympathetically and replied, "I'm afraid, so, Mr Zimmerman, client confidentiality forbids me." Heinrich Wagner started to speak, he appeared annoyed, but Claude Zimmerman quickly put his hand on Heinrich's arm, and he fell silent immediately.

Claude sighed, stood up and walked around the table which meant the meeting was over. Smiling politely, he firmly shook Joe's hand, and thanked him for his time, and said, "Withholding your information, Mr Makin, just wastes our time, and this meeting was pointless, so there's no reason to continue. By the way, have you spoken to the police yet about your investigation and hopefully been a little more forthcoming with them?"

Joe bent down to pick up his briefcase before replying, "My colleague telephoned them when the identity of Mr Harrington was made public, but to date, they haven't been back in touch for an interview" (another one of Jimmy's prompts).

Claude smiled that big false smile of his again and replied, "Too busy, I suspect, but I'm sure they will get around to you soon. Once again, thank you for taking the trouble in coming to see us, and I assume we won't be seeing each other again."

Joe smiled back, politely and tantalisingly replied, "You never know Mr Zimmerman, you never know!"

As if by magic, the lady from reception opened one of the doors, and Claude ushered Joe out of the room. As they waited for the lift to come, Joe heard raised voices from behind the double doors but couldn't make out what was being said! In the lift, Joe smiled at the receptionist. Commenting on her name tag, he said, "I see your name is Octavia, that's a very beautiful and unusual name."

She blushed slightly, and the lift doors opened, she replied, "Thank you very much; that's nice of you to say so, Mr Makin." At the front doors at reception, Joe thanked Octavia, returning his visitor badge; he gave her his best smile. It appeared to work; he was certain she held on to his hand a little longer than necessary when they shook goodbye. Coming out of the bank, Joe filed her name and face away for future reference, she could be very useful for finding out gossip inside the bank. Walking to the DLR station, he gave Sally a call as promised to see what kind of a day she was having. He never noticed the man who had been following him since he left the bank. The man kept a discreet distance behind Joe, but never took his eyes off him once, even when his mobile phone rang. He quickly took it from pocket and said "Pryvit" (*Hello*) without breaking stride.

After ending his call to Sally, he phoned Jimmy and told him quickly how the meeting had gone describing the three German exec's he had met with. He ended the call telling Jimmy he was at the tube station and would be in the office shortly to give him a full briefing.

Chapter Fifteen
Lorenzo the Butler

Jimmy had listened carefully to Joe's debrief, then finally asked, "And you couldn't make out what was being said once you had left the boardroom?" Joe was back in the office in Holborn and had sat in Jimmy's office briefing him fully on the meeting with Zimmerman and co.

Joe finished his mug of coffee and placed it down on the table, rubbing his chin, thinking he needed to shave. He focused and shook his head, replying, "No, I couldn't make it out, possibly sounded like Zimmerman, but I couldn't be certain. I think it was him doing the shouting, but I don't know who at, the HR guy or the head of security. The head of security guy started to say something towards the end of the meeting, and Zimmerman quickly stopped him, so it could have been him and Zimmerman. There's definitely something going on at LPZ. Jimmy, your three prompts worked a treat. I think the security guy was pissed that I didn't give them any information about our case. But they did appear rattled and might know something or even be involved in Nigel's murder."

Jimmy looked long and hard at Joe, taking in what he had just said, and eventually replied, "Maybe they do, but don't forget, Joe, they've just had a colleague murdered,

117

shot dead in a public park. Even if they are not involved, something like that is bound to rattle colleagues – even Germans! I'll have another word with Andy Sherry and see if there's any news yet from the boys at the Met. I'm sure they will have interviewed the directors at the bank by now. Also, DI Mooney rang this morning and warned us off interfering with a murder investigation. I told him we weren't and that we were just making our own enquiries because of our case and would never interfere with police business or witnesses."

Sitting back in his chair, Jimmy let out a big breath and continued, "When is it you are you meeting the butler? Is it tonight? We need to be careful the Met will only tolerate us for so long."

Joe agreed and replied, "Don't worry, I will be discreet, Jimmy. At least I've not heard from Mooney again, so hopefully he doesn't think I'm involved in any way. Did he mention me to you?"

Jimmy shook his head and replied, "No, he didn't mention you at all; he just warned us off getting in their way. I'm sure it was just one of their usual warnings."

They both fell silent for a moment, then Joe asked, "What about the real Mrs Harrington? Should I try and speak to her?"

Jimmy nearly choked on his drink and wiping tea off his chin with his hanky, he shouted, "Definitely not, Joe, don't go anywhere near her, haven't you been listening to what I've just said about Mooney? That would certainly cause us big problems with Mooney if she complained about us getting in touch. The Met would get a court injunction and have us closed down, no, stay away from Chelsea and her. Also don't forget she's just lost her husband, and it's been all over the TV and the newspapers."

Joe feigned regret and replied, "Okay, Jimmy, it was only a suggestion. Calm down. I promise I won't go near her." Jimmy gave him a withering look and poured the spilt tea from his saucer back into his cup.

It was just after eight pm and Joe sat in the Admiral Rodney pub in Covent Garden. It was busy, but he was sat where he had a good view of the door, so he would see Lorenzo when he came in. At eight twenty the door opened and in walked Lorenzo, he looked so different than when Joe had seen him before in his smart butler suit. He wasn't very tall; about five: seven at best, medium build and weight with dark hair and a few touches of grey in it. Joe guessed he was mid-fifties, he wore a stonewash jeans, a black tee shirt and a black leather jacket. Joe smiled to himself as he waved to Lorenzo who started to walk over to the table, he looked a real little Italian Jimmy Dean.

Joe stood up to greet Lorenzo and asked him what he would like to drink, he made his way to the bar and ordered another pint of lager for himself and a large gin and tonic for his new found friend.

Lorenzo filled Joe in on what had been going on in Adams Yard, the police hadn't had any more luck than Joe in speaking to the residents. Most of them were out of the country or out of town, they had spoken with house keepers and servants though about the comings and goings at number 53. He went on to say that a lot of them meet up for a drink in a pub off Oxford Street a couple of times a week and nobody had any news of what the police were asking them. From what he was saying Joe got the impression there was a pretty close-knit community amongst the servants, and they all liked to gossip to each other about their employers. Joe described his Mrs Harrington to Lorenzo who promised he would ask if anybody had seen her at number 53 when they next met up for a night out. A few men came over to say Hi to Lorenzo during the evening, he appeared to have quite a few friends in the pub. He told Joe that he was originally from a suburb of Turin and had come over to live and work in England in his early thirties. He didn't have any family alive in Italy so didn't see any reason to ever go back there. He lived with his partner Alan for the last eight years in a flat in Kilburn. They he had met here in the Admiral Rodney one Christmas Eve. Joe decided he liked Lorenzo a lot, he seemed a really nice genuine guy. He promised Joe he would report back to him on what he could find out from his friends and also on any more visits from the police. Joe slipped him £100 and remembered what Jimmy had said to him, he asked Lorenzo one last question, "By the way, who do you work for, you said I had to leave because her ladyship was on her way home?"

Lorenzo laughed out loud revealing a perfect set of pearly white teeth, "I was just saying that to get you to leave, I work for an IT bigwig he owns a few successful internet companies, it was his wife who was on her way home, let's just leave it at that, their name is irrelevant." Joe laughed and with that said goodnight to his new found friend.

Chapter Sixteen
A Possible Break-Through

Four days had passed since the meeting with Zimmerman and his cronies, Joe had been busy catching up on work stuff and when he had time going over his notes on Nigel's case. He had been in touch with Danny at Canary Wharf and asked if the police had spoken to him since Nigel's murder. Danny told him they did, but he hadn't mentioned the arrangement her had with Joe, for fear of getting Joe into trouble with them. Joe made a mental note to go and give Danny some money when he had time, he was a good guy. He had Sally around to his flat the night of the meeting at the bank and asked her if Nigel and his wife were regulars in the pub. She said, she couldn't really recollect seeing them that often even though they only lived down the street. He was thinking of trying to accidently bump in to Octavia the receptionist after she finished work at the bank one evening, it might prove fruitful, but he didn't mention it to Sally, she wouldn't understand it was just business.

He was frustrated about not making any progress on the case, everything had just seemed to grind to a halt. Jimmy heard back from Andy Sherry, who had told him they didn't have any leads and were no further on with coming up with a suspect Adding that they still didn't have a motive for Nigel's murder, but he told Jimmy he would come back to him and told him to be patient, it was early days. Then later that afternoon Joe got a text from Lorenzo saying he had something that Joe might find interesting and when could they meet up?

Joe walked in to the Killarney Castle pub in Kilburn and scanned the snug for Lorenzo. It was an old-fashioned London ale house the type Joe loved; they had lots of character. Apart from the odd lick of paint it probably hadn't changed one bit in fifty odd years. A big highly polished mahogany bar ran down the side of the room, bare floor boards and cast-Iron stools and tables and a cloud of cigarette smoke hovering just under the artexed ceiling. It looked like Joe was early, so he got himself a pint and sat at a free table. *Lorenzo must live locally,* he thought, it doesn't look like his type of drinking establishment, too down market for a Mayfair butler. After ten to fifteen minutes Joe was on his second pint when Lorenzo arrived, he smiled and signalled to Joe that he was getting a drink. Joe's thumbs up was taken by Lorenzo that he wanted another pint, so the little round table was filling up with beer glasses and the full foul-smelling glass ashtray. Lorenzo looked far too smart for the surroundings, even though he was only in plain black trousers and a smart white open necked shirt, which Joe suspected Lorenzo had worn for work earlier that day together with a tie.

After some small talk about work and their social life, Lorenzo told Joe, he thought he had something for him.

122

Joe smiled and leaned forward trying to hear above the back ground noise. Lorenzo said, he had been speaking to his friends, the other servants who work in Adams Yard. They met up on Thursday for drinks, nobody could recall seeing a woman at number 53 before the latest family arrived. However, one young chauffeur who worked across the across the road from number 53 is a real car nut. He went on to explain when he asked him about Joe's "Mrs Harrington" the young chauffeur told him he took a couple of photos of a Merecedes Maybach parked outside number 53 a few weeks ago. Lorenzo went on and on about the young driver boring him silly about how great a car the Mercedes was. Lorenzo asked him what the bloody hell all this had to do with a woman at number 53. The young man explained that when he took the photo of the car a woman came out of the house, and she was in his photograph of the car.

Joe could hardly contain his excitement to think he might have a photograph of the elusive "Mrs Harrington." He asked Lorenzo, "Do you think he will sell me a copy? How much does he want for it?"

Lorenzo laughed and held up his hands and said, "Slow down, Joe. Take a deep breath. It might not be the woman you want, she doesn't fit the description you gave me." Finishing the rest of his drink, Lorenzo continued, "He took the photo on his phone, and he's sent it over to me. Now calm down and go and get us another drink, and we'll see if the young chauffeur has come up trumps!"

Joe finished the rest of his drink and made his way to the bar, his mind was racing, we could have a break through at last, and his face broke out into a big smile. He ordered Lorenzo a large gin and tonic and another pint for himself, he quickly returned to their table. Lorenzo already had his phone out and was bringing up his photo file onto his screen, he turned his phone to Joe who was leaning forward in anticipation and said, "Here we are, Joe!" Joe took the phone from Lorenzo, narrowed his eyes and stared intently at the screen; using his thumb and fore finger he made the photo bigger. His focused concentrated face slowly turned in to a big smile has he slumped back in his seat.

He looked at Lorenzo, then back at the phone and said, "Bingo, bloody Bingo, Lorenzo, she's got black cropped hair, she must have been wearing a blonde wig when she came to see us, but there's no doubt, it's definitely her, our Mrs Harrington!"

Handing the phone back to Lorenzo, he asked, "How much does he want for the photograph?"

Lorenzo smiled and replied, "I'll send it over to your phone now. The lad never mentioned money, but it would be nice if you treated him, don't you think?"

Joe agreed and reached into his pocket and discreetly took his wallet out. He passed Lorenzo four fifty-pound notes under the table and said, "One hundred for him and the same for you; is that okay?"

Lorenzo smiled and quickly put the money in his pocket together with his phone. Lifting his glass to toast Joe, he said, "That's very kind of you, Joe. I hope it helps with your case, my friend."

Joe lifted his pint glass and chinked Lorenzo's glass. With a huge smile, replied, "I'm sure it will, Lorenzo. You've been an absolute star."

In the corner of the bar the well-built man took a slow drink from his pint of Guinness, he had followed Joe in to the pub and had been watching him and also Lorenzo when he arrived. It was the same man who had followed Joe when he left the bank the day earlier, but then he was dressed in a smart business suit, he had been watching Joe every day since. Tonight, he blended in well with the rest of the drinkers in the pub, black soft leather boots, denim jeans and a dark donkey jacket, the grey woolly hat covered his military style close cropped blonde hair.

He placed his EarPods in and dialled a speed call on his phone in a low voice. He said with a strong Russian accent, never taking his eyes off the table across the room where Joe and Lorenzo were sat. "It's me, Azim, he's with the butler from Adams Yard, and I knew he would be meeting him; the butler lives nearby. The butler has just shown him something on his phone; *(pause)* I don't know what it was. I think they will be leaving shortly. What do you want me to do? *(pause)* ... I can get the butler's phone. *(pause)* ... Yes, I agree, and it would be good to see what's so interesting. *(pause)* ... It's not a problem, consider it done." He ended the call and put the ear pods back in his jacket pocket. He picked up his drink and drained the glass, took one last look at Joe and Lorenzo across the other side of the pub, and left.

Chapter Seventeen
What's Happening?

Joe arrived in the office early at 9.15 a.m., Harriot was already there typing away on her laptop, she looked up and smiled at Joe has he walked in to the reception. She stopped typing and said mockingly, "So here you are, we've been waiting for you to finally decide to grace us with your presence! Jimmy was already here when I got in, I think he's a bit annoyed that you didn't send over the photograph when you text him last night with the news."

Before she could continue, Jimmy came out into reception and said, "Well, good morning, anything exciting happen last night when you were out? Come on, then let's see it. I hope to God you are right, and it is her, after all your drama!"

Joe looked from Jimmy to H. "Well, what do you think, it is her, isn't it?

Jimmy looked up at Joe and replied, "I only got a brief look at her, but it certainly looks like the same woman, what do you think, Harriot? You saw quite a lot of her when she was here."

Harriot looked up first at Joe then at Jimmy and declared, "I can't say for certain, but it does look like her. If it is her that was a fantastic wig she was wearing the day she came in for the meeting. I wouldn't expect you to notice Joe, but women are good at picking up on things like that, unless she had her haircut and changed the colour after she came in and hired us."

Jimmy added, "Well, considering what happened afterwards to poor old Nigel, that's very possible."

Joe sat there grinning like a Cheshire cat and finally said, "Right, Jimmy, so what do we do next?"

Jimmy replied, "Print off the photo from your laptop; try and increase the size of her face, but not so much that it distorts the photo."

Joe nodded and said, "I've already done that, and it's okay; it's pretty clear; I don't think there's a problem!"

Jimmy checked it out and agreed, then, looking up at Joe, said, "I'll ring DS Mooney and tell him the good news that we've found our mysterious Mrs Harrington and see if they can identify the woman."

Joe's smug look disappeared. He asked, "Do we really have to hand it to them on a plate, Jimmy?"

Jimmy looked shocked and scolded Joe, replying, "Don't be so silly; of course, we have to let the Met know, and it's a murder enquiry for God's sake, Joe. It's not your case to try and crack; anyway, how are you going to identify her? We haven't a snowball in hell's chance. They hopefully can do it in a matter of hours, if not sooner; besides, we can't withhold evidence from them; we'll lose our licence."

Joe conceded and said, "Okay, you're right, I was getting carried away with the breakthrough. Joe and

Jimmy walked back into reception and sat on the sofa. Joe asked H to call Mooney to arrange a meeting adding that she would be happy because he was Harriot's fancy man." H walking past the sofa stooped and smacked Joe around the back of head when he wasn't looking.

Jimmy let out a loud laugh and said, "Serves you right."

DI Mooney and his colleague Detective Brown arrived at the office just after lunch, Joe was already with Jimmy when Harriot showed them into Jimmy's office, she gave Joe a withering look when she saw his big cheeky smile, and his eyes with raised hi brows go from her to Mooney then back to her. Jimmy explained about Joe's relationship with Lorenzo the butler he lied that they had met when Joe was on the case for "Mrs Harrington." He went on and explained that they had met up for a drink and Lorenzo said, he would ask his colleagues in service at the houses in Adams Yard if they had seen anything.

DI Mooney threw a sideways glance at detective Brown, obviously thinking why the bloody hell didn't you guys do this, then look wasn't lost on Detective Brown who sheepishly looked down at his pad and continued taking notes.

Jimmy explained Lorenzo contacted Joe last evening and subsequently gave him the photograph. The look on DS. Mooney's face said he didn't believe a word of what he had just been told, but was prepared let it ride for now. He took the A4 Photograph that Joe had generated from her PC and studied it closely for a good minute, he finally looked up at Jimmy totally ignoring Joe, he asked, "And this is definitely the woman who came to your office and claimed to be Mrs Harrington hiring you to check on her 'husband', yes?"

Jimmy and Joe both answered *yes* at the same time, which prompted Mooney to look at the photo again. Jimmy eventually broke the silence, asking, "When you identify her, will you let us know who she really is?"

DS. Mooney looked up and replied, "That depends." Joe couldn't keep quiet any more, he had decided he didn't like this stuck-up pompous shit one little bit.

He jumped in, saying, "Depends on what? If we hadn't come up with the photograph, where would you be with the case? You don't seem to have made much progress and we've just handed you a good lead."

Mooney looked at Joe and replied officially, "It depends on telling you I am not hampering our ongoing investigation into the murder of Nigel Harrington."

Joe cut in again. "Hampering, how? How would we hamper the case when?"

Jimmy decided to bring the conversation to an end he could see Joe was beginning to lose his temper. He stood up and announced, "Okay, thanks for coming in, DI Mooney; we hope we've been of help giving you the photograph, and hopefully we might hear from you when she is identified."

He offered his hand, DI Mooney stood up and shook Jimmy's outstretched hand and replied again very officially, "Thanks for the photograph, it could be a big help." He turned and walked out in to the reception without giving Joe a second glance.

Joe was still sat in his chair, with a face like thunder when Jimmy returned from seeing the detectives out. He walked around his desk, sat down looking at Joe. He finally spoke, "For God's sake, Joe, what was that all about, how to make enemies in the Met?"

Joe let out a sigh and apologised, "I'm sorry, Jimmy, and it's just that he's such a fucking arsehole. He doesn't like me, and he shows it. Every chance he gets to stick it to me, he does. Also, just in case you missed it, the feelings mutual. I don't like him one little bit."

He stopped talking and looked up at the ceiling as if deep in thought. Jimmy said, "Well, let's see if he comes back to us; in the meantime, I will speak with Andy Sherry and see what he can tell us."

Joe stood up and put his "Mrs Harrington" file under his arm, rubbing the stubble on his chin he looked at Jimmy and asked, "Do you think I've blown our chances of Mooney telling us who she really is?"

Jimmy smile and replied, "I doubt it, young Joe, I don't think Mooney had any intension of telling us anything; he was most likely pissed off that his men hadn't done their job properly and spoken with all the servants, I know I would be."

Joe smiled and went back to his office closing Jimmy's door behind him. He sat at his desk staring at the photo of "Mrs Harrington" thinking who the fuck are you and why did you have poor Nigel murdered? His thoughts were interrupted by the ringing of his mobile.

Chapter Eighteen
A Coincidence?

Joe walked into the hospital ward and searched down the beds on the left-hand side and then over to the beds on the right. At the bottom bed of the row of eight beds, a man stood up from to the bed and waved to him. The man walked up the ward and met Joe half way, he had thick brown hair, short in height, but stocky build, with a ruddy outdoor complexion a builder would have. He firmly shook Joe's hand and walking back towards the end bed, told Joe, "I'm Fergal, Lorenzo's partner, he asked me phone you this afternoon when he came around. He was attacked last night on his way home after he left you at the pub."

Joe looked down at poor Lorenzo's bruised and battered face on the pillow, he looked so small in the hospital bed. Turning to Fergal, he asked, "How is he, and do they know who did this to him?" Fergal pulled up another chair from the side of the empty bed next to him and beckoned to Joe to sit down.

He went on to explain, "He's taken a beating; he's got a few cracked ribs, cuts and bruising to his face, as you can see, and he's lost three teeth. Why would somebody want to do this to him? What have you got him mixed up in?"

Joe was shocked at the forthright question, but felt guilty that this could have happened to poor Lorenzo because of him. He answered honestly, "I wish I knew Fergal; I really hope this wasn't connected to my friendship with him; was anything taken?"

Fergal looked from Lorenzo to Joe his voice cracking with emotion, he replied, "They took his wallet and his phone, they didn't have to do this to him; he isn't a fighter. If they had told him to give them his valuables, he would have just handed them over. They didn't have to do this to him, the bastards!"

Joe nodded in agreement, then waited for Fergal to compose himself before asking him another question. Smiling sympathetically, he continued, "Did Lorenzo speak to you about what I asked him to help me with?"

Fergal wiped his nose and struggled putting his hankie back into his jeans pocket. He finally looked at Joe and answered him, "Of course he did, we've been together for Many years, and we don't have any secrets. Do you think it was because of you this happened? If it was, I don't want you contacting him again."

Joe shook his head and said, "I honestly don't know Fergal; I hope not, and if it is, I can assure I won't trouble Lorenzo for any more help. Believe me, I don't want to put him or you in any danger."

He said, he believed Joe and thanked him just as Lorenzo started to stir, Fergal jumped up and told Lorenzo not to move, asking him how he was feeling. Lorenzo smiled at his partner and reached for his hand; he eyes focused on Joe. Joe smiled sympathetically and asked, "How you feeling buddy, can you talk about what happened or do you want to leave it for now."

Fergal gave Joe a withering look and went to speak, but Lorenzo waved him away and in a croaky voice told him to stop fussing. He looked back to Joe, smiled weakly and said, "Not too sure, my friend. We said our goodbyes, and I walked up the High Street, next thing I felt a blow to the side of my face, and that was it. I heard they took my phone and wallet, probably sodding kids, but I remember hearing heavy footsteps before it all went dark; it sounded like just one person."

Before Joe could reply Fergal stepped in and said, "That's enough for now you need to relax, my darling. Joe would you say your goodbyes and leave us now, please."

Joe stood up and said, "Of course, I understand." Looking down at Lorenzo, he said, "You take care of yourself and don't worry about your wallet.

"I will send you the money I gave you last night. I'll speak to you when you've recovered. Take care." With another disgusted look from Fergal, Joe smiled, turned and walked up the ward to the exit doors.

Joe returned to the office; Jimmy was stood next to Harriot's desk, showing a piece of paper in his hand. They both looked up as Joe closed the door behind him. Jimmy said, "You left in a hurry; is everything all right?" following Joe into his office.

Jimmy sat down while Joe hung up his jacket, he went on. "What's happened, Joe? I know that look on your face, it usually means trouble."

Joe plonked himself down behind his desk and replied, "Lorenzo the butler was attacked last night after I left him, and I've just been to see him in hospital. The poor bugger was beaten up pretty badly."

Jimmy looked long and hard at Joe and finally asked, "Do you think it's random or because he was meeting you?"

Joe shook his head, answering, "I don't know to be honest with you, Jimmy, probably random; it isn't the best of neighbourhoods."

Jimmy looked concerned, and rubbing his chin, replied, "If it was because he met with you, Joe, we have a big problem, it means you were being followed. Have you noticed anything lately? Have you seen somebody and then noticed them again, out and about somewhere?"

Joe stared down at his desk, shaking his head, he looked up at Jimmy and said, "Not that I can recall, but if that's what's happening, Jimmy, we must be on to something, don't you think?"

Jimmy agreed, adding, "Well, why else would somebody be interested in where you go and who you meet? Talk me through when you were in the pub with Lorenzo discussing the photo; did he show it to you on his phone? If he did somebody could have seen that and that could be why he was jumped."

Joe stood up and started walking around the office, thinking back to the meeting in the pub. He stopped and turned, pointing at Jimmy, he said, "You might have something; Lorenzo did show it to me on his phone, and when he sent it over, I checked my phone to make sure it had come through. That would be pretty obvious what we were doing to somebody watching us."

Jimmy half smiled and replied, "For God's sake, sit down, Joe, you drive me mad when you start padding around like a caged lion. If it wasn't random, which now I'm beginning to doubt, it could have been you in hospital and not Lorenzo."

Joe nodded and said, "Yea, I wish they had tried to jump me instead of poor little Lorenzo. They would have regrated it; I promise you"

Jimmy went quiet, he was sat in his chair, looking up at the wall. Joe asked, "What are you thinking?"

He finally looked back to Joe and replied, "If we are right, Joe, we've got to be very careful, we can't take any chances. Just remember, these might be the people who killed Nigel Harrington. When you're leaving the office, scan both sides of the road and see if anyone is just stood around. Take a good look at them, so you can remember their face, height, build, etc. When you are walking, stop and look in a shop window, good for seeing across the road for someone else stopping or that familiar face. Quickly turn and walk back the way you came from, carefully looking at people for any reaction. You can laugh, young Joe, but it could save your life. I've got a feeling this is starting to get serious. I'm waiting for a call back from Andy Sherry on where the Met are with the photo we gave them. I'll mention the attack on Lorenzo. I'll speak to Harriot and brief her; she can get an Uber home at night if it's dark. I don't want to spook her, but let's be doubly careful to all stay safe."

Chapter Nineteen
The "Mrs Harrington"

Looking at Joe, Jimmy smiled and announced, "Yulia Navarykasha." He then sat back in his chair with a triumphant look on his face.

Joe waited for an explanation and just stared at Jimmy, eventually said, "And that is?"

Jimmy took a deep intake of breath and smugly replied, "That! Young Joseph is our Mrs Harrington."

Joe let out a low whistle, and smiling at Jimmy, replied, "So Andy Sherry came good then, okay, oh font of all knowledge, go on brief me then; I can see you can't wait to tell me."

Jimmy threw his head back, let out a loud laugh and started with his briefing, "Yes, you're so right, Andy Sherry came back to me last night. He told me they had identified our 'Mrs Harrington' from the photograph supplied by your contact Lorenzo. Her real name is Yulia Navarykasha; she is Ukrainian and married to a Russian Oligarch. She arrived in London three days before she hired you and get this, and she flew out of Heathrow later that evening after you briefed her about old Nigel. She flew back to Boryspil airport, Kyiv, in the Ukraine. She was met at the airport by two unidentified men and has not been seen since. She flew in and out of here on a false passport in the name of Oksana Dobroshtan, and as we already know, she stayed at number 53.

"Navarykasha is her Maiden name, her married name is Yulia Novikov, and she married a Russian Andrei Novikov many years ago in Odessa, a port city on the Black Sea in southern Ukraine. She's originally from Odessa, she lived there with her parents, and younger brother Ivan, and her parents have both died, the brother's whereabouts unknown. She lives the good life with Andrei, they own several properties in Russia. They also own properties in Switzerland, New York, and Cannes and most likely many other properties not listed to them. Oh, and they have two children the eldest, a daughter called Zoya, and a son called Mykola, both of them, whereabouts unknown. They are mega wealthy courtesy of husband Andrei; he appears to have made his money in Oil and Gas after the fall of the Union. Like most of the Oligarchs he appears to have been in the right place at the right time, he has the usual luxuries, private plane, big yacht etc. He has friends in high places within the Government. Surprisingly, he is one Oligarch who doesn't appear have a registered home in London Officially! I would give odds on a bet that he is the owner of number 53 Adams Yard, and most likely other London properties that are registered to a shell company."

Joe had been listening carefully to Jimmy's briefing, he sat looking at Jimmy for a good thirty seconds without speaking even though he had finished and closed his folder. He finally sat back in his chair and let out a loud, "Wow! Andy certainly did his homework, didn't he? That is an incredible amount of information in a short space of time."

Joe's brain was working overtime, he continued, "Some things don't add up, though, Jimmy, after what you've just read out to me. What is she called, Yulia? Why would you send your wife over here to get involved in a murder? Surely, he's got people 'working' for him. Also, what puzzles me the most of all is why she came to us, why get us involved in this? Again, they could have paid people to check up on Nigel instead of involving a PI firm in London. Did Andy say anything else apart from the information on the wife?"

Jimmy smiled at Joe's perplexed face, he replied, "Regarding your questions, Joe, I don't know answers. I don't know why we got involved. I would think that it was 'them' that killed Nigel and put Lorenzo in hospital. If I'm right, they must be concerned we are on to something; otherwise, they would just ignore us. Andy did say something else, this briefing came from Special Branch, and he said, we need to be careful. These people don't mess around, and we could be in grave danger."

Joe let out a fake laugh and replied, "We've worked that out ourselves, haven't we? Also, what I don't understand is the way they killed Nigel; they could have done it a lot less publicly, they usually do. They could have kidnapped him, killed him, disposed of the body or poisoned him, which is popular with 'these' people."

Jimmy looked at Joe and nodded in agreement, he stared up at the ceiling as if looking for the answers. They both sat there in silence for a minute, each lost with their own thoughts of the briefing. It was Jimmy who was the first to speak. "Do you know what I think, young Joe? I don't think she came to London with the intention of killing or having Nigel killed. She came for something else, maybe business-related, or to see someone socially. Why come on a false passport and why not use their private jet? Something unexpected must have happened when she was here, and poor old Nigel ended up dead."

"Also, like you said, Joe, why shoot him and leave him in a park? I think that was done intentionally; it was a warning to others. A warning that maybe gave out the message: do what you're told or you will end up like this. Joe shrugged his shoulders and came in with 'Yes,' but a warning to who, Jimmy? That's the 65,000-dollar question, if your theory is correct."

Jimmy shrugged his shoulders and said, "Possibly Nigel's associates at the bank? I have a strong feeling that this thing is connected with the bank, and Nigel was in on whatever was going on. Maybe she met Nigel and/or his associates from the bank, and they upset the Russians somehow, so they decided to kill him as an example or a warning to the others involved."

Joe sat looking at Jimmy, he rubbed his hand down the side of his face and across his chin, taking in what Jimmy had just said. He smiled a cheeky smile at him and gently shaking his head, said, "Where the hell do you get your logical approach from? Does it come with old age or from being a detective for all these years? I think you might be right, or at least on the right track, what you said does make a hell of a lot of sense. Did you tell Andy Sherry that I had been for a meeting at Nigel's bank? And how's the Mets investigation going?"

Jimmy shook his head. "No, I didn't mention your meeting to Andy; he's a good, trusted friend, but he wouldn't hesitate to stop us if he thought we were interfering with the investigation. Anyway, you shouldn't offer up everything you know; I'm sure he hasn't, even though he has told us a lot. Regarding the Mets progress, they are working on the theory that the killer has flown out of the country straight after the murder. Also, they haven't ruled out the possibility that the killer could have been our Mrs Harrington." He paused and popped a mint in his mouth before continuing, "I doubt that very much, from what we've been told about her and her husband. People like them have 'specialists' to do their dirty deeds for them. I also spoke to Brian May at the newspaper; they don't appear to have any leads or anything regarding what Andy told us; that's probably why it's been pretty quiet in the press."

Jimmy continued, "I think we could be getting close to something, but hey, let's not take any chances, these are dangerous people, like Andy said. I wouldn't mention any of this briefing to Harriot; you know how she worries; I don't want her getting upset and nervous, okay?"

Joe nodded, saying, "Okay with me, I think I'll try and speak to that receptionist at the bank. Shit, what she was called?" He looked up over Jimmy's head, picturing them both in the lift, talking and glancing at her name tag. It worked, he announced triumphantly, "Octavia! Octavia Connelly! That was it, a pretty-looking young lady, you never know, she might know something that could help us."

Jimmy smiled and replied, "Don't you mean you are going to take her out on a date? What about your girlfriend? What's she called, Sally?"

Joe stood up, gathering his notes. He feigned shook and horror, smiling said, "It's all in the course of duty Jimmy, one has to make sacrifices to do what needs to be done to crack the case."

Jimmy shook his head, smiled, and said, "Go on, bugger off out of my office; I might be getting old, but I'm not stupid!"

Joe walked out in to reception, pointing at Harriot, who was sitting, typing away. He made her jump in fright when he shouted, "Coffee, young lady, and a chocolate biscuit in my office now!

H gathered herself together and threw her pen at him, shouting, "You dope, you frightened the life out of me. Get your own bloody coffee. I'm busy."

Joe shrugged his shoulders and with a big smile on his face, nonchalantly replied, "Okay, will do." He walked over to the coffee maker, chuckling quietly to himself, much to the annoyance of Harriot.

Chapter Twenty
LPZ, A Chance Meeting with Octavia.

Joe watched her come out of the bank, it was just after six pm, and he walked quickly down the road crossing between oncoming traffic, then casually walked back in the direction of the bank. Stopping directly in front of her, he smiled and said, "Hi, its Octavia, isn't it from the bank?"

She looked startled. She pulled the air pods out of her ears, then recognising Joe, smiled broadly and replied, "Hi, You're Mr... Umm, don't tell me I will get it."

Joe put out her out her misery and said, "Makin, Joe Makin, I was in your bank for a meeting with Mr Zimmerman and his cronies, and you looked after me."

She smiled, putting the air pods in her handbag, she said, "Yes that's right. It's very kind of you to remember me. How are you?"

Joe gently took her arm and moved her towards the wall of the building to get them both out of the way of the flood of people heading towards the station on their way home from work. He slowly removed his hand from her arm and replied, "I'm good, thanks. How are you?" He paused, but before she could reply, he asked, "Listen, I hope you don't think I'm pushing it, but would you like to go for a drink or a coffee, or something? It's a little busy around here? I'm really thirsty, and I've had a hell of a day. That's if you haven't got anywhere to dash off to, that is?"

He hoped she would be curious to learn what had happened in his day; it worked. She gave him another big smile and said, "Yes, I would love to, I could do with a drink myself."

"So, what would you like to drink?" Joe asked, they were in the cocktail lounge at The Alchemist, a trendy bar at Reuters Plaza. Joe hoped it was just far enough away from the bank that none of Octavia's colleagues would walk in and spot them together. Also, they had an excellent restaurant upstairs, where, if everything went well, they could have a meal and stretch the evening out further. Octavia was telling Joe about herself, she was from Fleet in Hampshire, where her parents still lived. She went to Bristol University and shared a house with four of her uni friends on Chenies Street next to the Pret a Manger. Which was off the Tottenham Court Road, she had worked at the bank for four years. Joe was half listening and also thinking, *She really is beautiful a lot more so than I remember.* He put her age at about twenty-seven to twenty-eight years old, she had big hazel eyes, full lips, beautiful white teeth, her long dark hair was tied up in a bun on the top of her head, and perfect unblemished pale skin.

He focused and said to himself, "This is work also I'm meeting Sally tomorrow for dinner, concentrate you dope."

He smiled and joined the conversation, saying, "Really? That's amazing; our offices aren't very far away; we're in Holborn. We're practically neighbours."

Octavia threw her head back and laughed. "Wow, how crazy is that? What do you do?"

Joe got the usual reaction when he replied, "I'm a private investigator."

Octavia's face went very serious, and her beautiful eyes widened. She said, "Really, I've never met a private investigator before; what's it like? Is it very exciting like you see in the movies?"

Joe laughed and was joined by Octavia, when their laughter died down, she added, "I sounded a little silly, didn't I? Just can't wait until I get home and tell the girls I've been on a date with a private investigator."

Joe smiled and replied, "Is this what it is, a date?"

Realising what she had said made her blush and splutter. "Well, no, I didn't mean a date as such."

Joe saved her embarrassment and gently touched her arm, smiling broadly and said, "It's okay; I know what you meant; I'm just teasing you. It's the job, it usually gets a reaction from people when I tell them what I am. Also, the answer to your question is no, it isn't exciting; a lot of the time it's just boring, let me get us another drink."

Walking to the bar he smiled broadly and thought, she is absolutely adorable; *I'm really enjoying my job tonight*. He returned with her Vodka and soda and his large Malt whisky. She smiled up at him has he went to sit down beside her, a little closer than before, he asked, "Are you hungry? They have a great restaurant upstairs, I can see if we can get a table, what do you think?"

She smiled that beautiful smile again and replied, "That would be nice. Thank you. After the drinks, I think I should eat something."

They had an enjoyable meal, like downstairs in the cocktail lounge, the restaurant was busy. They had chatted away like two old friends, Octavia appeared to be getting a little tipsy. Joe had ordered a bottle of Chablis with the meal and was going to ask if she would like a brandy with her Latte, but thought better of it. Octavia excused herself and left the table to go to the ladies, it gave Joe the opportunity to think if he should try to get her talking about her job at the bank, he wasn't sure. As luck would have it the decision was taken out of his hands, over coffee Octavia asked him why he had visited the bank to meet with Mr Zimmerman. With him being a private investigator, she wondered if there was any scandal going on that he could tell her, laughing she admitted that she was being nosey. Joe decided she definitely was tipsy from all the drink, he explained he was there because of Nigel Harrington being murdered. Joe wasn't surprised how quickly that sobered up Octavia, she had been leaning forward into the table, she sat back straight upright, her face serious.

Joe asked, "I'm sorry, have I upset you, and are you okay?"

Octavia smiled and appeared to relax a little. She replied, "Yes, I'm fine, I've been enjoying your company so much, it was a shock when you mentioned poor Mr Harrington."

Joe seized the opportunity and said, "Forgive me, you asked me, and I was just being honest. Did you know Mr Harrington well?"

Octavia dabbed the sides of her mouth with her napkin, sighing deeply, she replied, "Yes, I knew him; he was a director at the bank; he and would always smile and say good morning when he came in to work, except…" Her voice tailed off, she took a drink of her wine.

Joe was intrigued and leaning forward topped up her wine glass and quietly asked, "Except what?"

She thanked Joe and took another drink then continued, "Well, a couple of days before he was… you know, she stopped short of saying murdered. He stopped saying good *morning* when he came through reception. It was as if he had something on his mind; he would just walk straight to the lift, looking down at the floor. It was probably nothing, but it was just so out of character; he was always so nice and friendly. I saw it on the ten o'clock news about someone being shot dead in the park and said to my flatmates, it's so violent in London now. It was such a shock when we found out that it was poor Mr Harrington who had been murdered."

Joe ordered two more lattes from a passing waiter, turning back to Octavia, he said, "I can imagine; it must have been a terrible shock. What people at the bank thought it was all about, you know his murder?"

She gently shook her head from side to side and replied, "We didn't know what to think; it was just so awful, and we all received an email from HR saying we weren't to discuss Mr Harrington with anyone outside the bank. I suppose they were worried about the reputation of the bank."

Joe agreed with her, "Yes, I suppose there was that to consider; did the police speak with all the staff when they came in?"

Octavia smiled and replied, "No, not really; from what I can remember, they just spoke with some of the directors and also Mr Harrington's PA."

Joe thought typical Met laziness, he decided to take a shot seeing they were talking openly about the bank. He took out his mobile and brought up the photo, turning his phone to Octavia, he asked her, "Have you ever seen this woman at the bank?"

She looked at the phone and then took it from his hand for a closer look, handing it back to, Joe she smiled and replied, "Yes, I have, that's Mrs Dobroshtan." Joe couldn't believe what she had just said; he nearly choked on his drink. He tried to appear calm; he went to take another sip of his drink, but didn't trust his hand not to shake and spill it on the table.

He paused for a few seconds and continued, "Mrs Dobroshtan? Oh, so you know her?"

Octavia smiled, had another drink of wine and replied, "No, not really, but she came in to the bank to see Mr Zimmerman."

Joe smiled and tried to act nonchalant, he asked, "Can you remember when you saw her?"

Octavia thought for a while and replied, "It was only a few weeks ago, I remember her because she was so classy looking and attractive for her age, very expensively dressed. I telephoned Mr Zimmerman's PA, and asked her if she wanted me to bring her up to his office. But she said no; she would come down and get her, which was unusual for her. She's so up herself being Mr Zimmerman's PA, none of us receptionist staff like her, she's a real cow."

Her words were just washing over Joe, he was thinking what she had just told him, what a break through, he couldn't believe his luck. He realised Octavia was asking him something, he quickly focused back in to Octavia who he wanted to kiss for what she had just told him. He said, "I'm sorry; what did you say?"

Octavia let out that lovely laugh of hers and repeated, "Why do you ask about Mrs Dobroshtan? Are you looking for her?"

Joe played down his question, replying, "No, not at all, a friend of mine was trying to get in touch with her a few weeks ago and asked if I could help find her, something to do with business, I think."

He felt guilty lying to her, she seemed so innocent and nice, she would never know what a big help she had been. Octavia innocently said, "Oh, maybe I could help you with that. Would you like me to try and find out where she lives from the bank."

Joe shook his head and replied, "No, I don't think that would be a good idea; in actual fact, I wouldn't mention that we've been together tonight to anyone at the bank. You see, I think I might have upset Mr Zimmerman when I came in to see him. I wouldn't want to get you into any trouble, associating with a private eye, and they might not like it. I can't say any more about my visit to your bank; it was confidential, you see."

He hoped that would head off any further questions from Octavia, it worked. She lowered her voice and leaning in to the table, said, "Oh, I see, is it detective stuff?" Joe looked around as if to check that no one was listening, then smiled at Octavia and winked. He did his utmost not to spoil it by bursting out laughing, she was so gullible it was adorable. If he wasn't seeing Sally, he would definitely have asked her out, she was fabulous.

Joe felt as if he had won the lottery, the chance meeting couldn't have gone any better, this was big news. Also, it looked like they could be ahead of the Met, but they would probably check with Zimmerman now they had the photograph. It looked like Jimmy's theory was correct about the bank being involved in whatever was going on and Joe could now confirm it. He asked the waiter for the bill, Octavia said, "Thank you for the drinks and the lovely meal, you have absolutely spoilt me tonight." Joe told her it was a pleasure and hopefully they could do it again sometime.

Outside he hailed a passing cab, they both climbed in. Joe told the cabbie Octavia's address, but asked him to first stop at the tower block number one Canary Wharf just for a minute or so. He wanted to call in to see Danny and thank him for his discretion when he spoke with the police, Joe had a fifty-pound note in his top pocket that he wanted to give to Danny. As the cab pulled away from the curb, Joe turned and looked out of the rear window to the entrance of the bar. Nobody was outside looking in the direction of the cab, he turned back to Octavia and smiled.

A moment later, the door of the bar opened, and out stepped Lorenzo's attacker. He watched the taxi disappear down Cabot Square, then turn right. Pressing the speed dial on his phone, a voice answered, and he spoke, "He met with a receptionist from the bank; *pause*... it looked like a date, but I'm not so sure. *Pause*... I think that would be too much of a coincidence. Yes, they have just left in a cab; Paval is following them on the motorbike, and I will meet with him later, what do you want me to do?" *Pause*... Nodding his head, he answered, "Yes, I understand; it will be done, do-svidaniya."

Chapter Twenty-One
Slowly, Slowly Making Progress

Jimmy listened intently to Joe's meeting with Octavia the previous evening, stopping him occasionally to clarify a point here and there. Joe finished, threw his arms up in the air in triumph and sat back in his seat. Waiting for Jimmy to say something, he couldn't wait any longer, so he finally said, "Well, what do you think is that manner from heaven or what?"

Jimmy sat looking at Joe, slowly tapping his fingers on the arm of his chair. He sucked his cheeks in and then out again, thought long and hard, and finally said, "Several weeks ago, the young lady said? So that puts her visit to the bank before she hired us to check on Nigel. Did she know if Nigel was in the meeting with Zimmerman?"

Joe shook his head. Jimmy continued, "Something could have been said at that meeting, either by Nigel or if he wasn't in it by Zimmerman about Nigel, that she wasn't happy about, that could have possibly sealed his fate."

Joe nodded in agreement, replying, "It looks like it could have been that way."

Jimmy fell silent, Joe put his head back and adopting his usual pose, looked up at the ceiling. Jimmy finally spoke again, "Did Nigel meet up with anyone when you were on the case or break his routine and go somewhere differently?"

Joe shrugged his shoulders and replied, "Not as far as I can remember, I don't think so, it was all pretty routine, go to work, go home. Apart from going home to Chelsea that evening to see his wife and then for a pub dinner."

Jimmy asked, "And you had eyes on them all the time?"

Joe replied, "Well, yes, I was I was four tables down, and even when Nigel went to bar for the first drinks, I did to, it was a busy evening. Do you think he spoke to someone inside the pub about Yulia coming to the bank?" I didn't see him speak to anyone.

Jimmy said, "Oh, well, I suppose he could have spoken with someone on the phone in the evening when they went back to their house."

Joe stood up and said, "Wait a minute! I had forgotten one lunchtime he met a guy at the Lombard restaurant. They had a meal, talked a lot over the meal, and then Nigel left to go back to the bank. The other guy looked like a banker too. Smartly dressed, expensive suit, but quite bulky though, he looked like he could look after himself. I couldn't get a snap of them because I was sitting at the bar with a good view of them, which meant they would have had a good view of me too. Bloody well wish I had now, who do you think he could be?"

Jimmy shrugged his shoulders and replied, "It could have been anyone Joe, like you say possibly just a business meeting, we're just surmising and clutching at straws now.

Anyway, changing the subject; did you behave yourself last night?"

Joe smiled and said, "For your information, yes, I did; we got a cab back to hers, and I gave a peck on the cheek. I got her phone number just in case, and then the cab took me home to Fulham. She is such a lovely woman, a little naïve, but that just made her all the more loveable."

Jimmy threw Joe a "really" look, but Joe was ready for it, adding, "And tonight I'm having a nice romantic meal with Sally at mine."

Jimmy stood up, laughed and replied, "I never said a word; I never doubted you for a minute, always the perfect gentleman, young Joseph."

Joe stopped at Wholefoods on Fulham Broadway to get food for dinner and the weekend. He was glad it was Friday, it had been a busy week, but one that ended on a big high with what Octavia had told him. Preparing dinner, he thought about whether he should tell Sally about having drinks and dinner with Octavia the night before. He decided against it; he wasn't sure if she would be okay with it, that it was only business. He really liked Sally; they were getting on so well, and he didn't want to cause a problem. He took a drink of wine and put his glass down on the worktop. Just then the front door bell rang, wiping his hands on the tea towel, he pressed the buzzer and said, "Come on up."

Joe opened the front door and smiled at Sally who was stood there in a smart knee length camel coloured coat, he kissed her and said, "You look gorgeous, come in." He took her coat and hung it in the closet, her hair was parted down the middle. She wore very little make up with the exception of bright red lipstick. She wore a short beige fitted woollen dress that emphasised her fabulous figure and legs, finished off with matching beige high heel shoes. Joe turned, and stopped in his tracks, looking at her he said, "You look very sexy tonight, if you don't mind me saying so."

Sally laughed and thought mission accomplished, she replied, "Well, thank you, kind sir." Bowing slightly.

Joe walked over and said, "Let me put your overnight bag in the bedroom, do you want to pour yourself a glass of wine?"

Over the dinner of lamb cutlets, truffle mash, carrots and peas, Joe asked Sally how her week had gone, then added he was pleased she'd had a good week. She asked him how things had gone with the case seeing there hadn't been much about it on the television news. Joe couldn't say too much, but did tell her about Lorenzo coming good with the photograph proving that their "Mrs Harrington" had stayed at number 53 Adams Yard. However, he left out the part about Lorenzo getting mugged after they parted company at the pub. He didn't see the point of spooking Sally and the last thing he wanted was her worrying about him getting hurt doing his job.

Joe changed the subject and asked, "What should we do this weekend?"

Sally smiled, topped up their wine glasses and leaning forward replied in a low sexy voice, "Why don't we just chill, watch lots of TV, make love lots, and I will cook you some nice meals, seeing you did make me such a beautiful dinner tonight."

Joe let out a deep sigh and replied, "I'm not sure if there's anything good on the TV."

Sally had a drink of wine and running her shoeless foot up the inside of Joe's leg, whispered, "Well, that just leaves more time for making love then, doesn't it?"

Joe smiled broadly, adding, "Well, I think that sounds like a good plan, I'm all for it."

He stood up and said, "Why don't you make yourself comfy in the lounge and I'll l clear away the dishes."

After loading the dish washer, he poured himself a straight scotch and walked into the lounge, it was empty. He called out, "Where are you?"

"In here," came the reply from the bedroom.

Joe walked into the bedroom and there was Sally lay out on the bed naked smiling up at him, he laughed aloud and thought this is the perfect end to a bloody great week.

Chapter Twenty-Two
Octavia Connelly

Monday morning, Joe walked into the office, whistling and full of the joys of spring, despite it being a miserable summer's day outside. Smiling at Harriot already working at her desk, he asked, "Hi, H, how was your weekend? Good I hope."

Harriot looked up and smiled, replying, "It was good thanks, but not as good as yours by the way you cheerfully strolled in here."

Joe smiled, walked into his office and threw his briefcase onto the sofa, hanging up his jacket he shouted through to H for a cup of coffee and a digestive. He was in a very good mood, he had a great weekend with Sally, and they had a breakthrough with Nigel's case. He wasn't sure what the next move would be, he would wait for Jimmy to arrive and see what he thought they should do next.

Jimmy arrived shortly after nine thirty, Joe heard him greet Harriot and go into his office, and Joe would give him five minutes to set up shop as Jimmy liked to call it. Harriot popped her head around the door and asked, "I'm making Jimmy his pot of tea; do you fancy another coffee?" Joe smiled and gave her a thumbs up, smiling back she closed the door. Joe was thinking about what

Octavia had told him on Thursday evening about the visit of "Mrs Harrington" to the LPZ bank. Was that why she had come to the UK, for a meeting with the bank, couldn't she have spoken to them over the phone? Also, what happened that after the meeting that she hired us to spy on Nigel? He looked up at the ceiling for divine intervention, because he was buggered if he could work it all out! Instead of finding the way forward to the conundrum, all he got was H coming in, interrupting his thought process with, "Here's your coffee, dopey!"

Joe walked into Jimmy's office with his notebook in one hand and his coffee in the other, he greeted Jimmy, "Good morning, boss, how was your weekend; good I hope?"

Jimmy looked up and sat back in his chair and replied, "It was thanks, Joe, but by the twinkle in your eyes, I would say not as good has yours."

Joe had sat down and settled himself in for the morning meeting, smiled broadly and winked at Jimmy, who replied, "Okay, say no more then, let's get started." Recapping on Friday's briefing on what your lady friend Octavia told you about the meeting at LPZ.

It looks like the timeline from our, "Mrs Harrington going in for her meeting with Zimmerman, and we're not sure who else. It was the two days before she hired you to check up on Old Nigel."

Joe nodded and confirmed, "Yep, that's about right," Jimmy continued, "I had a drink with Andy Sherry on Sunday lunchtime and asked him if the Met had been back

158

to the bank since they discovered who our Mrs Harrington actually was; he said they had, and the director they spoke to checked it out, and they denied knowing her."

Joe let out a soft whistle, "Really, they said that? After they'd had a meeting with her at their offices, only a few weeks before, wow."

Jimmy smiled and nodded. "That's exactly what I thought; even if they knew her by a different name, surely they would have recognised her from the photograph. So that begs the question, Joe, why would they lie about knowing or having a meeting with her if they are not up to their necks in all this?"

Joe asked, "Did you tell Andy that we knew she had been to the bank?"

Jimmy shook his head. "No, we only have hearsay, they could just deny it. What we need is some proof that she was there. Did she sign in at the banks reception when she arrived?"

Joe shrugged his shoulders, replying, "I don't know, I could ask Octavia, what are you thinking, getting her signature and trying to match it?"

Jimmy said, "Not us, DI. Mooney's motley crew; we could tell them we believe she was at the bank for a meeting and ask them to check out her signature. They could easily get a copy of her writing from special branch to do that and then we would have solid proof that, the bank is lying. Could you speak to your young lady and see if there's a signature, and could she get a good copy of it? Even a photograph of it on her phone would be a big help."

Joe agreed enthusiastically, "Yea, I'm sure she would do that for us, but I just don't want to put her in any danger. She is an adorable lady; I don't want her getting on the wrong side of Zimmerman's people. I'll give her a call after our meeting, maybe see if she wants to meet up for a last-minute drink or meal tonight."

It was a typical London Street, identical terraced houses on both sides, each with a small garden in front of the bay window. Most of them had a small three-foot wall in front with wrought iron gates. Some were brightly painted and well cared for, probably owned. Others probably rented and split into flats downstairs and upstairs, but even they were still in good condition and well looked after. It was seven thirty in the evening, Joe walked down the path and rang the doorbell on the dark grey front door of the end terraced two-story house. He had left it until this time hoping somebody would be home from work by now. No answer, Joe tried again. Only this time left his finger on the buzzer for longer; it worked. He heard a female voice inside shout, "Okay, hang on, I'm coming!" The door was opened by a young woman, quite short, thick black hair, a rounded pretty face, wearing glasses. She was dressed in a white blouse, a straight grey skirt, with black flat shoes, Joe put her age at around twenty-three to twenty-four. He assumed this was the primary school teacher flat mate, Octavia had mentioned last week at dinner, she certainly looked like a school teacher. With one hand still holding the door she looked Joe up and down slowly and asked, "Are you the police, have you any news about my flatmate yet?"

Joe smiled and replied, "No, sorry; I'm not the police, I'm a friend of Octavia's, and I wondered if I could talk to her. I phoned her mobile this morning and then rang the bank; they told me she didn't turn up for work last Friday morning and wasn't in again today. I was with her on Thursday evening; she seemed fine not ill, worried or upset about anything. The bank seemed a bit annoyed that she hadn't been in touch. Are you one of her flatmates?"

The woman's face broke into a smile, she stepped back and said, "Oh sorry, come in, I thought you were them, the police, we reported Octavia missing at lunchtime. Although they didn't appear to be too concerned, they said it was early days yet, and she could just turn up with a logical excuse, bloody hopeless they are, if you ask me."

She closed the front door and Joe followed her down the hall into a cosy, but untidy sitting room at the back of the house. She turned to face Joe, moving what looked like dirty laundry, she offered him a seat on the sofa smiling, she said, "You'll have to forgive the mess, the bloody cleaners disappeared at weekend also, they were supposed to come on Saturday. I'm Karen by the way, one of Octavia's flat mates. What did you say your name was?"

Joe smiled and replied, "My name is Joe, like I said, I was with Octavia on Thursday night; we had drinks and dinner, and I dropped her off her later in the evening. Have you…"

Karen the flatmate cut him short and asked excitedly, "Wait a minute, are you the private detective? We were all here when she came home from your date, and she was telling us all about you. She was quite keen and hoped you would ring her. We haven't seen her that excited about anyone for quite a while, well, not since she split up with Gavin."

Joe smiled and replied, "I really enjoyed our evening, she's a lovely lady, and I thought maybe she was ill. I didn't realise she had gone missing; does she usually miss work days and not get in touch with them?"

Karen was now sat on the sofa next to Joe, the dirty laundry was now a heap on the floor. Despite Joe's question, she asked him, "What kind of private investigating do you do? I bet it's exciting? Is it dangerous?"

Joe thought this is going to be bloody painful, he smiled politely and nodding his head said, "Karen, Octavia? Missing?"

Karen blushed, sat up straight and said in her school teacher's voice, "Sorry, no, she left for work as usual on Friday morning. But she didn't come home Friday night, we thought she might have hooked up with you again. Fiona, one of the other flat mates, called her on Saturday afternoon and her phone was switched off. Then on Sunday, still no sign of her and her mobile was still off. Today, I phoned the bank to speak with her to make sure she was okay and find what where she had been up to, they told me she hadn't worked since Thursday.

"That's when I telephoned the police and reported her missing, they didn't seem that concerned. They took her name and address and the details, then said to see if she turned up in the next day or so, and if not, to go back to them. But I know Octavia; she loves her job at the bank; she wouldn't just go absent. I spoke with her ex-boyfriend Gavin, Gavin Ford, this afternoon, but he said he's not seen or heard from her since they split up."

Joe looked at Karen's worried face and tried to reassure her, "I'm sure there's a perfect explanation; have you tried her, parents? Maybe, something's happened, and she went back to her parents' house."

Karen's face lit up. "That's a good point, I never thought about them, but why would she turn off her phone or not get in touch and tell us what she was doing or where she was going? We're all very close, we're like sisters, it's so out of character for her to just vanish without saying anything or get in touch."

Joe took out a business card and passed it to her, he asked, "If and when she gets in touch, would you mind letting me know. Also, would you ask her to ring me, I want to speak with her?"

Karen looked from the card in her hand to Joe. "Do you think it's anything to do with you, like a case you're working on or something?"

They both stood up from the sofa at the same time, Joe feigned surprise and walking out into the hall answering, "No! Not at all, I'm not really working on anything at the moment, why do you ask that?"

Opening the front door for Joe, she smiled and replied, "Just with you being a private detective and seeing her the night before she goes missing, that's all. I'm not trying to accuse you of anything."

Joe smiled and said, "That's okay, I didn't take it that way, it was lovely to meet you, Karen. I'm sure Octavia will turn up soon, and please don't forget to ask her to get in touch. You're a good friend, and she's very lucky to have you looking out for her." Saying their goodbyes, Joe walked down the three steps and onto the pavement, closing the little wrought iron gate behind him. Walking back to the main road, he was deep in thought hoping that it wasn't his fault Octavia hasn't been seen since they met. He was concerned for her, especially after what she told him about "Mrs Harrington's" visit to the bank. Was it just a coincidence poor old Lorenzo gets mugged after their meeting, and now Octavia had drinks and a meal with him, and she goes missing?

Joe decided he would call it a day and head back to his apartment, maybe get some dinner from the Wholefoods store or one of the takeaways on Fulham Broadway. He couldn't stop thinking about Octavia, it did seem out of character for her to just disappear, according to her friend. She was such a lovely young lady, he really hoped he hadn't caused her any harm, bumping into her. He thought about Lorenzo and promised himself he would ring him tomorrow to see how he was doing. Taking his phone from his pocket, he speed-dialled Sally, he smiled when he heard her voice. He didn't pay any attention to the man sat astride his parked motorbike also talking on his mobile. His eyes followed Joe down the street, in a strong eastern European accent, said in to his phone, *"He's just walked past me now after leaving the girls house, he was in there about twenty minutes talking to one of her flatmates. What do you want me to do?"*

He listened carefully to the voice on the other end of the line and replied, *"Okay, will do, Do svidaniya."*

Chapter Twenty-Three
A Coincidence?

Joe walked into the office and went to say his usual good morning to H, only to greet by her empty chair. He called out through the open office door, "Morning, Jimmy, where's Harriot this morning?"

Jimmy's familiar cheerful voice came back, "Good morning, she's at the dentist; she should be in before lunchtime, she said." Joe put his suit jacket on the hanger in the small wardrobe and went back out in to reception to make himself a coffee and take advantage of H's absence by raiding the biscuit tin. He took his mug of coffee and four digestive biscuits in to Jimmy's office and smiling sat down facing him. Jimmy looked up at the biscuits now stacked on his desk in front of Joe and gently shook his head.

He sat back in his chair and asked, "Well, how did it go yesterday?" Joe explained about not being able to reach Octavia and the visit to her flat. Jimmy listened intently and looked hard at Joe when he finished for a good minute or so. He looked worried, standing up he slowly walked around the office with his hands in his pockets jingling his loose change and looking down at the floor.

He finally sat back down at his desk and said, "I don't like this, Joe, I don't like this, not one little bit. I think it's too much of a coincidence. The butler gets mugged after you meet him. By the way, I'm glad to hear he's on the mend. But last night when you phoned him, he told you that his wallet, with the money still in it, was handed in to the police by a member of the public the next day. What does that tell you, Joe? It tells me that the mugger only wanted his phone, his wallet probably fell out when he was being attacked. Sound a bit strange, hey? The phone that he had been passing over to you in the pub to look at the picture of our 'Mrs Harrington.' Sounds like they were very interested to see what Lorenzo was showing you."

Jimmy stood up and set off around the office again, he carried on, "Also, you meet up with the young lady from the bank. You go for a meal, quiz her, then drop her off at home and now she's disappeared. My honest opinion! I think we are getting in over our heads here, young Joe. Are you sure you haven't seen anyone following you?"

Joe who had been listening to Jimmy's logic whilst watching him do a circuit around the office, replied, "No, I haven't, Jimmy, honestly, when we left the bar in Canary Wharf in the taxi. I looked back at the entrance; nobody came out after us…"

Jimmy sat down again, rubbing his index finger across his chin, he replied, "They might not have been inside, Joe. They could have been waiting outside for you to leave."

"You went to see the doorman at Nigel's flat on the way back to the young ladies' house?"

Joe nodded. "Yes, I did, and I've had a chat with him too, I told Danny to be careful, watch to see he's not being followed, and he must let me know if anything seems odd, I think I nearly frightened the poor bloke to death."

Jimmy nodded and continued, "They must have followed you and seen you drop the woman home from the bank. I just pray that she's not come to any harm, her disappearance seems strange and out of character from what her flatmate told you.

"I think I need to speak with Andy Sherry and bring him up to speed with all this."

Joe let out a big sigh and begged, "Do we have to, Jimmy, really? They could stop us from carrying on with the case."

Jimmy looked annoyed and raised his voice a little, "That is utter rubbish and totally selfish, Joe; an informant has been violently attacked. A woman is missing and possibly could have been murdered, and all you're concerned about is carrying on to try and crack the case. This isn't a film in the cinema Joe; this is real life and people's lives could be at stake. I don't think you understand, Joe. The tables could be turning, we have been are out there trying to hunt down Nigel's killer, and the way things are turning out, I think now we might be the ones who are being hunted! We need to speak to Harriot, hopefully without spooking her. We all need to be extra vigilant. I don't want her going home alone, you can get a cab home and drop her off on the way. If the beating and the abduction are connected to you, Joe, and I really think they are, we must be close to something. I just can't get my head around it yet to join all the dots, but I bloody well will."

Chapter Twenty-Four
Out in the Open

Joe hadn't heard anything from Karen the flatmate, so he assumed Octavia was still missing. Harriot turned up at the office at lunchtime with the side of her face numb after two fillings. At six o'clock, they said goodnight to Jimmy, and headed off down Holborn. Joe suggested a couple of drinks, seeing it was a nice warm evening they could sit outside somewhere. They settled on The Doggett's pub just at the end of Blackfriars Bridge, on the river. They choose a table on the third-floor balcony overlooking the Thames. They chatted about what each had been up to recently, socially. With Harriot stating, she was as boring as ever and not much was happening in her life to talk about. She asked Joe if he was still seeing Sally and looked a little disappointed when he confirmed he was. She asked, "Is this the one then, are you going to make an honest woman out of her?"

Joe threw his head back and laughed out loud. "Good God, no, I wouldn't inflict that on the poor woman. Come on, you know my history, I'm not very good at being engaged, or married, twice is enough for me. Thanks, no more!"

H was laughing, to she defended him, "No, you are being too hard on yourself; neither of them were your fault."

Joe shrugged his shoulders and replied, "It was my fault picking the wrong women to propose to; I'm rubbish at it!"

They left the Doggett's just after eleven o'clock and were waiting to cross the road to try and grab a passing taxi. At the kerbside a bus was pulling away from the bus stop, when Joe saw a familiar face smiling at him. It was Danny the concierge, Joe gave him a little wave, Danny smiled broadly and pointed to H giving Joe the thumbs up. Crossing Blackfriars Road, after a few minutes wait, they managed to flag down a passing cab. Outside Harriot's apartment block Joe gave her a peck on the cheek, she asked him if he wanted to go in for a coffee. He thought, *Better of it, her perfume was fantastic.* He kept getting a smell of it all evening and after quite a few drinks he didn't feel he could trust himself. H smiled and kissed him back on the cheek lingering just a little longer next to his face. She said goodnight, and Joe climbed back in the cab; waiting until H was safely inside, he let the cab pull away, he gave the cabbie his address. His mind wondered a little about H, she was a lovely person, pretty and he had noticed in the past that she did have a good figure.

He stopped himself, blaming the drinks and the balmy evening air for his lurid thoughts. Jimmy would kill him if he had an affair with his darling Harriot, he thought of her like the daughter he never had. Also, Joe didn't want to spoil the great friendship they had built up working together. *Maybe Jimmy should make sure Harriot gets home safely in the evening,* Joe thought, smiling to himself. Danny certainly appeared impressed with H, giving Joe the thumbs up from the bus, the cheeky bugger, he obviously thought they were a couple.

The cab pulled up outside Joe's apartment, climbing out he paid the cabbie and thanked him. He was about to key in the four-digit entry code when a movement caught his eye on his right side. He heard a noise and turned, straining his eyes trying to peer into the darkness of the doorway, someone was in there. The click and sudden flame of the lighter startled Joe, a man's face stared at Joe as he lite his cigarette. It was only a few seconds, but it seemed like an eternity as they stood looking at each other in the silent deserted street. Then darkness again as the flame went out, just the small red glow of the end of the man's cigarette. Joe's concentration was broken by another cab turning in to his road and stopping a short distance from him. Joe decided to take the opportunity and went to walk through the main door

Smoke eerily drifting out of the doorway, Joe could see into the dark doorway, but the man didn't step out into the street. Joe keyed in the security code and walked in to the safety of the brightly lit hall of his apartment block. His old police training had kicked in, he was visualising and remembering the man's face. Short fairish hair a little like an old-fashioned G I crew-cut, cold steel grey eyes. A slight bump on the bridge of the nose, probably from an old break. Thin lips, but a strong square jaw, probably early forties.

Joe felt spooked by the incident, but with everything that had happened recently, it was no wonder. Why was the guy standing in the doorway, was he waiting for Joe? Possibly. If he was going to do Joe harm, why show himself? That was a stupid thing to do, but he didn't look stupid, he looked military and mean and that concerned Joe. He got a good look at the man, but that was intentional, but why, did the weirdo possibly want Joe to see who was about to kill him? Joe was grateful the cab arrived when it did, it could have maybe saved his life. On the other hand, it wasn't against the law to stand in a door way at night and have a cigarette, maybe it was all innocent. He went up the stairs and let himself into his apartment, he went to the window, but he couldn't see the doorway. He didn't know if the man was still there, maybe he had left after facing off Joe. He went over to the front door and clicked on the double lock then the top and bottom brass bolts, better to be safe than sorry, his aunts would always say.

Joe had a troublesome night's sleep, he kept dreaming about the stranger's face appearing out of the dark. Everywhere was dark, then a spotlight appeared and lit up the face, then flames surrounded it and then it started to melt like candle wax. Joe woke up with a start he was soaked in sweat; he lay there for what seemed like an eternity before he fell asleep again.

Jimmy briefed Andy Sherry the next evening over dinner and a couple of drinks, he wasn't going to mention it to Joe. Andy never told Jimmy to step back from the agency's investigations, just to be very careful going forward. He commented that Jimmy's agency was doing a better job than the Met, and he was grateful for all the information Jimmy had provided. Answering Jimmy's concern, he said it was possible the two incidents could have been connected. Also, he would check that Octavia's disappearance was being properly investigated, seeing she still hadn't turned up getting close to a week later. Brian May had managed to get a piece of her disappearance covered in his national newspaper asking her to get in touch, her parents were very concerned. The bank was helpful, but couldn't add anything, only saying Octavia was a valued and trusted employee of the bank, and they would cooperate in any way. There wasn't to be any suggestion of a link to the murder in the park in the story, Jimmy was very clear on that point when he asked Brian to do him a favour. It was just a straight forward missing person story; Brian had done well to get it carried. Jimmy told Joe to be extra careful now that this was out in the public domain, there could be reaction. It might go quiet with the villains stepping back into the shadows. The other option being, they could decide action was needed to quickly tie-up the loose ends and that could mean trouble for anyone involved. They would find out soon enough, how they might react (*whoever they were*), in the meantime, no taking any chances.

Chapter Twenty-Five
It Begins…

 Joe took the stairs two at a time to the office on the first floor, it was ten-thirty he was late, thanks to the crazy dreams he had again about the stranger. He was surprised, he hadn't had a call from H asking, "*Where the hell he was*." Finally, at the last step he paused, he was breathing heavily, he promised himself to start going to the gym more often.

Turning right on the first floor landing he stopped suddenly, his jaw dropped open, he said out loud, "What the fuck?" His heart was beating so fast, but not just from the run up the stairs. He narrowed his eyes trying to process what he was seeing, down the corridor he stared at the half open office door. The glass in the top half of the door was smashed with the broken shards littering the floor. He could see Harriot's desk on its side, her laptop was on the floor with all kinds of stuff, files, and pieces of paper. He dropped his briefcase and ran towards the office, calling out Harriot and Jimmy's names.

The office was a mess, it had been ransacked, good and proper. He frantically looked around the reception area again calling out to Harriot and Jimmy. He heard a noise coming from Jimmy's office, like a low gargled growl, he ran in and on the floor amongst all the debris, lay Jimmy. His face ashen, he had a deep cut over his left eye, and blood was pouring down his face and on to the carpet. Joe lifted him up as best he could and lay him on the sofa, he was in a bad way making moaning noises. He tried to speak Joe bent over him with his ear practically touching Jimmy's face. Joe managed to hear the murmur Jimmy was trying to get out, he said, "Harriot."

Joe replied, "Where is she, Jimmy, I can't find her?"

Jimmy's eyes closed has he struggled for breath. Joe put a pillow under his head and whispered, "I'll get an ambulance, Jimmy, you just rest, and everything's going to be okay." Joe's eyes filling with tears. He jumped up and ran into his office calling out for Harriot, he came out and looked around the reception, nothing. Dashing back into jimmy's office with his mobile in his hand, he knelt to Jimmy, Joe was breathing heavily and his heart was beating like a drum. Jimmy reached up and grabbed Joe's arm, he was struggling trying to lift himself closer to Joe, his face full of panic.

Joe put his hand over Jimmy's and gently said, "It's okay, you're fine, Jimmy. I'm here now, and I'll stay with you. Joe suddenly realised Jimmy's eyes full of fear were not looking at him, but over Joe's shoulder, Jimmy was looking behind him. Joe half turned, but it was too late."

Joe opened his eyes, his neck and throat hurt, he thought his head was going to explode, he tried to touch his forehead, but a hand stop his hand. A face came into his view above him, a female face, it was a nurse he was in a room, a hospital room. The face spoke to him in almost a whisper, "Just stay still, my lovely, you're going to be okay, but you must stay still for me." Joe tried to speak, but his throat just rasped, his eyes closed, blackness came again. He woke up he was looking up at a ceiling, in his view he could see a rail hanging down from the ceiling with a plastic curtain attached. He tried to lift his head, but the pain was just too much, on his fore finger was a pulse oximeter on the end of a lead. He pulled it off, it dropped onto the bedspread covering him, he heard a continuous bleep.

Soon a nurse came in and attached it back to his finger, she smiled at him and said gently, "How are you feeling? I'm glad you've come to." Joe tried to speak, but his mouth and lips were too dry, the nurse reached for a beaker on top of the bedside drawers, Joe drank the water from it. The nurse took his pulse while he was trying to work his mouth to ask her a question.

In a croaky voice a little more than a whisper, "How long have I been in here, is my boss in here too?"
She gave him another smile, a little more sympathetic than the last one. She replied, "I can't answer your questions, I only came on duty this afternoon. I will tell the policeman outside that you've regained consciousness, also I will also let the doctor know you're awake, he will want to come and examine you. In the meantime, just try and rest."

Joe was trying to take in what the nurse had just said, he watched her walking towards the door, and he could see a uniformed policeman looking in at him through the glass panel in the door. Joe closed his eyes, the throbbing in his head would have made him scream out in pain, if he only had the strength to scream. Instead, he just lay there trying to piece together what he could remember from arriving at the office, he drifted off again. Later he heard voices, he opened his eyes fuzzy at first and then he focused on the nurse and a doctor in a white coat who could have passed for a six-grade schoolboy looking down at him. After checking him over, temperature, light shone in his eyes, then checking some machine he was wired up to, he was given some medication. The doctor asked Joe, "How are you feeling? You came around this afternoon, but went to sleep again, which is good, it's important that you rest."

Joe took a gulp of water the nurse offered him and eventually replied, "What time is it, how long have I been in here?"

The doctor smiled down at him and said, "It's just after eight thirty in the evening, and you've been here for three days. You were the victim of a vicious attack, you suffered a wound to the back of your head, which required six stitches. Your skull wasn't fractured which is good news, you also have very bad lacerations to your neck where your attacker tried to choke you with rope or cord. You've got a few stitches in your neck also."

Joe's head was beginning to clear. He took in everything the doctor had said, licking his lips. He asked, "My boss was attacked in our office before me. Where is he? Was he brought here too?"

The doctor said, matter of fact, "I don't know anything about that; I'm afraid. The police want to speak with you obviously, there's an officer stationed outside the room for your protection. I'm going to tell them you're not fit enough to speak with anyone yet. We'll review it tomorrow and see if you're strong enough to speak to them. In the meantime, just try and rest." Joe wanted to argue the case for speaking to the police now in order to get some answers, but he didn't have the strength. He lay back looking up at the ceiling trying to relive what had happened apparently three days ago in the office, his head hurt, he slowly drifted back into a deep peaceful sleep.

Chapter Twenty-Six
The World Changes

Joe was checked over in the morning by a different doctor than the young one he had seen the evening before. This one was older and a lot more distinguished probably because of his slicked back grey hair, he also spoke quite posh. He told Joe he was over the worse, but would need to rest and it would be some time before he was fully recovered, it be a slow process. Also, he wasn't allowing the police to interview him, he wasn't strong enough yet. Joe wasn't happy with that, he wanted to know how Jimmy was. But then he saw the doctor giving DI Mooney a roasting outside his room and send him on his way, at least that brought a smile to Joe's face. The next day he mostly slept, the following morning for breakfast Joe managed half a cup of coffee and some orange juice, he couldn't eat his throat was too sore. Just drinking nearly wiped him out. The nurse said the doctor would be doing his rounds at eleven and if he thought Joe was up to it, the police could have a very short meeting with him in the afternoon.

Joe was propped up with pillows when DI Mooney and his trusty sidekick Sargent Brown walked in with the nurse. She smiled at Joe and reminded him that he could stop the interview at any time if it was too draining him, she fussed with Joe's pillows and left. The inspector took the nearest chair to Joe with the Sargent taking the chair at the bottom of the bed. Mooney took a long look at Joe, smiled sympathetically and asked, "How are you feeling?"

Joe looked from the Sargent, then to Mooney and wetting his lips as best he could with his tongue, replied, "Like shit!"

Mooney smiled again and replied, "Well, if it's any consolation, you look like shit, are you up to telling us what happened the other day in your office?" Joe wet his lips again and went through the events that morning from oversleeping to finding Jimmy on the floor of the ransacked office. Stopping occasionally to take a drink of water from the straw in his beaker that the nurse had left him.

Sargent Brown was writing away frantically. Joe took a big breath and finally said, "I'm afraid that's all I can tell you; I didn't see who was behind me; the lights just went out, and I woke up in here with the biggest headache you could imagine."

Mooney nodded, scratched his forehead, and replied, "Okay, what I need is you to tell me everything you know about Nigel Harrington's murder. From your 'Mrs Harrington,' who actually is Yulia Novikov, a Ukrainian married to one Andrei Novikov a Russian oligarch, to Octavia Connelly's disappearance, which we believe is all connected to the murder. We are aware you and Jimmy were investigating why you were hired to check on Nigel Harrington's personal life. Are you up to it today?"

Joe told him everything except the part that Octavia talked about "Mrs Harrington having an appointment at the bank. Like Jimmy had told him, never show all your cards, they certainly won't. Also, if those bastards at the bank were responsible for this, he wanted revenge."

This was a different DI Mooney that Joe had grown to dislike intensely, in the very short time he had known him. Today he was genuinely sympathetic to what had happened to him and Jimmy. Joe took another slurp of water, and he asked, "Where is Jimmy, have you spoken to him what did he have to say?" Mooney threw a glance at Sargent Brown who stopped writing in his notebook and looked up at Joe.

Joe knew by the expression on their faces what Mooney's reply was before he said it, but it still came as a shock. "He didn't make it Joe, I'm sorry."

Joe rubbed his mouth with his left hand and weakly repeated, "He didn't make it… what do you mean, they killed him?"

Mooney looked down either embarrassed by Joe's tears or his answer to Joe's question, "Yes, I'm afraid so Joe, he died on the way to hospital. You're at risk to now, we need to make sure you remain safe. You could have gone the same way, if someone hadn't called it in."

The sirens on the police cars racing down Holborn were what most likely saved you. We think the attacker or attackers fled out of the back of the building just as the squad cars arrived. Who do you think it was who called it in? Joe was shocked by the news that Jimmy had been killed, he hadn't looked good when Joe arrived and found him on the floor of the office.

Joe let out a long hard emotional sigh he looked at Mooney and replied, "I don't know, I didn't know it had been called in it wasn't me, was it male or female maybe it was Harriot, she's safe, isn't she?"

It was Sargent Brown who answered, "We can confirm, the caller was male, couldn't make out an accent, but English though, it was basically no more than hurried whispers. It's sounds like he was there and witnessed the attack on you."

Mooney picked it up from the sergeant. "So it wasn't Harriot, we haven't been able to locate her yet. We're not sure if they've taken her or whether she's running scared and hiding somewhere. Have you any idea where she could be."

Joe shook his head, Mooney continued, "I didn't think so, but it was worth asking, did Jimmy say anything else to you other than Harriot's name?"

Joe answered, his voice quivering with emotion, he suddenly felt all alone again in the world. "No, just her name, it took poor Jimmy all his strength just to say that."

Mooney cut in looking at Sargent Brown, "The attack and Jimmy's murder has had national news coverage on TV and radio news, also the press. There hasn't been any mention of all this possibly being connected to the murder of Nigel Harrington in the reports. We don't want it connected because we haven't enough information yet, although it looks like it definitely is from what you've told us this afternoon. Did you or Jimmy have any photographs of Harriot? We couldn't find anything at the office. I don't suppose you have one at home, do you? We wanted to put one out to the public in the hope that someone might have seen her. We want to find here quickly and keep her safe and out of harm's way, that's if she's still alive."

Mooney saw the pained look Joe gave him and regretted the slip of being so forthright with him over Harriot. Standing up, Mooney announced, "Okay, I think that's enough for today, you need to rest up, Joe, I promised the doctor, and I wouldn't wear you out. If it's okay, by that I mean if you're strong enough, we would like to speak to you again in the next day or two." Joe nodded agreement. Mooney and Brown said their goodbyes and left Joe to his thoughts, he felt sick, not just from his injuries but from the news about Jimmy. Poor Jimmy he didn't deserve to die like that, he didn't deserve to die at all. Joe prayed that Harriot hadn't been harmed and had managed to escape somewhere safe. When he got out of hospital he would search for her, and carry on until he found her. She might have fled to Brighton, she lived there with her mother; she could have friends down there. He should have told Mooney about Brighton, when he asked about H. If she was safe, why she hasn't gone to the police yet, they would protect her from these evil bastards. Joe wondered if she saw Jimmy's attack that would have frightened anybody let alone a gentle soul like Harriot. Maybe, they took her, Jimmy must have seen something to use all his strength to say her name to Joe. It was all too much to think about, Jimmy's death, maybe Harriot also or at best being held hostage somewhere. His mind was racing with all the scenarios he felt worn out, he closed his eyes and tried to clear his mind and sleep.

The next day, Joe got an unexpected visit from Andy Sherry, he was upset about Jimmy and wanted the killer or killers brought to justice. He asked Joe for an update on everything that led up the attack. Just like Mooney had. Andy told Joe this was personal, he and Jimmy went back a long time, they were very good friends. Joe told him everything he had told Mooney only he included what Octavia had told him about their "Mr's Harrington" having an appointment at the bank. Andy wasn't surprised and agreed with Joe that they or someone at the bank was involved in all this mess. Before he left, he gave Joe his mobile number and said to call if there was anything else or if he felt he was in danger when he was discharged.

He advised Joe to leave the case alone now, reiterating that they must have been close to something to warrant the attack and murder of Jimmy and attempt on Joe's life. Andy told him just like Mooney had that he would have been killed if someone hadn't called it in. Joe told him like he had told Mooney he had no idea who it could have been. He asked Andy to let him know if there was any news on Harriot and Octavia. Andy promised he would and again warned Joe about not carrying on with his investigation when he was discharged from hospital. Joe half smiled he was pissed off with everybody telling him to rest, he wanted revenge.

After Andy left, Joe lay there staring up at the ceiling, he said to himself, "Leave it alone, leave it to us, yea right,

Jimmy's death is personal to me too. The only difference is when I find the culprit, I'm not going to send him to prison, I'm going to fucking kill him, and that's a promise."

Chapter Twenty-Seven
Three Weeks Later

Friday morning, Jimmy's funeral was a solemn affair and not one of those modern. "Let's celebrate the life of James Daniel Daly." It couldn't be really considering the nature of Jimmy's death. Joe sat on the front row alone, gently shaking his head he thought, *God bless you, Jimmy, you shouldn't have died, it wasn't your time and certainly not to die violently like you did. Thank you for everything you did for me, you were my mentor, my father I never had. I owe you so much, rest in peace, Jimmy, and be assured I fill find out who did this to you and make them pay.*

It was a good turnout with lots of old friends turning up to pay their respects, probably from the social side of Jimmy's life that Joe never really got to know. It was all work really apart from the monthly review dinners the three of them would have. The police were in attendance, because it was a murder, also friends Andy Sherry and reporter Brian May. Joe scanned the congregation once more for Harriot, but to no avail, she hadn't been seen or heard of since that fateful day. That worried Joe, he knew if she could have made it, she would have been there. She wouldn't have missed paying her respects to Jimmy, she adored him. Also there hadn't been any news about

186

Octavia, nothing at all despite her photo and a missing-have you seen this woman? Story in the national press thanks to Brian May. The longer the silence went on it filled Joe with dread, it was as if they had disappeared off the face of the earth. If they were still alive, Joe prayed they were safe, being held captive somewhere by whoever took them. Andy Sherry told Joe holding hostages was dangerous and the safest option was to kill them and get rid of the bodies. Andy had had been true to his word and kept in touch and updated Joe regularly; Joe had only been discharged from the hospital the previous Saturday. He had told Joe, some known villains with form from Russia and the Ukraine had been brought in for questioning regarding the attack and murder of Nigel Harrington, but all interviews were fruitless. The choice of suspects and line of questioning was due to the fake "Mrs Harrington" being from Odessa and her Russian husband Andrai Novikov, it was a start at least. Andy did reiterate to Joe that the men interviewed were all hardened criminals, but when questioned about Novikov the very mention of his name appeared to unsettle them to a man. If the Met were asking questions about him and his wife, as far as the suspects were concerned, Novikov's people were involved, and they were feared by fellow Russians. This resulted in a wall of silence, on even with the most routine of questions. Novikov was obviously not a man to cross and was even feared by the hard men of Russian and Ukrainians living as far away as London. Apart from this update from Andy, the Met appeared no closer to finding anything about Nigel Harrington's murder, let alone Jimmy's. They had checked CCTV around Jimmy's office and surprise, surprise it was broken, it had been tampered with. Other CCTV on Holborn hadn't thrown up any leads

Joe didn't want to go to the wake at a pub near jimmy's home in Maida Vale that friends and neighbours had arranged. He didn't feel up to it physically and anyway he didn't know any of the mourners. He didn't want to talk about his times with Jimmy, not with strangers, it was too upsetting.

He desperately needed a drink, but had promised Sally he would go straight home afterwards. She was desperate, it was days before she could finally visit him in hospital and when she did see him, she was in floods of tears. She had wanted to go with Joe to the funeral, but he asked her not to, he didn't want her to see him upset, and she didn't really know Jimmy. She had been so good since the attack visiting Joe in hospital every day. When he was discharged, she moved into his apartment to look after him. She laughingly told him not to get worried she wasn't planning on moving in permanently, it was just for a week or so until his health improved.

Joe was fine with the arrangement for different reasons, he didn't tell Sally but he wanted to keep her close. He was worried that "they" might come for her, he had already "lost H and Octavia," he didn't want her to disappear like they had done. They could have been watching Joe for some time and most likely would have seen him with Sally. They obviously knew where he lived, he assumed because of the smoking man in the doorway that night. She came to Joe's apartment regularly and "they" could have followed her and knew where she worked and lived.

He took an Uber down to Covent Garden and got dropped at the Wheat Sheaf on Wellington Street. He had been there many times and just wanted a few quiet drinks alone with his memories of Jimmy. He couldn't believe it all had come to this, Jimmy dead and Harriot missing, possibly dead.

Jimmy Daly was the dad he never had, he helped him when he was at rock bottom, and he gave him a job and then made him a partner in his company. What a man, fate, Joe thought, *If he hadn't of ever met me, he would probably still be alive today*. That was something Joe could never forgive himself for, but his concern now was finding H. He was feeling so much better, he was restless in hospital that last week, he wanted to get back in the saddle. First find H and then settle a few scores, the Met didn't appear to having any more luck with Jimmy's murder than they did with Nigel Harrington's. They had said they needed to protect Joe in case "they" were going to make a move on him, well that didn't last long. Joe decided he would go back into the office tomorrow; the Met had finished their work there for what good it did. He didn't look forward to it, but it had to be done. He needed to get the window in the door repaired and everything tidied up. Why had "they wrecked the place? What were they looking for?"

After his third pint, he decided he would go on whisky, they were going down well, and the whisky was warming his throat. Jimmy didn't like him having a binge drink, it worried him, so Joe decided he owed it to Jimmy. One more large one for the road and then back home to Fulham. Sat on a bar stool, he ordered his last drink, glancing in the long mirror that ran the length of the bar, he could see all of the room. He was surprised it wasn't busier, Covent Garden is a tourist attraction as well as lots of offices in the area. His eyes settled on a thick set man sat at a table next to the door, he looked out of place. There were customers in suits, women shoppers, and some younger casually dressed people. Joe studied the face long and hard to make sure it wasn't the "smoking" man from the doorway. No GI crew-cut, it wasn't him, but this guy also looked military. He had a glass of beer on the table in front of him, untouched from what Joe could make out. He had a short hair, a stubble jaw, thick neck, he was wearing dark blue thick woollen jacket, black jeans, and black ankle height boots. Joe thanked and paid the barman for his drink and decided to swing his stool around to face the room. He looked over at the man, he was looking straight at Joe, he held Joe's stare. Joe swung his stool back to the bar and looked in the mirror again, he followed the man's gaze. There was another man, Joe had missed when he first scanned the pub.

He was stood across the room next to the gents' toilet by a gaming machine. He had dark hair a trimmed beard, about six feet, he wore a dark business suit with an open neck white shirt. He blended in with the drinkers in the pub. But Joe was certain when he turned back to the bar, he saw the two men look at each other and a slight nod of the head was exchanged between them.

Joe thought, *Shit! What do I do now, I still feel weak, but I think I could handle one of them, but not two? That's if there are only two.* Joe scanned the room again slowly, but everyone else looked "okay", was he being paranoid, it was possible. Joe took a drink of his whisky, and kept a close watch on both men, when the pub door opened and in walked a woman.

The man sat next to the door stood up and greeted her with a hug and a kiss, he downed his glass of beer and the two of them left. Joe let out a low whistle and thanked his lucky stars, for a minute there he thought he was in danger. The man by the toilets was now busy playing the gaming machine. Joe smiled. *Crazy how the mind can play tricks on you,* he thought. He felt relieved and relaxed; he downed his drink and ordered another one for the road.

Despite his promise to Sally he was feeling a little worse for wear from one too many whiskies. He went to the toilet for a pee after paying the waiter to call him a cab to take him home to Fulham. His phone had run out of battery on the way to the pub. Joe walked out of the pub and the cab was waiting outside the front door. The evening fresh air hit him, and he knew in his weakened state he shouldn't have had so much to drunk. They drive over to Fulham was in silence, he should have called Sally from the pub to let her know he was on the way home. The cab pulled up outside his block, he thanked and paid the driver. He awkwardly got out, still sore, took a deep breath and put his wallet away watching the cab pull away and disappear in the distance. He walked to the reception door and was about to enter the pass code when was conscious someone was right behind him. He was about to turn around, but he felt something press into the small of his back. It felt like the barrel of a gun, that didn't happen in Fulham, but it felt like one. Joe slowly raised his hands, the voice behind him said in a strong Russian accent, "Put down your hands, this isn't a fucking cowboy movie."

Joe looked in the glass reflection of the apartment block; it was the guy in the pub sat next to the door that left with the woman. The voice spoke again, "Don't turn around, just walk down the street slowly! And don't try anything stupid."

Joe did as he was told and started to walk. He calmly asked, "Did you murder my boss?"

The voice replied, *"Nyet."*

Joe asked, "Is that a NO?" His mind racing what to do next. If he didn't come up with something he was going to end up dead. Suddenly there were voices behind Joe's left shoulder. A young couple arm in arm had walked around the corner and were laughing and chatting away. The man lowered the gun so it was out of their sight.

He spoke to the back of Joe's head, "Don't shout out, or you will all be dead!" The happy couple only had eyes for each other and crossed past the back of them without giving the two men a second glance. They climbed the steps of one of the terraced houses across the street, unlocked the front door, and disappeared inside.

The Russian, hearing the front door slam, said, "Walk" and pushed Joe in the back with the gun. They continued in silence down Joe's dimly lit street towards the bright lights of Fulham Broadway.

The Russian walked closely behind Joe's left shoulder, further down the street a car flashed its headlights at them. They passed the corner of a side street on the left, there was a loud banshee shout and a rush of feet. A figure all in black wearing a ski mask ran out behind them, before the Russian could turn, he was hit across the small of his back. The Russian screamed out in pain the dull thud sent him staggering forward.

He fell into the back of Joe and crashed heavily on to the pavement; the gun fell onto the pavement. Joe quickly picked it up, he was facing the figure holding a baseball bat standing over the Russian. Joe looked at ski mask, then down at the Russian writhing on the floor, then back to ski mask. The noise of the car tyres screeching as it set off at speed up the street towards them focused Joe's mind. Ski mask grabbed Joe's arm and shouted, "Quick, come on, run for it!" They both ran up the side street leaving the groaning Russian half on the pavement and half in the gutter. They heard the car screech to a halt behind them, spurring them on to run faster.

They ran around the corner onto the well-lit Watling Street, Joe doubled over and emptied the contents of his stomach, mostly alcohol, on to the pavement. Ski mask stopped, turning to Joe, he said, "God, no wonder you can't run; it smells like a brewery. Come on, we need to get to my car and safety."

Wiping his mouth with the back of his hand, Joe stood upright with the help of the shop front window and turning replied, "I've got to get my girlfriend from my apartment."

"Ski-mask" gently pulled Joe's shoulder and said, "Don't worry, she's safe; I've got her out, she's at my flat. Look my car's just over there, do you think you can make it?" Joe nodded, Ski Mask ran, and Joe staggered across the road to the parked silver S-type Jaguar.

Safely in the car they pulled out and drove down Watling Street. As the passed the end of Joe's Street, they both looked, but the car and the injured Russian had gone. Ski-mask looked in his rear-view mirror and announced, "We're not being followed, and I think we got away with it."

He looked over at Joe and asked, "Are you okay? Don't be sick in my car, let me know and I'll stop. Where the fuck have you been anyway? Your girlfriend Sally said the wake was at The Stag in Maida Vale. I went there looking for you; nobody had heard of you. So, I came back to your apartment and waited around the corner. I waved at your cabbie, but he probably thought I was trying to flag him down for a journey. He just drove on past; I couldn't get to you in time before he pulled up outside your place. It was too late then; the gorilla was waiting opposite in the shadows, and I couldn't take the chance of him seeing me. So, I stood there to see what his move would be and waited to take my chance. We were lucky that he was going to kill you somewhere else and not outside your apartment block."

Joe didn't feel too good, his head was spinning, and it had all been too much for him. He belched loudly, bile coming up into his mouth, that didn't help, he swallowed hard and asked weakly, "Where are we going?"

Ski-Mask replied, "To my flat, Sally is there waiting for us, we can't go to her place, it's too dangerous. You've gone green, don't be sick in here, okay?"

Joe's mouth was so dry he couldn't get his words out, he looked across at the Ski mask and asked, "Just who the fuck are you and why are you helping me?"

Ski-Mask laughed out loud and replied, "So you've forgotten me already."

They pulled up at a red light on the busy Kings Road. He leaned over to Joe and took the revolver off his knee, he said, "I think I should look after this for the time being."

Joe didn't try to stop him, he was too weak from all the running, and he looked across at the driver and said, "Who are you?"

They pulled away from the lights, the driver pulled off the Ski-mask with his left hand. Joe's jaw dropped, not believing his eyes he leaned in a little closer to the man's face, trying to moisten his mouth. He said in a croaky voice, "Fuck me, Rob! Rob Fee, I don't believe it, shit, man, am I glad to see you." They stopped on the embankment and Rob got two large lattes from the burger van. The coffee tasted shit, but Joe needed it badly, it helped his dry mouth and helped to sober him up a little.

Chapter Twenty-Eight
Back from the Dead

They drove the remainder of the way in silence after Rob smiled and confirmed to Joe it really was him in person. Joe drinking Rob's coffee, looked over at Rob and said, "Are you still doing your impersonations of famous people; I must be honest your earlier one of James Mason was pretty good it certainly fooled me, so it must have fooled the Russian. But it wasn't necessary, it's been that long I wouldn't have remembered your Brummie accent. Also, you were the last person I would have expected to ride to my rescue."

Rob laughed loudly and said, "I had plenty of time to practice the accents while I was in Rehab."

The Jag pulled up outside a block of private apartments behind the Elephant & Castle. Joe was still in shock of seeing his old friend turn up out of the blue and felt better for it. Rob smiled and said in his normal voice, "This is where I'm living now; I'm renting, and I have been for the past month. After a lot of nasty shit, which I won't bore you with, I got myself into rehab and finally got sorted out, I've been clean ever since. I had to come back to see you, buddy. I can't begin to tell you how bad I feel about ruining your business and your life. I wasn't sure how you would take it seeing me again after what I did to you. So, I spoke to some of our old friends, and they told me you were doing well for yourself and that you were a private eye now and a partner in the agency. I had been watching you for about a few weeks, trying to pluck up the courage to show myself. But I didn't come forward, because when I was checking you out, that's when I realised. I wasn't the only one interested in you; I stepped back and have been watching the Russians monitoring you."

"One evening, you had a drink and a meal with a woman you purposely bumped into outside a bank. I followed you to the bar in Docklands. I was in there watching you both, but so was a Russian guy. I left while you were paying the bill and waited outside, just far away enough from the entrance so not to be seen. The Russian came out straight after you. I moved closer, and he made a phone call, that's how I knew he was Russian. A guy in rehab was Russian, and he taught me. I thought it would impress the ladies. The Russian was talking about you; he told who was on the other end that his colleague was following your taxi on his motorbike. From what I've seen, it looks like there's a team of three or four of them. Also, who's on the end of the phone giving the orders? I've watched two of the heavies for a while now, one of them was the guy I smacked tonight with my trusty old bat. Hopefully, I've put him out of action for a while. The other one is a mean-looking thick-set, bastard with a crew-cut;

he looks military. You look like shit Joe; I think they came to finish the job tonight."

"What the fuck have you been up to Joe to have these guys after you and now trying to kill you? They really are seriously bad bastards? I saw them smash up your offices and attack the old guy. Sorry, your boss, I crapped myself and got out of the corridor sharpish. I phoned the police and reported it. I was hanging around when I saw you turn up and go into the building. I followed you back in to try to warn you, but you were too quick for me. I hoped that with calling it in, the police would turn up and save the day. I had said I just witnessed a murder. I said that for a prompt response. I didn't realise I actually had witnessed a murder, at least not until I saw it on the news on the TV. I was going to come in and help, but I heard the police sirens outside. I worried that they had killed you too; I didn't want to hang around and get involved if you were dead. It was after seeing what they did, I went out and bought the baseball bat. I'm telling you all this out here, Joe, because I get the impression your lady Sally doesn't know about what's been going on, does she? She's a really nice lady you have got to be straight with her, Joe. Get her away from here now, for her own safety."

Joe had sat listening to Rob in silence, drinking his coffee, he hadn't said a word, and he let out a big sigh. Listening to everything be described by someone else, made him realise what a mess he was in. He gently shook his head and smiled, he said to Rob, "You don't know how glad I am to see you, old friend; I'm in way over my head with all this shit. When you disappeared, I felt guilty that I hadn't seen you were having problems and hadn't helped you. Yea, I lost the business, my home, oh and my misses, but I thank for that loss."

"Now, seeing you've saved my life twice already; I think we can call it evens, don't you? How long are back here for? Have you any plans?"

Rob's face broke out in a huge smile with relief, he replied in his best Jimmy Stewart voice, "I'm here for as long as you're in this mess, possibly even longer. As far as I'm concerned, we're in this together, and I'm definitely in now; I've smacked that guy with my baseball bat earlier."

They both climbed out of the car, and Joe said, "Come on, let's go in. You're right about Sally, so let me speak to her, and then tomorrow we'll get her away somewhere safe. I'll explain everything to you on how I got in all this mess after she's gone."

The next morning, Joe and Sally said their goodbyes and Rob took her to the station to catch the train to her parents. She didn't need too much persuading after the attack at the office, Jimmy's murder had really shocked her. Joe told her he wouldn't get in touch until this was all over, she understood it could put her and her parents in danger.

The apartment Rob was renting was very nice, it was a new build, in a block on the second of seven floors. Two bedrooms, each with on-suites, a large lounge, a generous kitchen diner, a balcony, and it was tastefully furnished.

Rob returned from dropping Sally off at the station about ninety minutes later complaining that he didn't miss London traffic one bit while he had been away. Joe had showered, shaved and looked a lot better than he had the night before.

Over a hearty lunch of scrambled eggs, bacon, mushrooms, buttered toast and endless mugs of fresh coffee, Joe told Rob the whole story, everything that had happened. From that fateful day when "Mrs Harrington" walked into their office to Jimmy's funeral the day before. He didn't leave anything out, he was glad when he had finished, it was a cleansing of the soul. Rob had sat eating his lunch and listening to everything Joe had said, he sat back and let out a long low whistle. "Fuck me, Joe, we are in at the deep end, aren't we? What do we do? Go to the police and tell them what happened last night? Shit, I know that look, you don't want to, do you? You want us. Sort it ourselves, don't you? From what you've just told me, Joe, and the look of them, they are professionals at this shit; I'm surprised you're not dead already. We can go head-to-head with them, the best we can without ending up dead. But we could still could end up dead, even if we do go to the Met, from what you've said, the Met haven't done much so far. I'm not sure I need to ask, but I will. What are you going to do about the gun you picked up last night?"

Joe, took a drink of coffee and wiped his mouth on the back of his hand and replied, "I've already made up my mind, Rob, I'm carrying on alone, and I'm not running to the Met. These fuckers killed Jimmy, I loved the guy, he was like a father to me, the nicest guy you could ever wish to meet, and this is personal now!"

Rob sat back in his chair and stared at Joe for a good minute or so without speaking. He poured himself another coffee, adding milk he finally answered Joe. "You are not in this alone, Joe, I'm with you all the way, I said that last night. Besides, I sort of get a kick out of saving your life, I've always wanted to be a hero."

Joe gave him a wry smile. "This isn't a game, Rob; this is serious shit we could and probably will end up dead, but hopefully not before we settle the score with these bastards who killed Jimmy.

"But I must say, I'm so relieved to hear you say you're with me."

Rob smiled, replying, "I'm in this with you, to the end, it's the least I can do after what my drug taking fucked up your life, I owe you that much."

They decided to come up with a plan of action, Rob showed Jimmy photos on his phone that he had taken following the Russians who were following Joe. He sent the file over to Joe's phone so he could memorise them and pick them out. Rob was going to go to the office in Holborn to see if the Russians were watching it, in case Joe was daft enough to go back there. Then onto Joe's apartment in Fulham, and if possible, slip in and get some of Joe's clothes and other items he wanted. Rob was banking on the Russians not identifying him. When he jumped in and saved Joe, he was wearing his ski mask.

Also, if they had realised, he was following them, they would have done something about it. They were hoping to keep Rob a secret, it would be a big asset, and like said, he couldn't walk around wearing a ski mask all the time it was too warm.

Meanwhile Joe was going to H's apartment in Kennington to see if anyone had seen or heard of her. He then planned to phone Andy sherry hoping to get an update on the investigation into Jimmy's murder and any news on Octavia and Harriot if she wasn't in Kennington.

When Joe got back to the flat at the Elephant, Rob was already there waiting for him. He showed Joe a photo he had taken of the two Russians staking out Joe's office when he was there earlier. They were two of the three Rob had sent Joe earlier. The good news was the one Rob floored the night before wasn't there, they hoped Rob had put him out of action. They called the two staking out Joe's Office, number One and number Two, "One" was the GI crew cut guy 5–10 to six feet, stocky build, square chin, blue eyes, and a nose that had been broken on a few occasions in the past. As for Number Two, Joe remembered him from the pub the previous night, he was the one stood near the men's toilets. He had dark hair, dark cold eyes, a long pale face, dark beard, tall, 6.2 maybe taller, a wiry build and like number One, someone you wouldn't want to mess with.

Rob was surprised that no one was watching Joe's apartment, they probably assumed Joe wasn't that crazy to go back there. Rob had managed to pack a large holdall he found in Joe's apartment and brought back his laptop, clothes, and a few personal items. One was a framed picture of Joe with Jimmy and Harriot celebrating their Christmas office party at The Savoy, Joe studied it for a couple of minutes and let out a long sigh. Rob smiled and said to Joe, "Come on, I'm sure Jimmy wouldn't want you to be sad for him and as far as Harriot is concerned, she might be safe and hiding out somewhere, you don't know. If she is, we'll find her Joe, don't you worry about that."

Joe stood up and stood the frame up on the coffee table and asked, "Is it okay if I leave it here?" Rob nodded.

Joe went on. "Do you know, Rob; I just can't believe everything what's happened and so suddenly. One minute life's good, everything's going along fine and pow! It all changes. All because of one thing, a simple case of a cheating husband, I regret taking the case on. If I hadn't, none of this would have happened, people wouldn't have been killed or disappeared."

Rob interrupted him, "Hey, come on, buddy, don't get all melancholy on me, and don't beat yourself up over what's happened. You weren't to know how it would turn out; nobody could have. When your Mrs Harrington walked into your office with a job, of course, you would take it; that's what you did for a living. Besides, we've got bigger problems now; some nasty bastards are trying to kill you, and you're not too sure why. Also, even more importantly, I could also end up dead!"

Rob was looking at his pal who's face broke out into a big smile, Joe shook his head and replied, "That was a nice speech, and you have to go and spoil it don't you, you Brummie lunatic."

Rob laughed loudly and said, "Of course, it wouldn't be me; otherwise, would it?"

Back to business Joe reported that he hadn't had any joy at Harriot's flat in Kennington, the place was all locked up, and it didn't appear to have been broken into. Everything looked normal, he managed to speak to one neighbour, an old lady who lived two doors down. She told Joe she hadn't seen Harriot for some time, and confirmed that she hadn't seen any strangers hanging around the apartment block either. Although if they had snatched Harriot there wouldn't really be any reason to go to her place. Joe had managed a bit of success; he got in touch with Andy Sherry on facetime. He told Joe the investigation to Jimmy's murder was in full swing, but nothing to report yet. He asked Joe what he knew the attack on the office. Joe told him the same has he told the Mooney and his sidekick Brown in the hospital.

Regarding the girls, Andy said they still weren't any closer to locating Harriot or Octavia and all enquires had hit a dead end. They had just disappeared into thin air, without anyone witnessing an abduction. He said the longer it went on he feared the worse, holding someone hostage was very risky so much could go wrong. He didn't continue that he feared they had been killed; he thought Joe had been through enough recently. Andy looked at Joe's bruised face and bandaged neck, and decided he was right to keep his theory to himself. He smiled and asked

Joe how he was bearing up, and said he his injuries looked a little better. Joe had told him he was fine and kept the attempted kidnapping the night before to himself, also he never mentioned his friend Rob turning up out of the blue.

Chapter Twenty-Nine
The Reason

Rob had ordered a takeaway for them from the local Chinese restaurant, and he had plenty of alcohol in his flat. They had a good chat about what had happened in their lives since they had been apart. Joe was exhausted, but Rob was up for a boozy night, but at ten-thirty they decided to call it a night, and they both went off to bed. The next morning Rob was up first, Joe ambled into the kitchen just before ten looking the worse for wear. Rob reminded him he was still recovering from his beating and that he probably shouldn't have had a couple of drinks the night before. He was feeling too week to argue, Rob topped him up with a coffee and made him a couple of rounds of toast.

After a shower and shave, they sat down to go over the day's activity, Rob decided to go first and asked, "You mentioned yesterday that Jimmy thought the bank was the key to everything, I think I agree with him. We have a foreign bank, a murder, and Russians, park the murder for a minute what does the other two parts point to?"

Joe stepped in right on cue and said, "Money laundering."

Rob smiled and said, "Exactly, I think jimmy was spot on, your Nigel Harrington was a director at the bank. His 'fake' wife had a meeting there, something happened, and he ends up dead. We need to establish what happened for 'them' to kill him. This house in Mayfair, what is it 53 Adam's Yard?"

Joe nodded that was correct. Rob continued, "Putting my accountancy hat on, I think that could be the main part of the jigsaw. I going to spend today doing some digging into number 53 and see what I can find out. What are you going to do? I suggest, my friend, you take it easy and just rest up here today. You're not looking too good, Joe." Joe wasn't strong enough to argue and agreed he would be best resting and building up some energy levels.

Joe woke up on the sofa at two-thirty, his head fuzzy from his deep sleep, like his dear old aunts would say, "You must have needed it." He went to the toilet and then washed his face in cold water, he felt better. Going back into the lounge he picked up the remote and put Sky News on the television to see what was happening in the world, apparently not very much. He sat with a mug of coffee, thinking about H and Octavia, the longer there was no news, he was certain it was bad news, he was sure of it. He felt so guilty especially about Octavia, she was so sweet and had everything to live for, and he put her in danger because he wanted answers. He regrets the day the Ukraine "Mrs Harrington" walked in to his office. Little did they know the devastation she would cause, Jimmy murdered,

H and Octavia probably dead, he would have been too, if it hadn't been for Rob's intervention.

The front door banged open it made him jump; he shouted out from the lounge, "Is that you, Rob?"

He was relieved to hear his friend Brummie's voice reply, "It sure is, and what a day. Have I got news for you, Joseph." Joe relaxed again, he sat back in to the sofa and let out a sigh of relief, he would never admit it, but the recent events had really rattled him. Rob walked into the lounge from the kitchen with two open bottles of beer, handing one to Joe, he sat down on the armchair with a big beaming smile then took a big glug of beer from the bottle.

Joe sat looking at him, impatiently and eventually, he held out the palms of his hands and said, "For God's sake, well?"

Rob cleared his throat and grandly announced to the whole of the lounge, "We have made a big stride today. Joe, my son, I have proof 53 Adams Yard is being used for laundering Russian money.

"Over 1873 companies have been registered there over the past two months; they probably have thousands registered to that address." Joe was trying to take in what his pal had just said, he opened his mouth, confused. All he could get out was, "What? How?"

Rob continued, "It's easy; they're exploiting a 'soft touch' in our system that lets anyone create a new business without proof of identity, neither proof of address, passport, nor driving licence. It takes less than fifteen minutes and costs just £12 to register a company on the government's company House website. Also, the downside is it takes weeks of form filling to get a bogus company removed. The soft-touch system for registering companies in the UK is a fraudster's paradise. A friend of mine who works for an accountancy company in the city helped me. Afterwards, I rang Companies House, saying I had received a letter to a Russian company at my home address. They said it would take eight weeks to even look into it. They told me it was happening all the time, and they couldn't do anything about it. Then listen to this. So ridiculously, you couldn't write this nonsense, they said I would have to send them proof of my address. Would you believe that, only then would they inform the Russian director that his company was being contested, and he would have twenty-eight days to reply. I assume that meant they would write to him at my address, you couldn't make up this shit, could you?"

Joe sat looking at Rob in complete silence trying to digest what he had just been told, he wasn't an accountant. It was a lot of information to take in over two minutes, but it all started to begin to make sense now. Rob asked, "Are you with me, are you keeping up? These are just shell companies; they have no staff and don't trade. They move assets on behalf of individuals or other businesses to launder billions of stolen or illicit cash through Britain every year."

Joe smiled broadly. "Yes, I think I am keeping up, you're a cheeky bugger, it's just a lot to take in all at once, well done you and they say accountants are boring bastards, we need to work out our next steps."

Rob cut in, "We could go to the bank and tell them we know that they are laundering Russian money!"

Joe stood up and walked over to the fireplace, tapping his hand on the mantle-piece top, he turned and said with a smile, "Or we can go out and jump under a bus or surrender to the Russians, what do you think you Dope? The bank is obviously involved, how do you think they would react to us telling them we know all about it? We would end up dead in Green Park like old Nige or disappear off the face of the earth like H and Octavia. You might be whizz with numbers, and accountancy, but you're a shit warlord."

Rob's smile fell from his face, at what his friend had said, he asked, "Is this what this is, war?"

Joe stared down at Rob's solemn face and replied, "What do you think, we've got a Russian hit team in London trying to kill us. They've already killed Jimmy and possibly H and Octavia for all we know; what else would you call it, Rob?"

Silence fell over the lounge; the seriousness of Joe's words had taken the bravado out of the room from Rob's break through news. The mood changed has they both reflected on the situation they were in up to their necks. Joe sat back on the sofa, he broke the silence, "When I went to number 53 with DI Mooney looking for our 'Mrs Harrington', there was an Eastern European family possibly Russian supposedly renting the house. I remember a leather pouch on a table against the wall halfway down the hall. The son shouted to his mum, 'It's the police Mum, not the courier.' The pouch looked pretty full; do you think they could have been documentation of the shell companies?"

Rob nodded, leaning forward towards the sofa, he asked, "Most definitely, what are you thinking?"

Joe sat back crossing his legs and said, "We stake out the house, follow the courier when he makes the pick up and see where he delivers the pouch. It might be where the Russians are staying, knowing where they are based must be an advantage to us. Don't you think? I haven't thought what we would next yet, but I will, I need to think what logic Jimmy would have used. He always said to me, young Joe do know how to eat an elephant? Slice by slice."

Rob stared at Joe in silence for a minute thought about it and nodded his head in agreement, "Well, I agree, Joseph, it wouldn't hurt for us to know where they are staying. We could even stake it out and follow them to see what they are doing. I should think they are probably looking for us, I think it's a bloody good idea, my son, not a war plan, but it makes sense for now."

Chapter Thirty
The Courier

After two days of Rob sat at the bottom of Adams Yard on a Honda motorbike that he borrowed from a friend, he hadn't seen anything that resembled a pickup by a courier at number 53. What he had seen though was a van parked across the road. Which may as well have had police surveillance in big letters across it for how inconspicuous the occupants were. Climbing in and out to stretch the legs, and even more obvious when they were swapping shifts. Rob told Joe about the stake-out when he got back to the flat, Joe just shrugged his shoulders and said, "Well, at least they're doing something positive, even if it is cack-handed."

It was six-thirty in the evening on a Tuesday, they were sat in the lounge enjoying an ice-cold beer, and it was one of those hot uncomfortable balmy summer nights. Joe sat upright and announced, "I know what we can do, I'll ring Lorenzo and see if he can find out when the collection made." Joe had to explain to Rob again who Lorenzo was also about him being mugged and ending up in hospital, but was convinced now it wasn't random, it was the Russians.

Thanking Lorenzo Joe ended the call, Rob looked at him waiting for the news. Joe said, "There's Russian's renting the house. Lorenzo said the staff had told him that they are over here on business for a few weeks. He's going to ask the cook and maid who are work at 53 for me tomorrow; he's a great bloke. Bless him."

Rob wandered off in to the kitchen and opened two more beers and replied, "Good, so no more stake outs for now then? Thank God, I was going bandy sat on that bloody motorbike all day. So, what's the plan for tomorrow then general?"

Joe ignored the title Rob had given him since his dramatic "War" speech and said, "I'm going to ring Andy Sherry in the morning and see if there's any news on their investigation."

Rob handed him a fresh beer and asked, "If they are making some progress in their investigations, do you think we should tell them what we know about the Russians trying to kill you and staking out your office. It might help catch these bastards and who knows, it could save our lives?"

Joe smiled and nodding replied, "Possibly, but let's see where they've got to, because so far, they haven't been doing that good, if that's still the situation I don't see the point. We can decide whether to tell them when we find out where the courier's delivering to, if they are holed up there, that would be a big bonus for the Met on top of what we know about the shell companies and them coming after me. Now what do you say we go out and have some dinner, somewhere local where we're going to be safe from mad killer Russians?"

Rob jumped up and replied, "Now that's the most sensible productive thing you've said all day, are you taking the gun, just in case?"

Joe nodded. "This is going everywhere with me from now on. If I'm going to cop for an unfortunate one, I'm going to take a couple of those murdering bastards with me."

Wednesday lunchtime, Rob came back with two carrier bags full of food and drink from the Sainsbury's local on the next block. Joe was finishing his call with Andy Sherry, dumping the two bags on the kitchen table, and he took out two beers. He took the tops off the bottles and handing one to Joe asked, "How did it go? I'll unpack that lot later." Following Joe in to the lounge, he flopped down on the sofa.

Joe stood by the fire place, took a large gulp of beer and replied, "Basically they've got fuck all, nothing on Jimmy's murder, no update on Harriot and Octavia's whereabouts and nothing on poor old Nigel's murder. All they do know is the Russians are involved, which is bravo the Met, seeing it was us who gave them the photo of Yulia Navarykasha who posed has Mrs Harrington.

"He did say that they know there's a team of ex FSA guys in town, but the Mets usual Eastern European snitches don't know why they are here. Or else they are too scared to give up any information they might know or have heard. He finished telling me to be careful in case it was anything to do with the Harrington case, I couldn't believe it, and they are supposed to be London's finest."

"So, for the time being, Rob, I suggest, we keep our cards close to our chests and see what Lorenzo can find out for us, do you agree?"

Rob nodded his agreement and said, "I feel a little vulnerable, Joe, so I'm going to see my old dealer in Camden. I think we need more than one gun between us; he'll sell me another handgun or maybe a shotgun and some ammo. Are you okay with that? I've already spoken with him."

Joe looked long, hard at Rob and replied, "You do realise; you just might have to use one, don't you, Rob? We're getting into some deep shit here, and it's not even your fight. I don't know the outcome, we could end up in prison for a long time or even dead. There's still time, for you to back off, that's okay with me. Once they know about you and that we're together, they won't hesitate, and they will kill you."

"The way I see it, Rob, is they don't want any loose ends, so that means getting rid of anybody and everybody who knows anything about Nigel Harrington's murder and the money laundering operation."

Rob made a decent attempt at a smile and replied, "Joe, I understand the consequences and I'll be honest with you; it scares me shitless sometimes. But I can't walk away and let you face all this on your own. I feel I owe you, and I know before you even say it, I don't owe you anything, but that's just how I feel. If I hadn't fucked you up, you wouldn't even be the private investigator that got you in this danger. So don't worry about it, I'm with you until the end, we're in this together, no matter how it ends, good or bad."

They stood looking at each other for a while, then Joe nodding his head gave his mate a hug, patting Rob's back, he said, "All right, that's fine with me, I couldn't think of anybody else, I would want by my side in this mess, I'm so thankful I've got you with me!"

That evening they went out in the East end, to The Merchant of Venice on the riverside. The pub served great seafood and good craft beers, they also felt safe from the Russians keeping away from the office in the city and Joe's apartment in the West end. The following morning Rob went up to Camden to see his ex-dealer and hire the merchandise. Joe saw he had a missed call from Lorenzo, he must have phoned earlier when Joe was still in bed. He played back a message Lorenzo had left him, he said Friday lunchtime every week was when the courier calls to collect the package from number 53. Joe made a mental note to arrange to see Lorenzo and give him some money for his help. Meantime, he texted Lorenzo thanking him for the info and that he would be in touch for a drink soon. Rob came back in the afternoon, carrying a tan leather holdall which he put in the wardrobe in his bedroom. Joe handed him a cold beer when he walked into the lounge, he asked, "Did you get what you went for?"

Rob flopped down in the armchair and took a big drink of beer, replying, "Yes, all went well, I think we're on a level playing field now if those bastards come for us. It will be like Gunfight at the OK Corral, I loved that film when I was a boy. Funny thing, on the way up to Camden, though, I stopped off at Holborn and walked past your office to see if they were still staking it out."

Joe asked, "And were they?"

Rob nodded. "Yep, two of them again, but the strange thing was, I'm certain that someone was watching them from across the road."

Joe looked puzzled and asked, "Plain clothes? Andy Sherry never mentioned stakeouts when I spoke with him. I never told him you saw the one at Adam's Yard, maybe he's keeping things close to his chest like us!"

Rob finished his beer, said, "God that hit the spot, I'm having another one, do you want one? No, this guy, I don't think he was a copper, he looked like the Russians, you know, tough looking, ex-military."

Joe followed him into the kitchen and when Rob took his head out of the fridge Joe, asked, "Well, what did he look like?"

Handing Joe another beer, he replied, "Well, like I just said, I managed to sneak a photo of him on my phone, I'm getting good at this private eye business, and he had no idea whatsoever."

He brought up his photos and handed his phone to Joe. Joe looked at the photo, and he looked shocked. "Shit!"

Rob stood up, surprised at Joe's reaction. "What? Do you know him? Who is he?"

Joe composed himself, handing back the phone to Rob and said, "That's Heinrich Wagner from the bank; he's their head of security. He was in the meeting I told you about that I had at the bank after poor Old Nige was murdered. What the fuck is he doing spying on the Russians? I thought they were all in on this together; it doesn't look like they are, does it?"

Rob said, "Maybe the bank is just being cautious; after all, they did have one of their directors bumped off by these goons. They wouldn't just say. Oh well, and carry on banking, would they?"

Joe nodded and drank some beer, he replied, "Well, yea, I suppose that could be the case. I wonder how they knew about the Russians being over here."

Rob answered, "Well, if they are laundering the money from the companies set up at number 53. It's all Russian money so they must have contacts in Moscow; they could have tipped them off, and don't you think?"

Joe nodded. "Yea, I suppose so, but they weren't quick enough with a heads-up to save poor old Nigel, were they?"

Rob added, "True, but possibly after they killed Nigel, the bank investigated why and were told then that the death squad had been sent over. If that was the case, like I said before, you couldn't blame the bank for wanting to know what they were doing. Especially, if they figured out the connection after your boss Jimmy was murdered by the Russians too."

Chapter Thirty-One
The Lion's Den

Rob was getting tired of trying to convince Joe that the bank must be involved in the laundering. He was losing patience, he said, "Joe, look just because their head of security is watching the Russians doesn't mean they are legitimate. It's got to be the bank that they are laundering the dirty money through. Nigel was murdered after Mrs Harrington went there for a meeting. We've established that number 53 is being used to register thousands of shell companies; of course, the bank is involved. Maybe Heinrich, or whatever is bloody name is, was told to make sure they didn't lose any more staff. First Nigel, then that Octavia Connelly disappears. You thought it was the bank who took her. My bet is that it was the Russians acting alone who took her and this team who have been sent over here are not in bed with the bank. If they were, why t would the bank be spying on them?" Joe had been sitting in silence listening to Rob's argument, and he admitted it did make sense, and he and Jimmy could have been wrong on how far the bank was involved.

He looked at Rob and said, "Okay, I think you have a good point, and it all does make sense. I agree with you that we shouldn't speak to the bank about joining forces against the Russians. Sorry, it was a daft idea, but you've got to admit I'm turning you from a dull accountant into a general on a war footing, yes?"

Rob burst out laughing and said, "Sod off, accountancy might be dull, but it's certainly safer than being a PI, you cheeky bastard."

They both laughed raucously, Rob continued, "So tomorrow I'll be at Adam's yard waiting for the courier, and hopefully we'll find out where the Russians are holed up. Then we tell your Andy Sherry so the Met can raid the place and hopefully pin Jimmy's murder and your attempted murder on them, yes?"

Joe agreed, "Well, that's the plan, then we can get them off our backs and stop hiding out here. Also, we can sort out what we do about the bank and the laundering without having to look over our shoulders all the time."

Rob laughed and said, "It sounds like a plan, Stan; where do you want to go for dinner tonight?"

Joe replied, "I know it's not the weather for a curry, but I really fancy one. There's a great little restaurant on the Mile End Road; what do you think?"

Rob replied, "Okay, by me, and seeing you picked where we are going to eat, you can pay tonight."

Friday morning, Rob left for Adams yard at ten-thirty he had his revolver from Camden tucked in the back of his black Armani jeans, just in case the plan went wrong. It worried him having a gun, because it was serious shit. It could be a jail sentence or shot by armed police. All sorts of things could go wrong, but at least it gave him a fighting chance if he was rumbled by the Russians and more importantly it could save his life.

Joe's phone went at one forty five, it was Rob to say the courier had just done the pickup and was about to leave, Joe told him to keep alert and ring as soon has he had the drop off point. Rob phoned back at two-fifty he told Joe. The drop's been made to number 12 Cornwall Terrace Mews, Joe said, "Where the hell is that, sounds bloody posh?"

Rob replied, "It is, it's between Baker Street and Regents Park; I think its Marylebone; not too sure though. The guy who answered the door was the one I smacked with my bat outside your place that night after Jimmy's funeral. He was still limping. I told you I got him a good one. I'll fill you in on all the details when I get back; see you in about an hour." Sounding very pleased with himself, he rang off.

Joe was finally beginning to think they were making some progress at last; Jimmy would have been proud of the way he had handled the situation. Every step of the way he asked himself, "Now what would Jimmy do." He never mentioned it to Rob, but he really missed Jimmy, he thought about him all the time. Always asking himself the same question, "What could I have done differently, that would have saved Jimmy's life." He never came up with an answer, not one, it tormented the hell out of him. Rob was true to his word, arriving back at the flat just over an hour later. He sat down in the lounge and was just about to shout through into the kitchen for a cold beer when Joe walked in holding two. Rob downed his in three gulps saying, in his defence as he went for another one. "It's bloody hot in those leathers and that crash helmet in this heat, I can tell you. So how do you feel, I think we're getting the upper hand, don't you?"

Joe nodded, taking a drink of his beer. "Same here, Rob, my old buddy; I think we've been playing a blinder lately!"

When Rob had finally quenched his thirst with his third bottle, he told Joe all about waiting for the courier. Then following him up to Marylebone and seeing the Russian again, sent a shiver down his spine he didn't mind admitting it. The mews house was very nice he had to admit, adding that they certainly weren't slumming it, while they tried to hunt down Joe. Rob mentioned eating out later, Joe was all for it he was going stir crazy being in the flat all day. They decided on a Cantonese dinner in Canary Wharf to celebrate how the day had gone. Rob said his friend was returning his car and collecting his motorbike, then they could get ready to go for dinner and some celebratory drinks.

Chapter Thirty-Two
A Bombshell!

They finally got out for dinner after waiting for ages for Rob's friend to come for his motorbike. He finally phoned and asked if he could come by the next day, so they finally got an Uber over to Canary Wharf. They had a great meal ordered a couple of extra dishes they struggled with and had a couple of drinks more than they should have. The restaurant, a floating Chinese boat moored in the South dock. It was popular with tourists and locals alike, not only for its novelty value, but the food was excellent. After the meal they walked up to the main road to flag down a black cab. One soon came their way, heading towards the tunnel, Joe shouted to the cabbie, "Just pull over will you!"

Rob looked worried and asked, "What's wrong?"

Joe laughed, replying, "It's okay, I've just seen a friend."

With that, he jumped out of the cab and shouted, "Danny!" He waved to a man back down the road. It was Danny Sumner the concierge from Nigel Harrington's apartment, he turned looked at Joe and waved back.

After a few minutes, the cabbie was getting restless, Rob paid him and let him go. He walked up to Joe and Danny who were still chatting and laughing like long lost brothers. Joe introduced Rob and suggested Danny should join them for a drink, adding they had had a good day. They crossed the road to a pub opposite, The Henry Addington pub was named after the British Prime Minister and one time Doctor to King George 111. Joe ordered a round of drinks, while Joe and Danny sat at a table outside the back overlooking the wharf, it was a lot cooler there with a nice breeze coming off the water. Joe asked Danny how the family were doing, he was pleased when Danny said everything was going well. He explained he had left the concierge job after Joe had visited him and explained that some dangerous men could pay him a visit over Nigel Harrington's murder. Which they did, luckily it was on his night off, but that was enough to scare him, he never went back to work. He explained he didn't feel safe and owed it to his family to stay out of danger. Joe and Rob both agreed he had made the right decision especially after what had happened since.

Danny said he had read about Joe's partner's murder in the newspaper, he offered Joe his condolences. It stopped the conversation for a while, the awkward silence gave them all time to have a refreshing drink of their beers. Joe broke the silence, asking Danny, "So, where are you working now, Danny?"

Winking at Rob he continued, "You certainly look like you've gone up in the world; you look very dapper in your business suit and briefcase."

Danny threw his head back and laughed confidently. "I'm doing good, thanks, Joe, jacking in the concierge job was a good move. A school friend of mine works for an insurance company in Canada Square. He got me an interview, and I got the job. I haven't looked back since. I'm taking the family away to Malaga for a holiday next month; it's our very first family holiday abroad."

Joe smiled and replied, "I'm so glad for you, Danny, I was worried when I came to see you that evening. I wouldn't have forgiven myself if those bastards had got hold of you for helping me."

Danny looked embarrassed and said, "Thank you, Joe, it was a pleasure, and you were very kind with the money, it really helped at the time. How's all that business going, it's all seems to have gone quiet in the papers?"

Joe's smile dropped from his face, he said, "It's a shitstorm, really, Danny, I can't believe what's happened after taking on a simple case. Anyway, the good news is we've had a decent breakthrough these last couple of days and we're hoping it will all be over soon."

Rob returned with another round of beers, sitting down he raised his glass and toasted. "And I will drink to that!"

They both responded to Rob's toast with a resounding *Cheers* and took a drink with Rob, they all laughed. Danny wiped his mouth and asked, "Did finding Mr Harrington's mystery woman help, Joe?"

Joe looked puzzled and replied, "Mystery woman? I'm not with you, Danny!"

Danny smiled, "Yea you remember, the dark-haired woman I told *you* about, the one who would come and visit Mr Harrington in his apartment."

Joe took another drink of his beer and said, "Oh yea, her; no, we never managed to turn up anything on her, Danny."

It was Danny turn to look, puzzled. "What are you joking? You found her; I saw you come out of The Doggett's pub together on Blackfriars Bridge that evening. Remember? I was on the bus that stopped outside the pub, and I knocked on the window. That's why I gave you the thumbs up to say, well done, you!"

Joe looked from Danny to Rob and back at Danny, open mouthed in utter shock and disbelief at what he had just heard. The colour drained from his face, bearing in mind Joe was still recovering, Rob asked, "Are you okay, buddy, you've gone a funny colour?"

Joe didn't reply he just continued staring at Danny, what he had just said was slow getting through to him. Seeing Joe's reaction Danny was worried he had said something out of order and was feeling uncomfortable at the atmosphere he had created. It was Rob who spoke again, "Joe, are you okay; what's wrong?"

He finally cleared his throat, ignoring Rob's question again, he said to Danny, "Are you saying that the woman you saw me with outside the Doggett's that evening was the woman who would call at Nigel Harrington's apartment and stayed the night… that was her?"

Danny was worried, by the look on Joe's face that he had said something seriously wrong. He began to panic and replied in a nervous voice, "Well... yes, that was her, Joe, the one I told you about. I wouldn't make up something like that."

Rob was completely in the dark, listening to this weird conversation that had turned fun drinks into something very odd, so he decided to join in. "For fucks sake, will someone tell me what this is all about. Who is this woman, Joe?"

Not getting an answer, Rob spoke again, only louder, so to snap Joe out of his thoughts trance, "JOE!" It worked, bringing Joe back to the table. He looked across at Rob, and he answered, "I was with Harriot that evening, our receptionist from the office."

Seeing the same look of horror now appear on Rob's face prompted Danny to splutter an apology, "Joe, I'm really sorry if I've said something out of order; I wouldn't do that intentionally, honestly." Joe was still trying to clear his head and compose himself.

He placed his hand on Danny's hand and replied, "Danny, you haven't said or done anything wrong, what you just told me, well... was just a big shock, that's all. Let me just ask once more, are you definitely certain that was her, she was the woman? If it was her, God, she played it so cool when you knocked on the bus window."

Danny looked from Joe to Rob and back to Joe, he replied, "Yes, it was definitely her; I swear on my children's lives, she probably didn't recognise me; don't forget she was only used to seeing me in my uniform and concierge cap, but yes, I swear it was her!"

Joe said, "Okay, Danny, I believe you really, and I'm sorry if I've scared the shit out of you, but I tell you her not recognising you on the bus that night was the luckiest break you will ever have. If she had recognised you, you would most certainly be dead by now." If that was supposed to reassure Danny, it had the complete opposite effect, it scared the life out of him. They sat there in silence drinking their drinks, each with their own thoughts going through their minds.

It was Danny who spoke, draining the remains of his pint glass, he stood up and said, "I really need to get going now, Joe, my dinner will be on the table."

Joe and Rob stood up and shook Danny's hand and wished him all the best. They sat back down again with Rob commenting, "I think you frightened the shit out of him, Joe. He couldn't get away from here fast enough, I don't think you'll ever see him again, that's for sure."

Joe was deep in thoughts again, Rob decided to leave him to it and didn't bother repeating himself. He went back inside to the bar and got two more beers and two large whiskies. He came back and placed the drinks on the table and sat looking at Joe. He was still lost in his thoughts and slowly started shaking his head. Rob knew Joe would speak when he was good and ready to. It didn't take too long; he drank the large whisky down in one and then had a big drink of beer.

Joe looked at Rob and finally said, "Can you believe it? That Harriot is involved in all this. With Nigel Harrington's murder, the Russians, shit! And Jimmy's death. For fuck's sake he was a father to the pair of us, we were like a family, Rob."

Rob gently shook his head and replied, "Now slow down a little, you don't know she's involved in everything that's happened, just because she was going and staying at Nigel Harrington's apartment."

Joe came straight back with. "Well, why would she keep it a secret then, if she had nothing to hide and was innocent, just tell me that?"

Rob shrugged his shoulders and replied, "I don't have the answers, Joe, but neither do you yet; all I'm saying is don't try and complete the jigsaw puzzle without having all the pieces."

Joe studied Rob's face for a while and then said, "I suppose you are right, but I think with what we now know, and it's safe to say she's involved in this and probably up to her neck. Why stay silent if you've nothing to hide? When you saw the trouble in our office, did you see Harriot there?"

Rob shook his head, replying, "No, I couldn't see if she was there."

"Oh my God! I've just remembered something."

Rob looked at Joe's shocked face, and said, "What now?"

Joe carried on, "When I found Jimmy, the last thing he said to me was *Harriot*! I thought he was trying to tell me they had taken her, but what if he was trying to warn me that she was involved?

Rob let out a big sigh. "That could be true, Joe, I don't know and neither do you right now. What are we going to do?"

Joe disappeared once more in his thoughts, so Rob thought, *Fuck it,* and went off to get some more drinks. When he returned, Joe was still away in his thoughts, so Rob just placed his pint and large whisky in front of him. Finally, he returned to earth and spoke, "When you were staking out the Mews in Marylebone, you didn't see a woman there, did you?"

Rob shook his head. "No why, do you think she might have been there with the goons?"

Joe replied, "She might be, it's a possibility, and can you ring your friend and ask if we can keep his motorbike for another couple of days?"

Rob laughed. "Of course, it sounds like I'm on stake out duty again, if she is there what do we do, tell the Met? After all she is a missing person in a murder investigation, they would go in all guns blazing with what we now know."

Joe shook his head, and explained, "No, I was thinking more along the lines of, if she was there, we grab her and find out exactly how involved she is, and if so, maybe we can find out what the fuck this is all about. We know it's about money laundering, but by the look of things, that's been going on for quite a while. But what's triggered all this violence – Nigel Harrington being murdered. A hit squad being sent over to tie up all the loose ends, or should I say kill all the loose ends, I need to know Rob, and I think Harriot's got the answers. Despite coming over as all sweetness and light, there's a side to her, Jimmy, and I didn't know."

Rob took a large swig of his whisky, and putting his glass down he said, "I needed that after what you just said… we grab her? Grab her? Are you mad or just pissed? That's easier said than done, Joe. How do you propose that we grab her, shoot our way in there? They are bloody professional killers." Joe was serious, it's possible, let's establish if she is there first hey, and in the meantime I'll go, and get us another drink.

Chapter Thirty-Three
Smash and Grab

The following day, Saturday, not surprisingly they both had massive hang-overs, Rob was complaining about going on a stake-out on a motorbike when he was probably still over the legal limit to drive. He went anyway after complaining about having to wear leathers and a crash helmet on such a hot day. The flat was quiet now, and it gave Joe time to think about what he had discovered the previous night from Danny. Despite all the drink it had taken him a long time to clear his head and go to sleep. Then he had a nightmare that a laughing Harriot attacking a defenceless Jimmy as he lay on the floor of the office. That must have kept him awake for another hour at least, he felt shattered. He was thinking what he would do if Harriot confessed to being involved in everything and was responsible for Jimmy's death. Everything was so fucked up, last night they were on a high because they felt like all this nonsense was close to ending. Then bam! Along comes Danny and everything is worse. He got his phone and text Danny apologising for last night. He felt guilty, poor Danny looked worried sick when he said his goodbyes and hurried off down the road away from the pub. He lay on the sofa thinking of different scenarios of how Harriot could be involved, but none of them made any sense, after a while he drifted off into a deep sleep.

The front door banging shut woke Joe with a start. Rob's voice carried through from the hall, "It's only me, I'm absolutely roasting in these fucking leathers, and I don't think I'll wear them again tomorrow." Eventually, walking into the lounge in a white tee-shirt, white Calvin Klein boxers and black socks, he dropped down into the armchair.

Taking a drink from a bottle of beer, he asked Joe, "Do you want one?" The very thought of a drink turned Joe's stomach.

He asked, "No thanks, how did it go, any joy?" Taking another drink, Rob shook his head.

"Nope, number one and number two came out and got into a Range Rover and drove off. Probably going to check on you turning up at your office; how much longer do you think they will keep watching for you there? Then another guy came out and got in to a silver Merc and drove off, I haven't seen him before. He came back after about an hour, but apart from that, no sign of her. How's your day been? You look like shit."

Joe got up to go to the toilet, he replied, "I feel like shit, I've been asleep for ages, didn't get much sleep last night as you would expect. What did the guy in the Merc look like?"

Rob shouted after him, "Pretty much the same as the others, a tough looking military type, I've taken a photo of him. I slept like a log, what should we do about dinner, fancy a takeaway? You don't look up to going out."

Joe shouted back, "Sounds good to me, what do you fancy?"

Days two and three were both fruitless, then day four (Tuesday), BINGO! Rob phoned about eleven thirty a.m. all excited and said, *"She's just turned up; she's here – that guy I told you about the other day with the silver Merc. He's just arrived here with her, and they've gone into the Mews. Strange thing, though. She was sitting in the back, and he jumped out and opened the door for her like a chauffeur would do. I'll tell you something, Joe, from the way you described her being a plan Jane with glasses, she must have had a makeover; she looked anything but plain; in fact she looked very tasty, and I managed to get a good photo of her. So, you can confirm it is her, but from what you've told me, I would say it's definitely her."*

Joe's head started to spin again at the news, but he calmed himself and replied, *"Okay, you stay there, when she comes out, follow them and see where he takes her. We might be able to grab her there, if she hasn't got any goons there."*

Rob asked, *"Are you okay, Joe. You don't sound too enthusiastic about her turning up. She's really fucked with your mind, hasn't she? You know, being involved, you've got to let it go; shit happens. It's better that you do know; it's what you do from now on that really matters."*

Joe cleared his throat and replied, *"I'm okay, Rob, to be honest, yes, I was hoping she wouldn't show, and it would all be a big mistake. I'm still having trouble getting my head around it, I'll be fine though, well done anyway, great work."*

Rob smiled into his mobile and said, *"Yea, I understand, Joe, and I also understand you've been through a hell of a lot these past few weeks. We'll get through it buddy I promise you, speak soon when I have some more news, don't wait up for me."*

Joe woke up early after having a good night's catch-up sleep, he got up and went to the bathroom for a pee. Rob's bedroom door was closed, he hesitated outside, but decided to let him sleep, he didn't have any idea what time he got in last night. He made himself an instant coffee and went and sat in the lounge. He was thinking about if they managed to grab Harriot would they bring her back here. That would mean one of them would have to guard her all the time and that wasn't ideal. Or do we take her somewhere else, find out everything she knows and hand her to The Met or let her go? He hated the uncertainty of all this, and the anger he was harbouring for Harriot.

Thankfully Rob appeared at the door of the lounge and broke his thoughts. He looked like something from another world. His hair was sticking up and out in all directions, he needed a shave, he had dark rings around his eyes and apart from his boxers he was wearing only one sock. Joe looked him up and down and mock horror, and said, "God, did the Russians work you over last night? They've made a hell of a mess of you." Rob collapsed in to the armchair threw his head back, he roughly rubbed his eyes. Gripping the arms of the chair, he asked in near-perfect Cary Grant voice, "Make us a mug of coffee, would you, a strong one, there's a good chap."

Joe laughed, shaking his head, he asked if they only showed old black and white films in Rehab. He walked off into the kitchen without getting a reply, he decided Rob needed time to "come around". He came back in with two coffees; Rob hadn't moved other than closing his eyes and going back to sleep. Joe put his coffee on the coffee table and watched him sleep, he smiled thinking what a great friend he was. He was so glad that he was back in his life, apart from his two aunts Joe never really had anyone else he was close to and cared about. He just wished everything wasn't so fucked up and life could be normal again, normal seemed like a lifetime ago now.

It was lunchtime before Rob woke and was ready to update Joe on the night before He had showered, shaved, got dressed in tan chinos and a blue Polo shirt. In fact, he looked quite smart, he came in to the lounge and sat down on the sofa. Joe spoke first, "How did it go last night, what time did you get in?"

Rob replied, "Two a.m., that's why I was so knackered; she stayed at the mews last night. I stayed watching in case she was going to leave later and go somewhere else. But all the upstairs lights went out at just after one p.m. I gave it another thirty minutes or so, but it was obvious they had bedded down for the night. So, what do we do now, General?"

Joe shrugged his shoulders and said, "Let's give it another day and see if she is stays there or goes somewhere else. How long have you got the motorbike for?"

Rob said, "Ahh, it's funny you should ask that, my mate text last night, he wants to come over this afternoon for it."

Joe stood up and walked over to the fireplace, Rob thought he seemed to do his best thinking stood at the fire place. After a minute or two, he said, "Okay, they don't know your Jag; we can stake it out in that alternating between the car and watching from the road. That should be all right, we'll do it together, it's good and sunny I can wear a baseball cap and sunglasses. I won't look out of place if they see me, I've haven't got anything else to do here, so it will be good, yes?"

Rob nodded in agreement, but said, "Just so there aren't any surprises, if we get the chance are we going to grab her?"

Joe in all seriousness, replied, "I think we have to if we get the chance, don't you? The longer this goes on, I feel our luck is going to run out, and they're going to catch us, whether by tracking us down or because we've got sloppy."

Thursday Morning 7.15 a.m., the Jag was parked across and three doors down from the mews, the row of mews were set back about four metres from the road. Sat in the Jag they had a clear view of any comings and goings, they could also see the Range Rover and the silver Merc parked outside on the road. The silver Merc was parked facing the Jag, so they would have to be careful when and if it drove off, it would drive right past them. Eight a.m., there was still no movement. Joe got out and walked down past the mews to the next road, he bought two coffees and some sandwiches. Back in the car, Rob reported all quiet, and asked, "What's on the sarnies?"

He pulled a face when Joe replied, "Egg mayonnaise." Just after nine-fifteen the Russians two and three came out and got into the black Range Rover. Rob said as they drove off down the road. "There they go to keep watch on your office; they've not got much imagination have they."

Joe shrugged his shoulders and replied, "Not a clue, but I'm glad they're now out of the way. Hopefully, Harriot is still in there and didn't bugger off somewhere else." There was silence as they both enjoyed their sarnies and morning coffees Rob lowered a couple of windows it was getting uncomfortable in the Jag.

Eleven-twenty, Joe had been watching the mews from further up the road, Rob was still sat in the car, Joe had said he needed some fresh air about twenty minutes earlier. After another seven or eight minutes the front door opened and out walked the "Chauffeur" of the silver Merc. Joe crossed the road slowly and started to walk down the pavement towards the Russian, hoping if he had seen him before he wouldn't recognise him wearing his sunglasses and cap. The Russian stopped at the back door of the Mercedes and looked back towards the mews; Joe quickened his pace. He took the gun from his pocket, and held it down by his side in case it wasn't Harriot who came out of the Mews.

The next few minutes were sheer pandemonium, it was Harriot who came walking out of the mews, prompting the Russian to open the back door of the Mercedes, and Joe was only a short distance away now. Because of how close he was, Harriot looked at Joe who was close to her. Harriot said something to the Russian who dashed towards Joe from the back door of the car. Joe arm came up and out, he raised the gun and shot the Russian in the thigh, the noise was deafening. Harriot froze in fear, open mouthed, she looked from the Russian screaming in agony on the floor to the man now next to her. Rob was watching all this from the car, he screamed out, "No, Joe!" even though nobody could hear him in the car.

Hands shaking, Rob started the car on seeing Joe roughly grab Harriot and pull her to the roadside, Joe frantically waved to Rob to drive up to them. Rob screeched to halt alongside the Mercedes, Joe tried to open the back door, but couldn't, he shouted, "For fuck's sake, Rob, you're too close, pull back." Rob did as he was told and pulled back away from the parked Mercedes. Joe dragged the screaming Harriot by the arm and bundled her onto the back seat of the car, jumping in, he landing on top of her.

Flailing arms and legs, he pushed Harriot still screaming along the back seat, his heart was racing, he shouted, "Rob, fucking go, NOW! Harriot, shut up for fucks sake."

Finally recognising Joe's voice, she stopped struggling and screaming and stared at Joe sat next to her. The sudden silence didn't calm Rob who roaring off at speed, taking off the wing mirrors of two parked cars further up the road. Joe shouted, "ROB... ROB! For fucks sake, slow down now, before you run somebody over or kill us all, just try to calm down." Harriot went to speak to Joe, but he glared and pointed the gun at her, he told to her to keep quiet. Shocked, she lowered her head and stared in silence at her shaking hands.

Rob shouted over his shoulder in a high-pitched voice, "Calm down! Are you having a fucking laugh? I can't stop shaking; otherwise, I would. Fucking hell, Joe, you're lucky; I'm not having a heart attack! You just shot someone and in broad daylight, we're lucky nobody was out on the road to see you. Why did you do that?"

Joe met Rob's eyes in the rear-view mirror, and he sighed, a little short of breath, he replied, "I don't know, Rob, I didn't mean to. I had the gun in my hand, he moved on me. It was an adrenaline rush, I pointed it at him and then there was this deafening bang."

Joe realised he was still pointing the gun at Harriot; he carefully placed it in the storage pocket of the door. Rob asked still in an unusual high voice, "Where are we taking her?"

Joe looked in Harriot's direction and answered, "Drive up to Hampstead Heath, but, Rob, nice and slow, hey! The last thing we want is to get pulled over by the police."

Rob said, nervously, "I will, I'm still shaking, I feel sick now. What about the guy we've left, bleeding on the pavement, what if he dies?"

It was Harriot who spoke, "There's a house keeper there, and she will get everything sorted out. They have people who 'clean up' so the authorities don't get involved." Joe and Rob made eye contact again through the rear-view mirror, neither spoke, but Joe raised his eyebrows, they were both shocked at the matter-of-fact nature of Harriet's answer.

They travelled the rest of the way to the Heath in silence, Joe and more so Rob was beginning to calm down. They turned in to the car park just past the Old Bull and Bush pub on the North end way side of the Heath. Apart from two other unoccupied parked cars, most likely dog walkers, it was all quiet. Rob brought the car to a halt and turned off the engine, he decided to let Joe do all the talking, and he was still shaken up from the shooting. He turned and sat with his back against the driver's window so he could clearly see Joe and Harriot. Joe was looking daggers at Harriot, he couldn't believe the change in her appearance, she had gone from looking a plain Jane to beautiful woman. Her deception annoyed Joe even more, it made him realise that both him and Jimmy had been fooled by her all along. To think, Jimmy told him not say too much in front of Harriot because he didn't want her to be frightened and upset. When all the time she had been involved in everything that was happening.

Joe still breathing heavily, he cleared his throat and asked her outright, "Were you involved in Jimmy's murder?"

Harriot looked shocked and genuinely upset by the question, she looked down and replied in an emotional voice, "No I wasn't, I tried to stop it… but I couldn't."

Joe instinctively moved forward, Rob thought he was going to hit Harriot so did she. She cowered and pushed back into the seat. Joe appeared to bring his anger under control after Harriot's reply. He shouted angrily, "Well, that sounds to me like you were involved, who did it, the Russians and don't you fucking dare lie to me?"

Harriot had started to sob gently, she answered without looking up to him. "Yes, it was them, they were sent over to clean up after everything that had happened."

"What do you mean, everything that had happened, do you mean, poor old Nigel's murder?" She nodded, Joe didn't know if the tears were genuine or another one of her shitty little tricks.

He carried on, "Do you know I've been worried sick about you since you disappeared and have been looking everywhere for you? I even went down to Brighton, and it was all bullshit."

This time she looked at him, making eye contact and answered, "I'm sorry for lying to you, and I'm sorry for the trouble I've caused you. I didn't mean for any of this to happen."

Joe let out a big sigh and said, "Well, how the fuck did you expect it all to turn out?"

She looked down again at her shaking hands and continued to cry quietly. Joe looked at Rob and rolled his eyes and slowly shaking his head. Looking back at Harriot, he continued with his questions, "Did you know the woman who came into our offices claiming to be 'Mrs Harrington?'" Harriot dabbed her eyes with a small white handkerchief from her pocket, she looked up at Joe and nodded. Joe still breathing heavily, raised his voice in anger again. "I fucking thought as much; how do you know her?"

She looked at Joe, red-eyed with tears running down her face, and replied in a trembling voice, "She's my mother…"

Chapter Thirty-Four
Odessa, Southern Ukraine

A port city on the Black Sea in Southern Ukraine. Odessa is widely known for its beautiful 19th century architecture. Despite being heavily bombed in the Second World War, its historical centre is well preserved. The Opera house is the second biggest Opera house in the world. Although Ukrainian is the official language, Russian is the dominant language. Odessa has a large fishing fleet and is also the hub of the Ukrainian navy.

Ukraine is the seventh largest nation in Europe, the Oblast region is very industrialised with coalmines and Iron works.

In 2014, Russia invaded and annexed the Crimea Peninsula from Ukraine. Because of the invasion, anti-Russian groups formed in the Donbas and escalated into a war between the armed forces of Ukraine and Russian.

Olek Navarykasha lived on Volzhskyy Lane a cobbled street in the centre of Odessa close to the magnificent building that housed the railway station. The lane had identical modest two-bedroom terraced houses on both side of the street. Situated in the city centre it was close enough to the port for Olek to walk to his job at the docks. He was quite short for a man 5–6 tall a ruddy complexion, losing his hair early, despite his height he was strong with powerful arms and big hands, he very rarely smiled. His wife Ionna still had her looks and figure despite her age and mothering two children, she towered over her husband at five-ten. Her thick black hair was complimented by her dark eyes, high cheekbones and full lips. She worked in a popular Patisserie on Kanathaya Street which ran along the side of the Railway Station. They had two children, daughter Yulia and her younger brother Ivan. They were proud of their terraced house which they bought with a mortgage. Ionna's mother had died two years after her father's death, being an only child was left an inheritance which paid the deposit with some left to help with the mortgage repayments.

Most of their neighbours rented their houses, not being able to afford to buy. They were all simple, honest hard-working people, who didn't have much money, but were happy to help each other if and when it was needed. They were proud Ukrainians who loved their country and loved their life in Odessa. Yulia was sixteen years old and in her last year at school, her parents couldn't afford to send her to the City University.

Her father said, she needed to get a job to help pay the family bills and take some pressure off her hard-working mother. She was happy with that, she loved her mother dearly and was like her in appearance with her lush black hair, high cheek bones, green eyes and tall with long shapely legs. Yulia and her mother were very close, mum Ionna doted on both her children. Yulia was the ideal

245

daughter whereas Ivan was getting troublesome. He was fourteen, a good-looking young man, tall like his mum and sister. He was well built for his age with thick curly black hair, hazel eyes and a strong square jaw. He was often in trouble at school, also he had some questionable friends in the city. An intelligent boy, but he found school boring and was always in search of excitement. His mother loved him for what he was, a free spirit, Ivan and Yulia although very different, were very close, Ivan was very protective of his big sister has she was of her younger brother.

Olek was an old-fashioned father who didn't show any emotion to his children. His father Petruso was tough on him, and he and his older brother Fedir, they would be flogged for the slightest misdemeanour. Their father was killed by the Russians, when they were teenagers, thankfully the brothers thought, they had to do numerous jobs to bring food to the table and look after their mother. They rarely spoke about their father, not because they didn't have feelings for him, but they didn't really know him except for the beatings. When he wasn't working, he was asleep in the armchair if they woke him up, he would shout and beat them, life was hard and tough in the old days. One thing Olek was passionate about was his hatred for Russia and its people. Not because it was a Russian who murdered his father, he found them arrogant and untrustworthy. There were many Russians that worked at the docks with Olek and his comrades, indeed there were many Russians living in Odessa. They were all the same they looked down on the locals and fights would often break out between the two factions. His wife Ionna said, their arrogance came from the Ukraine once being part of the USSR, they still thought and behaved like it was their country.

Because of his harsh upbringing Olek found it difficult to show his emotion, he was a tortured and troubled human being. Even when the children were very young, he never held them or played with them. Basically, he was a loner who unfortunately in a moment of madness thought he would give love a try and got married. His wife Ionna understood the miserable upbringing he had led and loved him nonetheless. She made up for love he couldn't give her or the children by giving her children all of her love, attention and affection. It also helped her, the love she gave and received back from her children more than compensated for being in a loveless marriage to a practical stranger. She never complained, Olek paid the bills and looked after them all in his own strange distant way. She was grateful for that and after all she had her children that was all she needed.

In early summer Yulia left school and got a job as a receptionist at the upmarket Potemkin hotel in the city centre. She looked stunning in her smart dark blue uniform, and her hair up in a neat bun or a simple ponytail. Her friendly personality made her a big favourite with the guests, she loved her job. On her first day, she came down the stairs in her uniform, her mother cried and hugged her. She told Yulia how proud she was and how beautiful she looked.

Meanwhile, Ivan was in trouble with the police, they came to the house and took him away to the police station. Apparently, him and his friends had been gone to the Moldavanka district and robbed some tourists. One of his friends had been caught by an undercover cop trying to sell an expensive watch they had stolen and named the rest of the gang.

The Moldavanka district was next to the old town and consisted of narrow back streets. Where there were dwellings mixed with brothels, gambling clubs and drinking dens of the local gangsters. Tourists were warned off going into the district, but with the close proximity it wasn't uncommon to stray from the charming old town into the dangerous streets. Ivan along with his friends were sentenced to a year in a young offender's institute a few miles outside of the city. His father wasn't interested or concerned, his mother Ionna and Yulia visited Ivan every fortnight without fail and took him treats that the prisoners were allowed. His mum always cried on the way home, it tore her apart that he had fallen in with the wrong crowd, he was still her baby. Yulia would get upset, but for different reason, not for foolish Ivan, but for her mother. She knew the life her mum had gone through with her dad and had always done her best for her and Ivan, with no help whatsoever from her dad. Yulia was a good daughter and gave her mum housekeeping money each week from her wages at the hotel. Her mum always put her family first, so Yulia tried to make sure her mum spent some of the money on herself, they would go shopping and buy a new dress or shoes.

They were happy times despite, the absence of Ivan, their father never once went to visit him or spoke about him. His excuse was he said, he had washed his hands of Ivan, for bringing shame on the family name. Also, when he was released from prison, he would not allow him back in the family home. Ionna pleaded with him to change his mind, but he wouldn't and told her not to speak Ivan's name in front of him again. Ionna told Yulia that she would speak with her brother Boris who had a tailor's shop in Luhansk, in the Donbas region. Luhansk was on the eastern region of the Ukraine close to the border with Russia. Far enough away for Ivan not to shame the family with any more trouble as far has his father was concerned. She hoped he would take Ivan in because he and his wife Anastasia couldn't have children. Yulia remembered them from when she and Ivan were young, they would go and stay with them during the summer holidays. They always had a wonderful time and would be very spoilt by big Uncle Boris and pretty Aunt Anastasia. Ionna said, she was sure Uncle Boris take care of Ivan when he came out of prison. Also, both Ionna and Yulia thought be it could a good thing to get Ivan away from his friends who were a bad influence on him in Odessa.

Chapter Thirty-Five
Yulia

Yulia worked hard at her job at the Potemkin hotel and in time was promoted to a job in the guest relations department. The department looked after VIP guests and especially the frequent returning guests who spent a lot of money with the hotel. Yulia was one of three staff who looked after the VIP's, and it was very important that their every wish was carried out. Yulia, kept a book and after looking after them would log details about them for the next time they checked in. Details of where they lived, their business, their likes and dislikes, the name of their wives and children. Even the names of any pets they might have mentioned, also names of other family members who had stayed at the hotel with them. When a VIP had booked a visit, she would get her book out and remind herself of their details. They were impressed with her not only remembering their name, but their wife's and children, asking how they were by name. She once asked a guest's little daughter how her dolly was that she was holding, she had even made a note of the dolls name. She asked a male client how his dogs' operation had gone, again by his pet's name. This friendly detailed attention made her very popular and guests would ask for her by name when they booked a reservation. Her popularity also got her very generous tips when they were checking out. When a client brought their wife, Yulia's good looks didn't harm her relationship with them. Knowing all about the family, the wife's name and also the children's names. This made the wives warm to her and many considered her a friend. Sometimes a very trusted friend with the things they would tell Yulia about their husband or marriage, again she would also note them down in her book.

She made a point of never going out on any dates with any of her VIP clients when asked, it was frowned upon by the hotel boss. She knew a lot of the young women had relationships with guests, especially the wealthy Russian ones, who came to Odessa on business. They would take the young women to the best restaurants and nightclubs and give them gifts of money and jewellery. Yulia didn't judge them unlike some of the older female employees. A lot of the young women who worked at the hotel, came from poor families, the money and jewellery they got really helped their families at home. The women were seen out and about with the wealthy hotel guests, staff would talk about them. The hotel would on occasions turn a blind eye, to staff fraternising with guests. It was very important they didn't upset the wealthy guests for fear they would take their business to another hotel in the city. Yulia understood, but never talked about it at home, if it came up in conversation, she would always say see didn't know anything. Her mum never raised it, it was always her dad, saying he heard things about the women who worked at

251

the hotel at work. He said, it was nothing more than a high-class brothel for the rich Russians, who he hated, and that the staff were just prostitutes. He would look at Yulia and tell her she shouldn't work there and to never bring shame on the family by doing what the other women do. Her mum would always calm him down by saying Yulia was a good girl, and they had been raised her properly, despite her father never having helped with the children growing up, ever!

Yulia loved her job at the hotel and would never complicate her life by doing what some of the other young women did. She wasn't short of admirers, but she kept her dates to the local men and not guests of the hotel. However, there was one VIP who would set her heart a flutter when she heard he was coming to stay at the hotel. He was a Russian businessman by the name of Andrei Novikov. Twenty-three years old, she checked his age in his passport one day, Tall, over six foot, an athletic build, dark hair, a neatly trimmed beard, gorgeous blue eyes that she could get lost in. He lived and worked in St Petersburg and was single. She would fantasise about him taking her away from Odessa, and they would live together in the country with their children. She would have her mother living close by and her brother Ivan, so she could take care of them both. Andrei would flirt with her when he was at the hotel on a business trip, he usually stayed Monday to Thursday every third week of the month. She would try her hardest not to blush, but he always managed to make her go red as a beetroot. Despite all his flirting she always maintained a profession relationship with him and would never become overly friendly, after all he was a paying guest and a VIP at that!

One day when he was staying at the hotel, Yulia was in town after finishing her morning shift, her mother had asked her to collect some dry cleaning. It was a warm spring day; she had changed out of her uniform into a blue flowered dress. It was much cooler in the spring sunshine than the uniform, and it was her favourite summer dress. She saw him walking up the street towards her, it was Andrei looking so smart in his blue pinstripe suit, white shirt and red tie, highly polished black shoes. He looked cool despite the hot weather; he looked like he had just got showered and dressed and not like he had been in meetings all day.

She panicked she didn't know what to do, maybe go into a shop until he had passed by. Unfortunately, for her it was too late he had already seen her and started to smile. He flashed that gorgeous smile that he always had when he saw her in the hotel, true to form she blushed as he drew closer, she thought she would faint. Her heart was beating so fast her legs were shaking, she did her best to look relaxed, and she smiled back at him. He stopped directly in front of her, stopping her from saying hello and quickly walking on. Another pearly white smile, and he said, "You look gorgeous in your summer dress, I'm not saying you don't look gorgeous in your uniform, you always look beautiful."

She blushed even more if that was possible, she was looking into those beautiful blue eyes of his. Trying to concentrate and not stammer, she replied, "Well, thank you, kind sir. How has your day been?"

He smiled again and said, "Very good, thank you, but all the better for seeing you. I've just closed a big deal, and I want to celebrate, but I don't know anybody in Odessa to celebrate with. What about you, will you celebrate with me? Please say yes."

She opened her mouth to speak, but nothing came out, Andrei took that as a yes, he laughed and said, "Excellent, thank you, are you okay, not too hot, your face is very red?" his teasing just made her blush even more. He took her arm and led her to a table under the canopy of the coffee shop they were stood in front of. The gentle touch on her arm, was like an electric shock that surged through her body. She had never felt that way before, his touch was so innocent yet it made her go weak at the knees.

He sat her down at an empty table and said, "Let's sit here, and I'll order us two coffees; is a latte okay?" She nodded and smiled at him across the table, two women walking past and gave him an admiring glance has they passed the table. He said, he couldn't see the waitress and got up and disappeared inside the shop. Yulia quickly opened her handbag and took out her compact, touching up her face, she checked her hair and tided her ponytail.

She looked inside, he was paying for the coffees, and she told herself to stay calm and not say or do anything silly that will make him think you're mad. But she knew from that touch that her principles had all vanished, she wouldn't be able to resist him, and her stomach was turning over and over.

In a strange way it calmed her nervousness, knowing what was going to happen later that evening. She blushed, smiling to herself at the thoughts she was having, she wondered what his body was like, imagining him on top of her. His voice ended her day dream, "Here you are one latte. Sorry for the delay."

She looked at him across the small pavement table and smiling said, "Thank you, so what are we celebrating?"

He threw his head back and laughed loudly. "This isn't the celebration; this is a getting to know you chat. We will celebrate later; we'll go to the best restaurant and drink champagne and really celebrate. That's okay, yes? You haven't got to be anywhere have you or meet anyone, like a boyfriend?"

She thought his smile was irresistible, she heard herself replying, "No, no plans at all, no boyfriend either." She blushed again; she didn't mean to be so straight forward.

He laughed loudly again and replied, "That's excellent news, there's no one I would rather celebrate with than you!" She smiled broadly had a sip of her coffee and asked him again what he was celebrating.

He told her about his life, he was an only child, his mother had died when he was in his early teens, and he still missed her. He explained that the company he was working for belonged to his father. He was learning all about it, so one day he would take over the business when his dad retired. His father bought a gas and Oil company from the government following the political reforms in the Soviet bloc in 1989. His father had been a high ranking official in St Petersburg's government. This, he told her was one of the reasons his dad was allowed to buy the company, that and of course the big bribes over the following years. She was shocked at his candidness, she told him she didn't think he should be telling her, a virtual stranger these dangerous things. He just laughed and said, he didn't care because it was all true, the government thrived on corrupt deals. He said, they were celebrating because he had met some people from the Donbas region. They owned an Engineering company, and he had done an excellent deal with them for equipment for the family business back in St Petersburg. Later, he had met with another business group and bought a forty-five per cent stake in their company. He went on to explain that with coal being Donetsk's dominant industry; it was the centre of the iron and steel industry which was in the Donetsk metallurgical plant. The Donbas was rich in hard coal particularly anthracites, rock salt, lignite, marl, limestone, mercury and various ores. He and his father had been buying stakes in the companies over the past five years. Later they would eventually sell the coal and Oil business back to the government for a huge profit. Their stakes and ownership of the companies in the Donbas region were illegal as so far as the Ukrainian government were concerned. The deals were all done in secrecy with payments to the present owners being paid into accounts in the Cayman Islands. What they didn't know was that in the future Russia would unlawfully annex the Crimea Peninsula from Ukraine. Andrei's father believed that in time Russia would move further in to the neighbouring Donbas region and also take that from Ukraine. The companies he was buying up now in the region would be worth millions under Russian rule.

She had never met anyone like him, he made his business deals sound so exciting and interesting, and her previous boyfriends had all been locals. He was different, so confident, so much passion for life and business, so carefree and above all in her eyes, so gorgeous looking. They went to the best restaurant in Odessa, she had said, she wasn't dressed for it and wanted to go home to change, but he wouldn't hear of it. He told her she looked beautiful, and he hadn't changed from his meetings that morning, but he said, it didn't matter, it was good to be impulsive.

The meal lasted long into the night, they talked endlessly about their lives, their goals, their hopes for the future. Yulia couldn't believe how easy he was to talk to; he was a very good listener. She was so relaxed and was telling him things that she wouldn't tell her friends, they just spilled out. She told him about Ivan being in prison for getting in with local a gang, he was sympathetic not judgemental. One thing she didn't tell him her father's hatred for Russians and all thing Russian, she didn't think that was a good idea. Also, he would never meet her parents so why did it matter. They had finished their

257

second coffee; he paid the bill and asked the waiter to arrange a taxi for them.

He asked Yulia where she lived, explaining to the driver the first drop was her house and then on to the hotel to drop him. Yulia was surprised he hadn't suggested they go back to his suite. She felt embarrassed because she had already decided that if he had asked, she would have said, yes. The taxi pulled up outside her parents' house, he followed her out and walked her to her front door. He asked her if she would like to go out for dinner with him again, adding that he didn't want to get her into trouble with the hotel management. She said, they could be discreet, and she would love to see him again. He placed his hand around her waist and pulled her towards him, he kissed her hard a long lingering kiss, and she melted into his body. She regretted, they hadn't gone back to his suite and spent the night together. She knew that the next time they met they would end up in bed, there was nothing more certain.

Chapter Thirty-Six
The Affair

The next six months were heaven, they met every time Andrei came to Odessa on business. He admitted sometimes he could have done the business over the telephone; but he wanted to come to see Yulia. They would speak every day when was in St Petersburg or elsewhere on business. She missed him terribly when he was away from her, and he said the same. Later that year, Andrei bought an apartment in the north of the city close to the harbour. It was near the Potemkin Steps; the giant stairway was the formal entrance that led from the port into the city. The love nest was on the top floor of an eight-story building with a balcony with stunning views that looked out over the harbour. Even when Andrei wasn't in Odessa, Yulia would go there and tidy up and water the plants. It was their secret and their escape from the outside world. She had told her mother about Andrei and their apartment. Mum Ionna was shocked at first and worried Yulia's dad would find out about the Russian boyfriend. Eventually she would go the apartment with Yulia, and they would sometimes have lunch there after going shopping while her dad was at work. One thing Ionna wouldn't do was met Andrei when he was back in the city. She told Yulia it was wrong to deceive her husband, but at least if it came out and asked her if she had met him, she could honestly say no! Yulia understood, she didn't want to cause a problem for her mother.

Ivan was released from prison, his father wouldn't allow him in the house, and Andrei agreed he could stay at the apartment when they weren't using it. Mum Ionna was making arrangements to get Ivan out of Odessa to live with his Uncle Boris and Aunt Anastassia in Luhansk and work in his shop. She was worried about him getting into trouble and going back to prison, but this time it would be for longer. He was happy to go, he remembered his uncle and aunt, and they were nice people. One thing was for sure he didn't want to go back to prison, also he felt there was nothing for him in Odessa. Three weeks later his mum and sister kissed Ivan goodbye at the railway station, he was on his way to a new life in Luhansk much to the relief of his doting mother. He had met Andrei the week before he left, he had gone for dinner with him and Yulia. He could see how in love they were, especially Yulia, he was happy for his big sister and delighted her by telling her he liked Andrei.

Unfortunately, Yulia's dad found out about her Russian boyfriend, a waiter who knew her saw them in a restaurant and told his parents, his father worked at the docks with Olek. There was big fight and Yulia ran out of the family home in tears when her father called her a Russian prostitute. She went to the apartment, the next day she collected all her belongings when her dad was at work.

Her mother was heartbroken, she told Yulia that her dad said, she must never go back to the family home again. Ionna had now lost both her children, the only two people in her life that she truly loved. She was now left alone in a loveless marriage with a man who was like a stranger to her. Yulia begged her mum to leave him, telling her she could live with her until they found her somewhere to live.

She wouldn't, she said a wife's place was next to her husband and to provide a home for him, even if there wasn't any love. When Yulia told Andrei, he offered to speak to her father and explain that he loved his daughter, but Yulia said, it wouldn't do any good. Andrei told her he would be in Odessa the next morning, he would come directly to the apartment, and it was Yulia's day off work.

She was excited to see Adrei and was thrilled he said, he would come straight away; it had been a horrible couple of days. With Ivan leaving the city and then the big fight at home with her father and the horrible things he shouted at her. She had made a big effort to look good for Andre, she had full make-up on and wore her favourite dress, the one that he loved, and she wanted to look nice for when he arrived.

The apartment was neat and tidy with flowers on the dining table and on the coffee table in the lounge, and she had his favourite red wine with beers chilling in the fridge. He arrived at the apartment just after ten thirty, she ran into the hall and threw herself into his arms and burst into tears. He gently led her back into the lounge and sat her down on his knee, telling her everything would be okay, he would

261

look after her now. She felt safe in his arms and told him about the problem with her father and about him not liking Russians. He said, it was fine, he understood her father's feeling towards Russia, adding that they hadn't actually endeared themselves to the Ukrainians over the years. He showered, and they spent the rest of the afternoon in bed, making love. The heartache of the last few days washed away now she was in Andrei's arms once again; he was worth the trouble as far has she was concerned.

Two months later Andrei proposed and three months afterwards they were married in St Petersburg. She adored her new father-in-law Artyom, from the very first time she met him. When Andrei told him they were going to get married, he cried and hugged her so tight, she thought she was going to faint. He wiped his eyes and told her he had always wanted a daughter and now he was finally going to get his wish. Yulia cried at his lovely sentiment, her father never showed her any love, even as a little girl. Yulias mother said, she couldn't come to the wedding; her father wouldn't allow her to, he wouldn't even let her speak to him about her or Ivan.

Her "new father" proudly walked her down the aisle to give her away. It was a spectacular wedding, with lots of important Russian people there who she didn't know, she had never seen so many bodyguards before in her life. She was so happy, but also shed a tear, she would have given anything to have her mum and brother sat there on the front row of the beautiful old church smiling up at her. She liked Russia and all of Andrei's friends, though it wasn't lost on her that she was living the privileged life. There was a lot of poverty in Russia and despite the harsh government, most people were simple, honest, and kind. They lived in Andrei's father house in St Petersburg, it was like a palace, and there was plenty of room to have their privacy when they wanted it. She loved cooking on the cook's night off and would invite Artyom to join them. He enjoyed her home cooking, and they had some wonderful family evenings after dinner, with Artyom telling Yulia all about his childhood and family history.

There was also a ten-bedroom apartment in Moscow again stunning and filled with expensive antiques. They would go to Moscow usually about once every three weeks to see friends and go to the Ballet. They still owned the apartment in Odessa for when Yulia wanted to go home and see her mother. Her mum had a key and would make sure everything was okay, she enjoyed being in the apartment she felt close to her daughter in there. Yulia would send money to the apartment for her mum, that way her father didn't know about it, and it couldn't cause trouble. Ionna led a simple life she never wanted for much; she opened a bank account to save the generous amounts of money from Yulia. She would send money every month to Luhansk to Ivan her son, she didn't know that Yulia was also sending him money each month. What with the money from his mum and big sister and his wages for working in his Uncle Ivan's shop Ivan was building a nice nest egg in his bank account.

Chapter Thirty-Seven
The Children

Andrei had taken over the family business, his father Artyom had retired and was enjoying a carefree life. He had bought himself a huge ocean-going yacht, a retirement gift to himself, he would tell everyone. He enjoyed travelling around the world on it and spent a lot of time in the Caribbean, Yulia missed him not being around. Andrei would take August off, and they spend a few weeks on the Yacht with Artyom either in the South of France or the Bahamas. Then they would then have a few weeks holidaying by themselves, somewhere exotic. Yulia's father had died the previous year from a heart attack, she had gone to the funeral with Andrei, it was the first time her mum and husband had met. They got on famously, and her mum said, she had found a good man and not to ever let him go. Brother Ivan didn't come back from the Donbas for the funeral, he had told his mum it would be hypocritical. He said, his father didn't like him, and he certainly didn't like his father. Despite Yulia begging him to come for his mum's sake he refused, she understood, but like her mum she still thought it was their family duty to attend and pay their respects.

Her mum promised to visit them in Russia to see their wonderful homes, but never made it. She died six months after her husband, in a hit and run accident on her way home from work one winters evening. Yulia was heartbroken. Now that her mum was finally free from the restraints of her loveless marriage. She wanted her mum to experience the fabulous lifestyle she had, she wanted to spoil her mum. Take her with them on the family holidays to exotic places she had only read about in magazines. It was not to be and the missed opportunities were gone through a cruel twist of fate, so unfair, after the hard life her mum had in Odessa. After the funeral she cried and hugged Ivan, she said, he was all the family she had left now. Ivan promised her he would be there for her whenever she ever needed him, all she had to do was whistle, and he would be there by her side. He would say that when they were children, and it always made her laugh, but this time he promised he meant it. When Adrei shook Ivans hand and began speaking with him, Yulia noticed a little resistance and coldness from Ivan. He answered Andrei's questions with a one word reply and never made eye contact. Yulia never got the chance to ask him what was wrong, she assumed he was upset about the nature of their mum's sudden death.

Yulia's good life continued in St Petersburg, with Andrei working harder than ever. He was trying to negotiate a deal with the Government to buy the families Oil and Gas Company. He told Yulia if that happened, they would be wealthy beyond their wildest dreams, and he would retire like his father. She was pleased for him, but how much money did they need or want? They were rich already and had a fabulous life. A few weeks later she had some important news for Andrei, she cooked a wonderful meal for them both, she had let the cook go after Artyom retired, she did all the cooking herself. After the Lobster she poured him a glass of his favourite brandy, they went and sat in the lounge, and she told him she was pregnant. He was absolutely delighted and only stopped hugging and kissing Yulia because he wanted to phone his father to tell him he was going to be a papa.

Artyom insisted on speaking to Yulia and between sobs he told her she had made him the happiest man in the world. He was so emotional that he made Yulia cry too, she put Andrei back on the phone and dabbed her eyes dry. They talked long into the night about the baby, what the sex would be, how great holidays would be, schooling. Yulia fell silent and Andrei knew what she was thinking, he pulled her lose to him and said, "Your mum will know you are having this child, and she is probably with him or her in heaven right now telling it what a wonderful mother it is going to have."

His lovely words started Yulia crying again, he tried to lift her mood. He laughed. "What a weepy family I have, you are her crying, my father is somewhere in the Caribbean crying. This is a happy time and all you two can do is cry!"

It worked. She burst out laughing and wiping her eyes said, "It is a happy time, I've known for a little while, but

I didn't want to say anything until Dr Vinogradov confirmed everything was good this morning."

Daughter Zoya was born the following summer on 30 July, she was beautiful and reminded Yulia of her mum, with her black hair and full lips. Andrei was besotted with her and has she grew she could she could twist him around her little finger, she was every bit a daddy's girl. She was four when her little brother Mykola put in an appearance, she was very jealous of him at first. She would often ask her mum and dad, "When is that baby going back to where he came from?" They had a very privileged life; Andrei had sold the company to the state, but part of the deal was he had to take up a post in Moscow with the government. Yulia didn't know what it was all about, she never got involved with his business life. They went from rich to super rich, they had homes around the world. Zoya went to school in Switzerland and didn't have an accent, her English like her mum and brother was perfect. They had a home in Switzerland where Yulia stayed so Zoya could come home at weekends from school. Mykola went to boarding school in St Petersburg the same strict school that his father and papa attended, Andrei never said anything to Yulia, but he didn't want his son to be too westernised like his big sister, he wanted him to be foremost Russian. The family spent a lot of time in the apartment in Moscow with Andrei's meetings with government officials. They had full time staff, a butler, a maid, and a top chef. Andrei said Yulia had to stop cooking and serving meals they had staff to do that. Andrei said, it didn't look right when colleagues visited on business or came over for dinner. She concurred, but enjoyed nothing more than cooking for the children, when Andrei was away on business Yulia wasn't tied to Moscow and would spend family time with the children at their homes in Switzerland, and the South of France in the summer. She spent less time with Andrei, he always appeared to have a business excuse for not joining them. The only exception being the summer holiday on his father's yacht. She felt like they were growing apart, and it troubled her, she was worried her marriage would turn into her parents' loveless marriage. He still worked long hours despite his supposedly retirement, she couldn't complain too much, it provided her and the children with a fabulous lifestyle.

Mykola and Zoya would go with their mum to visit their uncle Ivan in Luhansk, Mykola was sixteen and Zoya nineteen. Before the first visit their mum told them to never tell anyone in Luhansk that they were Russian, but just to say they were from Odessa. They found it strange considering a lot of the people in Luhansk were Russian. At first, they didn't really know Uncle Ivan, apart from the fact he was their mum's younger brother. But they were soon in awe of this popular tall dark haired tough man who was related to them, they had never met anyone like him before. They loved visiting Uncle Ivan he was such good fun, when their mum left them with him when she went to Odessa on business. He would take them deep into the forest camping while their mum was away. He swore them to secrecy never to tell their parents, he would take rifles and taught them to shoot and hunt. Because of the privileged lives they led, big homes, servants, a private jet, holidays on Grandpa's yacht this was a whole new experience, a completely different life, they loved it.

They loved living in the forest and hunting so exciting even if it was only for a few days at a time, they never wanted it to end. They would make a camp fire and after dinner Uncle Ivan drank whisky from the bottle while he told them stories about fighting the Russian gangs in the Donbas. Also, now the Russian gangs were trying to take over the Donbas and their government in Moscow was supplying the gangs with guns and money.

Everywhere they went people knew their uncle Ivan, he was very popular, he took them everywhere with him. They also loved staying with great Uncle Boris and great Aunt Anastasia, where Uncle Ivan lived. It was a very small house to what they were used to, but it was what their mum told them real life, real people. When they were out with the town with Uncle Ivan, he would put his arms around Zoya and Mykola and introduce them as his family. Being his family made them very popular with all his friends in Luhansk. Mykola worshipped Ivan, one night during family dinner he asked if he could go to see Uncle Ivan in the summer holidays. His father refused telling him he and Zoya shouldn't be spending too much time with those peasants in the Donbas. There mum protested saying those people were her family, it started a row, which ended with their mum in tears.

Zoya became involved and told her father she loved her mum's family; they weren't peasants, but good honest people. Her father's response was that they weren't to go to Luhansk again and that was to be the end of it. Mykola argued with his father, he said, they loved staying at his great aunt and uncle's home with Uncle Ivan. He then asked his father was he banning them because of the Russian gangs who were being bankrolled by the Government here in Moscow to cause unrest in the Donbas. His father was horrified at such talk, he demanded to where Mykola had heard such lies, despite having a good idea who had told him. Mykola shouted back his Uncle Ivan had told them all about how evil Russia had been to Ukraine, and how his people were going to stop them. Yulia and Zoya stood there in shock as the argument became violent and Andrei punched Mykola to the floor and started kicking him. The screams and tears from the women and finally Yulias intervention stopped the fight. Andrei turned on Yulia, shouting this was her peasant families doing, filling their sons head full of lies. They helped Mykola up from the floor and took him upstairs, his father shouting threats after Mykola from the doorway of the lounge. Mykola shouting back anti- Russian taunts has he was being helped up the stairs, despite his mother pleading with him to be silent. Later that evening, they heard their father and mum having a loud conversation. It was about Uncle Ivan, and Mykola's behaviour was because of going to the Donbas to see her family. Zoya and Mykola were both listening on the upstairs landing,

Mykola wanted to go downstairs and confront his father again, but Zoya stopped him.

Yulia was shocked and upset at what she had witnessed, she told Andrei, "I've never seen you behave like that before; I feel as if I don't know you any more. He is your son Andrei; how could you attack your own flesh and blood like that. Is all this because of your involvement here with your government friends? Andrei, we have everything we could ever wish for, good health, wealth, privileges, also two beautiful children, is all this now not enough, why is that, why have you changed?"

Andrei sat silently in his high-backed dining chair with a half tumbler full of his finest scotch whisky in his still shaking hand. Looking at Yulia, he replied, "I'm so sorry; we do have everything like you say, because of my father's sacrifices over the years. But all those things, the wealth, and privileges we enjoy – come with conditions. Don't you realise that, it is the way of Russia, my country? We must be grateful for that and always show our allegiance to Rodina *(the Motherland)*. Because if not, we would be in great danger, our lifestyle is at the whim of the powers that be. If the blood connection between you and your brother and his activities in the Donbas were to ever come to light here."

"Well, we could all be killed; we would be classed as traitors, even though we haven't done anything wrong, but because of your brother. If that did happen, there wouldn't be nowhere to hide in the world. No matter how great our wealth, they would track us down and deal with us all of us. Surely you must be able to see and understand that, Mykola repeating his uncle's mad rants out loud are very dangerous. He must never repeat them here in Moscow what he said about Ukraine tonight, or anywhere else for that matter. Do you understand, my darling? Also, I must forbid you and the children from ever visiting your brother again this is for all our safety." The conversation ended with Yulia excepting about the dangers that Andrei had explained. She asked him to go and apologise to Mykola for attacking him and not to be harsh with him for repeating what Ivan had told him.

The next weekend Zoya asked her mum if they could go to their home in Switzerland, she didn't want to stay at the apartment in Moscow. The fight had really upset her, she was still shocked seeing her father behave the way he had. Also, with Mykola being a hot head like Uncle Ivan, she didn't trust him not to argue his father again. Her mother had also realised that son Mykola was becoming like her brother. She agreed it would be good to put some space between him and his father for a while and hopefully let things cool off.

When Yulia spoke to Andrei about them spending time in Switzerland, he said, "Fine, stay there for a while, and it's probably better. Mykola doesn't stay here in Moscow with his treacherous opinions. Besides, he hasn't spoken to me since the incident last week; he just scowls or ignores me if I speak with him. I will be busy for the next few weeks, so a break might be good for all of us."

Yulia nodded in agreement and replied, "I think it would be best, like you say, why don't you try and apologies again to Mykola before we leave? It will be good to heal the wounds between the two of you rather than letting it fester in our absence. Andrei smiled and nodded and promised he would try and apologise again, but Mykola must never repeat what he said the evening of the fight."

Yulia tenderly kissed her husband on the forehead and left the room knowing that she would to speak to Mykola beforehand. She had to convince him, to accept his father's apology and to agree to keep his thoughts on the Ukraine to himself.

She smiled, thinking it shouldn't be too difficult to convince him, when we're at the Chalet in Zurich, we can secretly go and visit Ivan in Luhansk. After all, he was her brother and her only family now, in a conversation with Zoya about spending time in Zurich, she had mentioned that with her father working in Moscow, he wouldn't know if they did visit Uncle Ivan. Her mum added, that they would have to make the visit on a commercial flight, they wouldn't be able to use the private jet because it would show on the flight log and Andrei always signs it off. Hopefully that would keep the peace between Mykola and his father, after that terrible night.

Chapter Thirty-Eight
Young Ivan – The Early Days

His Mother and sister Yulia saw Ivan off at the train station heading for Luhansk to live with his Uncle Boris and Aunt Anastasia following his release from the young offender's prison. The plan was for him to work in Uncle Boris's tailor shop and learn the trade. She knew this all his father's doing, he wanted Ivan out of Odessa and out of their family's life. His mum and sister were in floods of tears at the station waiting with him for the train, they promised they would come and visit him soon. There was no mention of his dad who he hadn't seen since being released from prison. The journey wasn't too bad, it was under two hours from Odessa, and his Uncle Boris was waiting for him on the platform. He hugged Ivan and took his worn old case, they walked to his car parked outside the station, he looked older than Ivan remembered. But they were only young when he and Yulia would visit during in the summer holidays. Boris was his mum's older brother by eight years, and he had done well for himself. Uncle Boris had thick dark brown hair with grey at the sides and now sprouting out all over, even in his big bushy highbrows. His ruddy complexion, was a result from drinking too much wine, Ivan remembered him being drunk most evenings when they visited. Uncle Boris was also shorter than Ivan remembered, he had a slight build with little narrow shoulders, and Ivan was a good foot taller than his uncle now.

Uncle Boris looked across at Ivan, smiled broadly and said, "You've grown since I last saw you, boy, but it has been a good few years ago since you were last here. Your mum was very upset that you got into trouble. She asked us to take you in, so you wouldn't end up back in prison. You must behave here Ivan; your aunt Anastasia and I are responsible for you now. Promise me you will behave yourself here."

Ivan looked at his uncle's troubled face. He had forgotten that he never used his name but had always called him boy, Ivan replied, "Don't worry, Uncle, I won't cause you any problems, and I don't want my mum to be upset because of me, she's had enough heartache being married to my dad."

Boris let out a big sigh, he slowly shook his head from side to side and said, "I know, boy, they should never have got married, and your mum was a real looker and had lots of young men chasing her when she was single. I always thought she felt sorry for your father, but I told her that wasn't a reason to get married, but she wouldn't listen." They did the rest of the journey in silence, Ivan looked out on the city as they drove through, and it was busy with people on their lunch break from work. Uncle Boris lived about five miles outside of the city limits in a semi-rural area. From what Ivan could remember it was a pretty house, in a nice suburb. It had a large back garden; the house was more like a cottage with white washed walls. When they pulled up on the short drive, it was just how Ivan had remembered it only a little tired now. Before they the car stopped aunt Anastasia came running down the path, wiping her hands on her apron, she came around to Ivan's side of the car and opened the door for him.

She gave him the biggest hug and kissed him on both cheeks before stepping back and said, "Now let me look at you, my darling; how you have grown and so handsome with it. You will be a big hit with the local girls, Ivan." She was just how Ivan had remembered her, only obviously older, but still very attractive. She had a gorgeous smile, her blond hair tied up in a bun, medium height, a full figure and a bigger bust than Ivan remembered. She put her arm around Ivan's waist and walked him back up the path into the house. As she always did when they were kids, she took him straight through into the kitchen, sat him down at the table and asked him what did he want to eat.

The kitchen hadn't changed, it was how he had remembered it, smelling of baking, it was a lovey homely warm smell that filled the room and had always made Ivan feel quite hungry. Uncle Boris walked in and said, "She's been baking your favourite cake and cookies for two days now, Ivan, she still thinks you're twelve years old. You'll be fat inside a month, mark my words, you will."

Aunty shushed Boris, "Hush you, go and take Ivan's case up to his bedroom and be off back to the shop."

Wiping her hands again on her apron, she turned to Ivan and said, "Now, my darling, how about a cup of coffee and some cookies?"

Feeling at home, Ivan smiled broadly and replied, "Aunty, I would love nothing more, and I must say you look gorgeous, even more than I remembered."

His aunt threw her head back, let out a loud laugh and said, "My God, a good-looking boy and a smooth talker to boot, the local girls are going to absolutely love you!"

After a couple of coffees and a few too many cookies, Ivan went up to his bedroom to unpack and change. Upstairs there were three good sized bedrooms and two bathrooms. Ivan's room was at the back of the house with a large window looking out over the garden, with fields and hills off in the distance. The Donbas was a heavy industrial region, but still had some beautiful countryside. The bedroom was a bright room with a double bed, chintzy duvet, and matching curtains, very country cottage-like. The family bathroom was across the landing, a big bath with a separate shower cubicle. This was to be his new home until he was old enough to live where he wanted to, he smiled and thought I could have done a lot worse. In the meantime, he was sure he was going to like it her living with his aunt and uncle. His uncle was a good man who just wanted his business to do well and live a quiet life. Aunt Anastasia, loved her home, she had everything she ever needed or wanted, except for a child that she could love. Now she had Ivan, who would live with them, she could love and would spoil him, just like she would have done with her own son. If God would have blessed them with children, they would have been the best parents ever. Ivan was relaxed about being exiled with his aunt and uncle, after all there were worse places, and all he missed was his mum and sister Yulia. Even after only a few hours he had settled in to his new home, his aunt gave it a loving, happy atmosphere. Not like in Odessa, where his father had always cast a long shadow over their home. When he was out working or drinking with his friends it was good happy place. His mum and sister laughing and happy together it was different, but when his dad came home it all changed. His mum always made excuses for him saying it was his upbringing, but Ivan and his sister could never understand his total lack of emotion or interest in them. Lying on the bed looking up at the ceiling with his hands behind his head, he thought, *Yes, I'm going to like it here, what with aunt Anastasia spoiling me terribly and all the new girls in town to meet, it's going to be good.*

Chapter Thirty-Nine
Three Years On

Ivan and Fedir lay in the wet grass, Kalashnikov rifles in their hands, ready they waited for the signal the truck was near. Ivan looked beyond the large fractured tree stump across the road blocking the way through the forest. On the opposite side he could just make out the blacked out faces of Taras and Marko. They were all waiting for a call on the mobile from Lyaksandro to warn them their prey was nearby. Ivan's racing heart was beating so fast and loud he thought it would give away their position, his mouth was bone dry. He licked his lips and swallowed hard, but it didn't help, the silence was deafening. Everything was so still and quiet, not even a sound from any of the many animals that lived in the forest. It was as if they knew that danger and death was close by, so silent, not one single noise except for the beating of Ivan's heart. A clearing appeared in the clouds; Ivan looked up as a bright ray suddenly appeared from the full moon. It shone down through a gap in the dense trees, lighting up a circle on the road like a spotlight on a stage. He wondered if it would cause a problem with the truck, thinking that the light might spook them, but the moonbeam disappeared as quickly as it came and the "spotlight" went out.

The silent vibration and light from Fedir's mobile startled Ivan and made his heart beat even faster, Fedir whispered, "Okay" and hung up. He nodded to Ivan and said, "This is it, get ready, they are here." He waved over to Tara and Marko, who responded with a quick return wave, guns at the ready they waited in silence. They heard the rumble of the truck in the distance, Ivan swallowed hard as the noise from the diesel engine grew closer and louder. After what appeared to be an eternity the truck finally came in to view, its headlights lighting up the forest, the four pressed their bodies deeper in to the wet undergrowth. They heard the squeal of the brakes as the truck stopped a few metres from the huge tree stump blocking the road. They could hear a muffled conversation from inside the cab, they waited poised, ready to strike, and they had rehearsed over and over what to do next. The passenger door of the truck opened and a man in a flat cap and black leather jacket climbed out, looking around in all directions, gingerly he walked towards the tree trunk, still looking to his left and right, he stopped at the stump after studying it for what appeared like a lifetime. He stared to the forest again, turning around he shouted that he would need help to move it. Two men jumped out from the back and walked up to help; Ivan could just about make out Lyaksandro appear from the shadows around the back of the truck on the driver's side. He slowly started to make his way up the towards the driver's window. Ivan's hand was sweating so much he had trouble holding his Kalashnikov. "This is it," he said to himself any second.

Lyaksandro shouted at the same time he fired his revolver through the side window of the truck killing the driver. The three men in the road were startled by the shout spun around to the direction of the shot. Has they started to crouch; the bullets flew from both sides of the road cutting them down. It was over in a matter of seconds, a deafening noise then, and the eerie silence again, with just the smell from the Kalashnikov's. At first nobody moved, then Ivan and the other three men slowly immerged from their hiding places onto the edge of the road, rifles still pointed at the three bodies lying in front of the stump.

Lyaksandro had walked down from the truck to join his men, he turned and shot one of the men who was groaning twice in the chest, his body heaved from the bullets, the groans stopped. He looked up to his colleagues and said, "Well done, quickly now, let's move the stump and get to the barn. We need to unload the weapons and store them, and destroy the drugs. Move the bodies off the road so we can pass, after all, we are not animals."

Ivan never spoke on the journey back to the barn the cargo guns and drugs had just come across the border from Russia for the gangs in Luhansk. He felt sick, his hands shook, he had just killed a man, and he aimed and shot him down dead, all in a matter of seconds. Did the man have a family back in Russia, that were waiting to have breakfast with him in the morning when he returned from work? Yes, they were the enemy, and they were in his country, but at this moment in time he felt ill that he had taken a life. Lyaksandro sat next to Ivan was driving the truck, he looked across at the young man. A sideward glance, they made eye contact, he could read Ivan's mind, and he knew his thoughts. He gave Ivan a resigned smile and said, "Don't worry, it gets easier; the first kill is always the worse. We have all felt what you are feeling at this moment. You will be fine; do you have a girlfriend?"

Ivan shook his head. Lyaksandro smiled again and said, "Well, go out with your friends tonight and get steaming drunk; it will help, trust me, okay?"

Ivan nodded and gave a half smile and looked back out of the windscreen at the headlights lighting up the road back in Luhansk. He wondered what his mum and sister would think if they knew he was a killer, a patriotic killer, but still a killer none the less. Would they think any better of him because of that, if they knew he was fighting for the freedom of his Uncle Boris and Aunt Anastasia, he wasn't too sure they would. You had to live in Luhansk to know how oppressive and corrupt it was living under the LPR's rule, his family wouldn't understand.

Basically, living under corrupt Russian control in your own country, even when the region is still international regarded as Ukraine. Regarded, Internationally or not, counts for nothing in the Oblast, it is up to the Ukrainian people living here who struggle, to stand up for themselves, because nobody else in the world will. After the war the previous year in 2014, the government recognised its own military was too weak to fight off the pro- Russian separatists and relied on paramilitary volunteer forces in the region to fight. The forces were funded by wealthy patriotic Ukrainians, including the then governor of the Dnipropetrovska region. The forces grew and spread quickly throughout the region, forces such as Dnipro 1 and Dnipro 2, Aidar and Donbas units. They exist and fight because they are passionate and love their country. The LPR and Moscow despise them and spread lies that they are just Nazi and white supremacy thugs, but that is just propaganda, they are patriotic warriors.

Ivan put the guilty thoughts out of his head regarding his mum and sister, he knew he could justify to them his actions, and they would forgive him. Just has his Uncle Boris and Aunt Anastasia have done, they understand the fight and support him. He smiled at the thought of the relief on his aunt's face when he would come home from a mission. When he goes out at night she never asks where he is going nor when he will return. She knows, and she worries about him just like she would her own son. He loves her dearly, in the time he's been living with them, he had never felt more like part of a family, and he would do anything for them.

Chapter Forty
The Luhansk People's Republic

The Luhansk Peoples Republic a breakaway quasi-state within the territory of the Ukraine. The LPR claim the Luhansk Oblast in the Donbas region is Russian territory, after the invasion of 2014. They are Russian government backed, and turn a blind eye to the Russian separatist gang's evil money-making rackets like drugs, extortion, protection racketeering, Loan sharking. Prostitution, money laundering.

Ivan first became aware of them, after a month or so on Luhansk, he had heard talk of the Separatists from friends he had made. When they were out in a bar the friends would tell tall stories about things that the gang did. To Ivan it all sounded exaggerated nonsense, like stories you read about or see in the movies about the Italian Mafia in New York. However, one night he heard his uncle and aunt talking about how *"they"* had increased the monthly payments. His uncle said, there was nothing he could do, if he refused there would be trouble, he and the other businesses just had to go along with it. When Ivan walked in, they quickly changed the subject, he said, he couldn't help over hearing, but his uncle just laughed and said, "It's nothing for you to concern yourself with boy, don't worry about it, it's just business matters." His Aunt Anastasia looked upset and close to tears and that did concern him.

Ivan enjoyed working in his uncle's shop, at first the other staff were suspicious of him and were wary of speaking in front of him. However, once they got to know him, they realised that he was a genuinely nice young man. There wasn't any favouritism from his uncle, he started work at the bottom running errands, brewing up, sweeping the floor in the cutters room. He enjoyed the work, and he liked the people who worked for his uncle, he was enjoying his time living with his aunt and uncle and had become very fond of both of them. His mum and sister had come to visit one weekend; it was good to see them. They told him all the gossip and things that were happening in Odessa, but he wasn't that interested, he had settled down in Luhansk, and Odessa seemed like the distant past. They also said his father sent his regards, which he knew to be a lie, his father had probably already forgotten he had a son.

Ivan had made a friend who worked in the bakery next to his uncle's shop, his name was Fedir, he was learning to be a baker and his uncle was the owner. Fedir lived just across the Lugan River not too far out of town, he lived there with his mother and sister. His father had been killed when Russia invaded the Donbas region. Fedir was born and raised in Luhansk, he was seventeen the same age has Ivan, a tall skinny lad with an unruly shock of red hair and a face covered in freckles. Ivan and Fedir hit it off and became good friends; they slept over at each other's homes. Fedirs mum was a big jolly red-haired lady, with a

285

ruddy complexion. She was always smiling and couldn't do enough for her children; anyone could see she loved them dearly. She was a matron at the local hospital in the city, and worked additional shifts to earn extra money for the family. Fedirs sister Nyura made up the family of redheads, she was thirteen thin and tall like her brother. But with beautiful green eyes, also she appeared to have a teenage crush on Ivan. At the end of his shift each day, Fedir was allowed to take some home bread and pastries, he would call in at the tailors next door and give Ivan some to take home to his Aunt Anastasia.

The Speakeasy was a bar in town, an old-fashioned place, wooden floorboards, a long dark wooden bar and wrought iron stools and old cracked red leather seats. Dimly lit, the big green neon signs behind the bar advertising Budvar beer and a Donbas Vodka gave the place an eerie glow, but none the less very popular with the locals. The Landlord a fat man named Petruso, allowed the boys to drink in there on Friday nights providing they behaved themselves. They rule was they had to stay in the back room, not be loud and not get drunk, well not too drunk to annoy any of the regulars. It was Ivan, Fedir and their pals highlight of the week, it made them feel all grown up, like proper men.

The end of the bar was unofficially reserved for a group of local men, tough looking men. Rumour was that they were Dnipro 1, but nobody ever talked about them. One of the men, a really tough looking man, always wore a long black gabardine overcoat, he had short black hair.

A scar on his face, from his left ear down to his chin, dark eyes, and his nose had obviously been broken a few times, thick lips and dark stubble covering his square jaw. He looked like the leader when he spoke the rest of the men always stopped talking and paid attention. Fedir appeared to know things about the tough guy, he had told Ivan that his uncle the baker knew him, his name was Lyaksandro. One night when he was sleeping over at Fedirs s uncle's place on Friday night he was drunk and told Ivan what his uncle had told him.

Fedirs uncle said the big man, Lyaksandro lived alone on the edge of town. Word, was he had left the SBU which is a national law enforcement force and also the government's main security agency. He had left the agency with the governments blessing to form a vigilante group to fight the Russians in the Oblast. Ivan was fascinated hearing about the groups fighting the Russians, he had heard talk, but thought it was all urban legend. He wanted to know more, he asked Fedir, "Did he form a group?"

Fedir replied, "What I am about to tell you, you must never repeat; otherwise, my uncle could be in grave danger, okay?" Ivan nodded, eager to hear more.

Fedir continued, "My uncle told me Lyaksandro is in overall charge of the groups Dnipro 1 and Dnipro 2, the Russian gangs are afraid of both these gorilla fighting forces. Their reputation is legendary throughout Ukraine not just in the Oblast, also they hold no fear of Moscow." Ivan told Fedir that he had heard his uncle speak of Dnipro once outside his shop in a hushed tone to one of his customers. But when Ivan approached them, they stopped talking. Ivan laughed when he heard Fedirs snores he had fallen asleep and didn't hear a word Ivan had said. Ivan hadn't had has much drink has Fedir, he was wide awake after what he had been told. He lay in bed looking up at the ceiling and thought, *God I love living here, you wouldn't get exciting stuff like this in Odessa.*

One Monday lunchtime, Ivan and Fedir were walking back from the café down the street where they had been for lunch. They were making arrangements to go fishing when Ivan saw his uncle stood outside the shop speaking with a tall skinny man. His uncle handed the man an envelope then went back inside. The man turned and walking towards them; Ivan interrupted Fedir, "Do you know this skinny guy coming towards us?"

Fedir looked and replied, "Yes, I've seen him around, the cocky bastard," as he approached them.

Ivan said, "My uncle gave him something."

Fedir replied, "It will be the monthly protection money; he's in the Russian gang that run the rackets!" Ivan's blood was angry, he was certain this was what his uncle was discussing the other week, when his aunt was upset. The skinny guy was close now, he had really bad skin, Ivan said, "Look down, don't let him see your face."

Fedir replied, "What?"

Ivan said, "Look away." Skinny swaggered past them and turned right into a side street.

Ivan pulled Fedirs arm and said, "Come on." The street was quiet only Skinny was walking down there towards a parked car.

Ivan quickened his pace and seized the moment, right behind Skinny now, he said loudly, "Hey!" Has Skinny turned, Ivan punched him hard in the jaw, he collapsed unconscious in a heap on the ground. Ivan quickly knelt down and took all the envelopes from skinny's pocket. Turning to a mesmerised Fedir who was stood watching with his mouth open in total shock at what had just happened.

Ivan said, "Come on, run." He ran back up the street in the direction of the shops. At the corner Ivan turned and looked down the street, Skinny was still lay there on the deserted street, nobody had seen what Ivan did. They ran around the corner onto the main street, both burst out laughing and were panting heavily.

Ivan slapped Fedir on the back and said, "Okay, just walk slowly now; we don't want to draw attention to ourselves."

Fedir slowed and walked alongside Ivan, catching his breath, he said, "I don't believe that; what a punch. I don't think he even saw who it was that hit him. Why the fuck did you do that? You do know it will cause problems now with the Russian gangs."

Ivan looked at Fedir, who was sweating a little, winked and said, "Do you know what you need to worry about – getting fit, fatty? Go back to work, don't say a word to anyone, we'll meet up after work at our spot on the river; oh, and don't forget to bring your fishing rod."

Fedir was right, the mugging did cause problems, and the Russian gang members were out in town in force asking questions, threatening people. They didn't get any information because nobody witnessed anything, which just pissed them off even more. Also, none of the shop owners mentioned to the Russians that the following morning their cash envelopes had been returned to them, pushed under the door of their shops. The mugging was the talk of the town, even his uncle and aunt were talking about it over dinner the following evening. Ivan waited for a lull in the conversation, he took the envelope from his pocket, the shop name written in the top corner, and he placed it on the table in front of them, without saying a word.

The look of shock and horror on their faces made Ivan smile, his uncle looked up at Ivan and said, "My God, it was you!" His Aunt Anastasias burst into tears and made the sign of the cross on her chest. She said between sobs that Ivan was going to get into trouble, he gently squeezed her hand and assured her that he was going to be fine. He explained to both of them that Skinny couldn't recognise him, also nobody apart from Fedir saw the mugging. His uncle said, he was brave, but foolish he shouldn't have got involved. He said, he would speak to people he knew to help Ivan and Fedir, when Ivan asked who they were, his uncle wouldn't be drawn on the matter, he made Ivan promise he wouldn't tell a soul what he had done. Ivan said, he wouldn't and had also made Fedir promise not to speak or brag about what he had done.

Ivan came home on Thursday evening with Fedir, Aunt Anastasia had been invited him around for a meal with them. They were in the kitchen washing up after dinner, as a thank you to Ivan's aunt. They hadn't heard the knock at the front door, they could hear a muffled conversation going on in the hall. Ivan went to hand Fedir a plate to dry, but he was stood staring across the kitchen, Ivan looked over his shoulder at what Fedir was mesmerised by. At the kitchen door stood his uncle with Lyaksandro, they both stood and stared at the big man in awe. Their hero, the legend, the man who the boys and their friends had talked about and worshipped from afar for ages. He was even wearing his long black coat that they had seen him in at the bar. In his aunt's kitchen the man looked even bigger and meaner. Ivan's uncle introduced him to the boys, but it hadn't been necessary, they knew who he was. He shook hands with both of them, a strong firm handshake, he told them to sit down. Uncle Boris told them both he had asked Lyaksandro and his people to protect them after the mugging of Skinny. Lyaksandro asked Ivan why he had mugged skinny. He added it was a dangerous thing to do, and could end up with the Russians killing him has an example. Ivan said, he wasn't afraid of the Russians, and it was wrong what they were doing in his country. He saw a slight smile cross Lyaksandro's lips so he continued. He added that he would do it again, when he got the chance and also, he and his friends were planning to attack the Russians selling drugs. Which was utter bullshit, they had never discussed anything of the sort.

Fedir jumped on the bandwagon reaffirming what Ivan had said, and asked, if Lyaksandro could get them guns adding that they were prepared to pay for them. The big man raised his hand to stop Fedir continuing, he looked over at Uncle Boris and smiled, he said, "It looks like you've got more trouble than you first thought, Boris; we've got a couple of wolves here pulling at their leases to be let loose." He told the boys they couldn't do any such thing, but he admired their spirit and patriotism. He added that he could help if they were genuine about driving the Russians out of the Donbas, both boys enthusiastically nodded their heads.

The big man spoke at great length about the fight against the LPR and the Russian gangs also about how they were backed and armed by Moscow. He asked them if they were genuine about loving their country and being prepared to fight for its freedom, they both said they were. Uncle Boris told Fedir not to mention to his family about what had been said tonight here in the kitchen, also that Ivan wasn't to speak about this in front his aunt. They following month evenings and weekends were taken up being taught how to shoot a variety of weapons, and how to fight including killing moves. The two young men were captivated by the local fighters who were teaching them battle skills. They enjoyed every minute of the strenuous training, they felt like they belonged and knew all their new comrades had their backs. That night in the forest, the ambush and their first kill affected Ivan more so than Fedir who justified what happened with. "Well, they shouldn't be in our fucking country, should they? It serves them right; they deserve everything they get."

Chapter Forty-One
Present Day-Fighting for Freedom

Ivan had remembered what Lyaksandro had told him that night in the forest, when they ambushed the arms and drugs shipment, he was right the first kill was the hardest. They had been in many gunfights and ambushes since that night and yes it did get easier. Ivan wouldn't admit it to anybody but Fedir, for fear of appearing weak, but it still troubled him. Some nights he would wake up soaked in sweat reliving killing a Russian gang member. It was always the same nightmare, different faces, but always those dark eyes, bulging in pain and then the haunting look of bewilderment on the face has he took his last breath. Staring through Ivan's eyes right down into his soul and that ear-piercing scream KILLER! He didn't even tell Fedir about the dreams, he kept them to himself. Although sometimes he would catch his Aunt Anastasia looking at him with such a sad expression. She would hug him and kiss him on the cheek, she never spoke, but it was as if she knew about his tormenting dreams. Ivan had become well respected in the group, a good fighter, and tough and with a good organised brain. He had risen quickly through the ranks and was trusted and respected by Lyaksandro. His Uncle Boris was proud of him, although Ivan never discussed anything in front of his aunt, but he had the feeling she was proud of him. His uncle had told Ivan several times to be careful talking about any business they were involved in when his aunt was around. However, Ivan knew she was aware of everything that was going on and acted naïvely for her husbands' benefit and his peace of mind.

Ivan's sister Yulia and her children Zoya and Mykola would come to visit and stay at Uncle Boris's house regularly, he loved to see them. One warm balmy evening when Ivan, his uncle and Yulia were at in the garden after dinner, having a drink. Yulia told them of the time her husband Andrei had banned them for coming to Luhansk, because Mykola had repeated what Ivan had told him and his sister about how the Russians were treating Ukrainians. Also, that Andrei had lost his temper and was so furious he beat Mykola. Ivan said, "What do you expect from a Russian, they are all the same. One day, we will drive them from this region and out of our country."

Yulia laughed and said, "You sound like a freedom fighter." She saw the withering look Boris gave Ivan, he fell silent, and she knew that what she had just said in jest was true.

She looked from Boris to Ivan, her lips trembled with emotion, and she asked Ivan, "Are you? Please, say you're not, Boris how could you let him, our mum sent him here in your care to keep him out of harm's way."

It was Ivan who replied, "Yulia, I'm fine, really; it's not Uncle's fault. You don't know what it's like here – the corruption, the injustices, and the violence. We have to no option but to fight back. You have a different life now – a life of luxury, servants, five-star treatment wherever you go because of your husband's wealth. That's fine; I'm so happy for you, and Zoya and Mykola are great kids; your wealthy lifestyle hasn't spoiled them. But here in Luhansk, we have a different life, and we have to fight the Russians who try to rule us in our country."

Yulia started to gently cry, Uncle Boris who had been silent, leant over and gently squeezed her hand and said, "It is true what Ivan says, Yulia; ours is a different world to yours, but we live here and have to defend our land and people; they are just gangsters; we have to pay them protection money or our shops will be bombed. Ivan and his group defend the businesses here, and they are heroes."

Aunt Anastasia with Zola and Mykola appeared from the kitchen with fresh drinks and snacks. Yulia quickly looked away drying her eyes, the conversation stopped. They thought Mykola had gone back into the kitchen to help; he had been around the side of the house listening to their conversation. His chest swelled with pride when Boris said his Uncle Ivan was a hero. He smiled when he heard his Uncle Ivan praising him for standing up to his father. He already idolised his Uncle Ivan, he was like his uncle, and he wasn't frightened of the Russians either. Standing in the dark at the side of the house, he looked up at the stars shinning in the clear sky and vowed there and then he would join his Uncle Ivan and fight long side him for the freedom of Ukraine.

The next day when they were leaving, Yulia pulled Ivan close to her and gave her brother a big hug and kissing him on the cheek, whispering, "Please take care of yourself and look after Aunt and Uncle, I didn't realise things were so bad here. Tell me how I can help? I can send money, that would help wouldn't it?"

Ivan laughed and replied, "It certainly would be ironic, that we're using your Russian money for arms to fight the Russians. If it doesn't get you into trouble, his money would be a great help."

She looked into Ivan's eyes and stroked his face lovingly and said, "Do you know something, if Dad was still alive, I really think, he would have been proud of you. Take care, my brother, you're all I have left of my family from Odessa. Leave it with me, I will finance your fight here, it's the least I can do. I'm also Ukrainian, don't forget."

Ivan was in the cutting room at the back of the shop, but he could see his uncle and that arsehole skinny through the window. They appeared to be arguing, he saw Skinny give his uncle a back handed slap across the face. He grabbed a pair of cutting shears and ran towards the door, he was furious, his uncle had fallen back against the window. Petruso the head cutter, walked in to Ivan's path and stopped him with a bearhug. He whispered in Ivan's ear calm down man, you will get you and your uncle killed, you well know there's a time and place for what you want to do right now. Petruso relaxed his grip when he felt Ivan relax and stop struggling, Boris had come back into the shop, Petruso still practically face to face with Ivan, said, "Now go and make sure your uncle Boris is okay."

At the next Dnipro gathering, Ivan spoke with Lyaksandro at a group meeting, and said, he wanted permission to kill Skinny. A heated discussion followed about it being pointless, the argument being that another collector would just take over his stores and businesses. It was Fedir who stood and said, "Why stop at Skinny? Let's kill all the collectors."

He felt embarrassed, all eyes were on him, with some colleagues shaking their heads slowly at his proposal and others laughing out loud. Fedir raised his arms and said, "No! Here me out, if we hit their finances and cause disruptions. Instead of just stealing their shipments and killing the drivers and guards. Well, if we kill the collectors and the drug dealers, they are Russians also, aren't they? If we rob the collectors when they have finished their rounds, it's a double bonus. They would have to give the collectors more security, taking up gang members' time for their collections. When the time is right, we can hit the drug dealings, more security needed again. We then alternate and hit the collectors again and their bodyguards; they won't know when attacks are going to happen. What do you think, Lyaksandro?" Fedir sat down next to Ivan and winked at him, his plan had certainly caused a stir.

Everyone started talking at once, the room was filled with loud voices, Lyaksandro stood and the chatter started to die down. Finally, silence, the big man spoke, "Fedir's got a good point, but I think his plan would bring down the wrath of the Russian gang on the shopkeepers and the local community, that would cause problems and wouldn't help. However, the plan does have legs, if we scale it back somewhat. We hit, say, two of the collectors, then leave it for a couple of collections, and then hit two or three drug dealers. It would have the same effect; they would have to give all of them extra protection because they wouldn't know where or who would be hit next.it could have the same effect, but without putting the lives of any shopkeepers and locals at risk." It was decided that was worth doing, and Fedir was so proud that his plan was being put into action. Afterwards, at the bar, Ivan asked him when he had come up with the plan.

Fedir laughed and replied, "As I was speaking, I made it up, as I went along." Lyaksandro's revised plan worked well and caused the Russians a lot of trouble and money.

Chapter Forty-Two
Russian Ambush

The plan to hit the collectors and drug dealers was working well, the first hit was on Skinny and another collector over the other side of town. It was the talk of Luhansk, everyone including the Russians knew it was the work of Dnipro. Lyaksandro wouldn't let Ivan carry out the hit on Skinny because he said, he was emotionally involved which wasn't a good thing. Instead Fedir and a veteran called Oleksly shot and killed Skinny, he was the one that also collected from his uncle's bakery, so as far as Fedir was concerned justice was done. Things were tense afterwards the LPR questioned lots of people, shopkeepers were warned if it happened again, there would be consequences and the collection fees would increase. There weren't any attacks on the collections over the next two months. But there were three on the drug dealers as expected security had been increased after the collector's attack. The LPR and separatist gang obviously thought the increased security had frightened off any further attacks on the collections. The fourth collection the following month was hit, three collectors and six guards were killed. Unfortunately, reprisals were swift and vicious, two shops were burned down, a butchers and hardware store, and the staff were badly beaten. The people were afraid, but the search for information on the attacks on the collections came to nothing, they were given no leads whatsoever, everybody remained tight lipped. Money taken in the attacks was given to local builders working on rebuilding the burnt-out butchers and hardware stores. Further attacks on the collectors were put on hold for the foreseeable future, so the local community would be safe.

Three months later, news came through of another large shipment of arms and drugs was due in from Russia. The Intel came in from the Dnipro's informant in Moscow, plans were put in place for a meet and greet on the motorway outside Luhansk. This attack would take place after the convoy had driven through the forest. They would feel safe once they were through the forest after previous attacks in there. However, when the Intel finally came through, the plan had to be changed, the shipment was coming up through Mariupol via the Crimea and not the usual short route from across the border in to Luhansk. It was of no concern, there were lots of ideal spots for an ambush along the route. Changing the plans for the attack Lyaksandro had chosen an old derelicts steel works on both sides of the M04, the M04 motorway started at Debaltseve and went straight through Luhansk and up to the Russian border check point. A lot of the surrounding countryside was cropland and flat, the attack and getaway had to be swift. It was a clever route coming up from Crimea in the south, the local separatists would provide protection which could be a problem. Because of the route, the ambush would consist of a large squad of both Dnipro 1 and 2 fighters. Also, Dnipro 1 would provide cover after the attack on route to the storage place. The drugs would be destroyed as usual and the arms stored in a safe location near Makiyivka, a small town north of Donetsk. Ivan and Fedir were stood down from the operation because of both squads being involved. They weren't happy about the decision; this wasn't like the forest ambush they both took part in. This was going to be a full-on battle with large numbers of separatists giving the convoy protection. They were both veterans now and wanted to be take part, but they knew better than to complain at the briefing. They listened to the plan along with the rest of the squad, it sounded dangerous, but that just added to their disappointment. They helped load the trucks and stood after watching as they trundled off into the night, they went to the speakeasy for a last drink.

The news of the ambush came through, first on the lunchtime radio news broadcast the following day, with a more in-depth report on the early evening TV news show. As expected, it had been a bloody battle with both sides taking losses, the news reporter said the Dnipro squad were outnumbered but fought courageously. Ivan rang Fedir who was also watching the news report, but he hadn't heard anything other than what was on the news broadcast. They agreed to meet later at the bar, hoping that by then there would news on the squad. News came through later in the evening, but it was sketchy and varied, a lot of it didn't make sense, Ivan and Fedir went home really none the wiser. Hopefully the next day a proper update would come through from Dnipro 2 of casualties and if the mission was successful. Facts like a shipment from Russia was the cause of the battle was never mentioned on the News broadcast, they just reported there had been a clash.

It took another two days to establish the extent of what happened that fateful night and the consequences of the attack. The LPR and separatists were guarding the shipment in numbers. Most likely anticipating an attack on the convoy somewhere along the route. Dnipro 1 &2 fought valiantly, but sustained heavy casualties, they included Lyaksandro and also the deaths of some of the top men. Lyaksandro was badly wounded, and he died three days later from his injuries. Dnipro was in disarray and down on numbers, they had lost good experienced men and also their leader. Ivan was asked to step up and take charge of Dnipro 1, he had worked closely with Lyaksandro and had been coached by him since joining the group. He made Fedir his number two, and they set about recruiting more fighters and rebuilding their group. After news of what had happened there were plenty of volunteers, young, willing and prepared to fight.

Chapter Forty-Three
Two Years Later-Luhansk

Dnipro 1 & 2 had recovered, they were strong and taking the fight to the separatists despite the efforts of the LPR. Ivan had become a good respected leader, not unlike Lyaksandro. He was prepared to lead from the front, which earned him respect from the men. Fedir was by his side all the way and the both of them were very popular, not only with the locals, but also the Ukrainian Government in Kyiv. They had both been to Kyiv and met with the president who personally thanked them. He also asked Ivan to pass on his best wishes to his sister Yulia for her generous funding of the cause. On a personal front, back in Luhansk Uncle Boris had died of heart attack just before Christmas when they were visiting friends in Svatovo town in Luhansk. Aunt Anastasia took it badly, she sold the tailor business and also donated some of the proceeds to the cause, on the good side, and she had another "son" to dot on. Mykola against his mother and sisters wishes had moved to Luhansk and joined his Uncle Ivan in the fight. His mother had forbidden him to go, but to no avail and then tried to dissuade him. He wasn't a boy any more, but a young man, his mind was made up and nothing his family could say would change it. His father was too busy in Moscow to have any idea where his children were in the world. It appeared that he was happy with that arrangement, he just had the close business relationship with his wife, Yulia. When he did occasionally ask about them, Yulia would tell him they were fine and making their way in the world and that was more than enough details for him.

Yulia was still bank-rolling the fight in the Donbas region from the wealth that was available to her. After all, being married to an Oligarch, with homes all across the world did have its benefits. She only wished she could get Mykola away from Ivan in Luhansk; it was too late for Ivan; it was his life now. She was worried it would also become Mykola's life, and she needed to get him out ideally to one of their homes in Europe or New York before it was too late. She would visit regularly to see Anastasia and would spend time with Mykola and Ivan, Mykola would also phone her, they would have long chats, and he was a good son. At the end of every phone call, she would ask him to come back to her and leave the fighting to Uncle Ivan, but her efforts were futile, he idolised his uncle. On her last visit to see them all she took Zoya with her, they had a family week together. Anastasia loved fussing over them and cooking all her old recipes for dinner. She told Yulia not to worry about Mykola, Ivan was very protective to him. As usual when she was leaving, Yulia made Ivan promise he would take care of his young nephew. He would laugh and make the promise adding that Mykola was becoming a fine warrior. That was the last thing Yulia wanted to hear, she had given up talking Ivan to walk away. But still hoped that one day and soon, she could get Mykola away from the fighting, as noble and patriotic as it was.

Dnipro were taking the fight to the separatists and making good ground in disrupting their cash flow and attacking their ammunition and drug supplies. Moscow was becoming frustrated that the LPR couldn't control what they saw as trouble makers. But the facts were, the top men at LPR were too busy making their money, ready for when they retired to Europe. As long has the LPR were making money from their corrupt business deals that Moscow was unaware of They weren't bothered by Dnipro's activity, they were happy to leave that to the Separatists. Who were also busy making money, like LPR their top men didn't plan on living in Ukraine forever. They, like the LPR were moving money out of the country to Swiss bank accounts, unknown to Moscow, to enjoy later.

Chapter Forty-Four
The Demand

Not long after Mykola arrived Fedir had got him a job at his uncle's bakery after Anastasia had sold the Tailor shop. He took to baking very well and was becoming quite the pastry chef; he enjoyed baking and was getting a reputation especially for his ideas on celebration cakes. He had made three wedding cakes on recommendation of the first one and numerous birthdays, retirements and anniversary cakes. Fedirs uncle was delighted with the attention and indeed business Mykola was bringing in. He would bake novelty cakes that would go on display in the shop window until they were quickly bought, more often the same day. He still went out on Dnipro business with his colleagues fighting the cause. His mum had heard from Anastasia about his new found celebrity status and the demand for his baking. When they next spoke on the telephone, she begged him to leave Luhansk she promised she would set him up with his own bakery business wherever he wanted in the world. Yulia spoke with Ivan about trying to get him out of Ukraine, he promised he would suggest that he should leave and become a professional baker. One the downside to his rise to fame in Luhansk, the separatists had increased the bakeries protection payments. Fedir was furious, but his uncle was resigned to it and just said it was to be expected. Fedir spoke with Ivan about hitting the collectors and drug dealers again, but on a bigger scale this time. Ivan reluctantly agreed when other members also thought it was time to start the campaign again.

The following months both the collectors and dealers were the target, the plan was to hit all twenty plus collectors and as many dealers as possible. It was going to cause trouble, but they were ready with Dnipro 2 from the Donbas offering their support with the aftermath. Things had been too quiet for too long; it was time to take up the fight again. All members were involved, hoping to catch out the separatists after how quiet it had been these past months. Since the previous attacks on them they always had back-ups, but never more than one or two men. After being safe for so long, they had become slack on their operation. Dnipro would take advantage of this with the element of surprise, and what a bloody surprise they had planned. The attacks went to plan more or less, but with some casualties, Fedir suffered a shoulder wound, the back-up on their attack were alert and fought well. Mykola was one of Fedirs men, and helped get Fedir away from the fight after he was shot. Apart from four other separate casualties, the operation was a success with no fatalities on Dnipro's side.

Enquiries were ongoing the following days by the LPR and the separatists who had taken a big hit in the attack, in money and body count. Fedir had to lie low, he stayed at his mother's sister's house out of town. Enquiries got violent, but after six or so days things started to calm down. Ivan had gone to visit Fedir when he received a phone call from the bakery. Some separatists had raided the shop and grabbed Mykola, taking him away in a grey van. They threatened the staff with guns when they started to intervene, announcing Mykola was a member of Dnipro and was involved in the collection attacks. Ivan then had a call was from his Anastasia, someone from the bakery had phoned her and told her about Mykola. She sobbed that Ivan had to save him from the Russian gang and soon before they killed him. Ivan rushed back home to make sure she had calmed down by the time he arrived, but broke down again when they talked about why Mykola was taken from the bakery. Fedir rang to say he would come over in the evening, adding that he had reached out to their contact in the LPR offices to try to get news of Mykola. Fedir arrived just after eight p.m. with two heavily armed colleagues, he didn't look too good, and he hadn't recovered from his injury. They all sat at the patio table in the back garden, Anastasia brought out a tray of drinks and savoury snacks for them.

She kissed Fedir on the forehead, and asked in an emotional voice, "How are you, my darling? We live in dangerous times. Please bring my young boy back to me safely, I wouldn't be able to face his mother if anything happened to him."

Fedir squeezed her small trembling hand and replied, "I'm fine, I will survive, and we will get him back, if we have to rip Luhansk apart to find him, don't you worry Anastasia."

She gave him a half smile. "I know you will, you're a good boy." With that she made her way back inside making the sign of the cross again has she left.

Ivan looked round and checked; she was back inside the house and out of earshot. Turning he asked Fedir, "What have you found out, anything?"

Fedir took a drink of his beer and replied, "It's too early yet, I've spoken with Taras, our man inside LPR. He said, they will most likely hear where Mykola is being held and also what's going to happen to him."

Lowering his voice slightly, he continued, "Taras said, they won't kill Mykola without the say so from Moscow, which is reassuring, but that doesn't mean the bastards won't torture him to find out the names of other Dnipro fighters."

Ivan nodded and asked, "Did Taras say why they took him and how they found out that he was involved?"

Fedir shrugged his shoulders at the question. "He doesn't know yet; he thinks somebody might have recognised him in the firefight, after all, he has become a bit of a celebrity around town with his baking, hasn't he?"

Ivan frowned and nodded in agreement, looking each of the men. In turn he said, "We must get him back before they torture him for our names; our future depends on it. Also, his mother has been bankrolling us for some years, but more importantly; he's family, he is my nephew, my flesh and blood."

Nothing came through from Taras at LPR which was strange, they were usually kept informed what was happening with the Russian gang. Ivan needed to find out where Mykola was being held, the longer the silence the more concerned he was for his nephew's and members safety. Then it all became clear why LPR had been kept in the dark, the separatists made contact. Two of them went to the bar, they spoke with the owner Petruso and gave him a letter for Dnipro. They told him his bar was well known for being used by Dnipro, and he was lucky it hadn't been bombed. Despite his denials they said, he had to get the letter to the leaders. Without implicating himself he said, he would do what he could, after they left, he phoned Ivan. That evening they met at the bar, Ivan read out the letter aloud to the other members present. It read that they knew who Mykola's parents were, and they wanted a hefty ransom not to kill him. But also, not to tell the authorities in Moscow that one of their richest members had a son who was fighting against them, murdering Russians in the Ukraine. Ivan continued to look at the piece of paper in his hand even though he had finished reading. It was Fedir who broke the silence, "That is not good, Ivan, even if his parents were to pay the ransom. It doesn't mean the bastards won't kill Mykola and tell Moscow who his parents are. Even if they do release Mykola, they could carry on blackmailing your sister and her husband for years to come."

Ivan folded the piece of paper up and carefully placed back in to the envelope. Laying the envelope on the table, he looked up at Fedir and said, "I agree with you entirely, but what do I do? I was hoping we could get him back without telling my sister, but now I have to tell her. Her life could also be in danger if they have already told Moscow. I doubt Taras will get any news from the LPR; the gang won't tell them they don't want to give them a share of the blackmail money. That's why the LPR doesn't know anything, the ransom money will go straight to a bank account in Switzerland. I'm not bothered about Mykola's dad; he's a Russian, and he deserves everything that comes his way. It's my sister I'm worried about. I must keep her safe, she's not bothered if she never sets foot in Russia again. They have homes all over the world, but they can find her wherever she is, we know that from experience. Have we not got any leads on where they might be holding Mykola?" The six men around the table all shook their heads when Ivan looked from one to the other.

He let out a big sigh and looking at Fedir said, "Okay, well, I'm going to have to speak to Yulia and tell her that her son's been captured and that her whole life is about to change!"

Chapter Forty-Five
Yulia's Despair

Yulia had flown in to Kyiv airport from Switzerland and was being driven south to Luhansk. Since the Russian annexation of Crimea in 2014 and the trouble in the Donbas, the Ukrainian aviation was forced to revoke certificates for airports within the military operation area. This was due to there being no positive control over airports in Crimea and the Donbas regions. Anastasia had spoken to her and asked her to visit, on the pretence of missing her. She hated having to lie to Yulia, especially when she was asked by her how Mykola and Ivan were. It was Ivan's suggestion he wanted to be face to face with Yulia when he told her the bad news about the situation they were in. He was also aware from their childhood days of her bad temper and expected to a slap or two for not keeping Mykola safe. He was more nervous about telling Yulia about Mykola than ever going in to any battle with the Russian gang.

Ivan took Yulia's bag upstairs to her room and left her talking with Anastasia in the kitchen. When he came down to join them, Yulia was holding Anastasia they were both weeping, they both turned and looked to Ivan stood in the kitchen doorway. Anastasia said between sobs, "I'm sorry, Ivan; she asked me where Mykola was."

With a look of horror on her face, Yulia asked, "What's happened to him, Ivan. Is he dead? What's happened?

Yulia rushed at Ivan, hitting him in his chest, she screamed at him, "You promised you would take care of Mykola; what's happened?

Ivan tried to calm her; he held her tight to him. He answered, "He's okay, he's alive, please just calm down and let me tell what's going on." They all sat at the pine kitchen table, Anastasia quietly sobbing head down, wringing her hands. Yulia tears running down her face gently shaking her head looking at Ivan intently. Ivan told his sister everything that had happened including that they were still searching for the place Mykola was being held and still hoped they would find him. He explained about the huge ransom demand to be paid in US dollars, also that they had demanded a photograph of Mykola, and he was fine. He didn't mention is face, the black eyes and spilt lip, where they had beaten him for information.

Yulia started to compose herself and reached for Anastasia's hand. She let out a huge sigh and gently squeezing Anastasia's hand, she managed to smile at her and said, "Okay, my darling, dry your eyes it's going to be okay; we will get him back."

Ivan let out a long, silent breath. Yulia had obviously thought the worse with Anastasia breaking down, and she was so relieved to hear Mykola was alive. Ivan said, "What about your husband? Are you going to tell him? Even when we get Mykola back, there could still be big problems if this gets back to Moscow."

Yulia stared at Ivan for several moments, as if mulling everything over in her mind, she replied, "No, definitely not, he will panic and probably tell the authorities before the separatists do. He will try to save his own skin; he would sacrifice Mykola and me, and he mustn't now anything of this."

Ivan nodded, leaning forward and clutching her hand, said, "The problem, my darling brave sister, is, even if they don't tell, you could be held to ransom for the rest of your life. They would probably still demand hush money in the future." He stopped short of saying they might renege on the deal, take the money, then still kill Mykola and tell Moscow.

Yulia was being so brave, he wouldn't upset her with that, even though knowing her she had probably already considered it. She looked Ivan in the eyes and replied, "I don't care about the future, and I just want to get Mykola away from them, away from here and safe with me. I will deal with anything that comes once I have him back in my arms."

Ivan nodded and said quietly, "I understand, Yulia. I am so sorry I let you down. I promised I would look after him, and I didn't, but we will do everything in our power to bring him back to you safely."

Yulia took her hand out of Ivan's and placed her handbag on the table, taking out her mobile she announced, "I need to get my car to pick me up. I have to start making plans to get the money together, there's no time to lose."

Chapter Forty-Six
Hampstead Heath, London

All three sat in silence following Harriot's stunning confession that "Mrs Harrington" was in fact her mother Yulia Novikov. Rob in the driver's seat had closed his eyes and was finally calming down after the shooting at the mews. Joe deep in thought was looking out of the side window on to the heath at a woman throwing a ball for her over-excited French bulldog to chase. Harriot in the back next to Joe was thankful all the questions had stopped, at least for the time being. She was calm and had stopped crying, she wanted to check her makeup, but didn't dare in case it appeared flippant, and it threw Joe in to another rage. She was genuinely frightened earlier she thought Joe was going to kill her, she had never seen him like that before. She sat there afraid of breaking the silence, it was peaceful and for the first time she felt safe. It was Rob who finally spoke and broke the silence, looking at Harriot, he said, "So, what do we do now? Where do we go? I guess that if '*they*' were trying to kill us before, now we've shot one of *them*, they will definitely want to kill us?"

Harriot looked from Joe to Rob and answered him quietly, "Yes, they will, but because you've taken me." Then turned and looked out of the window.

Joe exhaled loudly and rubbed the side of his neck, he looked at Rob and raised his highbrows. He cleared his throat and said, "Well, there you have it, straight from the horse's mouth, and we're dead men. Let's go back to the Elephant?"

Harriot turned and when Rob started the engine, she asked, "The Elephant, is that some sort of code."

Looking at Harriot Joe answered sarcastically, "No, it's not a code, its Rob's flat at the Elephant and Castle, just down the road from your flat in Kennington remember? After all, we can't go back to my flat, you know the one you found for me, and helped me furnish, can we? Especially, after your friends tried to murder me there the other night, after Jimmy's funeral. You remember Jimmy, don't you?"

Joe's cutting words started Harriot sobbing, in between sobs, she managed to say, "They're not my friends." The rest of the journey back into town was in silence, Joe was trying to get his head around everything that he had found out, to say it was overload was an understatement.

Rob showed Harriot his bedroom where she would sleep, he said, he would sleep on the couch since Joe still had some problems following the attack. Harriot looked upset, she asked Rob, "Was he badly hurt?"

Rob nodded, adding, "So badly, he didn't have the strength to defend himself after the funeral, if I hadn't been there to get him away from them, they would have killed him."

Harriot went to speak, but stopped because Joe walked in, ignoring Harriot, he asked Rob, "Are we going to eat? I suggest a takeaway."

Rob smiled and trying to lighten the mood, replied, "That sounds like an excellent idea to me. What does everybody want?"

The meal was more or less eaten in silence, with Joe and Rob tucking in, but Harriot only picked at her food and pushed it around the plate several times. She did join them with the red wine though, they were well in to their second bottle. The wine flowing appeared to put Joe and Harriot at ease, Rob was in good form, Joe even managed to raise a smile at least once or twice, even Harriot smiled at Rob's attempts to cheer everyone up. Harriot made eye contact with Joe and asked him, "What are you going to do with me?"

Joe took a drink of his wine and calmly replied, "I don't know yet; I could ring Andy Sherry and tell him everything and hand you over to him. He would be interested to know that you've got a Russian death squad over here. He could get promoted, clearing up quite a few murders and missing person's cases, courtesy of you, Harriot. Actually, it's just hit me, if you're Russian, Harriot isn't your real name, is it?" His coldness upset Harriot, but she didn't want him to see how it affected her.

Still looking him in the eye, she said, "No, it's not, my name is Zoya... Zoya Novikov, and I'm not Russian; I'm Ukrainian.

"Also, I didn't bring a death squad over here, it was my father, and he ordered them over from Moscow. They are here to take me to him in Moscow after they tidy up all the loose ends here in London. I told you the truth, and when he gets me back to Moscow, he might have me killed. I am not your enemy Joe."

Her straight forward reply stunned Joe, he just sat there staring at "Harriot" digesting what she had just said.

Rob looked from Joe back to "Harriot" and said, "Wow, you're the daughter of the Oligarch Andrei Novikov? I've read about him, he's worth billions, isn't he?"

Still looking at Joe, she answered Rob's questions, "Yes, I am his daughter and yes it's true what you say he is worth!" Rob slowly shook his head from side to side and let out a low whistle.

He replied, "Wow, and you're working here in London at Joe's detective agency, has their receptionist?"

Growing in confidence seeing how her news had affected Joe, she said, "Actually, I was working for the boss of the agency Jimmy Daly."

Looking back to Joe, she continued her voice, starting to crack with emotion, "And I would have given my own life gladly to have saved him. He didn't deserve to die because of me; nobody did, and I loved Jimmy more than my own father. I will never forgive myself for what happened to him. My father's people are monster, they just follow orders, and they don't care about anybody." She wanted to say more, but she couldn't speak, she looked away, she started to sob loudly. Joe stood up and walked around to where she was sat, he gave her some tissues. Taking them, she looked up at him and threw her arms around his waist and buried her face into him sobbing uncontrollably. He went to place his hand on the back of her head but resisted, he looked over at Rob. Who made a sad face at Joe and nodded towards Harriot, Joe placed his hand on the back of her head and gently stroked her hair.

Harriot pushed the chair away and stood up pushing her body into Joe's throwing her arms around his neck. He held her tight, his arms around her waist, they just stood there, eventually her sobs quietening down. Rob sat there unsure whether to get up leave them alone, or try and speak to break the silence. He decided leave them alone, pouring himself another glass of wine he went to his bedroom. Joe and Harriot stood silently holding each other for a good twenty minutes or so. It was Joe who finally spoke, he said, "Come on, its late you need to get some rest." He walked her into his bedroom, she lay down on the bed, and Joe bent over and tenderly kissed her on the forehead.

He walked to the door and flicked the light switch, out of the darkness, he heard Harriot's say, "Don't leave me alone tonight, Joe, stay with me, please." They lay on top of the bed in each other's arms, not speaking. Harriot just relaxed after everything that had happened that day, cuddling in to Joe just felt right. She made the first move, nuzzling into Joe's neck she slowly lifted her face up to his and kissed him gently on the lips. He responded and kissed her back, a long lingering kiss. They undressed and got under the duvet, Joe was gentle making love to Harriot, and she responded arching her body up into his. She loved his firm body, the way he kissed her, she hung on to him like her life depending on it, and afterwards they fell asleep exhausted in each other's arms.

The next morning, Rob knocked and after a good few seconds popped his head around the bedroom door. He announced, "A cooked breakfast is on the table and ready for eating lovebirds, a Rob special, come on get up before it gets cold." They were sat around the table enjoying a Rob special fry up. Rob was dressed, Harriot wore Joe's towelling dressing gown, and Joe was in his boxers and a white tee shirt. Rob sat back down at the table after making another pot of fresh coffee. Joe looked across at Harriot even with no makeup and her hair up in a bun she still looked beautiful, he was amazed at the difference in her appearance.

For a moment he felt a wave of anger about the way she had deceived him and Jimmy. She met his gaze and smiled a little embarrassed, she started to tidy her hair. Rob broke the silence, taking the words out of Joe's mouth, "So, Harriot or is it Zoya, what do you prefer to be called? Know that we know your real name. Are you going to enlighten us on what this mayhem is all about – that people have been killed and abducted, probably all killed?"

Harriot flushed at Rob's abrupt questions, she looked from him to Joe, he added, "I think Rob's right, it's time now, we need to know everything, especially what caused this shitstorm in the first place. Once we know all the facts, we might be able to figure out, how we can get out of this alive."

Chapter Forty-Seven
Harriot's Story

Harriot took a big drink of her coffee, cleared her throat and started to tell her story, "You already know my father is the Russian Oligarch Andrei Novkov. My mother Yulia is Ukrainian, they had two children me and my brother Mykola. We have homes in many countries, but my father lives almost all of the time in Moscow, this is because of his work with some important people, high up in the government."

Rob interrupted, "Work like what?"

Harriot answered the question, "He launders his and their money through a German bank here in England."

It was Joe's turn to interrupt, "LPZ that German bank in Canary Wharf."

Harriot nodded and continued, "He has been successfully doing it for himself for years, with the clean money eventually ending up in numbered accounts in Swiss banks. This means whatever political or economic unrest that might happen in Russia or government clampdowns or policy changes, their wealth is safe and cannot be touched. He included some close friends, and he was made to start doing it for some important government figures; he had no choice. My mother has a brother Uncle

Ivan; he lives in Luhansk. When we were young, we would go there and holiday with him, and we had some wonderful times. Years later, my uncle joined the government-backed Dnipro fighters to against the Russian gangsters in the Donbas. They would hijack the arms and drug shipments sent over the border from Moscow. They would fight against the Russians and disrupt the gang's racketeering, like selling drugs, protection payments, prostitution and lots more. They were parasites, sucking the life out of the Ukrainian people trying to live peacefully in their own country.

"My father found out about my uncle's involvement in the fight against the Russians in the Donbas and forbid us and my mother to have anything to do with him ever again. He said he was worried his powerful friends in Moscow would find out and that we could all be killed. Our mother took us to live most of the time in Switzerland; we felt safe there, until one night, on the way home from dinner, a car tried to force us off the road. We didn't wait around; she flew us out a few hours later on our private jet here to London. Apart from the Adam's yard mansion in Mayfair, we have a large estate in Sussex; my brother and I stayed there. My mum was flying in and out of the country back to Moscow on business. My father told her that whoever had tried to hurt us in Switzerland, it wasn't on the orders of anyone in Moscow, I'm not sure she believed him. My brother Mykola flew out with her one day to Odessa and decided to stay, he never came back. After a month on my own, I was lonely and bored. So, I leased the flat in Kennington and moved up to London. My mother allowed it on the proviso I didn't contact with any of my friends here in London in case it got back to Moscow. So, I had to live under the radar, as my mum called it. I got a job with Jimmy at his private eye agency. I adored it; it was my very first job, and he was such a lovely man, I had some of the happiest days of my life working has his receptionist. I felt so safe, my mum approved, she said, 'It was perfect; I was hidden in plain view.' She continued to fly in and out of the country, doing liaison work with the bank for my father, he never mentioned the trouble in Switzerland and neither did she." Harriot paused to gather herself talking about Jimmy had upset her. Joe was sitting next to her, rubbed her back, and she leaned into him. He gently kissed her on her forehead, taking a glass of water from Rob, she had a sip and continued.

"Everything was fine for a long time, and there didn't appear to be any issues with Moscow. The operation at the bank was going well as usual; everything ran through Adam's Yard. It was a perfect operation. Simple yet perfect, the bank did a good job and were well paid for their services. One day, when my mum flew into London, we went out for dinner; she broke down in the restaurant, and she told me we had a problem. My brother Mykola had joined my uncle in the Donbas fighting the Russian gangsters. She was heartbroken, worried that he could get hurt, or even worse, she went to see them, but Mykola wouldn't leave; he said the fight for his homeland was his life now. She was also worried that his actions could put us all at risk if it got back to Moscow and my father."

"There wasn't any trail to identify my uncle Ivan that would connect him to us, but with Mykola, it was different. Despite our fears, my mum managed to keep what he was doing away from our father; he was unaware that Mykola was in the Ukraine. Life carried on as normal; I was happy at work, and I would meet up with mum when she flew in for meetings with the bank. My brother Mykola was still with Uncle Ivan fighting in Luhansk; my mum visited them there a lot. She said my brother was okay, but was still being stubborn about coming home

"Then everything changed in a heartbeat. Mykola had been caught by the Russian gangsters following an attack on one of their convoys in the Donbas. Then it went from bad to worse; they found out who he was and more importantly, who is father was. My uncle Ivan received a ransom demand for Mykolas's release and also for their silence. I got another shock, I found out that my mother had been bankrolling the Dnipro group via the Ukraine government for a number of years. My uncle and my mum had a big row; Uncle Ivan was against her paying the ransom. He said they would keep making demands, and what was to stop them informing Moscow who Mykola's father was. He promised her the fighters would find where they were holding Mykola and save him."

"However, against my uncle's advice, my mother was obviously prepared to do anything to get Mykola back. She flew over here and told Nigel Harrington about the situation and asked for his help to arrange to divert money from the bank's operation to pay the ransom demand. He was heavily involved in the operation at the bank, but my mum trusted him. There wasn't anyone else at the bank she could trust, and she couldn't turn to my father. It was a big sum of money, but the amount of money running through the bank on a weekly basis was huge, so it could work. Thankfully, Nigel agreed. I would go around to his apartment in Canary Wharf and help with the figure work so everything matched as far as the bank and more importantly, Moscow were concerned. It was arduous work, but we were getting there, but it wasn't happening fast enough; as far as my mum was concerned, she was getting desperate."

"Nigel said, we had to be careful and not make any mistakes by rushing and get found out. Skimming money from Russians is definitely not recommended and definitely not good for your health. It made sense; it was a dangerous game my mum and I were playing. Then one evening, when I was working on the figures in Nigel's apartment, I noticed an anomaly on the amount Nigel said we had accrued against the actual amount. From the figures, I could see we were already at the amount that we needed to pay the ransom. I double-checked the figures again the next evening when I went to help; they were above the figure that we needed. I told my mother, and she flew over the next morning, and we met up. I explained what I had found out about Nigel's figures; she said by her calculations, we should have had the amount over a week ago. We had to be careful; we couldn't just ask Nigel or accuse him; first, we needed to see if anyone else was involved. That's when we came up with the plan to hire you, Joe, to try to find out if he was meeting up with anyone who could be involved."

She paused and looked at Joe embarrassed, she said, "I'm so sorry for deceiving you, Joe, but we were desperate to get Mykola back safely."

Joe brushed the hair away that was hanging down over one eye and replied, "Don't worry about it, now I know the truth, I would have done the same in your position." Harriot smiled, and held onto his hand.

She continued, "You reported to my mum that he had lunch one day with a foreign-looking chap, but you couldn't get a photograph of him because you were seated at the bar. Time was of the essence, we decided the only option we had was for my mum to confront Nigel. To our horror, Nigel confessed to double-crossing my mum, he came straight out and admitted it. He said the money had already gone to an account on the Cayman isles. He laughed in her face and boasted it was the perfect crime. After all, he said, what could she do about it? Report him to the police, tell the bank? who would tell her husband"

Rob cut in and asked, "So your mother killed Nigel Harrington because of his treachery, yes?"

Harriot shook her head, she paused to compose herself. She was getting tearful, reliving it all. "No, it wasn't that simple, my mother flew back to Kyiv and met up with my uncle Ivan." Her voice started to break, and the tears came. Joe asked her if she wanted to take a break.

But Harriot shock her head, dabbed her eyes and blew her nose, composing herself, she continued, "No, my mother didn't shoot him in the park that evening, my uncle Ivan did. You see because of the delay getting the money because of Nigel Harrington's treachery, the Russian gang murdered my brother Mykola. So, you see it was a matter of honour, my uncle flew into London with my mother, she arranged to meet Nigel Harrington one last time. She told him what his treachery had done and my uncle Ivan executed him in the park. They both flew back to Kyiv the next morning; Uncle Ivan is hiding my mother in the Donbas somewhere.

"The bank was in total shock and panic when it broke about Harrington's murder, they carried out a full audit and discovered the missing funds. I believe they are still trying to retrieve the money from the bank in the Caymans. They panicked when they found out what had happened, the managing director flew to Moscow to explain the theft to my father. Explaining that my mother must have been involved and probably me also. It was in both the banks and my father's interests to keep what had happened secret. It would be disastrous for the bank, who earns millions from the operation. Also, it would be life-threatening for some of the directors at the London branch, as an example. Insofar as my father's safety is concerned, if it ever came out that his wife stole funds from the operation, that would definitely be the end for him and also me and my mother. That's why my father sent his people here to clear up the mess and get rid of anyone who had any knowledge of what had happened. These men are professionals, but instead of poisoning the victims, they are being high profile to set an example to the directors of the bank, also fellow countrymen here in London to mind their own business. It would appear that Moscow haven't been told about my brother fighting for Dnipro in the Donbas, at least not yet anyway. Otherwise, my father could have been killed, and we would be hunted down like dogs and also killed.

"My father has also got his people in the Ukraine searching for my mother, but she's under the protection of the government, and more importantly, my uncle Ivan. My father also told his men they must return with me, hoping that taking me back will get my mother to return to Moscow to try and protect me, so no loose ends. But with my uncle Ivan protecting her, he would send my father's people back to Moscow in boxes. It is a very serious situation that we have got my father into, and I'm not sure if he will ever forgive us. It's possible he could have us killed to save himself; that's a bad thing to say about your own father, but I just don't know."

She looked from Joe to Rob and back to Joe, for reassurance. Rob let out a low whistle and said, "That's one hell of a shit storm you've been going through, young lady, and a hell of a father you've got there. Who would have his family killed to save himself, I don't know what to say!" Joe was lost in his own thoughts, looking at the wall he slowly rubbed his chin with his thumb and fore finger. Harriot looked at Rob, who just shrugged his shoulders back at her. The three of them sat in silence for a while, the only noise was the ticking of the clock on the wall.

After what seemed like an eternity, Joe stood up and walked over to the window looking down on the back of the Elephant and Castle shopping centre. He turned to face the room and said, "You can't go back to Moscow Harriot. From what you've just described to us, I think you and your mother would both be killed. If not by your father, by the people he's in business with. That would be your father's only saving grace; he wouldn't want what Harrington, you, and your mum did – hanging over his head for the rest of his life. By sacrificing the two of you, it would show that he was completely innocent of the scam and dealt harshly with it. It most likely could save him from his powerful partners; also, I don't want you to go back, I will protect with my life if necessary." Harriot stood up from the couch and slowly walked over to Joe stood in front of the window, she put her arms around his waist and kissed him passionately on the lips.

Rob shouted out, "Oh come on, I don't want to see that!" Joe and Harriot stopped and looked over at Rob, all three of them burst out laughing.

Joe and Harriot came over to Rob, they group hugged him with Harriot planting several kisses on his cheeks and forehead, Rob feigned disgust and wiped his face. Joe announced let's party tonight and get drunk, then tomorrow we can sort out what we need to do, but Rob, "You need to leave London and go somewhere safe, buddy; this isn't your fight. Being serious for a moment, you've been brilliant; I can't ever thank you enough for everything you've done for me, and you saved my life."

Rob let out a fake laugh and replied, "Oh, I get it; you want rid of me now, do you. Now you've got the girl? You're both going to ride off into the sunset; well, my Geordie friend, you don't get rid of me that easily."

Joe interrupted him, "They haven't seen you, they don't know you, so you're in the clear, you can walk away without any worries, you dope."

Harriot snuggling into Joe's chest laughed and said, "Is he always like this, stubborn?"

Rob smiled. "You're finally getting to know me, Zoya, Harriot and Elsie, whatever your name is, yes, stubborn to a fault. I'm in this for the duration, whatever it takes we will see this through together. Now after that stirring speech, I'm off to the supermarket on the corner to get some more booze."

Chapter Forty-Eight
Hiding

They finished with the remains of the pizzas they had delivered; Joe refreshed the wine glasses before going back to sit with Harriot on the sofa. Rob was lay on the rug on the floor in front of the fireplace looking up at the ceiling. Everyone was relaxed after the recent activity and Harriot's harrowing family revelations earlier in the day. It was a chilled atmosphere because of all the wine they had drank. Rob broke the silence, "We need to get out of the country; there's no other option. We can't hide away here for ever; they are sure to track us down eventually. For all we know, they could be onto us right now; they might be looking for my Jag; it's possible one of them could have seen it when we were getting away with Harriot."

Joe joined in, "I think you're right, Rob, what you saying makes sense. We'll need our passports, mine's at my apartment in Fulham, where's yours Harriot, and did they take it off you?"

Harriot turned to face Joe, smiled at him and replied, "No, mines at my apartment in Kennington, I haven't been back there since they took me from the office when they..." She stopped short of saying *when they killed*

Jimmy. "I'm not sure if they know about my apartment; if they had, they could have taken me from there anytime they wanted to."

Rob offered up, "Well, why don't I go to both your places tomorrow; get the passports, and we can all bugger off somewhere safe and preferably warm? I would love a bit of a holiday after all this shit."

Joe asked Harriot, "Is that sensible, I am right, aren't I? He is safe, they don't know about Rob, do they?"

She answered, "They know you have someone helping you, and I heard them discussing it. But from what they said, they don't know who it is, they mustn't have seen you, so they won't know what you look like."

Rob smiled. "Perfect, I'm going to borrow my mate's motorbike again, just in case something goes wrong, and I end up being chased through traffic."

Joe stood up, drained his wine glass and replied, "Let's think about this; we're talking about dangerous shit here, it might not be a good idea. Especially going to my place, they will definitely be watching that, even if not Harriot's flat in Kennington."

Before Rob could protest, Harriot stood up and put her arm around Joe's waist. "I agree with Joe; let's sleep on this and discuss it tomorrow when we're all sober. I'm tired. Take me to bed, Joe, please!"

Rob, looking to worse for wear, struggled rolling over and standing up shouted after them, "Yea, you go, you two. For a night of passion, I'll just tidy up all this mess in here."

Looking around the lounge, he added in his best Clint Eastwood voice, "Fuck it! No, I won't. I'll do it tomorrow when I get up." With that, he swayed over to the door, flicked off the light switch and walked down the hall in to his bedroom, and fell on the bed.

Across the road the thick set man stepped out from the shadows, lighting his cigarette he looked up at the lounge window of the flat on the second floor that was now in total darkness.

It was eleven thirty when Rob stirred in his bed, he could hear Joe and Harriot talking in the lounge. He climbed out of bed and lurched towards the bathroom, stood peeing in the toilet he glanced to the left at himself in the mirror over the sink. It wasn't a pretty sight and once again he declared, he wasn't ever going to get drunk again. He turned, and headed towards the familiar voices in the lounge, passing the open kitchen door the smell of bacon wafted past his nostrils.

He was greeted with a cheerful, "Good morning" from Harriot and Joe, who added, "For God's sake, go and put some trousers on, and you should buy some new boxers." Ignoring Joe's comments and Harriot's giggles, he dropped down heavily in the armchair and rubbed his eyes for a good twenty seconds.

It didn't really help, Rob looked over at Harriot, and half smiled and asked, "Is there any bacon, left my love? I could murder a couple of bacon sarnies, and a mug of coffee, with milk please, no sugar."

Harriot was already up and on her way to the kitchen, walking past the armchair, she ruffled his hair and replied, "Yes, of course, handsome."

Smiling Rob shouted after her, "Oh and thanks for tidying up the lounge, I was going to do it this morning, really.

Looking at Joe's disbelieving face, he added in a good Geordie accent, "I was, honestly pet." By the time Rob had finished his breakfast, showered and made himself look presentable it was just after two pm. He phoned his friend and arranged to borrow his motorbike collecting it around six that evening.

Harriot came in, carrying a tray with a mixture of club biscuits and three mugs of coffee, Rob asked her, "Where is the passport in your flat, I'll be going over there early tomorrow morning."

Handing Rob his coffee, she sat down next to Joe and replied, "I left my door key in my drawer when they took me from the office. But I've been thinking, Sally my neighbour has got a spare. I can ring her, ask her to go in to the flat and get my passport and meet you with it. Just in case, they are watching my place it will be safer, what do you both think?"

Joe nodded his head in agreement and Rob said in a decent Humphrey Bogart voice, "Sounds good to me, kid."

Harriot smiled, pleased that they liked her plan, she carried on, "Now, where are we going to go? I'm due to facetime, my mum. I'll ask her if we can go to the Chalet in Switzerland, she would have let the housekeepers go, but that's okay. You will love it, it's a beautiful place, just a few miles outside Zurich."

Joe shook his head and replied, "Won't your dad's people be watching for you or your mum turning up there?"

Rob added, "That's a good point, Harriot, it could be being watched."

Harriot was deflated that this idea had been shot down in flames, but admitted, "Yes, it's possible, I suppose, let me speak with my mum and see if she's got any suggestions, also I've got a spare phone in the flat, I'll ask Sally to give it to you with my passport, Rob."

Rob rubbed his hands and spoke, "Good we seem to getting somewhere now, Joe, where's your passport."

Joe thought for a while then said, "It's either in my bedside drawer, if it's not there, it could be in the top drawer of the cabinet in the lounge… If not there, and it might be!"

Rob cut him short laughing, said, "So, basically you haven't got a fucking clue where it is in the apartment, have you?"

Joe relied sheepishly, "That's correct, it's there somewhere, Rob."

Harriot threw up her arms in the air in despair and asked, "Can I lend your laptop, Rob? I'm going to facetime my mum, I'll go in the bedroom, are you coming, Joe?"

Joe hesitated, then said, "I would rather not H; it would be strange after meeting her that day she hired me to check out Nigel Harrington."

Harriot looked at him for a while without replying, then said, "That's okay. I understand. I suppose it might be a little weird. Is it all right if I tell her about us?" She turned to walk to the bedroom, a big smile crept over her face. She said to herself, "He called me H, that's 'the first time he's done that since before the trouble started. He's forgiven me, I think it's because he loves me too." She felt like a school girl with her first crush on a boyfriend, despite what had happened and the trouble they were in, she was so happy and felt safe with him. Making love to him was just how she had dreamed it would be like. Falling asleep in his arms, nothing else compared to how she felt, she went weak at the knees every time she looked at him. The beginning of a relationship was always great, so exciting when you couldn't keep your hands of each other.

Harriot got upset when Uncle Ivan called her mum to the screen. She missed her mum so much, and seeing Uncle Ivan made her think of Mykola again. It all came flooding back, she explained how Joe and Rob had taken her away from her father's people and now she was safe now with them.

They both cried when her mum told Harriot about Mykola's funeral and how proud she was at all the people who came to pay their respects. They had taken him back to Odessa and buried him in the local cemetery next to his grandmother. "Such a waste of a young life, Harriot," her mum said sadly, dabbing her eyes with a handkerchief.

Harriot asked if she had spoken to her father, her mum said, "Yes, he demanded that I went home to Moscow, and

I had to bring you with me." He kept saying, did I realise the trouble I had caused by allowing Mykola to fight in the Donbas. I had put all our lives at risk, and it was all the fault of my trouble making brother, your uncle Ivan. I tried to explain, Mykola was a strong-minded young man, and I couldn't order him leave Ukraine. Well, my darling, I think you know what your father is like, it was pointless trying to explain to him. I asked him if he was sad that his son had died, and he just laughed, a sarcastic laugh, it broke my heart. Apparently now, there is a bounty here in Ukraine to kill your uncle Ivan, also a bounty to capture me so I can be sent to back to Moscow. Your father's put a bounty on our heads and sent his killers over to London to get you, what man would do that to his family.

Harriot replied in a quiet voice, "A frightened man, Mummy."

Her mum scolded her, "Don't defend him, Harriot, don't! He's selfish, and he's only trying to save himself. If he has to sacrifice you and I – me to do that, he won't hesitate.

Harriot bowed her head and started to gently weep, her mum said, "Oh! I'm sorry, my darling, I didn't mean to shout at you, please don't cry. I'm frightened for us, but what was I supposed to do? You and Mykola are my life. I had to try and save him, it was an unavoidable outcome, your uncle Ivan told me, but I had to try."

Harriot, looked at her mum and touched the screen tenderly, she replied, "Don't blame yourself, Mummy, you did the right thing. We will be okay; you're safe with

Uncle Ivan. I've got Joe and Rob looking after me here now, and I will be safe with them. But we do need to leave London before we are caught. Would it be safe to go to the chalet in Switzerland?" Her mother said no, it wasn't a good idea. She suggested they should go to America. She explained she had a friend who had a holiday home in the Hamptons, in east New York. Adding it would be a good place to "disappear," while she tried to straighten everything out with Harriot's dad Andrei. They finished the call again, tears flowed, saying how much they loved and missed each other and desperately wanted to meet up again soon. Harriot's mum said, she would text her about New York, but agreed they should leave England as soon as possible. They said their sad goodbyes and promised to speak again at the weekend.

Harriot went back in to the lounge all red eyed and sad, she snuggled into Joe's warm body and gathered herself together. She told Joe and Rob what she and her mother had spoken about, also that they should get over to America to be safe. Rob said, he quite fancied hobnobbing it in the Hamptons, adding they could bump into Paul McCartney, apparently, he had read that the ex-Beatle had a place there. With that snippet of useless information, he said in a Liverpudlian accent he had to go and meet his mate. He left to exchange his Jag for his friend's motorbike for a couple of days. Joe and Harriot went to the local supermarket to buy some food, Harriot had promised to cook them a nice meal after they all agreed they were getting sick of takeaways. It was good to be out and get some fresh air, Joe wore a trendy flat cap with his jacket and sunglasses to hide his face. Harriot wore a pink woollen beanie to attempt to hide her face. Joe was relieved when they got back to the flat with the shopping although everything appeared okay outside, he was still very nervous and took a gun with him.

Rob arrived back an hour and a half later, after parking the motorbike in the resident's car park beneath the flats on the ground floor. They sat down for dinner at eight thirty, Harriot had cooked Scallops in garlic for a starter and a beef stroganoff for the main course. The men teased her about how good a cook she was, Rob said, "Great, isn't it, Joe? Here we were struggling with horrible takeaway food, and we had a Michelin-star chef in the flat all this time." They jeered her and made fun calling her a little rich girl, when she told them she was taught to cook at the finishing school in Switzerland.

Harriot told them to sod off, she topped up the wine glasses and laughed. She added, "I know you two are just trying to get me to cook all the time. Well, I will cook a meal again, but only for a special treat."

They relaxed after dinner, drinking wine and discussing their getaway and how they were going to get over to America, possibly via Ireland. Rob was the first to turn in for the night, saying he wanted to be alert in the morning when he went to get the passports. Joe hugged him and said, "Stay safe, if you see any of them or if anything at all doesn't look right, just get the hell out of there fast. What time are you leaving tomorrow?"

Rob replied, "About ten-ish, I'll nip around to Harriot's first meet her friend then shoot over to yours in Fulham and grab yours; do you think I should take a gun with me?"

It was Harriot who replied, laughing, "If how you carried on when Joe shot the chauffer, I would say definitely not; you might end up shooting yourself in the foot."

Joe and Harriot roared, laughing and lay on the sofa, Rob pretended to be insulted and sniffed, "Well, thank you very much for that vote of confidence. Here I am putting, my life on the line while you two are here kissing and cuddling, and that's all the thanks I get. Also, for your information, I would be fine now; it was just a shock seeing Joe shoot that bloke." Joe and Harriot looked at each other and started laughing again.

Rob walked out of the lounge and slammed the door behind him, shouting, "I'm buggering off to bed, good night."

The next morning, Joe and Harriot were still in bed when they heard Rob leave. They made love and lay there discussing leaving London and England, Joe wondered if it would be best if the three of them went to Ukraine and stayed with Harriot's mum for a while before heading off to New York. Harriot liked the Idea, she said, she would love to go and spend some time with her mum and Uncle Ivan and also if it was safe visit Mykola's grave in Odessa. It was decided she would speak with her mum to see what she thought of the idea and if they would be safe there.

Lunchtime flowed into the early afternoon and Joe was getting agitated, Rob hadn't returned. Joe had tried him on his mobile a few times, but it was just going to answerphone. Sensing Joe's anxiety Harriott started get upset, she asked, "Do you think something bad has happened to Rob, Joe?" Her voice cracking with emotion.

He pulled Harriot to him and hugged her, replying, "I honestly don't know, H. I'm not sure what to do, I want to go looking for him, but I don't want to leave you here alone." They stood silently, holding each other in the lounge, Joe thinking what to do for the best. The buzzer on the wall startled them, they both jumped and looked at the intercom on the wall, and then looked at each other.

Joe ran over to the buzzer; he pressed the intercom, but didn't speak. A voice with a foreign accent came through loudly, "Hello, can you hear me, Mr Makin. I know you are in there with Miss Novikov. We need to speak urgently, you are both in danger, and they are coming for you." Harriot went to speak, but Joe put his finger up to his lips to quieten her.

He spoke into the intercom, "Who are you and who do you mean they?"

The loud voice came through again, just as agitated as before, "We have met before Mr Makin; my name is Heinrich Wagner, and I'm head of security at the bank LPZ. We met when you came in to meet Herr Zimmerman after they murdered Nigel Harrington. And I think you know who *'they'* are, they are the Russians who killed your partner, Mr Daly, and have been trying to kill you ever

342

since. Also, I have some very bad news. I'm sorry to have to tell you this, but they have just killed your friend whose flat this is; they got him in Fulham."

Joe looked at Harriot in horror, her scream filled the room, it was full of pain, and she staggered backwards and dropped onto the sofa crying hysterically. Hugging herself, her sobbing and screams sounded like the noise a wounded animal would make. Joe ignored her screams, he stood like a statue staring at the intercom, his finger still pressing down on the button. The news about Rob was like an explosion had gone off in his head, his knees went weak he thought he was going to collapse on to the floor. His eyes filled with tears, he couldn't concentrate, he looked back at Harriot on the sofa screaming in horror, but his legs wouldn't carry him over to her. He focused back on the intercom, as Wagner's voice came over again, "Mr Makin, please let me come up, there isn't much time, and you both have to get out of there."

Joe took his trembling finger off the button and pressed the entry button. He cleared his head and ran to the bedroom, he came back with the handgun, and he helped Harriot off the sofa and guided her into the bedroom. She fell on to the bed, still sobbing, he brushed the hair off her face and said shakily, "You stay here, don't come out, do you understand, don't come out for anything?" She nodded and rolled over, burying her face in to the pillow, sobbing uncontrollably. Closing the bedroom door behind him, the sound of the doorbell startled him. Holding the gun behind his back, he walked over to the door and looked through the door-viewer.

He recognised Wagner's concerned face from the meeting at the bank, he slipped the lock and stepped back from the door saying, "Come in slowly."

Wagner did as he was told, slowly walking into the hall with his hands in the air. Joe grabbed the back of his collar and roughly bundled him into the lounge, he pushed him down in to the armchair. Wagner with his hands still up in the air said, "Your hands are shaking, Mr Makin, please take that gun out of my face. I will slowly stand up, and you can check that I haven't got a weapon on, my person."

After Joe had quickly frisked him, he slowly sat back down and asked, "Can I please put my hands down now?"

Joe nodded okay, still pointing the gun at Wagner, he sat down on the edge of the sofa. Joe said aggressively, "How did you know we were here. What's happened to Rob, my friend?"

Wanger replied, "I've known you were here for a few days now, I followed you up to Hamstead Heath, after you shot the Russian and took Mrs Novikov. Then I followed you back down here to your friend's flat, I've been watching the place ever since."

Joe studied the Germans face, not sure whether to believe him, he was still on his guard. He poked Wagner with the handgun and said, "More importantly, what's happened to my friend Rob, you said he's dead?"

Wagner lent forward a little and looked genuinely sad, "I saw him come back with the motorbike yesterday, and consequently, I hired a motorbike courier for today. When he left this morning, we followed him, he went to Miss Novikov's apartment block in Kennington. He met with a woman outside she gave him something, and they talked for a short while and then he left for your flat in Fulham. The Russians were there and saw him outside Miss Novikov's apartment block. I don't think they recognised or knew him, but they must have followed us to over to Fulham."

"When he went into your apartment block, I suppose they decided it was too much of a coincidence, from Kennington to Fulham. They were waiting outside in their car, and when he came out, he was walking over to his motorbike, and they just ran him over. He must have been thrown at least two or three metres into the air. It was horrible to see, the bastards; they ran him down like a dog. They drove off at speed down the street. I ran to him along with the courier, two other people who had witnessed also came over to him. I'm afraid he hadn't survived he was dead."

Wagner appeared to relax a little has Joe lowered the gun. "I wanted to try and protect you if they came for you. Herr Zimmerman at the bank assigned me to find Miss Novikov for her father. He's a very important client to the bank, as you are now no doubt aware. But I'm not sure now who I can trust at the bank, so I didn't tell Herr Zimmerman that I had found you all."

Joe looked long, hard at Wagner and finally asked, "I'm curious, why are you trying to protect us? Why do we deserve your protection?"

Wagner gave him a half smile and continued, "I don't agree with what's been going on at the bank for the past number of years. Also, Nigel Harrington used to be a decent man, and look how working for the Russians changed him. He was murdered because of his greed for the dirty Russian money. I don't want to be part of it any longer, and I certainly don't want to work for people who are partners with murderers."

Joe's eyes had filled with tears, and he looked down at his shaking hands. Wagner said, "I'm so sorry to have to give you such bad news about your good friend." He nodded towards the bedroom door, Harriot was sobbing loudly.

Wagner continued, "Miss Novikov is taking it very badly also, isn't she? They are animals, I won't have anything to do with them; we are not like them, and we are bankers, Mr Makin. There is an old German saying, if you teach a bear to dance, you only stop dancing when the bear stops. All this aside you and Miss Novikov must leave here. I received a call from Herr Zimmerman a short time ago saying to call off my search for you both. He said the Russians know where you are and are awaiting instructions from Moscow. I don't know how they found you, but they have. Please for your safety, you must leave now. I don't want to know where, that would put my life in danger. I am leaving now, please leave straight after me;

I don't know how long you've got, and they could even be on their way here now." Joe stood up and followed Wagner to the door. He turned to Joe and offered his hand, and Joe shook it and nodded.

Wagner gave a wry smile and said, "God speed, Mr Makin, and may he be with you both." With that, he turned, and headed quickly towards the stairs.

Chapter Forty-Nine
The Escape

Joe finally calmed Harriot and told her everything Wagner had said, except how Rob had died. He told her to pack some clothes and accessories she might need, explaining they had to leave immediately. He packed a few items of clothing in a tan leather holdall, but he wasn't thinking straight because of Rob. He told himself to get his shit together, their lives depended on it; he couldn't protect Harriot if they caught them. They would kill him and take her back to Russia, where her father could possibly have her killed or hidden away for the rest of her life.

Harriot wasn't functioning very well, so he shouted to her what he had been telling himself, "Harriot, for God's sake get your shit together!"

He felt guilty, and it only started her off shaking and sobbing again. He hugged her to him; she had stuffed the laptop and a few items of clothes into her holdall, and it was open on the bed. He held her face in his hands and gently said to her, "Let's go; we can buy whatever we need when we get somewhere safe. Don't worry, my darling, I'll protect you, I promise." He kissed her on the forehead grabbed the holdalls, and they left. To be safe they went through the side door into the car park and climbed over the short wall onto the street at the back of the apartment block. Joe looked left and right up and down the street, he said to himself, "So far so good." No suspicious looking characters, just an elderly man walking his happy tail wagging white hairy dog. They walked down to the end of the street and turned right heading towards the main road. At the corner Joe peered around the edge of the building looking up towards the front of the apartment block, again no sign of the Russians. They turned and walked along the road heading away from the block and the Elephant and Castle roundabout. Joe waved at a black cab approaching them on the opposite side of the road, it swung around through a clearing in the oncoming traffic. Joe unceremoniously bundled Harriot and the two holdalls into the back of the cab and jumped in himself and said, "Knightsbridge, please, Cabbie."

Harriot sheepishly looked over at Joe and asked, "Where are we going to?"

Joe replied, "We'll check in to a hotel for the time being."

She replied, "I know a small boutique hotel near Buckingham Palace."

Joe shook his head and said, "Too dodgy; we need somewhere quite big, so if we need to, we can escape. I know the Savoy is ideal. It's big enough, and it's got two entrances, the main one on to the Strand and one at the back of the hotel on the riverside."

He tapped on the partition to the cabbie. "Change of plan, the Savoy, please." The cabbie flicked open the

Perspex hatch behind his head and replied, "Okay, guvnor, no problem." They checked into a suite at the rear of the hotel, with views over the Thames. It was an elegant suite, a large lounge with a three-seater sofa in pink and grey crushed velvet. A large off-white glass coffee table with two tan leather armchairs either side of the coffee table. The large bedroom had a very inviting king-size bed, the duvet covered with a pink throw and huge pillows, the furnishings were in a soft pink and taupe colour. The on suite had a huge marble bath, separate walk-in shower, toilet and bidet. Altogether, a perfectly luxurious place to hide when you are being hunted down by killers, Joe looked around and said to himself, "Well, if they get us, at least we'll be going out in style." Harriot had stopped crying, but she was very pale and looked completely washed out. Joe suggested that she should lie down and try to sleep for a while, she agreed, undressed and got into bed.

Joe quietly closed the bedroom door; he turned on the huge television on the wall over the marble fireplace in the lounge. He turned to the news channel to see if there was any news about Rob's murder. It came up on the "local!" London news after the National coverage, they were asking for witnesses to come forward who might have seen the hit and run accident. It also said police they would like to speak to two witnesses who left the scene before the emergency services arrived. Joe assumed that must have been Wagner and the bike courier, Wagner wouldn't go forward, but the courier might. Joe thought about speaking to Andy Sherry at the Met, but what could he tell him, that it was a Russian death squad who had done it, but he didn't have names, only a couple of vague descriptions, and he didn't where they might be found!

Joe turned off the television and looked around the lounge, he saw a highly polished sideboard against the back wall, inside on the left was a drinks cabinet. Smiling to himself pleased for his find, he opened a bottle of twenty-five year old malt and poured himself a large glass. Sitting back on the sofa his mind went to Rob, they'd had a good night the previous evening, a smashing meal, quite a few drinks and the usual good laugh. Letting out a huge sigh, he started to get emotional, he thought and now he's dead, first Jimmy, now Rob also probably that lovely innocent young lady Octavia too. What a fuck up, how did I get to this point in my life where I've lost people who meant so much to me? Am I fucking cursed? Parents who didn't give a shit about me, a new life, special friends, who become my new family and now gone, all of them, because of me. He finished his glass and went over to the cabinet to pour himself another one.

He looked around the elegant lounge, he smiled and thought, *Not bad for a Newcastle boy, a suite at the Savoy, my aunts would have been proud. Although I'm sure it's nothing to places Harriot's stayed in with her father's wealth. I really feel like getting absolutely pissed tonight, it would be very easy on this malt, it's beautiful, but better not, I need to be alert in case those bastards track us down here.* He drained the glass and placed it on the coffee table, he rested his head on to the top of the sofa, and he stared at the ceiling and then closed his eyes. He woke with a start, Harriot was standing in front of him, her face pale and red-eyed. He held out his hand and pulled her down beside him. She cuddled into him, and he asked, "Have you been crying thinking about Rob?" already knowing the answer.

She nodded and replied in an emotional voice, "I can't stop thinking about poor Rob; it's just so sudden. We were all laughing and joking last night, and now he's dead, all because of me."

She burst into tears again, sobbing loudly, Rob hugged her tightly and said, "It's not your fault, H, you and your mum didn't know how all this was going to turn out; all you were trying to do was save your brother's life. If anyone is to blame, it's that weasel Nigel Harrington, and he got what he deserved from your uncle Ivan. You can't blame yourself; your brother's life was at stake; anybody would have done the same in the same situation."

Harriot climbed off the sofa and said between sobs, "I can't take these murders, Joe; if anything happened to you, I would kill myself, and I really would. I don't want to lose you too. Mykola's gone; I can't see my mum, Jimmy was killed, and now, Rob, I can't take any more of this, Joe." With that she sat down on Joe's lap, her arms around his neck, her face buried into his shoulder.

He gently rocked like you would a baby, kissing the top of her head, quietly saying, "Shush, it will be okay."

Joe opened his eyes after a surprisingly good night's sleep, Harriot was close just staring at him, and she smiled and kissed him gently on the lips. Stroking her hair, Joe asked, "How did you sleep? I can't even remember us coming to bed."

Harriot moved loser and snuggled in between Joe's outstretched arms, as he hugged her, she let out a contented purr. She replied, "Not too bad, I couldn't stop thinking of Rob, but I finally fell asleep.

Then I woke up in the middle of the night, thinking it had all been a dream and Rob was still alive. When I realised that it had really happened, I got panicky and upset again. Joe kissed her forehead and said, "Well, you are safe in my arms now, and I won't let anything happen to you."

She let out a loud Hmmm and said, "I wish I could stay her for ever just safe in your arms."

Joe kissed her forehead again and replied, "So do I, but unfortunately, we can't. First, I need a pee desperately and then a shower. Afterwards, we need to decide on our next move. Have you any ideas where the Russians are holed up?"

Harriot sat up with her back against the pillow and thought for a few seconds, then replied, "No, not really; they blindfolded me when they took me from the office. Then they brought me up to the house at Regents Park, where you and Rob came and saved me. I heard them say one of them was going to take me to Battersea heliport and fly to a private airfield; they had a plane ready to take me back to Russia. Why do you ask?"

Joe looked at Harriot, a little puzzled by her reply, for some weird reason he didn't feel that she was telling him the truth, *Why blindfold her, then they brought her up to the house in Regents Park,* brought her up from where? She broke his thoughts repeating, "Joe, why do you ask?"

He said, "Sorry, I was thinking I could go to my friend Andy, the detective at the Met, but we need enough information on them to get them arrested; it was just a thought."

Harriot shook her head and said, "It wouldn't help our situation; my father would just send more men to finish the job."

He smiled and replied, "Yes, I suppose so. I'm going for a pee and that shower I mentioned." After his shower he shaved and dressed, he ordered breakfast and coffee from room service while Harriot used the bathroom to freshen up. After the food was delivered, she joined him in the lounge, she looked stunning in the hotel white heavy towelling dressing gown. He enjoyed his full breakfast and three cups of coffee, Harriot settled for a piece of brown toast, one black coffee and a glass of iced water.

Wiping his mouth on the white serviette he stood and asked Harriot, "Will you be okay here for a little while?"

He could see the panic suddenly, cover her face like a cloud drifting across the sun, and she nervously asked, "Why where are you going to go? Please don't leave if anything happened to you, I wouldn't know what to do."

Joe sat down next to here on the sofa, holding her hand, he said, "Don't worry, nothing is going to happen to me, I know a villain in Camden. I think he will be able to get us fake passports. I was hoping Rob would get back with ours but…" His voice tailed off.

Swallowing hard, he continued, "I'll go to Camden on the tube and then come straight back here. Don't worry, I'm taking the gun, I'll be back before you know it. Why don't you have a nice long soak in the bath? If my guy can get them for us, we can get out of the country. Hopefully, that will be safer than trying to dodge them here in England. If I don't have any luck with them, can you try your mum? Maybe she could get us passports and even help us get out of the country. I'm sure your uncle Ivan must know people over there who can get fake documents." Harriot had started to gently cry; she nodded her head, and Joe lifted her face up to him.

He said, "Look, I promise, I will be careful; besides, I've got to look after you, I can't do that if I'm dead now can I."

His humour didn't go down well, Harriot wiped her eyes and said, "Don't joke, you know what they are capable of, you are all I have left. They know that once they kill you their job is done here. Then they can get me and take me back; you are the final piece in the jigsaw, and they have to kill you." Her chilling words were so matter of fact, so cold, if she wanted to stop him being flippant about being in danger, it certainly worked. They sat looking at each, looking in to her eyes, Joe was confused who was the real Harriot. The lonely naive receptionist, the beautiful heiress, the scared frightened hunted woman, who might have lied to him. Now very matter-of-fact telling him her fathers' people had to kill him, as if things like this were the norm.

Joe smiled he was just being paranoid after everything that had happened, he told her, "Don't worry, they won't get me; speak to your mum in case I can't get the passports for us; oh, and it goes without saying, don't go out and don't open the door, okay?" She weakly smiled back and nodded. He kissed her on the forehead, told her he loved her, and left.

Joe stopped in the front foyer and had a good look outside the main entrance for anything or anyone looking suspicious. Everything appeared to be okay, he walked out and jumped into the back of the first taxi in the rank. "Camden, please, cabbie," he said, and then looked out of the side window as the cab pulled up waiting to join the traffic on The Strand. He had decided against the tube, for all his bravado with Harriot, stood in the foyer he suddenly felt very vulnerable and nervous. Like Harriot had told him these people played for keeps, and he was their number one target. He met his contact Mattie at a coffee shop on Camden High Street. They had a good chat about what had happened and Mattie confirmed he could help Joe and his mystery girlfriend. However, it would take four or five days at best to get the passports done, also he would need photographs of the both of them. It wasn't ideal, but if Harriot's mum could help, he doubted it would be any quicker.

It was strange, he had never felt this vulnerable since his mum died, and Rob's murder had really started to get to him. He felt safe sat with Mattie and his men safety in numbers probably, also the fact that he knew every one of them was carrying a gun. If the Russians came into the café now it would be like gunfight at OK corral. However, the nerves came straight back once he said goodbye walked out of the cafe and hailed a cab to take him back to the Savoy. He really was getting paranoid, he wanted to phone H to make sure she was okay. But he thought she probably wouldn't pick up, and it would most likely only freak her out.

Chapter Fifty
The End?

Joe paid the Cabbie and felt relieved when he walked into the foyer of the hotel. His heart had been racing on the journey back from Camden, he told himself he had to get a grip. He didn't think he would be affected like this, but Rob's death had really brought it home that he too could be killed anytime, anywhere. He walked into the suite and double locked the door, he shouted out, "It's only me."

He heard Harriot shout back from the bedroom, "Okay, won't be a minute. I'm just on facetime."

She was sat on the bed with the laptop on her knees. Looking back to the screen, she said anxiously, "Daddy, I've got to go, thank you. I love you, see you soon, bye... bye." With that she quickly closed the laptop and placed it on the bed, she tidied her hair and wiped her eyes and went to join Joe in the lounge.

Joe was pouring himself another whisky from the cabinet, he smiled and asked, "Did you have a good long soak in the bath?"

She walked over to him and hugging him, she kissed his neck and lied, "Yes, I was in there for ages, it was so soothing."

Joe lifted her face up to him with his crooked finger under her chin and asked, "Hey, why the tears?"

She wiped her eyes with her fingers again and raised a half-smile, she replied, "I've just been speaking to my mum; we both had another good cry. She said to tell you she's sorry about what happened to Rob."

Joe nodded and asked, "Did she say, she might be able to help us get out of England? My friend said, he can get us the passports, but it's going to take about a week."

Harriot sat down on the sofa and beckoned Joe to join her, she replied, "She said she should be able get us out of the UK, but like your friend she said, it would take her several days to sort everything out."

They sat on the sofa in silence, Harriot leaning into Joe, and her head resting on his chest. It was Harriot who was the first to speak, "Do you know what I would like to do tonight? I would like to go out for a lovely meal, take me somewhere nice and romantic Joe."

He rested his chin on her head, sat up, and looked down at her, surprised. "Are you sure you want to go out to a restaurant, with your dad's people out there looking for us? We could eat downstairs in one of the hotel restaurants if you like."

Harriot smiled and replied, "They can't look in every restaurant in London, Joe. I'm sure we will be okay. Meanwhile, take me to bed and make love to me... please!" Joe stood up, looked down at her, and held out his hand, "Okay, it's a deal; you've talked me into."

Harriot raised her champagne glass and with the widest of smiles, said, "I love you; I always have done Joe Makin from first getting to know you when you came to work in the office. Whatever happens, promise me you will always remember that. Promise now."

Joe smiled and raised his glass and gently chinked her glass. He said, "I've never had much luck with women. I always seemed to pick ones, and you know, women who would run away with my friend or leave if things got tough. I really gave up looking for someone who I could spend my life with, but then we got thrown together through circumstances. I promise you now that I've found you, I'm never going to let you go, and we will have children and grow old together."

Harriot started to gently cry, she dabbed her eyes with the servette and apologised, Joe smiled and teased her. "That was supposed to make you happy, not start you off crying all over again. You've done enough of that recently to last you a lifetime." She smiled and then laughed; Joe looked around the restaurant it was busy. They were in The Ivy Joe had phoned his friend the Maître De, he had sorted them out with a table. You normally had to book months in advance, but they always held back a few tables for celebrities, who's PAs would phone up at the last minute to get their client a table.

Joe was pleased that Harriot was enjoying herself, he was still a little edgy when they got a cab from the hotel, even though it wasn't that far to the restaurant. Although he drew the line when Harriot suggested walking back to the hotel because *it was such a lovely warm evening.*

To appease Harriot for insisting they got the cab back from The Ivy, he took her to the American bar in the Hotel for cocktails. It was the perfect end to a perfect evening, after all the recent trouble they totally relaxed in each other's company. After quite a few cocktails they went back to their suite made love again, then fell asleep in each other's arms.

The next morning, they had a lazy start, they lay in until eleven a.m., then ordered brunch from room service. They chatted about what they would do, where they would live, Europe or the States. Harriot appeared subdued, Joe put it down to the champagne and cocktails the night before. Harriot said her mum would help them to hide away somewhere safe, hopefully until this all blew over. Joe made sure he didn't mention Rob, he didn't want to upset her again, but he was certain she was thinking about what had happened. Against his better judgement he agreed to go for a walk along the embankment, because Harriot wanted to, and it was a lovely summer's day.

They left from the riverside entrance of the hotel and walked through Victoria Embankment gardens. They continued down towards Westminster, Harriot linked arms with Joe and teased him about looking so serious. They looked like two people in love strolling along in the sunshine. Only Joe had a handgun tucked in the back of his jeans and his eyes were furtively looking around at people walking near them. They enjoyed the fresh air, but

361

didn't speak much, Harriot still appeared a bit sullen, she asked Joe what was going to happen regarding Rob's body. Joe explained that as far has he knew Rob didn't have any living relatives. He would get in touch with his friend Andy Sherry at the Met and ask him to speak with the undertakers to arrange the funeral. Joe said, "I will have to go; there won't be anyone else there. I don't give a stuff if the Russians are looking for me; in fact, because it was a hit-and-run, I think the police will have a presence at the funeral. I'll ask Andy."

Talking about Rob's funeral darkened Harriot's mood even further, shortly afterwards she said, she wanted go to back to the hotel, much to Joe's relief. Back in the suite, Harriot said, she had a migraine and wanted to try and sleep it off.

Joe used the time to contact Andy Sherry to ask him about the release of Rob's body. Joe was finally put through to Andy. He wasn't in a very good mood when he heard Joe say hello, he got straight to the point and said, *"Good of you to get in touch. I've been trying to contact you for over a week with no luck. What the fuck is going on?"*

Joe said, *"I lost my phone and had to buy a new one, different number, though. What do mean, what's going on?"*

Joe's reply just seemed to annoy Andy even more, *"Don't treat me like a twat, Joe. You know what I'm talking about – the hit and run outside your apartment block. The guy, Rob Fee dead at the scene, and what does*

362

he have in his pocket? Your passport. Also, the passport of a Russian woman, Zoya Novikov, who, if my memory serves me right, your mysterious Mrs Harrington had the same surname. Also, Zoya Novikov looks the double of Jimmy's receptionist, Harriot. Do you remember my friend Jimmy, and do you, Joe? You know your boss who got murdered; just what the fuck have you got yourself involved in?"

Joe was originally going to lie that he had seen the story of the hit and run on the six o'clock News, he had forgotten about the passports. There was no point in lying to Andy now. He answered him, *"It's complicated, and I promise I will explain everything when we meet up."*

Andy asked, *"And when will that be?"*

Joe said, *"The hit-and-run guy was a very good friend of mine, Andy. I want to give him a decent burial. I don't think he's got any family, so I want to take care of it; we could meet up after the funeral and have a chat."*

Andy came straight back with, *"A good friend of yours, was he? Well, seeing friends of yours keep ending up dead, my colleagues here want to have a little chat with you. Should I tell them you've been on to me?"*

Andy's sarcasm was beginning to piss Joe off, he quickly replied, *"Ouch, that was below the fucking belt, Andy, and uncalled for. You know full well I'm in the clear regarding what happened to Jimmy and also Rob's death. So, give me a fucking break, okay? Unless I keep my wits about me, I'll be next."*

Andy appeared to calm down after Joe's retaliation. He said, *"Well, come in then and let us protect you. Tell us what you know and who's doing this shit!"*

Joe was still angry, he said, *"Don't think so, your colleagues haven't done much good up to now, have they? They still haven't a clue about Nigel Harrington's murder, have they? Trust me, it's not that simple, I don't think you'll be able to arrest these guys. Look, if I will give you my number, would you let me know when Rob's body is being released?"*

Andy said, he would get the undertaker to contact Joe to arrange a funeral. Andy signed off the call, with what seemed like genuine concern. *"Okay, I'll see you some time after the funeral then, if you won't meet me before. In the meantime, try and make sure you don't end up next to your pal in the police mortuary. Take care?"*

The phone went dead, Joe hoped he could trust Andy that his colleagues wouldn't track his phone and come bursting in on them. He poured himself another whisky from the drink's cabinet and sat back on the sofa, resting his head on the top of the cushion, he studied the ceiling. One thing was certain, he wasn't leaving the country without giving Rob a decent funeral. He was racked with guilt about him, and Andy's sarcastic comments didn't help. A decent funeral was least he could do for his best friend, he had come back to see Joe and got involved in all this shit, after saving Joe's life. Wow, Joe shook his head and thought, talk about fate. He now wished Rob hadn't come back, if he hadn't, he would still be alive today. This was how it had ended up for Rob after the shit childhood he had, then the problems with the drugs, and all because Joe was his best friend. His life cut short and a funeral with no one there except Joe and maybe a couple of coppers. He would probably end up having an argument with Harriot, because he definitely didn't want her to chance going. Joe really didn't like himself at this moment in time. Andy Sherry was right, Rob gone together with Jimmy, the kindest man who had showed Joe nothing, but kindness. He had been a father to Joe, he drained his glass and poured himself another large whisky. After another couple of drinks, he checked on Harriot, peeping around the bedroom door, she was still fast asleep. He was hungry, most likely because of the drink, he ordered a club sandwich and a pot of coffee from room service. Harriot got up just after six thirty, said her migraine wasn't much better. Joe nipped down to the hotel shop for her and bought Paracetamol. She took them with a glass of iced water and went back to bed, Joe decided he would have a few more drinks, watch some TV and then turn in for the night himself.

The next morning, Harriot was up before Joe and was in the bath when Joe got up. She dressed and ordered them breakfast from room service, while Joe had a shower and shave. They sat talking about Joe's conversation with Andy Sherry and how he would organise Rob's funeral. Surprisingly, Harriot didn't mention about wanting to attend, Joe changed the subject and tried to lift her mood, to no avail. She ordered a pot of tea and coffee for Joe from room service, she asked Joe if would call at the chemist down towards Charing Cross for a few toiletries for her. He welcomed the chance of a bit of fresh air, and probably like Harriot was beginning to get a little stir crazy. He had another cup of coffee got his coat, slipped the gun in the waistband at the back of his jeans and was good to go. Harriot gave him her shopping list, she hugged him and gave him a passionate lingering kiss; he smiled at her and asked, "Is that my reward for running errands for you?"

She laughed and replied, "Oh, I can think of a far better reward that I could give you when you get back." They kissed again; Joe left for the Boots store along the Strand. On the way down in the lift he looked at his list, six items shouldn't take too long, he would come back via the embankment for some exercise and fresh air.

He stopped at the doors in the foyer and took a good luck around, the doorman gave him a look and asked if he could help him with directions to somewhere. Joe thanked him and asked him where the nearest chemist was. While the doorman was directing him to the Boots store, Joe had a final look around, everything looked clear. Joe was enjoying the warm sun on his face and also just being out of the hotel room. He bought Harriot's toiletries then walked along to Charing Cross Station turning left towards the embankment. He got to the riverside entrance of the hotel and reluctantly went inside, on the way up in the lift to the fifth floor he wondered whether he should suggest a walk to Harriot. It was another beautiful day it would cheer her up, she must be pissed off like him looking at the same walls.

He opened the door and dropped the key card on the hall table, and he light-heartedly shouted, "Hi, honey, I'm home." Walking through the lounge door, he felt the barrel of a gun jab into the right-hand side of his neck. The gunman's left hand went straight to the back of Joe's jeans and roughly pulled his gun out from his waistband, stood in front of the fire place was Harriot, with her holdall and two men.

He recognised the two Russian stood on either side of her, the gunman next to Joe pushed him forward and said, "Don't be stupid and try anything." Joe looked slowly to his right in the direction of the voice, he recognised the gunman. He was the one who had lit the cigarette in the doorway next to Joe's Apartment that night. Joe felt his anger rising, he was in the same room with Jimmy and Rob's murderers. His fists down by his side clenched tightly, he was thinking about his best move.

Harriot realising what he was thinking of doing, said, "Joe, please don't; I don't want you to get hurt, it will be okay."

She was starting to get upset, he was angry and confused, he asked, "Are you okay. Have they hurt you?"

She answered her voice started to crack with emotion, "No, they haven't, Joe, and they wouldn't dare!"

Joe looked at Harriot and said, "I'm sorry, I should never have left you alone, and I should have been here for you. I never for a minute thought they would track us down to here."

Harriot gave him a faint smile and slowly shaking her head, replied, "Oh, darling, don't blame yourself, they didn't track us to here. I spoke to my father and told him where we were." Joe looked at her open mouthed, he couldn't believe what she had just said, tears started to run down Harriot's face.

Joe was dumbfounded at what she had just said to him, his angry started to rise again. In a raised voice, he asked, "Why the fuck would you do that?"

These bastards killed Jimmy and Rob and most likely a couple of other people who had done absolutely nothing wrong! "Harriot sobbed." Exactly that's why I did it, because I couldn't live with any more people dying because of me. Joe continued to stare at Harriot with a puzzled look, trying to digest what she said to him.

With a wry smile, he said, "So you sold me out, and I thought you loved me. Shit how good am I at picking women to love? You're just the same as the others, you have me killed and run off to Daddy in Moscow. Wow, you really are something; do you know that? If I hadn't come back when I did, you would have just gone and left one of these clowns to kill me, wouldn't you?"

Joe quickly stepped to the side away from the man next to him, looking at him and the two men next to Harriot, he shouted, "Well, come on then, let's get this done!"

They made a move towards Joe. Harriot held up her hand and shouted, *"NYET HE!" (No don't)*. They stopped where they were. Sobbing Harriot said, "It's not like that at all, Joe. I rang my father to protect you and keep you alive. I've done a deal with him; if I go back to Moscow, he's promised me you won't be killed. But you mustn't ever tell the authorities about what you know about the operation at the bank. Please forgive me, Joe, I'm not like the others, I promise. I love you so much I couldn't take the chance they would eventually find us and kill you. Don't you see this? You are free of them, and you can get your life back without having to look over your shoulder for the rest of your life."

Joe answered, "No, I don't see. Wasn't I worth fighting for? We could have made it, at least we would have had each other. What makes you think I can have a life without you, Harriot? Without you, I may as well be dead."

Harriot, trying to control her tears, said, "Don't say that, Joe. This is hard enough; please try and understand."

Joe replied, "Understand what? That you're running out on me; also, how do you know you can trust your father; he has people killed without a second thought. Also, what will he do to you when he gets you back to Moscow?"

Harriot replied, "That's a chance I'm prepared to take, Joe, for you."

One of the Russians said to Harriot, *"My Dolzhny uyti"* (*"We must leave"*).

Harriot walked over to Joe and said tearfully, "We have to leave now." She hugged Joe, he didn't respond, she pulled back from him slightly and kissed him tenderly on the lips then walked to the door. The three Russian were behind her, one walked backwards watching Joe, the lounge door closed, Joe heard the suite door bang shut. He stood looking at the door, his hand went up to his cheek, his fingers wiped tears from his face, staring at the wet tip of his fingers he wasn't sure if they were Harriot's tears or his own.

Chapter Fifty-One

Joe sat in the front row of the chapel in the Crematorium and thought, *This is dire.* Rob deserved better than this. Joe was sat on the front row all alone, the only other people were way back on the last row next to the doors, and they were two plain clothes detectives. That was it, apart from the vicar who was at the front finishing off saying a few words about Rob's life that Joe had supplied him with. How could someone live for thirty odd years and not have anybody. Joe frowned and felt depressed, he realised his funeral would probably be just as bad, unless... his mind drifted to thinking about Harriot.

He hadn't heard anything from her since she walked out of their suite at the Savoy, that was over three weeks ago now, but it seemed longer. He was back in his apartment which wasn't good, he had visions of Rob being mowed down outside on the road. He would probably sell up and move to another part of town. The office was back to normal, cleaned up and looked good, again though just bad memories of Jimmy dying on the floor. It was strange walking through the door and Harriot not sat at her desk in reception. His life was getting back to normal, but everywhere was filled with bad memories. He had advertised that the business was up and running again and had received a few jobs and also some calls making appointments. He had advertised for a receptionist with the business picking up. He concentrated on working again, his savings were pretty low and Rob's funeral has small as it was, still cost him. He was to be interviewed by the detectives at the Met about Jimmy's death and Rob's hit and run death. He had spoken with Andy Sherry on the phone and pissed him off big style. When he told him he couldn't tell him anything or his life would be in danger. Andy angrily replied that he could have him charged with perverting the course of Justice and with that slammed down the phone on Joe.

Joe had tried to keep himself busy to stop thinking of Harriot, but it wasn't easy when you are all alone. He missed Rob, even his daft impressions, some very good, some not so good, he missed Jimmy, and how bloody unfair it was, he lost his life. Most of all though, he missed Harriot, he really did love her, and he knew she loved him. To sacrifice her life, her freedom for him, well, after a couple of bad choices she was the best love ever, and he still lost her. Even though his life was getting back to "normal" after all that had happened. He had never felt so alone in all his life, it was probably on par with when his mum died and later also his aunts when they died so close together back in Newcastle. He had toyed with the idea of going back to the North East to get away from all the sad reminders all around him. He decided against it because if he did, how would Harriot find him if she ever came back to London.

He had a couple of jobs that had come in, ironically both cases were "straying!" Husbands, thing were looking up businesswise. It was Friday Lunchtime, he had no plans for the weekend, and he closed the office for the day. He had arranged to go to the Met at two p.m., for their meeting about Jimmy and Rob's deaths coming out of the office into the sunshine on Holborn. He had decided he would go for a drink to the pub where he worked when he first met Jimmy. He smiled and thought I might get to sit in Jimmy's favourite seat at the end of the bar. Has he walked along he hadn't noticed the burly Russian with the old-fashioned crew-cut hairstyle watching him from the other side of the road. He smoked while he waited across the road from the pub, then followed Joe down to the Met building. He watched Joe go inside and speak with one of the receptionists. He took out his mobile and dialled a number, and after a few rings, he heard a voice say, *"Da"* (yes). Looking at Joe through the glass doors being ushered to sit down by the receptionist, he said, "He's gone into the headquarters of the London Police; what do you want me to do?"